GOLD
COAST
DILEMMA

GOLD COAST DILEMMA

NANA MALONE

GALLERY BOOKS

NEW YORK   AMSTERDAM/ANTWERP   LONDON
TORONTO   SYDNEY/MELBOURNE   NEW DELHI

G

Gallery Books
An Imprint of Simon & Schuster, LLC
1230 Avenue of the Americas
New York, NY 10020

For more than 100 years, Simon & Schuster has championed authors and the stories they create. By respecting the copyright of an author's intellectual property, you enable Simon & Schuster and the author to continue publishing exceptional books for years to come. We thank you for supporting the author's copyright by purchasing an authorized edition of this book.

This book is a work of fiction. Any references to historical events, real people, or real places are used fictitiously. Other names, characters, places, and events are products of the author's imagination, and any resemblance to actual events or places or persons, living or dead, is entirely coincidental.

First Gallery Books trade paperback edition April 2025

GALLERY BOOKS and colophon are registered trademarks of Simon & Schuster, LLC

Simon & Schuster strongly believes in freedom of expression and stands against censorship in all its forms. For more information, visit BooksBelong.com.

For information about special discounts for bulk purchases, please contact Simon & Schuster Special Sales at 1-866-506-1949 or business@simonandschuster.com.

The Simon & Schuster Speakers Bureau can bring authors to your live event. For more information or to book an event, contact the Simon & Schuster Speakers Bureau at 1-866-248-3049 or visit our website at www.simonspeakers.com.

Interior design by Hope Herr-Cardillo

Manufactured in the United States of America

10 9 8 7 6 5 4 3 2 1

Library of Congress Cataloging-in-Publication Data has been applied for.

ISBN 978-1-6680-6118-3
ISBN 978-1-6680-6119-0 (ebook)

*To the firstborn Ghana girls who carry the weight of their families
with grace and strength—you inspire me every day.*

*To my mom, who showed me what it means to love fiercely
and dream boldly. Thank you for being my forever muse.*

*And to Cuzi Love Productions, for the endless love,
unwavering support, and believing in every story,
even when I wasn't sure myself.*

This one's for all of you.

OFOSUA

ADINKRA SAYING:
(Odo Nnyew Fie Kwan) Love does not lose its way home.

HELEN ADDO:
Don't waste your time waiting to fall in love.
Find a lawyer, doctor, or engineer. You can learn to love him.

TWO YEARS AGO . . .

I was late.

For my first publishing industry party, no less. I repeatedly stabbed the elevator button, willing it to hurry the hell up. I'd been put in charge of getting the drinks for the interns and assistants, and Nazrin, the publicity assistant, would have my head for messing up her timeline.

I took a deep breath as a prickle of anxiety tickled the hairs on my neck. I wanted—needed—to prove myself. Being late was *not* the way to do that.

When the deep breathing didn't work, I rubbed my forefinger

and thumb together on my free hand, trying to remind myself of small truths.

I was good at my job. I was persistent. I'd stuffed hundreds of padded envelopes for press mailings without complaint, made persuasive phone calls to bookstores, and scoured Instagram and BookTok on my own time for appropriate influencers for this launch, finding key voices even the seasoned members of the marketing team didn't know about yet. All with a genuine smile.

I was good enough, even if I was ten minutes later to this party than I should be.

And honestly, nothing was going to make the sad Trader Joe's veggie platter awaiting me any more appetizing. It was fine. Totally fine.

Ding. The elevator arrived and I stepped inside, wishing it were a teleportation device and not an actual antique.

Drake Publishing was my dream job. It was a boutique agency and just the right size for me to be noticed. I might be just an intern, but I had my sights set on being a senior editor one day. Preferably before I was thirty so I could soften the blow to my parents about my occupation not being lawyer, doctor, or engineer.

But would even senior editor be substantial enough?

I focused on the floor indicator's curlicue brass arm marking the rise up, up to Mr. Drake's sprawling co-op.

The apartment was a real estate agent's dream, a penthouse perched atop a gleaming prewar building located on Central Park West at Eighty-First Street, built sometime in the 1920s. With panoramic views of the park's canopy of trees, it was, in a word, stunning. Even my traditional Ghanaian mother would have to acknowledge the apartment's elegance.

I'd poked around Mr. Drake's apartment earlier that morning

when I'd come with two of the publicity interns to set up the displays of glossy jacket blowups and stacks of the new novel *plus* gold-plated backlist. We'd arranged lush, literary tablescapes complete with floral arrangements in colors to complement the new jacket art in the main hall, the library, and the gallery. The idea was that guests would flow effortlessly from one room to another and onto the wraparound terraces, which were decorated with soft lighting and latticed vines to provide privacy.

When the elevator finally stopped and the doors slid apart, I quietly lugged my wine booty along the back hallway.

The interns and assistants wouldn't be enjoying the beauty of the stone terraces, the sunlit gallery, the wood-paneled library, or the velvet and leather seating in the main living area. We were under strict instructions not to be seen nor heard, unless we were needed for something, like clearing away stray glasses or fetching a specific title for a reporter. Our little enclave consisted of a tucked-away card table in the corner by the kitchen with a dodgy vegetable tray.

Jane, a petite redhead fellow intern with slightly ruddy cheeks, met me with a grin and clutched an empty plastic wineglass as if she might will some wine into it. "Thank God you're back." She helped me set the bottles down then appraised me. "That mustard color is amazing on you."

"Thanks," I said, tucking my waist-length braids over one shoulder and spinning to show off my outfit. I'd never understood why the girls in the office preferred black, navy, gray, or other neutral colors. I ventured a glance at the group of executives and authors gathering in the living area. Not a spot of color.

Only one woman, a tall silver-blonde with the coolest bright red glasses and a warm smile, had worn something even remotely interesting: an all-cream pantsuit. She stood out like a speck of salt in a pepper shaker. I'd heard Mr. Drake call her Ruby earlier, so I assumed that was his wife, Ruby Drake. I'd yet to meet her. The word was she rarely, if ever, came to the office. Which was too bad, as she looked like someone I might want to get to know.

Jane sighed melancholically at the celery she'd dipped into hummus. "You guys want to get real food after this?"

"God, yes." I was already regretting passing on the fried kelewele my mother had offered as I rushed out the door. I'd been worried about my breath, but now my tongue begged for the taste of sweet plantain and ginger with a pepper chaser.

None of the food trays laid out were remotely palatable. Even the carrots looked limp. No one liked limp carrots.

"I'm going to bribe one of the waitstaff to sneak us a canapé or two," Jane said.

"You are a goddess if you can pull that off." I glanced around and leaned over to her. "Let me go wash my hands first. I think I touched something sticky in the elevator."

"Good call."

A few minutes later, I stepped into the hallway after I was done in the bathroom. Party chatter greeted me from either side, but I'd gotten turned around and wasn't sure which way would return me to intern purgatory.

I hung a left, but nothing looked familiar. Instead, I came upon one of the open terraces and paused, uncertain. *Shit*, I'd gone the wrong way. But I couldn't resist the spectacular view and a moment to decompress.

"I see you had to escape too."

I whipped around, teetering on my Gianvito Rossi slingbacks as I searched for the source of the rich baritone. "Jesus, you scared me."

I'd never seen the guy standing in the doorway before. But he had a plate of real food in his hand and two bottles of champagne under his arm, so it was unlikely he was there to murder me.

The corners of his mouth tipped up in a lopsided smile as his eyes drank me in, his gaze direct and bold, making me feel like he could see right through to my La Perla.

I was momentarily stunned into silence by his good looks. The height struck me first. Over six feet definitely. Lean swimmer's build. Broad shoulders, but that jacket was tailored to perfection to drape him nicely. The simple white T-shirt he wore underneath looked to be of a soft jersey material and clung ever-so-nicely to his pecs as he lounged. Of course that insane body had to come with a ridiculously square jaw and beautiful, dancing gray eyes framed by sooty lashes. He looked roughly my age, maybe a little older. And when he smiled, he sent my stomach into free fall.

He was the definition of "pretty." So pretty.

And *so* not for me.

"I'm sorry. I'm not supposed to be here. I can go." I tried to sidestep around him, but he coaxed me to stay.

"You're not going to leave me to eat and drink by myself, are you? Even influencers need to eat and drink champagne."

Before I could correct him, my stomach, ever the traitor, thinking only about filling itself with the delectable Brie, assortment of meats, and delicious-smelling hors d'oeuvres on his plate, growled. *Loudly.*

"Looks like your decision is made for you. And I get to escape the pretentious bores with a beautiful woman."

I licked my lips, shifting nervously from foot to foot as I stuffed down the flare of anxiousness. This man really was too good-looking for my own good. I knew it like I knew the sky overhead was Tiffany blue. I had to snap out of it. "I'm sure you say that line to all the girls. I'm not impressed."

He chuckled softly. "Only when I mean it. Just as long as you don't dive into a twenty-minute diatribe about how novelists today owe everything to David Foster Wallace. I just escaped one of those."

My lips twitched. He was cute. And funny. *And you know better than to go chasing after a pretty boy.* But I wasn't chasing. He was the one offering food and champagne. "I can only stay for a minute."

He offered me his plate while he opened one of the champagne bottles. I tried not to stare at him as he took a long swig before passing the bottle to me.

My first thought—taking the bottle from his mouth was almost like we'd be kissing. His lips had been where mine were about to be, and that knowledge gave me another butterfly flutter.

My next thought—where has his mouth been?

My final thought—was I *really* going to drink contraband champagne at my boss's party?

Taking the bottle from him, I took a delicate sip. I'd sipped enough champagne to know that the bubbles went straight to my head.

He grinned at me widely as he took the bottle of champagne back. "So, I assume you're an influencer? But I can't say I've seen your content before."

"That's because I'm not an influencer. I'm an intern. Ofosua Addo. Just call me Ofos."

His gaze slid over me. "I'm Cole. And I have to say, you certainly don't look like the typical intern."

My back stiffened. I was a little older than most of the interns. I'd graduated with a business and creative writing double major. I hadn't been able to get a paying job at Drake right away, but I had managed to snag myself an internship. I didn't love living off of my trust fund, but it was what it was. I had a plan.

All I had to do was prove myself and work my way up. "What is that supposed to mean?" My question came out harsh and icy slick, daring him to put a foot wrong.

"You're dressed for a party. Not an ass-kissing snoozefest," he said with a roll of his eyes and another deep swig of champagne.

I cocked my head, assessing him further. "And you certainly don't look like the publishing type, at least not the Drake Publishing type. No wire-rimmed glasses. No seen-better-days blazer tossed over a fraying shirt. You look entirely too comfortable in that *really* nice suit. *You're* the one out of place here, not me. So what's your story?"

His eyes darkened, and he frowned briefly before recovering himself. "You are sharp. I was summoned. Think of me as a reluctant plus-one. So the moment I could, I swiped some champagne, and here we are."

I was desperate to know more. Who did he work for? Who was he? Or was he an author? But I had just met the guy. Maybe I should wait at least an hour before interrogating him, so I changed course. "This is my first publishing party. I'm not sure what I expected, but I thought it would be splashier. I mean, this home is gorgeous, of course. But . . . seems kind of dull in there."

He laughed. "Ah, so no one warned you about the de rigueur depressing hummus platters?"

"No! And I'm quite irritated about it really." I popped one of the warm canapés into my mouth and tried not to moan in delight at the melted cheese and spiced crabmeat on a perfect mini toast point.

He watched me intently with a curious smile. "All right, let's play a game. Tell me your favorite book right now. But it can't be anything by Wallace, anything considered a literary darling, and it can't be on a damn list."

I took the bottle of champagne from him, took another small sip. "That's easy. *The Count of Monte Cristo*, Dumas."

His brows lifted. "An adventurous woman. I have to say I'm thrilled you didn't say *Pride and Prejudice*."

Oh no. Tell me he wasn't one of those tedious Austen-hating men. Well, he was too pretty to be perfect. "That's my second favorite, actually. I'm a sucker for a love story. But I might love a good twist more."

One bottle of champagne and one empty plate later, I realized this had been easy . . . too easy. My guard was down. I was having a good time.

This is not a guy you can like, Ofos.

I'd known too many Coles. I'd gone to prep school with them, occasionally hung out with them, but trying to date one of them had never gone the way it was supposed to. Still, there I was on the terrace with one, and the rest of my world had completely fallen away.

"I'm telling you, you haven't experienced any kind of reading restrictions until you've had to sneak a romance novel past an African mother. Particularly a romance with a clinch cover," I said.

Cole tried to argue with me. "No way. Some of the horror novels I used to read had my mother convinced I needed a psychiatrist."

"Hardly the same thing. My mother marched into my middle school once to drag me out into the hallway and ask me how I could disgrace her like this. She'd found one of my library books, an old-school historical romance by Johanna Lindsey. There was hell to pay, and publicly."

With a laugh and a lift of his hands, Cole admitted defeat. "Okay, fine. That's worse. Getting dragged out of class by a parent." He laughed. "Granted, *I* usually got dragged out for other reasons. But for a book you were reading? That's brutal."

My phone vibrated just then, and I took it out of my pocket to see who was daring to interrupt my expert-level flirting. It was Jane.

JANE:

Where r u? Nazrin is looking for you.

Shit. I was supposed to be working. Making a good impression. "I've been out here way too long. I need to go."

His smile fell, and his gaze searched mine. "Who's going to help me finish the rest of the champagne?"

"That's a very good question, but I still need to go. I'm an intern, remember? I can't just vanish."

"Let's meet up later, then. I can feed you properly."

My brain stutter-stepped, and I flushed from my feet to my roots. "You want to feed me?"

The smile he gave me was slow and flirtatious. "That's usually what happens on a date, right?"

A date? He was asking me out? "Yeah. I'd like that." There was no hiding my grin. Who was I kidding? I liked him, even if I did know better about guys like Cole. Besides, I hadn't had a proper date in a while. When I turned to leave, he took my elbow gently.

"Me too. And thank you for making tonight interesting," he said.

The wind blew, and I tucked one of my braids behind my ear, but neither of us moved. This party wasn't turning out anything like I'd expected.

He was closer now, close enough to kiss. My heart thundered

so hard behind my rib cage that I had to force deep, steady breaths. I was not going to blow this by saying something stupid to chase him off.

He leaned in, closing the gap between us. His hand slid up to cup my face, and he gently brushed a thumb over my cheekbone. He was waiting. I could feel it. The implicit, *Is this okay?*

I gave him a slight nod. I couldn't have found words in that moment for all the books in the world.

My heart raced as he inched closer, his lips almost touching mine. Every nerve and cell in my body was on high alert, my breaths coming in shallow gasps.

The gentle brush of his lips made my breath catch. I didn't know a kiss could feel like this. Was it the champagne?

He paused for a moment, whispering a hushed "Wow," his gaze searching mine until I dug my hands into his lapels and pulled him forward. I had to know if what I'd just felt was real.

The electricity between us was palpable, setting every inch of my skin ablaze.

When he kissed me again, his hand slid onto the nape of my neck, pulling me even closer, making sure I stayed pressed against him.

I melted into him, feeling the heat of his body against mine as he deepened the kiss. As his tongue teased mine, my head swam in that foggy dreamlike way of fantasy kisses.

And I would have fallen deeper and deeper into the thrill of the kiss if the buzzing of my phone hadn't interrupted us, jolting me back to reality and the danger of my situation. What if someone saw us out here? I'd be the talk of the office and not in a good way. Plus, I'd never, ever be offered a permanent position at Drake. "I'm sorry. I really, really have to go."

"Wait. Don't go. Please. Stay."

God, was I tempted. "I wish. But I can't."

"I need to see you again. I don't have your number." His expectant smile made my heart leap.

"You have the proverbial glass slipper of information. You can find me."

With a lopsided smile he whispered, "Then this is just the beginning."

CHAPTER 1

OFOSUA

ADINKRA SAYING:
(Nkonsonkonson) A symbol of unity, community.
HELEN ADDO:
Marriage is not about you the person, but family. You will know happiness when you grow your family . . . especially if you pick someone from a good home.

TWO YEARS LATER . . .

I would have done things differently if the choice had been mine. But it wasn't.

I had no say in any of it.

But I forced myself to swallow. Panic was not welcome here today. I was not going to lose my shit.

I was getting married.

Utilizing my breathing techniques didn't change the fact that my mother and my mother-in-law-to-be had turned this perfect fall day into a spectacle. Worse, the monstrosity going on a few yards away without me was *just* the traditional marriage ceremony. It wasn't even step two, the white wedding.

Since my mother, Helen, claimed mostly her Ga side and not her Kwahu roots, we were doing a traditional Ga wedding, otherwise known as an engagement, only because it came before the big white wedding most couples *also* had.

In Ghanaian culture, traditional marriages were just as binding as a marriage ceremony is in Western culture. We just also liked the white wedding in the church for flair. This traditional ceremony meant the two families would be joined forever. And the official white wedding ceremony? That further cemented the permanence of it all in front of God. But honestly, it was a colonialist holdover, because traditional marriages were blessed by an osofo, or priest.

Glancing out the window at the three hundred or so guests outside, I couldn't believe the white wedding would be an even bigger spectacle than what was happening under Central Park's Wisteria Pergola right now. We had so many people, we'd spilled onto the main lawn of the Conservatory Garden.

It was all too much. In most instances these days, the couple didn't even have to be present at the ceremony. There was just a nominal exchange of, *Oh, yes, you know, the family bought these jewels and these clothing items.* And the other side would say, *Oh, look, we brought a cow, and money.* The cow would be a real show-off item.

No one brought a cow these days.

But when my mother was involved, there was no such thing as simple. Our ceremony was taking up half of Central Park. Every influential Ghanaian from Accra to London to New York was in attendance. Hell, a hundred of the guests were parental invites of business associates, dignitaries, Fortune 500 titans of industry.

I didn't even know them.

My mind was spinning at the expectation that we were going to go next level *from this* for the actual church wedding.

I had wanted to do this in Accra. That had been the original plan, but at the last minute Yofi said he couldn't get away from work, which I hadn't understood. He was Yofi Tutu. *Forbes* had named him Up-and-Comer of the Year. Surely he could dictate his own vacation.

All I could do was sit and worry silently as my auntie Ruth finished rebraiding my hair into the tightest cornrows of my life. She wasn't my actual aunt, but one of my mother's friends. Half the time, I wasn't even certain who was actually related to me and who wasn't. Every person who was at least fifteen years older than you was auntie or uncle.

She didn't like the hairstylist's work, so now she was redoing the braids toward my crown, then releasing the hair in a massive Afro with extensions to make it even bigger and fuller. My hair was intertwined with pieces of kente cloth with the family colors we chose of green, fuchsia, and cream.

My mother had insisted that only the best would do. *Her* idea of the best, not mine. I knew this was what she was used to. In Ghana, every celebration was over the top, from weddings to outdoorings, which were traditional presentations of new babies to the friends and family, to funerals. But, God, not a single person, *not one*, had asked me what I wanted.

My only contribution had been selecting Yofi. Luckily, I had done that myself.

Our parents had been friends for years. I had been aware of him because we were in the same circles and always at the same events.

Handsome Yofi had gone to Harvard, was an investment banker, and came from money. He was also one of those guys who seemed like they'd never settle down. But two years ago, he had. With me.

I'd been bored stiff at a Ghana Association dinner, when Yofi had sat down beside me, asking me why I looked like I wanted to poke an eyeball out. Instead of the simpering flirtation my mother would have preferred, along the lines of how my night was better now that he'd shown up, I'd been truthful and direct.

I told him I would rather watch paint dry in a humid room than be at this dinner.

To this day, I remember his laughter at my answer. Full-bodied, head thrown back, arm placed over his trim waist, his amusement had been infectious. His gleaming white teeth were a stark contrast to his smooth, ebony skin.

To say that Yofi was attractive didn't even begin to hit the mark. He was what I thought of when I heard *tall, dark, and handsome.* He looked like a very tall Michael B. Jordan, that actor my auntie Ruth lamented she should have married.

And honestly, finding a Ghanaian man over six feet tall who didn't think beer was a food group and didn't eat fufu for every meal? That was like winning the lottery. Add gorgeous on top of it all?

He seemed perfect. But more important, he *was* perfect for Ghanaian moms. For the first time in my life, I'd managed to satisfy my parents with my choice.

Yep, I'd landed the Holy Grail and everything that came along with it, including the circus I could hear going on outside.

My okyeame—the linguist meant to be the intermediary for us—was negotiating my bride price with Auntie Wenda, Yofi's family's okyeame. I loved the idea that it was two women who were getting what could sometimes be a tense negotiation done.

For a lot of tribes, okyeame were usually men. But the Gas

were more matrilineal, so we had women. My mother had told me to keep my mouth shut around them, though, because, God forbid, I might let slip the radical things I believed, like that love was love and that people should be allowed to marry anybody they wanted.

No, no. Never say that.

I had asked for someone open-minded. Mom and I had fought bitterly.

I had lost.

Now my auntie Phoebe was loudly talking about how I was pious, served Christ, and would make a good Christian wife who would listen and obey. Little did she know that I had asked Yofi to strike the word "obey" from my white wedding vows. Because if we were all being honest, everyone knew there was no way in hell that Ofosua Addo was going to obey anyone.

I had a mouth. Sometimes it said things.

I relaxed a fraction when she moved on to how my future husband's family was going to have to show that they were worthy, that they had the gifts and the means to look after me.

There was a commotion outside the door, but I ignored it and forced myself to breathe despite my far-too-tight kaba and slit. The traditional blouse and skirt set was made of white lace, with a patchwork of kente woven around each piece of lace. It was stunning.

The top was strapless, showing off my shoulders. My mother had been scandalized at first, but she'd eventually relented. It was basically a corset, shoving my boobs up under my chin, which I honestly felt was false advertising. Yofi knew what he was getting.

Hell, we lived together. None of this would be a surprise.

Finally, the commotion outside broke through my thoughts when the door was jimmied open. "Cuuuuzzz!"

I had to laugh. My cousin Kukua was not known for her subtlety. Her mom and mine were sisters. Her father did something for the World Bank, as was the way. They were Ghanaian, but her mother was half-American, so she had been raised to believe in freedom of choice in what you were going to do and study, and how you were going to grow up.

So Kukua became an artist and the wild one in our family. Every rule I at least attempted to follow, she blatantly broke. Hence, she was my favorite cousin.

"How are you, my darling? Are you ready to be shackled forever?"

"You make marriage seem amazing."

"Mark my words, I am never getting married. I prefer freedom of choice, freedom of movement, freedom of *dick*."

I snorted a laugh, which set Kukua off into a fit of giggles until she was snorting too.

And that was when my mother walked in. "Oh my God, the two of you. Can you keep it down? The okyeame are about to present the gold and gifts."

Most couples just presented jewelry and traditional cloth that the bride's mother already had in the house, but not my parents. My mother had insisted on a new gold wedding jewelry set to show what a good home I came from.

Some of the pieces were so intricate, heavy, and ornate that I'd never wear them. They were more showpieces. After that was done, Yofi and his family would arrive in style from the west side of the park. If we had been in Ghana, they would have had a massive caravan, likely stopping traffic in Cantonments, the posh neighborhood in Accra where my parents had their compound. With traditional marriages in olden times, the richer you were, the more likely you were to have cows to offer your new bride.

The exchange of drinks would be next. The drinks sealed the deal. For some reason, over the centuries, schnapps had become a vital part of the drink exchange, but in Yofi's case, they'd also bring Lagavulin and Macallan. He knew my father loved scotch. I knew for a fact there would also be a bottle of 2013 Goût de Diamants in the drinks they brought. Yofi had been so excited to show it off. But it felt like such a waste. Who needed a million-euro bottle of champagne? It was all for show.

In traditional marriages, on the off chance you were granted a divorce by the families, all you really had to do was return the drinks and fill out paperwork for the court. But getting one granted was so difficult.

And I always wanted to know what happened if you drank all the drinks at the reception.

My mother looked stunning in an elegant mother-of-the-bride off-shoulder kente kaba and slit in green, fuchsia, and cream. She also wore beaded dangling feathers from Kenya in her ears, and around her neck was the simple gold cross necklace she always wore.

But even now, she was busy bemoaning the fact that there wouldn't be cows. I should've known she hadn't really made peace with doing the ceremony in the States.

"Be practical! Where the hell were we going to find a cow in the middle of Manhattan? And where would we put said cow, honestly?" I asked.

I know she thought if Yofi wanted to show off appropriately, his family would have found a way to bring one. Kukua wrapped her arm around me. "Auntie Helen, look at your beautiful daughter. Can't you leave her be for one small moment?"

My mother sniffed and gathered herself. "I have never been prouder of you than in this moment. When your child looks beyond themselves to the future and future generations, it's a beautiful thing. I have done what a mother is supposed to do. Soon it will be your turn."

I heard a lot of hooting and hollering and laughing outside. Kukua leaned toward the window. "Ah yes, they're presenting the jewels."

My head throbbed, the stress of the day seeping in. "What are they saying?"

"That before your husband presents these to you as you lay naked on the marriage bed, which is what got all the aunties hollering, he will present them to your family to show that he is worthy of you. Did you know they brought you boudoir clothes to tempt your husband?"

My eyes went wide. "No, they did not."

Auntie Ruth stepped back, and I propped myself up just in time to see Auntie Phoebe pull something out of the adinkra-decorated chest and hold it up . . . Oh my God, was that a lace teddy?

My mother laughed. "Ruth, how are we coming?"

I could hear the smile in her voice. "Auntie, we're almost finished. Doesn't she look beautiful?"

Mom glanced down at me, and for once, I saw satisfaction on her face. I was making her proud by doing this, by letting her go as wild as she wanted. I loved her. I did want to make her happy. It was just that usually what filled her with joy and what revved me up were at opposite ends. I really hoped this would be the exception. "Are you happy, Mum?"

"As long as you're happy, that's all I've ever wanted."

Kukua tried to hide a giggle behind her hand, because we both knew that what she really meant was that as long as I was getting married to a man like Yofi, she was satisfied.

I loved my parents, but as long as I had been alive, I had never done anything to satisfy the Doctors Addo. There was never a straight-A report card that was enough. The question was always . . . How can you be better?

Mom made her way back to the door as Auntie Ruth released me. "Ah, and you are finished, my dear," Auntie Ruth said.

Kukua helped me to the mirror. Wow. The makeup artist had highlighted my cheekbones to perfection. And my hair really did look like the best kind of crown.

I turned to see Kukua was beaming at me. She took my hand as the commotion outside swelled once again. Yofi and his family were arriving. I could feel the drums in my blood, thumping through my veins. I could almost picture the dancers because I had watched them rehearse a thousand times. I moved my feet in time with the beat as I closed my eyes and took a deep breath.

When I released my breath and opened my eyes, Kukua met my gaze. "Before we go out there, you know as your cousin and your maid of honor . . . Honestly, let's face it, I'm no maid. I like *woman of honor*, personally."

I laughed. "Okay, woman of honor it is."

"Are you *sure* you want to do this?"

My brow furrowed. "Of course I do. Why wouldn't I?"

Her brown eyes bored into my soul. "I'm not saying you don't, but I know you. You have this deep need to keep your word and see things through. If you have any hesitation whatsoever with any of this, now is the time to say so because I will sneak you out of here so fast."

Unexpectedly, there was a part of me deep down inside that wanted to scream, *Oh my God, yes, please*. But that was one percent, the part of me afraid of the unknown, afraid of things that weren't in my direct control. I was getting married today.

I *wanted* to get married. I loved Yofi. I did.

I did.

But then a sneaky memory barged in.

A kiss from long ago, from someone who was *not* Yofi. From someone *before* Yofi. And just the memory was enough to make me feel ashamed. Deeply. But I swallowed it. From this point forward, I would think only of Yofi. "No. I want to do this. This is the right thing to do."

Her gaze searched mine, but then she relented. "Okay, if you say so."

I nodded. "I do," I said, grinning. "See what I did there?"

She may have rolled her eyes at me, but still, I let my cousin take my hand and lead me toward the drumbeats. I was getting married. And nothing was going to ruin this day for me.

CHAPTER 2

OFOSUA

ADINKRA SAYING:
(*Dwennimmen*) It represents strength (in mind, body, and soul), humility, wisdom, and learning.

HELEN ADDO:
Love makes us all fools. We must learn never to be fools again.

By the time we arrived in Brooklyn at the Weylin for the reception after the trad wedding, my cheeks hurt from smiling. I had never smiled so much in my life, and my mind was spinning. The valets were bringing in all the gifts, weaving between the tuxedoed waitstaff. "Relax, relax." My mother kept trying to make me enjoy this beautiful venue. And it *was* beautiful. The domes and architecture were breathtaking; the coffered ceiling, limestone walls, and mosaic marble floors so elegant.

So many names and faces. Yofi and I thought we'd be able to cull some of the folks from the ceremony to the reception, since we'd scheduled the reception for seven in the evening and moved venues from Central Park to Brooklyn, but no. There were people *everywhere*.

A little sliver of panic tried to wind around my lungs. Suddenly,

I was hyperaware of the din of chatter, the brassy tone of the trumpet as the band warmed up, and my beautiful gold-and-white reception kaba and slit trying to choke the life out of me. Two hours ago I'd felt confident and happy, and now . . . now my new corset was squeezing the life out of me. And every time I took a step, the slit left a tiny little slice on my thigh.

Truly death by a thousand cuts.

Take a deep breath. You've finally managed to make your mother proud. Enjoy it.

Guests poured in, excited to come and eat, or "chop," as we said at home. In no time, they'd be full on a fusion twist of old favorites like kelewele, jollof, and kenkey, prepped by the famed Ghanaian chef Adowa Blankson. And of course they'd drink as much free top-shelf liquor as they could. It was why they were there, after all. The spectacle of the ceremony was just icing.

I was elated.

Is "elated" the right word?

Yofi was too. While he'd not exactly been *demonstrative*, he was gripping my hand tightly.

We had a room full of gifts. Our town house in Park Slope was spacious, but not whole-bone-china-department-of-Bloomingdale's-with-settings-for-fifty kind of room. As it stood, we'd already received some wedding gifts at the town house that included Royal Doulton and Spode. What were we going to do with all that china? Obviously, people had ignored our registry. Some of the presents would have to go into storage or to my parents' houses. They owned two apartments in Greenwich Village.

My mother would gladly store anything we wanted. It would earn her bragging points, like *My daughter was given so many blessings for her wedding she couldn't even store them all.*

I'd crossed the finish line. Her job was done. I'd never seen her glow quite so brightly. When she danced over with a grin, I had to smile back. "Oh, my beautiful daughter, *married* at last. I have to tell you, I was so worried you wouldn't make it this far."

"Thanks for the vote of confidence, Mum."

"I just know how you are sometimes. But, Ofosua, know that I'm always proud of you, no matter what."

"Thanks, Mum. Now you can finally let me breathe for a minute, at least."

She laughed. "No, no. I want my grandchildren."

I sighed, because even though I'd hoped that we'd be left alone to get used to being married, I knew how it went. Even tonight, people had already commented, "Ah, you shouldn't wait too long before having children." And psychologically, I understood. Our family and guests wanted to perpetuate the culture in the US.

They wanted to plant the seeds, because in essence, the trad wedding wasn't about Yofi and me getting married, but rather about our *families* uniting. The merging of bloodlines, bringing us together, making sure we could not be separated. Because even, God forbid, in the event of divorce, I would still be their daughter-in-law in the eyes of our culture, whether I liked it or not. It was a lot of pressure.

I needed Yofi to reassure me, but he had vanished. "Mum, have you seen Yofi?"

"Oh, you know how men are. He's probably with his friends. You'll have to get used to not being the center of his world. A good way to keep busy is to finish your master's in finance. I wouldn't oppose you going to law school either."

Of course. "Mum, it's my wedding day. We're not doing this."

She pursed her lips and sighed. I learned early on that it was best to cut it off when she was about to embark on a lower-yourself-esteem tangent. It was safer that way. "Mum, excuse me. I'm going to go find him, okay?"

"Okay, but don't take too long. I have more people to reintroduce you to."

I laughed. "I'll be back soon."

I found his group of friends on the dance floor. One of them dragged me out there, trying to show me his moves. "Oh, Kpakpo. Don't you know I can shake 'em better than you?" I asked.

For a few minutes I let the bass and the drums take over as hiplife music played. When the song changed to "City Boys" by Burna Boy, I begged off to continue the hunt. And I laughed as the younger guests flooded the dance floor.

I found my father at the bar wearing his cream caftan, which resembled a long tunic with intricate embroidery near the V-neck collar. He was nursing a scotch, judging by the tone of the liquid. "Having fun, Dad?"

He gave me a misty smile that lifted his cheeks and had his ebony-dark eyes vanishing in the creases of his face. He lifted his glass to toast me with his deep baritone, "My little girl is married. I'm stuck somewhere being so proud and happy for you and sad that you're not mine anymore."

I wrapped my arms around his tall, slim frame in a tight hug, and I felt like my heart was going to burst. "I'm always yours, Dad."

When he pulled back, he scrubbed a hand over his close-shaved white beard and gave me a somber smile, all the while blinking the tears from his eyes. "You're happy, though?"

"Of course. I just wish I could find my groom. He's completely disappeared. Have you seen him?"

There was a tight narrowing of my father's eyes for an imperceptible moment, but his gaze quickly warmed again. "Where could he be but by your side?"

"That is a good question. I'll try the balcony. Enjoy your drink. I won't tell Mum you were sneaking one."

He harrumphed and deliberately took a sip. "One article she reads about how detrimental drinking can be to your health as you get older, and I have to go dry? What nonsense is that? I'm the head of the house. I can have a drink if I want to."

"In semisecret?"

The chuckle he gave me warmed me from the inside and reminded me of my childhood, when he would sneak me chocolates. "It is your mother. She can be quite formidable."

With a kiss to my father's cheek, I continued my search. Our party occupied both domes of the Weylin, and the white-wedding crowd in a month's time would be even bigger. My brain kept doing mental calculations of exactly how much the trad ceremony and reception would cost my parents. We were well into six figures already, between the outfits, venues, food, and alcohol. Then all the gifts brought to presentation, especially the gold. But I tried not to think about it because I knew that this traditional ceremony made my parents happier than anything else I'd done lately, so it was better to just let them have their moment.

On Monday we'd go to the courthouse, and then we'd be *officially* married in the eyes of New York State. And after that, I had had a lot more input in the big white church wedding in front of even more family and friends.

Hopefully.

I turned down one of the halls where the restrooms were. It was eerily quiet, with only the faint beat of the music in the background. In the skylights above, the moon hung low and bright, giving us additional light for our party. For the first time in the last twelve hours, I was *actually* breathing instead of doing that shallow-breath thing. I felt good, despite having been on my feet in these Louboutins for over four hours since I'd changed into my reception outfit. I felt like I was where I was supposed to be. Today was the first day of the rest of my life with Yofi.

When we got home I was going to crash and probably sleep for three days, but it was worth it.

I was *a wife*.

And then I heard something.

Muttering and then muffled moaning. The sounds were coming from behind one of the closed doors just beyond the women's restroom. But I didn't think there were any guest rooms down here. An office? I knew it was a good general rule to stay out of people's business, but something made me take a step closer to that door. And then someone said, "Oh God, right there. Right fucking there. Don't stop. Don't you dare stop."

I staggered back. I knew that voice, but this wasn't right. There was no fucking way. Even though some primal part of me sensed the danger, I stepped closer.

My brain refused to believe.

I heard another moan and, "Fuck. You're so good at that. I needed that so bad."

The bottom fell out of my stomach. A shiver racked my spine as I stood rooted into position. Unable to move.

Yofi was behind that door. And someone was getting him off. *At our reception.*

From that moment on, everything seemed to happen underwater. Time slowed and sound became warped. Through what felt like a tunnel, I heard, "I have to get back. It's been too long."

How long had I been standing there? A minute? Five? When my brain came back online, the same Burna Boy song was playing, so it couldn't have been more than two minutes.

The door opened, and I stood there in the dim light, staring at my husband. Was that a mop and a bucket just behind him?

He immediately stepped out and slammed the door behind him.

His normally open smile was nowhere to be seen. Instead, a myriad of emotions played on his face. The wide eyes and lifted brows of surprise, the furrowed forehead of confusion, and finally, his face set in a grim mask, his full lips pressed together. He reached for me. "Ofosua, it's not what it seems."

One breath. Two. My heart squeezed hard as my lungs fought for air, fought for oxygen, fought for life. "You, y-you, you were ch-cheating on me just now."

He didn't even have the good sense to lie as he quickly led me down the hall, away from the cleaning closet he'd just been in. Classy. "Ofosua, I didn't want to hurt you. It's just—"

I shook my head. This was not happening. Here. At my *wedding*. "No. No. No. Please, God, no." My voice rose higher and higher.

His all-too-familiar impatience sparked. "Don't get hysterical. Just calm down."

Calm. Down.

I stared at him, my disbelief, and pain, unspooling into horror and humiliation. "You do this to me, on the day of our traditional marriage, and you're telling me not to get *hysterical*?" Somewhere in the deep recesses of my brain, my control lost its slippery hold on the temper I never let out. "You cheating asshole, pathetic little-dicked—"

"Quiet, Ofosua," he barked.

"Who is she? Who. Is. She?"

Yofi didn't answer. My heart splintered. *This is what heartbreak is.*

Out of the corner of my eye, I saw my mother hurrying toward us with Yofi's mother, Auntie Judy, and his brother Martey trailing behind her. But I wasn't really paying any mind to them. Yofi had all of my furious attention.

I'd taken enough self-defense classes to know how to land a hit, yet violence wasn't part of my nature. But something overtook me in that hallway. I drew my arm back, but just before it connected, Martey grabbed me around the waist.

"Yofi, Ofosua, what is happening?"

At my mother's appearance—even Yofi wasn't so far gone that he would disrespect her—he stood up straight and smoothed the front of his caftan. Only his glassy eyes and slight sway gave away that he'd been drinking. Though that was the least of our problems. "Auntie, please. We are having a misunderstanding. That's all."

No. He was not going to pin this on me. "I didn't *misunderstand*, Yofi. I caught you cheating on me."

My mother gasped. "Whaaat?"

"Yes, Mum. Your perfect son-in-law. I caught him in a closet having sex with someone else. Just now."

My mother blinked in confusion, looking around for the offending closet. "What closet? Who?"

"Hell if I know. Care to enlighten us, Yofi?"

Yofi stared out at the party. He didn't deny anything I said. Which meant none of this was a bad dream. It was real. And that's when the thumping in my ears started to get louder and louder, like a herd of elephants thundering toward me. My palms started to sweat, and the edges of my vision started to gray.

Oh God. No, God. No, not in here. Not right now.

I sucked in a breath and released it slowly. Bring it down. Bring it down. Bring it down to a manageable seven. Hell, an eight. I would take an eight right now.

Instead, the panic kept rising.

As my mother marched away, presumably in search of my father, Judy ran after her. "Helen, wait, wait. I'm so sorry."

I stared up at the man who'd sworn he loved me. The man who had told me countless times on lazy Sundays in bed that he loved me a thousand different ways. When they say you never really know someone, this is what they mean. There was something in his eyes that almost looked like an apology, but then his gaze hardened abruptly. "It is what it is. You pushed for this marriage and spectacle. I didn't want to get married. But you pushed. Now, if you can learn to be a proper wife, then maybe we can work."

Martey couldn't stop me any longer, and I released a front jab to Yofi's nose. Blood was suddenly everywhere. Bonus, it was accompanied by a satisfying crunching sound.

I turned on my heel and I stalked back through the party toward the exit. I had to get out of the Weylin. Away from all of this. My mother appeared at my side, yanking me back.

"Mum, what are you doing?"

My mother didn't even meet my gaze as my father approached.

"Helen, what is happening? People are starting to make noise that something is wrong." And then he saw the look on my face.

My mother, for once, stayed calm. "That man cheated on your daughter. Today of all days. During what was supposed to be a joining of the families. The disrespect." And then she flung open the display chest Yofi's family had brought and threw out all the jewels and the money. They scattered, jewels pinging on the marble floor as they rolled.

The thundering was getting closer. Closer and closer.

Yofi reappeared, holding a towel to his face, his white caftan, a bloody mess. *Good.*

Auntie Judy came forward. "This is a misunderstanding. Yofi and Martey, you will clean up all the jewels and the money and take the chest back. Ofosua, we're going to talk about this because we are now family. You can't undo—"

My mother stepped in front of her. "Judy, if you ever want us to speak again, you will get out of my daughter's face. We are leaving."

"Mum . . ." My voice was weak, and I could feel the dizziness coming for me. The clapping sound of my heart in my chest was too loud.

And then, in front of everybody, that ring of light that had turned gray, and then charcoal, went totally black.

CHAPTER 3

OFOSUA

ADINKRA SAYING:
(Adwo) Calmness. A symbol for peace, tranquility, and quiet.
HELEN ADDO:
Strengthen yourself. Do not embarrass your family by carrying on.

Having a Ghanaian mother, especially a Ga mother, when there was a crisis, you might as well be listening to an announcer at a football match. With African moms, it didn't matter where they were from—they always had a specific decibel of volume.

And in the emergency room of NYU Langone Hospital, my mother was in full form.

"Eh, Ofosua, what is this nonsense? A heart attack? My child, you're only twenty-five. Hmm. I told you this job of yours is no good. You should have been a lawyer."

Since my symptoms were no longer acute and my heart rate was mostly stable, and since this was my mother's former hospital, I'd been seen quickly then temporarily placed on a stretcher in the in the hallway until a bed in the private wing opened up. I was already hooked up to an IV and a monitor just in case. I knew it wasn't a heart attack. But there was no getting Mom to stop the steady stream of admonitions. Unless . . .

"Why don't you go and see if you can force them into giving me a room?"

She patted my hand and was off at a clip that belied her age and Stuart Weitzmans. I knew Kukua was on her way. If I could just get ten minutes to myself, I'd be fine. I would figure this out.

In and out. Steady breaths. In for three. Out for three. Visualize my calm place. Just ten minutes. Long enough to—

"Ofosua?"

I peeled my eye open to find the last person I ever wanted or expected to see, ever. And definitely not today, the worst day of my entire life. *Cole Drake.*

It couldn't be. What the hell? What was he doing in Brooklyn?

No longer was he the sexy stranger I'd met on a balcony who gave me a kiss full of promises. The best kiss of my . . . no. No, I would not be thinking that. Now, two years later, Cole Drake was my coworker, possibly future boss . . . and nemesis.

Though I was reasonably sure he was unaware of being that last part. I hid it. Plus, how could anyone not like Mr. Gorgeous, Rich, and Charming?

I'd be happy to tell them exactly how.

I still thought back to the moment we met often enough to make me want to stab things.

I'd finally clawed my way out of free-labor hell and gotten promoted to editorial assistant a year and four months ago, eight months after he'd asked me out then vanished. It had been my first day, and I'd been so excited because it finally seemed as if all the hard work had paid off.

I had, of course, worn my good-luck outfit. Fuchsia wide-leg, high-waisted pants; a more conservative silk cream blouse with slightly puffed sleeves; and my classic black red-bottomed slingbacks. I felt and looked amazing.

I was being introduced around by Brittany Mills, who had been at Drake for a year longer than I. As an intern, my interactions had been mostly limited to my team, and other interns. I didn't get to interact with a lot of senior members of staff.

I remembered it like it was yesterday. We'd been right by the elevators when they opened and out stepped Mr. Drake and an all-too-familiar man. My brain had a hard time reconciling him there, in front of me, instead of on that long-ago balcony from months before.

Honestly, I'd thought I had imagined him.

I'd thought he was a figment of my imagination.

I'd thought at any moment the world was going to swallow me whole.

Instead, I'd had to stand there awkwardly that horrible day, in shoes that suddenly felt too tight and pinched my toes.

His uncle had stopped and welcomed me. He'd been one of my mentors when I was an intern. Then he'd turned to introduce me to his nephew. *N-E-P-H-E-W*. As in, a *Drake*.

I had made out with my boss's nephew.

Cole did a stutter step and stared at me. For a moment I thought a spark of recognition was going to flicker. I prepared myself for hella awkwardness. But instead, when his uncle made the introduction and I stuck out my hand to shake his, he just *stared* at me.

And not just stared, but blankly stared. No recognition, no warmth, no apology, nothing.

What was worse, was he didn't reach to shake my hand, which left me standing there like a fool for several long moments.

When I finally drew my hand back, he mumbled a greeting

before following after his uncle. Fair enough that he hadn't called, but why act like we'd never met? And worse, act like he couldn't be bothered to shake my hand?

All I knew about Cole Drake at that moment pointed to him being an ass. Not only had he given me the kind of kiss that curled my toes, but he'd made it seem like . . . *something more.* He'd said he wanted to take me on a date, then ghosted me.

Which would have been whatever. To then be introduced to me again months later and pretend not to know me and be a total asshole was too much.

He'd established our new rules of engagement in that moment. I'd just matched his energy. We'd been doing the same dance for nearly a year and a half now.

I blamed myself, though. How could I have not recognized immediately that he was a Drake? My boss's *nephew,* no less. Surely, I'd seen a photo of him somewhere in the office. After all, Drake was a family-run publishing house.

But mostly, when I thought back to that first night, I wondered how I could have been naïve enough to believe he might be different from every other rich nepo baby asshole just like him. The city was full of them.

Aren't you currently enjoying the perks of being a nepo baby . . . and rich?

Not the point.

Shaking myself out of my reverie, I said, "Cole. What are you doing here? Isn't Brooklyn off the beaten path for you?"

"My dad. He had an accident and is getting checked out, but they won't discharge him without someone to take him home since he's been sedated, so I got drafted. Wait, you're on a gurney hooked up to a monitor. What happened?" He looked genuinely concerned. But I knew better.

I could imagine how I must look. My once-beautiful Afro now misshapen, streaked makeup, and threadbare blanket. To my horror, tears sprang to my eyes.

Of all the people to look weak in front of. It was too much on top of an already horrendous day. I didn't want gossip at the office. And I especially didn't want pity. I wanted respect. I needed it.

I'd started the day excited to get married. And now I was being humbled for the second time in a way I couldn't ever have imagined. What were the fucking chances?

"Please, please don't tell anybody at work you saw me here."

His brow furrowed. "Why would I—"

My mother chose that moment to save the day. "Ofosua, your room is ready, although, I will say the nurse was very rude. I had to remind her that I am a former hospital administrator and that she had to treat me with—oh, I see your aide is finally here. Young man, please wheel her into room three-fourteen."

God, I know you stopped listening to me ages ago, but can you please make her shut up? Ooh, or swallow me whole? "Mom, he doesn't—"

"It's fine. I'm happy to do it." Cole's voice was low as he lifted me easily, his cologne triggering a memory of the brush of his lips on that balcony.

He settled me in the wheelchair and hit me with one of his Cole Drake smirks, and I scowled at him.

"I need you to promise."

"Relax, Ofosua. I promise. As far as I'm concerned, this never happened."

On second thought, I knew for a fact that Cole Drake could deliver on that promise. He was good at forgetting me. I did relax at that. A little.

Then, with a little bow to my mother, he left.

Thirty minutes later, still wearing nothing but a hospital gown and a plastered-on smile, I watched my mom circle the room for the hundredth time and clenched my jaw to keep from saying what I was really thinking. Instead, I said, "Mum, please calm down. Your blood pressure."

"*My* blood pressure? Apparently, I'm healthier than you are. A heart attack. What child of mine has a heart attack? And on her engagement day. The way everybody will be talking . . ."

They'd be talking, all right. I wondered how I could have been so stupid about Yofi to have missed the signs.

I could feel it again. That sharp, stinging pain in my chest like I was being pierced by an ice pick. And the shortness of breath, and then that weird skipping beat, slow, slow, slow, and then rapidly catching up. Oh God, it was happening again. I tried to breathe through it because, God, I couldn't lose my shit right now.

"Mum, stop. It's not a heart attack. You're exaggerating."

All around me, machines beeped. And the faster my heartbeat got, the faster they chirped. Next thing I knew, some nurses ran in to check my vitals, and then a man followed. Tall, nicely built, lean but with broad shoulders. Light brown skin, dark eyes. Hair closely cropped.

My mother, catching one glance at the doctor, stopped talking and stared. "Eh, you're the doctor?"

He nodded, his smile flashing. "Yes, I'm Dr. Banks."

My heart was still doing that beating-too-fast thing, but the machines had stopped blaring.

Dr. Banks looked at them as the nurses checked my vitals, then he came over with the stethoscope, putting the ends in his ears and looking down at me with a broad smile and a nod. "May I?"

I nodded and shrugged.

He lifted the gown and pressed the cool stethoscope to my chest, right above my heart. Completely professional.

I tried to breathe evenly and not think about the night. To not think about how my husband had been screwing someone else at our reception. Humiliating me in front of all our family.

And . . . there went my heart again, running a race for the hills even when my feet were stationary. I tried to breathe properly, but all that came out was shallow little huffs . . . like that horrid moment. I knew. I knew what everyone would say. That I hadn't been able to satisfy him. After all, why else would he cheat?

Everybody would be looking to place blame. Culturally, no one ever blamed the man.

When the room started to spin, Dr. Hot Stuff glanced down at me and frowned. "What were you thinking about just now?"

I shook my head. "Nothing."

His eyes were kind. "I can't help you if you don't talk to me."

I slid a glance over to my mother. "It's really not—"

My mother jumped in immediately. "Ofosua, what is this nonsense? Tell the doctor. Eh, you would think I didn't raise her right. Hmm, she caught her husband cheating at the big party to celebrate their union. Then she fell over. We couldn't wake her."

As she spoke, my breathing shallowed, and the edges of my vision started to gray. Legitimately anyone else could have kept me calmer than her. Hell, even Cole Drake had managed it. And we despised each other.

A nurse brought over one of those oxygen masks and placed it over my head. The doctor took my hand, squeezing it gently, then met my gaze.

"Ms. Addo, I want you to take one breath, as deep as you can. In, two, three, hold it for a moment, and out, two, three."

What the fuck? This didn't feel like any other panic attack I'd ever had. This was far worse. And he wanted me to breathe?

I kept trying to take off the mask, but he squeezed my hand in a firm way that told me he brooked no argument, his look reminding me of the one my mother always gave when she meant business. So I breathed like I was told.

My gaze kept sliding to my mother. All five foot two of her was pacing impatiently. I could tell she wanted to run over and shove the doctor aside to berate me into behaving, but she didn't. I knew she was worried. Her wig was slightly askew. She had as much hair as I did. More, even. But dutifully, every week, she went and had her hair washed, pressed, braided, and tucked away under one of her many, *many* wigs.

She was still dressed to the nines, but she'd swapped her Weitzmans for the emergency Louis Vuitton flats she carried in her Birkin.

After the machine stopped beeping and my chest stopped hurting, Dr. Banks patted my hand again and then sat on the edge of my bed. "Ofosua, it would seem that you have been suffering from acute anxiety. More severe symptoms resemble a panic attack."

"But my chest was on fire. And it feels different this time. More severe."

He nodded. "Oh, I understand. But I'm telling you, it's not a heart attack. It's your body reacting to your senses being overloaded."

Over his shoulder, I could see my mother staring at me. A heart attack was one thing. But good Ghanaian girls did not have *panic attacks*. You needed to be poised and always composed. My mother slid in with a cool, assessing smile as she looked him over.

"What do you mean, 'panic attack'? She's never had panic attacks. That's a white people problem."

Dr. Banks shook his head as he glanced over his shoulder at my mother, his smile wavering but never losing his patience.

"No, Mrs. Addo, I assure you, panic attacks are not just for white people. Your daughter has been experiencing them. How long now, Ofosua?"

"It's *Dr.* Addo, actually. Tell him, Ofosua. He's wrong about the panic attacks."

I swallowed, not willing to think about the times before a big presentation or every time someone brought up the wedding. Or before that, in college, high school, all the times I'd been under extreme pressure, when I'd felt that little twinge and too-fast breathing.

But all those times, I'd managed to suck it up, hadn't I? I'd gotten myself under control. I rarely lost it. It was my one amazing quality. If I were a vampire, like in those *Twilight* books, super self-control would be my superpower. But my superpowers had seemingly fled. "I-it's fine. I have the twinges all the time, and—"

He glanced at my mother. "If you'd like, we can speak privately."

My mother was not having that. "There's nothing that she's going to tell you that she can't tell me. I'm her mother."

I sighed, then the pain twinged again, and he frowned, reading my charts and the machines around me. Softly, he said, "Dr. Addo, if you wouldn't mind leaving us—"

My mother opened her mouth to yell at him and me, and to avoid it, I blurted out, "I've been having them for years. Since I was little. The only thing different about today was I was publicly humiliated in a way I could never have imagined, so that probably made it worse."

The wave of silence that fell over the room was deafening. I'd never really understood what that meant before, but right now, it was as if someone had plugged my ears, complete with pressure. And even though I could see people walking by the doors and nurses rushing to call things out to one another, and the machines around me continuing to beep and blip, I heard nothing. I watched as my mother's face crumpled, and she blinked at me. I don't know how many seconds passed before the sound came back.

"What do you mean, for years?" my mother prodded.

The machines started to go again, and Dr. Banks took my hand. "Uh-uh-uh, no, we aren't going to do that. We're going to practice that breathing I showed you. In you go. And out. That's good. Mrs.—erm, *Dr.*—Addo, if you can't help keep my patient calm, I will have you removed."

My mother rose to her full height. "You will *not* have me removed. Do you know my husband and I donate to this hospital? I can have the board—"

"Oh my God, Mum, stop it. Stop." She blinked at me as if I'd slapped her. I rushed to defuse the impending bomb. "Mum, please, I beg you, I'm so tired."

But she was not quite ready to put it to bed. "Why, Ofosua? You've had access to everything you could ever need. But you went and picked up anxiety." As if I'd picked it up from the store when I was supposed to be shopping for badassery.

I sighed. "I didn't really know something was wrong until college. And then I figured it was something I could will away."

Dr. Banks pulled his hands away and glanced around as if uncomfortable.

My mother's voice went shrill. "What could you have to be anxious about? We've given you everything. Besides, you've never said anything. This can't be right."

"Mum, can we *not* right now?"

I watched the implosion in her head, her annoyance at the absurdity, then the slow dawning and the fury. But this was a fury I knew would be aimed at Yofi, his mother, his whole family. Helen Addo was ready for war.

Dr. Probably-Wished-He-Never-Met-Me turned back to me. "I'm so sorry. I'm going to prescribe something that you can take when you feel an episode coming. In the meantime, I also suggest maybe finding someone to talk to. I can give you some recommendations."

I frowned. "No. I mean, I can get it under control. It's fine."

He shook his head. "As your doctor today, I am telling you not to do this alone. And when you say you have these twinges all the time, what does that exactly mean?"

"I don't know. When I get stressed out or things seem over-whelming, I get that pinched, rapid-heart-rate feeling."

"Okay, what do you do to alleviate it?"

I frowned. "I tell myself to suck it up and then go get it done."

Something told me that was the wrong response. He blinked at me. Blinked again. And then his brow furrowed. "You're serious?"

I nodded. "Yeah. But this time, I couldn't. I don't know. I couldn't move."

"Okay, so we should discuss some stress management tools."

"Yeah, good luck with that."

"This is important. It's for your health. Do you understand me? I'm going to give you a couple referrals for people to talk to, as well as some simple basics, like the deep breathing you were doing earlier, meditation, yoga even."

I nodded slowly. He was right. I'd never been rushed to the hospital before, and it was terrifying. Whatever I was doing hadn't worked tonight. "I understand."

He gave another squeeze of my hand and stood up, and then he gave my mum a fast nod. "I'll be right back with her prescription. Hang tight."

"Eh, I will get rid of the stress. Once I speak to Yofi's parents—"

We were Ga. Which meant my mother would lean toward

revenge. "No, Mum. I want nothing from him. I just want this over. I need to call Kukua and see if I can stay with her for a few weeks while I find a new apartment."

"Hmm, I will make sure his mother knows this shame lies at her feet."

"Mum, please . . . This isn't Auntie's fault. I need to get my life together and figure out where I'm going to stay tonight, and I don't want to—"

Her brow furrowed. "What do you mean? Of course, you'll come home."

Oh God. No, no, no, not home.

The machines started to go again, and Mum scowled at them. "They need to take care of these stupid machines. We know now you're not going to die."

That was my mother for you, really boiling things down. "Mum, I'm not going to stay with you and Dad. Remember when I moved to Ghana after I graduated, and we were under the same roof? How we fought?"

Right after I finished high school, my mother had left her position at Mount Sinai West and taken a position with the WHO working in the West Africa region, stationed in Accra. Dad already did a lot of technology and investing work around the world, so he'd gone with her and just flew out for meetings and conferences.

Like a fool, I'd thought it would be good to go home for six months after graduation to regroup and relax before coming back to hit the ground running to pursue a job in publishing. I'd finally gotten an internship at Drake and jumped at the chance. I'd been okay with an internship to start because I didn't need the money.

But those six months had been torture. I'd vowed to never live with them, my mother in particular, ever again.

She waved a dismissive hand. "Oh, nonsense. We have the

extra apartment here in the city. Right next door to ours. It's a doorman building, so it's safer. And your father bought it to take the wall down to give us more room, because the 2,500 square feet we have feels a bit cramped, as you know. But we can hold off on that. I keep telling him we don't absolutely need to increase our square footage. Who does he think will clean all that extra space? Not to mention, even though it was renovated to add all those floor-to-ceiling windows, I'll want to change some of those back to stone. I don't like feeling like strangers can see inside. But that's a large project I do not have time for at the moment. This is a better arrangement. You will have your own space, and that way I can cook for you every day."

I blinked at her. "Mum, I don't need—"

"Don't be ridiculous. What, you're going to stay with your cousin and live in Brooklyn on her couch?"

That sounded fabulous, actually. "Yes, why not?"

Kukua had her own place, completely free from her parents. But she only had one bedroom, and she had an active dating life, so if I moved in, I *would* have to make myself scarce often.

"Mum, I don't want to move home."

"You're not *living* at home. This is just until we get you someone new."

My voice was small when I spoke. "Mum, I don't want someone new."

She clucked her tongue. "What did that stupid, foolish boy know about love? When you make a commitment, you stay with it. This is nonsense. When I speak to his mother, we'll sort it out."

I could see it then. Yofi hadn't only broken my heart today, he'd broken my mother's too. All her plans. The way she'd intended to lord our brilliant marriage over her friends. This wasn't about *me*. Culturally, when you agreed to get married, it was the *families* agreeing to get married. Not two people. "Don't worry," she said. "We'll fix all of this."

That was what I was worried about. My mother jumping in to try and *fix* everything. She thought this would be as simple as returning the drinks presented, but it wouldn't be.

To have this whole thing reversed, we would have to go through the process. First, she would have to call the church elders. And that would be a shit show where they all met and if not blamed me, at least put the onus on me to fix the marriage.

They would meet to discuss how I could better sexually satisfy my husband. Because of course, what was poor Yofi to do since I was so bad in bed? Next would be how I should bring myself closer to God and learn forgiveness. Not once would anyone lay any kind of blame at Yofi's feet.

Though his parents would plead their case and try to save face and say I was excitable and a small thing like this shouldn't dissolve a union. My personal favorite would be them suggesting that I needed to learn to accept his failings. And the sooner I had children, the more settled Yofi would become. And then everyone would meet with me and my parents to try to force me to do the legal courthouse thing and stand by my cheating man.

I'd seen this before with my friend Ursula. She was two years ahead of me at school. Her divorce had been more traumatic, though. He'd put his hands on her and the elders had *still* tried to make her stay. She'd left. And wouldn't you know it, when the asshole's father died, his people still called her with tasks that she needed to perform.

None of this would be simple. But it would be worth the pain.

In the words of a certain perky blonde pop star, Yofi and I were never, *ever* getting back together. He'd humiliated my entire family. They had no choice but to release me from this farce of a marriage. But there would be a song and dance to play out first.

"Don't worry. When you come home, we'll fix everything, and then it will be better."

I tried not to show her, but I saw the panic I felt reflected in her eyes. The Tutus were wealthy. Yofi's father was some multimillionaire hedge fund manager. His mother worked at the World Bank. Some high-up VP.

My mother was probably concerned I would never make another match like this again. Possibly true. Or worse, worried that public humiliation would taint future prospects. She and Dad had stood by me, but I think that was more about their public embarrassment. Women of her generation had been taught to stay. After all, family was the bedrock. Once you picked your family, you made it work.

There would be whispers. So many whispers. But this blatant insult on my wedding day was pure disrespect. We'd lost face. The only way to save my reputation—and hers—was another match. A better one.

The pressure would really be on now. Now I had something to prove.

But I wanted nothing to do with that. I was so tired.

"Mum, we'll figure it out, but now I need to sleep."

"Fine, you sleep. When you wake up, I'll take you home."

"I don't want to go home."

Her eyes were dark. Everyone said I looked like her. The same high cheekbones, wide-set eyes, hair, lashes. "This isn't over. Trust me. Everything will work out. You're twenty-five, still plenty of time to find you someone better. He will see."

All I could do was blink up at her. The exhaustion threatened to overwhelm me like a tsunami. "I know you believe that, but I really, really don't."

CHAPTER 4

COLE

ADINKRA SAYING:
(Nkrabea) Everybody has their own distinct destiny.

HELEN ADDO:
Destiny doesn't happen by accident. It needs a nudge from your mother.

SAMUEL ADDO:
Your mother isn't always right.

I should have been enjoying the May weather and the sundress season it signaled. But eight months after that fateful day seeing Ofosua Addo in her hospital finest, she was still on my brain.

When is she not?

Even now, at the Clubhouse, one of the hottest brunch spots in all of Manhattan, in the packed crowd, I would have sworn I saw her crossing the street.

I needed help at this point.

We often crossed paths at work, but neither of us ever brought up that night in the hospital. Once or twice, I'd wanted to ask her about it, since she'd stopped wearing her engagement ring. But I knew that fell under the none-of-my-business category. Since we weren't exactly friends.

Whose fault is that?

I lounged casually as the line for the restaurant wrapped around the block. It paid to have a standing table.

My best friend Tallon jogged through the front door. His father owned a dozen Manhattan restaurants, including this one. He gave me the easy smile he'd had since we were kids. "Sorry I'm late. I didn't want to come."

I rolled my eyes and dragged him in for a quick one-armed hug. "You're a dick. And you're not late."

He grinned. "Asshole. Ouch. But you know, that's what Stefani, or Sarah, or Stacy . . . whatever the fuck her name was, said to me when I booted her from my apartment."

I choked out a laugh as he sat down. "You go through women like candy. What is wrong with you?"

"Well, I can't decide. Also, I may or may not have a memory problem. I don't know. Whatever."

I rolled my eyes again. "Did it ever occur to you that maybe *you're* the problem? The past lineup of girls that you can't remember names of would indicate perhaps a fuck boy."

He laughed. "Yeah, it's occurred to me. But that's deep-thought shit that I don't want to look too closely at. It makes me feel bad about myself." He clutched at his chest and then grabbed one of the croissants that I'd ordered for the table. The pastries here were stupid delicious. Tallon glanced around. "Where's the asshole?"

I rolled my eyes. "I don't know why you keep inviting him."

No one liked Chad. And I hated getting double doses of him, especially since he worked for my uncle as a financial analyst at Drake.

Your company.

I shoved aside that uncomfortable thought. Basically, Chad crunched a bunch of numbers to tell us if an author, book, or brand would be profitable or not. All he cared about was money and his own opinions. The type who thought he could buy his way into everything. Like my uncle.

"You know he's a dick. I don't want him messing up our morning."

"Well, tough, he's coming. And besides, Chad's all right."

He was not all right, but Tallon had a soft heart.

Speak of the devil and he shall appear. From the periphery of my vision, Chad casually sauntered into the restaurant as if he weren't already ten minutes late.

Tallon leaned forward. "Don't forget that his parents have that sick yacht. We could go to Ibiza."

"You hear yourself, right?"

He shrugged. "I'm an enigma. You see, I like to hold on to *my* money. If I can get some other idiot to buy a yacht and sail it to Ibiza to go party on, I'll do that."

These are your friends.

Tallon might think of himself as a dick, the kind who fucked around on girls and pretended to forget their names, but he was softer than he projected. And if he saw someone who needed help, he couldn't refuse. It was why he kept most people at arm's length. So they could never see that vulnerability and take advantage of it because he couldn't help himself. He kept everything surface. No one ever really got to know him very well. Except me.

I'd been there when he lost his mother. He'd been there when my drunken father tried to physically wrestle my trust fund out of my eleven-year-old hands at my grandfather's will reading.

And that's why you keep him around: because you hope he's secretly a good dude in other ways.

If your friends are only good in secret, what does that say about you?

I was not going to look too closely at that.

Chad threw himself into a chair, grabbed the pitcher of mimosas, and poured a healthy serving. And then, to three girls that waited patiently in the line on the other side of the barrier of hedges, he raised his glass and grinned. "Hey, ladies, you three can join us, but only if you climb over the planters and show us what's under your skirts."

Christ. I blinked at him. "Bro, is your asshole meter permanently set to 'on'? Is it stuck?"

Chad grinned. "Come on, they're hot."

"You're a dick." I turned my attention to the women. "I'm sorry. Let me make up for him being an asshole."

I waved over the hostess and quietly asked her to seat them inside. I also paid for their breakfast.

Chad laughed. "Man, you're going to empty your trust fund like your daddy did with his."

A shadow of dread danced up my spine. I turned my attention to him. "What the fuck did you say?"

He held up his hands. "Sorry, sorry. I mean, I was just looking out for your finances. Since you're the heir apparent."

Of course . . . When I was a kid, I'd followed my grandfather around relentlessly, trying to learn everything about the business. But then he died, and I didn't want anything to do with it. That would only last for so long, as I was meant to take over in a few years. At first I'd resisted. Though, as it turned out, I liked it.

I liked the challenge. I loved the books. I loved seeing where publishing was headed. I wanted to make a mark. It connected me to my grandfather, the only person who really gave a shit about me.

"You worry about yours. I'll worry about mine."

I held Chad's gaze and didn't let it go until he finally blinked and looked away, backing off. "All right, sorry, sorry. I'm being a dick. I'm just hungover. I need coffee. Happy now?"

No, I wasn't happy. But what was I going to do, kick his ass in the restaurant? Then I really *would* be like my father. I shook my head. "Yeah, whatever."

Suddenly, the hairs at the back of my neck stood at attention. I immediately started glancing around for what was causing my sudden irritation in addition to Chad. The usual cause for that electrical-zap-to-the-balls feeling was Ofosua Addo, the one girl at work who didn't give a fuck that I was a Drake. The truth of it was, she didn't have any fucks to spare for me regardless of who I was. When I couldn't find her in the restaurant, I turned back to my drink and pastries.

Ofosua fucking Addo.

Good thing she wasn't here, because Chad couldn't help himself but to be a total douche to her. He didn't care, and I knew it pissed her off. And while I liked seeing Ofosua pissed off, it wasn't because I wanted her to be upset but because it made her eyes bright and sparkly.

She hated me too.

And okay, fine, I was aloof to her sometimes. All right, *all* the time. It wasn't my fault though. On the very first day I'd started in publishing, when my uncle had introduced her as one of his brightest stars, she'd put her hand out for me to shake, then given me a warm bright smile. But I'd been struck stupid. Incapable of speech. She had these ridiculous cheekbones and incredible skin, dark brown and impossibly smooth.

So, like a moron, I'd stood there staring at her, my dick begging to do a happy dance. And I'd said nothing. She'd been standing there with her hand out to shake mine, and all I'd been able to do was stare at her. I hadn't even introduced myself or shaken her hand. Suddenly, that warm light that had flashed in her eyes had gone glacial.

Her gaze swept over me, and she'd dismissed me like I didn't matter. I'd tried to fix it afterward by going back and telling her some lame excuse about how I'd been focused on something else, and she'd been cold. Since then, our relationship had never improved. No matter how hard I tried to make her like me, she hated me even more. Which made me even more hyper-aware of her.

I hated the way that she would march down the hallway like she owned the building in her no-nonsense, take-no-shit, never-bother-with-prisoners kind of way. I hated the way I couldn't take my eyes off her ass when she did it.

I thought we'd had a moment months ago, when I'd seen her in the hospital. But she still treated me the same as she always did. She was beautiful but, Jesus, such a fucking pain in the ass. She was so annoying. Opinionated. Infuriat—

"Look, it's Ofosua," Chad said, breaking into my reverie.

There was that electrical zap again. Arousal with just a hint of a warning. "She's not here. Stop fucking with me."

Chad laughed. "God, you really do hate her."

"Yup, absolutely."

Liar.

Tallon glanced at me narrowly. "Man, I've been trying to get a glimpse of this woman. I have never seen Cole like this. It's fascinating. Where is she?"

Chad pointed, and like a glutton for punishment, my eyes followed the direction, finally focusing beyond the wrought-iron fence, and there she was, standing with what I assumed was part of a congregation, based on all the suits and dresses.

She looked outstanding in an outfit completely unlike anything she ever wore to work, some kind of African-printed pink-and-purple skirt-and-blouse combination, with her hair wrapped up tight with more fabric. Some of her curls came out to frame her face and tickle her clavicle.

I wished to fuck I hadn't seen it, because I knew from this moment on, I would forever be looking to see those curls tickle that bone. Holy hell. Her skirt was fitted tight, hugging every single curve. Her shoes matched the pink on her dress perfectly.

Chad grinned. "Oh, Ofosua. What an ass on her, but then she talks. Always, in every single meeting. 'We have to pay less attention to the bottom line and more to underserved communities,' or 'We need to use the influence we have,' blah, blah, blah, bullshit. She should talk less and bend over more."

My gaze snapped away from Ofosua to Chad. "Watch your mouth."

He laughed. "What? Oh, come on, even you have to agree. I know you hate her, but even you have to agree *that* is a juicy peach. I mean, I don't even fuck with Black girls, but you know, if what I heard is—"

I clasped my hands together in front of me. "Chad, before you finish that statement, I'm giving you a warning. Whatever the hell you think is going to be a funny commentary or a hot take, it's not. So keep it to your fucking self."

Chad's eyes went wide. Across the table, Tallon lifted a brow, studying me. I hated that he'd seen it. He could see what I'd hidden from most people: that little chip on my shoulder when it came to Ofosua Addo.

Chad lifted his hands. "I thought you hated her."

"I do. But I hate pricks like you talking about their colleagues like this even more. Do me a favor: take her name out of your mouth. Never say it again in my presence, yeah?"

He opened his mouth to argue, but I think he must have seen the look on my face, the truth behind it, that I would annihilate him if he did. And he shut his mouth. "Yeah, cool. I'm done."

We went back to eating, and I could tell by the way Tallon was watching me that he had a lot to say. But he would be saying it without Chad present. He'd be grilling me because now he knew how much I wanted Ofosua Addo in my bed. And like an idiot, even though I had told myself to keep my eyes off the woman, I couldn't help an occasional glance. And the final one was going to give me another sleepless night. It was as she reached the top step, and she backed up slightly to help the older woman. At the last step, the woman teetered on her heels, causing Ofosua to bend ever so slightly, accentuating the curve of her ass.

Fuck, my dick jumped straight to attention.

Hello, beautiful.

Damn it.

As much as I hated him, Chad was right. Ofosua Addo's ass was a thing of beauty. I'd spent the last two years staring at it. Imagining things I could do to it, wanting to touch it. Of course, I kept those thoughts to myself and tried not to think with my dick, because if I did, I was no better than Chad.

No better than your father.

It would ruin everything. One day, I planned to be in charge of Drake Publishing, and letting Ofosua distract me wasn't the way to get there. But now she was *here*, on a Sunday, intruding on my carefully drawn lines. My mask was slipping now. Tallon could see. I hoped that *she* never saw it, because if she did, she would eviscerate me.

CHAPTER 5

OFOSUA

ADINKRA SAYING:
(Pempamsie) A symbol of foresight, readiness, steadfastness,
hardiness, valor, and fearlessness.

HELEN ADDO:
Eh, sometimes running is the only answer.

Eight long months of avoiding the elders as they had tried to piece together the wreckage of my marriage. In the weeks after the wedding, there had been many a group chat about how I needed to seek guidance from God on how to be a better wife.

My favorite was how they prayed for me so I could find forgiveness. Not once did anyone pray over Yofi to keep his dick to himself.

The final straw for Mum and Dad had been when the pastor suggested he come and pray over our marital bed . . . while we were in it.

Surprisingly, Yofi had been helpful in the separation negotiations by adamantly stating he did not *want* to be married to me. That and the fact that we hadn't done the legal bit at the courthouse made things smoother.

Considering the traditional ceremony had happened in New York, my parents and I had still gone home to Accra to meet with the elders and take care of the simple returning of the drinks. Normally, going home to Ghana was a way to breathe and relax and unwind. But the few weeks we'd been there had been tense and fraught.

Interestingly, the Tutus had refused the jewelry and cash, so Mum was holding on to them for me, but she could keep the money and jewelry for all I cared. I wanted nothing from Yofi or his family.

It had taken eight long months, but I was officially "divorced." A twenty-five-year-old divorcée. It was wild enough that I'd been getting married so early. At least among my American friends.

But for the last eight months, I had been a Ghanaian social pariah. As if divorce were something you could catch. Or being bad in bed were contagious.

The real insult to injury was, since we'd finally gotten divorced, Yofi had called me a couple of times. He hadn't left a message either time. But every time I'd seen his name pop up on my screen, I'd gone full blank zombie for several minutes.

What the hell did he want? Why wasn't ruining my life enough for him?

"I don't remember agreeing to go to church with you. It's my day off."

"I don't remember asking," she said forcefully as she tugged on my duvet.

My mother had a round of churches she liked to attend. Ghanaian church was really the see-and-be-seen of the Ghanaian community in New York. The Ebenezer Williams church was in the fancy part of Brooklyn and attended by Ghanaians all over Manhattan. Let me rephrase that. The *right* Ghanaians. The ones my mother insisted that I was going to get to know: sons of captains of industry and daughters of would-be royal lines. Everybody would be coming in full shada, which meant the right outfits, the right makeup.

I knew people who had a glam squad prep them for church. After all, the makeup and hair had to endure, because church would be at least a six-hour affair.

I was going to need snacks. I was going to need to hydrate. *Or . . . you don't go.*

I dragged my duvet off my face for a moment. There was another option. "Ghana church or African church?"

African church was His Holy Spirit Church, located uptown. That one was all the upper-class Africans in New York, not just the Ghanaians. It was massive. One of those megachurches with another five- to six-hour service. But with that one, it would be less conspicuous if I made an early escape.

"African church. I still don't feel like dealing with Yofi and his people."

My heart squeezed. I had done this. It was my fault she was hiding from her favorite church. She didn't want to face the judgmental stares and whispers.

Her poor mother. Do you think it was because she doesn't have a master's?

Her poor family. She couldn't even satisfy him in bed.

Her poor mother with a daughter who is a failure.

"Wait," I said, suddenly realizing the disturbance in the force. "How did you get in? Did one of the girls let you in?"

She sucked her teeth. "I believe this is *my* house." She reached down and tugged my sheets. "Come on, we're going."

Ah yes, that constant reminder. I was in my *parents'* spare apartment. At least I had somewhere to go. And I hadn't moved back in *with* my parents, because that would have been even worse.

But they were next door. One thing I had insisted on, though, had been roommates. I knew my mother. Not allowing me to pay rent would be one more way to control me, and roommates made this place more affordable.

You have a trust fund.

Okay, yes. But it was the principle.

Glowering up at her, I muttered, "Mum, I don't want to go. Please, can you go back to your own apartment? Remember, you're my landlord; you're not my roommate."

"I can come in whenever I please. This is *my* house."

"Mum, that isn't how landlords work."

"I don't need permission to enter my own flat."

I knew it was futile. She wasn't going, and she wasn't going to acquiesce. All I could do was drag the covers over my face and silently scream into the nothingness before dragging my ass out of bed. "God, I need to sleep."

She tutted. "No, you don't. You've been asleep long enough. Time to wake up. Because we are going to solve your Yofi problem. And you can't do that if you're moping around in bed all day."

And with that, she strutted out. And then I noticed her outfit. She was wearing a kaba and slit, and white Manolo slingbacks, looking like hot stuff. She was fifty-one this year and honestly looked like she was in her late thirties. "Nice shoes," I muttered.

"Thank you. They're from your closet."

I had no choice but to give another silent scream because I knew they looked familiar. There was no stopping her. When she wanted something, she was going to make it happen. Regardless of what the doctor said about my stress levels, she obviously really didn't even think that panic attacks were a real thing.

Well, you haven't told her how bad it's been getting.

And I wasn't going to. She wouldn't believe me anyway, so what was the point? I would be screaming into the ether. Nope, I would keep popping Xanax like they were Tic Tacs and working out like it was my job, and I would eventually get far from my problems.

That sounds like a fantastic solution.

I scowled at my inner self as I climbed out of bed. From out in the hallway, mother called back, "And for the love of God, Ofosua, put on something nice, eh? Some makeup, lipstick, and look like you're trying, yeah?"

—

Dressed under duress, I shuffled into the living room, hoping that I could somehow yank my white slingbacks off my mother's feet, only to find my roommates howling with laughter, sitting around our massive glass dining room table, scarfing down Ghana pancakes.

They were like the thicker, sweeter cousin to the crepe and my absolute favorite breakfast food. My mother had been buttering up my roommates. I could see where this was going. She was about to enlist their help in her torture.

I glanced at Megan, whom I'd interned with one summer during college. Megan was all East Coast liberal crusader. She liked to say she used her blonde American Girl looks to help even the playing field. Every time I turned around, she was fighting for some cause. That traitor had five pancakes on her plate, all rolled up and dusted with sugar.

Cora was just as guilty as she spread Nutella on one of her pancakes. She shrugged and tugged on one of her locs as she made an *I'm sorry* face. She was one of my closest friends from college. She and her boyfriend, Travis, had been fixtures in my life since my first day of freshman year at Columbia. I'd thought their twenty-four-hour Black lovefest would have been like a knife wound to my soul. But it was comforting to have her here with me. Until this.

"Et tu, Brute?"

Cora laughed. "What? Your mum can cook. And you know I love these pancakes."

"Traitors, both of you."

Megan swallowed and then took a swig of . . . Was that fresh-squeezed orange juice?

They at least had the grace to look ashamed. I shook my head and then marched into the kitchen. As I started stacking pancakes on my plate, my mother counted and slapped my hand at four. "Eh, we're going to church. There will be men there. You don't want to look bloated."

I stared at her. "Mum, you know that these outdated ideas of the perfect woman are just that—*outdated*—and a little misogynistic. Who cares if I look bloated? Also what's wrong with bloated? It's still me. If someone can't like bloated me, they're not worth it."

She rolled her eyes. "Mmm, you can mumble your big words at me. You're not the only one who went to school. As for me, I am *old*-school."

I rolled my eyes. "Please, God, don't say 'old-school.'"

When she turned her back to fry another pancake on the stove, I snatched a fifth. If I was being dragged to church, at least I was going to be well-fed.

When I rejoined my friends at the table, Megan leaned forward. "I'm sorry. I let your mum in this morning."

I shook my head. "She has a key. She would have come in anyway."

"Well, if she'd come in any earlier, she would have seen Emily leaving," she said with a wry smirk.

My brow furrowed. "Which one is Emily? The brunette?"

Cora shook her head. "No, you're thinking of Elsa. Elsa is the one with the tongue trick."

I laughed. "Wait, am I late? Because I thought it was Max."

"Uh, who said it wasn't all three?"

We all choked on a laugh. Megan laughed the hardest before Cora lifted her glass to lead us in a salute. "All hail to the queen."

Megan's relationships were legendary. She was that girl who was the definition of free-spirited. Did she get a little messy sometimes? Sure. Overlapping partners, forgetting to notify one that she was already in a relationship. But everyone loved her. Men, women . . . didn't matter. She was a dating rock star. I needed some of that energy in my life. The thing was, I hadn't really dated much.

Until Yofi. And then he'd broken me.

Cora leaned forward. "You have that look on your face."

Megan leaned over and pinched my arm.

"Ow, what was that for?"

"You don't remember? You insisted that anytime one of us caught you thinking about Yofi, we were to pinch you, slap you, hit you. Do you want me to take a jab at you, or do you want Cora to do it?"

I scowled at them both. "Fine. Yes, it was a brief thought." I grabbed my arm where she'd pinched me. "I don't like you."

She grinned. "I love you, though."

I grumbled at that. Why would I ever ask them to do that? God, I was an idiot.

"You don't look dressed for church," my mother called from the kitchen.

I rolled my eyes. Cora stepped in. "Want me to help fix you up?"

Oh Lord, I needed her to. I really, really did. But I didn't want to say that.

"Okay, fine."

Cora squealed and pulled out the makeup bag she obviously had ready for this. Megan grabbed my purse and began stuffing it with several snacks and a bottle of what didn't look like water. "You think we don't know what you need?"

I glanced around at them. Knowing exactly what I was going to need and what I was going to want. With friends like these, who needed a man?

My mum came out with the rest of the pancakes. I looked at them longingly through one eye as Cora applied shadow. "Eh, okay, since you're all here," Mum said, "I want to tell you the plan. We're getting Ofosua a man."

I blinked at my mother. "Excuse me?"

She shooed me. "Hush. If you won't do it yourself, it's our job. We love you. So I'll be bringing by some possible prospects."

My eyes went wide. "Uh, Mum, maybe—"

My mother shushed me again. "Eh, you small girl, sit down. Be quiet. It's been eight months. Time to get back on the market."

I dutifully shut my mouth. Cora and Megan trailed their gazes to me, and it was Cora who tried to help. That fool. "Oh, um, Dr. Addo, maybe—"

My mother tsked at her. "Didn't I tell you to call me Auntie Helen? Everyone calls me Auntie Helen. Please."

"Okay, Auntie Helen, maybe we should give Ofosua time to, you know, get back out there on her own. We can get her on some apps, maybe, but I don't think *you* finding her a boyfriend is going to be a good idea."

My mother was in no mood to listen. "You do your part in your way. But my part, I'm doing in *my* way. This is how it's done in Ghana. How do you think people meet other people? Introductions are made. Besides, you young people with your dating apps and things, you don't get the right kind of people. You know what I'm saying?"

I stared at the three of them as they chatted about my dating life, makeup forgotten as if I wasn't there. I cleared my throat. "Um, is anyone going to ask me what I want?"

My mother turned her attention back to me. "No, staying single and living your life on your own is not an option."

"Mum, haven't I had enough fanfare? Can I have like a year before you try and marry me off to the next eligible bachelor? This isn't the Middle Ages. I'm only twenty-five. Maybe I'll meet someone at the library."

She laughed. "What kind of men are you going to find in a library?"

"You know, ones who read."

"Listen, he must be educated, obviously. But you know how it is: lawyer, doctor, engineer, those are the only acceptable professions. Not some bookworm or, God forbid, librarian. You want someone who can take care of you."

"I can take care of myself, Mum."

She glanced around at all of my belongings in her apartment. "Uh-huh, sure you can. Look, I know what's best for you. Matter of fact, my friend Wanda has a son. His name is Peter. I can bring him by. He's a doctor."

I stared at her. "If I say yes, will you stop talking?"

She laughed again. "No. Also, I see you took a fifth pancake. You don't listen to me. Now you will be bloated."

I sighed, smoothing down my own simple three-piece kaba and slit. The skirt fell to my knees with a split up the center to below midthigh with a simple purple-and-pink kente design. The top was like a halter and came with a crisp peplum jacket to go over it.

I knew it was stunning. If I was going to have to show my face, then at least I looked good. "Mum, maybe I can try meeting someone myself. You don't have to push me into it. No stress, remember?"

She waved her hand. "Tsk, don't go buying into these panic attacks. That's not who we are. That's not what our people do, eh? Besides, we'll find someone better this time. I have a plan. You'll have a new Ghanaian fiancé in no time."

An hour later I was seated on a pew in the middle aisle and already bored. The church could seat a thousand in their dark wooden pews. The saving grace was the soft cushion on top to save our behinds. To the far right there was a section for the first choir of sixty people. The children's choir of about twenty kids were seated in the first few pews to the left. The band had a setup just to the right of the massive altar.

The cross that hung from the ceiling was twice the size of a man. And the sunlight streaming through the stained glass windows made it appear that there was a halo around the cross.

Up front, there were five large calabash containers with painted-on adinkra symbols that would be used for the collection. We'd be seeing those come around at least five times during the service.

"Where have you been hiding, gorgeous?"

I turned around to find my cousin in the pew behind me, looking absolutely amazing in her wide-legged red, white, and blue trousers with adinkra symbols sewn on the white patches. Kukua also wore a white wraparound top that looked vaguely familiar with a crisp blue blazer over it. And her bag was Hermès, *obviously*. Because if it wasn't the most expensive one you could find, had you even come in full shada?

I squinted at her blazer, getting a better look. Was that a crop top underneath? Leave it to my cousin. Oil on canvas was her art specialty, but fashion was her life. And while the old folks had all lost their collective minds over her pursuing something like art, there hadn't really been much they could do about it. She'd done a double major in art and finance at McGill. Then she'd handed her finance degree off to her parents and told them she was pursuing her dream. She'd moved to New York and within a year had her first gallery opening, much to everyone's exaggerated horror.

"Cuz!"

"I knew Auntie Helen was only going to let you avoid church for so long before she had you back on the marriage market. Figured I'd intercept you here."

"Weren't you supposed to come around earlier this week?" I asked.

She leaned back. "Apologies, but I had a date. I should be sorry, but I'm not because he was very good with his hands," she said with a smirk.

"At least one of us is appeasing the aunties."

"Who said anything about appeasing the aunties? Mr. Nice Hands is not Ghanaian." She shrugged. "Once a rebel, always a rebel."

I snorted a laugh. "Next thing you're going to do is tell me he's Irish. The aunties would have much to say."

She sucked her teeth. "We all know that generation loves to gossip about the scandal of interracial dating and then show off their korkor grandbabies with pride. The colonialism and hypocrisy run deep with us, love. In better news, I am so glad she dragged you to church."

Kukua wasn't wrong. All that complaining and it was as if the more korkor, or light-skinned, the babies were, the happier they were. Which was asinine.

"Only because I'm the one with the good snacks," I said as I handed her the wrapped contraband, while keeping an eye out for my mother, who had been waylaid by an auntie.

She took a bite of the meat pie I'd made earlier that week and moaned. "Oh my God, I love you. Why don't you tell your mother you can actually cook?"

"Because she will never let me live it down. So, if I act like I can't cook around her, she does most of the cooking."

Kukua shook her head. "Machiavellian."

"I learned from the best." I frowned as something occurred to me. "Wait, what are *you* doing in African church?"

She answered my question with the gossip. "My mum and your mum were talking. Apparently, Yofi's mum had something she wanted to tell them, so they are deliberately avoiding her. They want a united front, so for now we hide in African church. Are you ready for a six-hour stint?" She leaned back and groaned dramatically. "I'm going to need a drink."

I took out my metal water bottle and handed it over.

Knowing me well, she raised her brow. "What's in here?"

I grinned. "It's a national."

Her eyes went wide. "You brought a mixed cocktail . . . to church?"

I clutched a hand over my heart. "It's just pineapple juice with extra ingredients. Yesu Kristo, you act like you never had a cocktail before. And the way I figure it, you're probably still half-drunk from last night. Consider this cocktail medicinal."

My cousin grinned at me. "I'm only *slightly* inebriated." She took a sip and then moaned. "Oh my God. This is amazing."

"Hey, not so much. This has to last six hours, okay?"

At least I wouldn't be forced to endure this on my own. We cackled and gossiped about my work people, and Kukua regaled me with tales of her date's very unfortunate bent penis. "So, I was saying, hey, we can work with this, but then he . . ." Her eyes went wide, and she froze.

"What's wrong with you?" I glanced surreptitiously around.

Yofi.

Something pinched in my heart, sending a stabbing, shooting pain throughout my body as all traces of oxygen evaporated. It was like getting an involuntary ice bath and being blasted with a flamethrower all at once.

Yofi was here, at African church, with his mother, talking to someone at the front of the church. But Yofi and his family always, always went to Ghanaian church. Why were they here? Auntie Judy looked like she'd been dipped in head-to-toe Fendi. Mom said you could tell the nouveau riche because they always wore the designers wrong. Logos everywhere and far too much. I once saw one of the latest up-and-coming boxers covered in head-to-toe Louis Vuitton. Every article of clothing he wore was emblazoned with the LV logo.

Yofi was wearing an ice-blue traditional suit with traditional leather sandals. He was far more understated than his mother. The quality still screamed money.

As I stared, my stomach knotted. His perfectly shaven dark skin gleamed. And that jaw . . . I had built temples to that jaw. Worshipped at his gorgeous face.

Fuck me sideways.

From the looks of it, he was with just his mother. There was no woman with them, hanging on his arm. I had avoided any news about him. I refused to stalk him on social media. Kukua did it for me. But he hadn't hard-launched anyone. So at least I'd be spared that embarrassment today.

If I didn't do something, he was going to see me.

While I was drinking.

In church.

I was going to hell. No, scratch that. This *was* hell. I was in some kind of horrible, hell-like purgatory. And I was trapped there with my mother at the end of the pews, still talking and laughing. I could feel it then. The dimming of the edges of my vision and the too-rapid breaths. I couldn't get enough air, I couldn't think, and I . . . *Oh God, oh God, oh God.*

I quickly slouched down in my seat, grabbing my purse to toss over my shoulder.

Kukua leaned over the pew. "What are you doing?"

I reached for her and grabbed onto the lapel of her blazer. "We have to go *right now*," I whispered. I could feel the walls vibrating closer and closer, inch by inch. I was going to suffocate if I stayed there. I knew it in my bones. I tried to remind myself that the fear wasn't real. This was a panic attack. I was *not* going to die.

She must have seen the look in my too-wide eyes. "Okay, okay. Yeah, let's go."

Except as she scooted up her pew, I realized I couldn't move. If I went toward the center aisle, Yofi would see me. If I turned to go the other way, it would be my mother. I was trapped.

There were two options. Stand my ground and face him. Or hide and live to eat jollof another day.

I dropped to my hands and knees on the teak flooring and crawled forward just as Yofi noticed me.

One day, I would look back on this moment of me scrambling across a pew, in church, with my skirt pulling across my ass, crawling away from the man that I used to love as he called my name. And I would reflect that this was not a good look.

But that would be *another* day.

Today, I was running. Or . . . erm . . . crawling. Chasing off the panic, running from my past, running from the truth. I had failed.

We finally reached the end of the pew, and Kukua reached out her hand and helped me to my feet to shuffle-run through the throngs of people from Kenya, Nigeria, and Cameroon, as they all piled into the unifier that is church.

There was no way we were getting a taxi, at least not unseen, and no way I could move fast enough to make a run for it in this outfit.

"Where do we go?"

"Restroom. He can't follow us there."

Finally, I got to safety and locked myself in a stall.

There was a knock on the wall next to me. And when I looked over, my cousin's long nails held out a tissue. "Hey, here you go. In case you want to let out your feelings. I won't tell."

I took the tissue, but I did my best to suppress the anger, the humiliation, the sadness, and the fear, which all threatened to bubble up. I shoved them back down where they belonged. Deep, deep, deep down, so that they would never surface again. And I held it together. I had embarrassed myself enough over Yofi Tutu. I wouldn't be doing it again.

"I'd rather die."

CHAPTER 6

OFOSUA

ADINKRA SAYING:
(Akofena) A sword of war.
HELEN ADDO:
When a man vexes you, say nothing, but empty your vex account and go on holiday. When you return, his attitude should be improved.

I was off my game.

The whole debacle at church yesterday combined with a missed call from Yofi after had me on my back foot. What the hell did he want from me? While there was a teeny-tiny part of me that was itching to know, I quashed it. Whatever he wanted, I didn't care about. And not once in the months since the wedding had he tried to explain why, who'd been in the closet, and how he could do that to me. I wasn't going to give him the satisfaction of taking his call.

Especially not in the one place I always found solace. *Work.* I was so busy wondering why my world was tilted on its axis that I didn't even notice someone was leaning over me as I was previewing the images for an upcoming cover meeting.

"Did you realize you make a face when you're concentrating? You stick your tongue out a little."

Flustered and surprised, I shoved my chair back, rolling so far that I hit the cabinet behind me. "Ow."

"Wow. You do know how to make a fast getaway, don't you, Addo?"

"Is there something you need, *Mr.* Drake?"

I watched the muscle in his jaw tick. He really, really hated to be called Mr. Drake.

"Yes, *Miss Addo.* Allison Kent's new book? We're going to have to adjust the original marketing budget."

I blinked up at him. This happened often. Books were given a projected print run fairly early in the process. But once the sales teams got ahold of the booksellers and tried to pitch a writer, print runs were adjusted to what accounts ordered. That number was then reflected in the marketing budget.

"No. You can't slash the budget. We're on a shoestring as it is. We can't depend on *her* platform entirely. We have to provide some support here."

"Sorry. The decision is final, numbers being what they are. And if you checked your emails as opposed to automatically deleting everything coming from me, you'd have been aware."

One time I'd accidentally deleted an urgent email from him, and he'd never stop reminding me. "You're going to hear from her agent."

"Actually, *you* have to deal with her agent."

As an associate editor, yes, I spent some time smoothing things over with agents. But this was beyond my pay grade. "You've got to be shitting me."

"I'm not. Allison's got no social media presence for her pen name. Just for her real name. Readers don't know anything about her except what she used to do. And let's face it, booksellers still have a hard time selling romance. And this book is so different from what she's done before."

If that wasn't some sexist, misogynistic bullshit. Allison was a former romance author–turned–thriller writer. Great plot, an excellent hook, and well-executed characters.

"Maybe *you* don't love a billion-dollar industry because you don't understand it, but I assure you booksellers do care about romance novels and their readers. Anyway, we're pitching them a psychological thriller, not a love story. And you can't tell me that's not a successful category."

He rolled his eyes. "She has no social media presence for the thriller, ergo, no access to that billion-dollar market. And the orders from the booksellers for the thriller you're trying to school me on reflect that."

No. I wasn't going to let him do this. I narrowed my gaze. "Don't bullshit me. We've got our own marketing efforts, plus we have access to her romance newsletter, with over a hundred thousand subscribers. If even ten percent of them convert to sales, this book could hit the *USA Today* bestseller list."

He shrugged. "Don't know what to tell you. Other than this is a part of the job."

I normally prided myself on not losing my cool at work, ever. But Cole Drake and his smug smile had a way of getting under my skin. Not to mention those slate-gray eyes had a way of hyp-notizing you, pulling you into a trance so you felt compelled to say yes to whatever he was asking for. He leaned forward on the table so I could just smell a hint of his cologne. The sandalwood and leather notes tempted me to lean in.

But I knew better. I'd learned to keep my distance from him, so I just waited him out.

"Now, if by chance you wanted to work out an arrangement where Evan Miles releases his book the same week as Allison, I might be able to pair them together for some events, primarily using Evan's marketing budget."

No. Not Evan Miles. "You are *blackmailing* me?"

He put his hands up. "Don't think of it as blackmail; think of it as doing business."

"We are *not* giving him another deal. Do you understand the pain and harassment I had to go through the last time trying to get him to revise his book? I thought his last book was the last one. It didn't even work. Readers have moved on. We all agreed."

I thought I was done with Evan's bullshit and microaggressions. At one point, he'd requested that Amy Green, my department's shared assistant, replace me as his editor. Once, he'd even asked me to make him coffee and balked when I'd made her do it instead. He was always taking her suggestions and praising her for her ideas. She wasn't even particularly good. Everyone knew she'd only been hired because Daddy happened to be an editor at the *New York Times Book Review*.

When I'd finally gotten up the nerve to tell my boss about Evan's behavior, I'd been met with what honestly felt like mock horror, but at least I was promised I'd never have to work with him again.

Apparently, this had been forgotten.

I opened my mouth to remind Cole of why I didn't have to work with Evan, but I knew how this would go. Even if I took this to my senior editor, Lila Garret, I'd only get pretend platitudes and I'd end up right back here. Did I have the energy for that? *No.*

"I understand, but the reps insist that most independent booksellers still love him and that buys will be strong enough. Especially in the South."

No way, no how. "Absolutely not. Besides, didn't he try to shop his book?"

"He did. But no one took the bait, so he's back. We have an opportunity here. We have his backlist. And your last edits, despite his combativeness, were terrific. You're familiar with his style and you can handle him. You're strong-willed."

I crossed my arms. "If I refuse?"

"It's your choice. Have fun explaining to Allison's agent why you decided you'd rather see Evan Miles fail than her client succeed."

I seethed but said nothing. In the office, there were three factions when it came to Cole. The wish-they-could-fuck-him faction: the girls, gays, and theys at Drake that salivated whenever he walked the hallways. Which, could I really blame them? Because Cole in a three-piece suit was mouthwatering. And he knew it too.

Then there were the haters who thought he was a nepo baby. They didn't realize he was intelligent enough to get into Yale without using his father's name. Not that I had dug up that little tidbit. Because it was none of my business.

And then there were the users, who wanted to be close to him to secure their own futures at Drake.

Where do you fall?

I was the rarity. The outlier. I hated him because he'd kissed me on a balcony two years ago and then he had totally and completely forgotten me. I had never happened. But that was neither here nor there. Right now, he was fucking with my career. Right now, he was blackmailing me, although I couldn't help but notice that he wasn't using his trump card. He was my true nemesis, and he hated me—why hadn't he taken the opportunity to embarrass me with the information about my hospital visit? Not a single rumor.

It didn't make sense given our enemies-to-nemeses relationship.

"Why go to war over Evan Miles? You don't actually read any of these books."

"I read some of them," he countered.

"You read the first three chapters of many books. Do you actually finish any?"

Okay, yes. That was a low blow. The night we'd met, we'd discussed our favorite books and what we loved about them in depth. I knew he read. But it was easier to treat him like he was just a pretty face and not like we were standing in the halls of a prestigious publisher that he would eventually inherit.

It made it easier to compartmentalize him.

He sighed. "Look, I know Evan Miles is old and crotchety. I know his sales aren't what they used to be, but they are sales. He's in the black, not the red. And he is one of the last authors my grandfather personally signed on. I want to keep him."

I narrowed my eyes. "Bullshit. You're really going to use what you call your 'grandfather's legacy' to mess with my list?"

Did I really see a minute tick in his jaw? But then he shook his head slightly, grinned, and winked. "One hundred percent. You have to learn how to play ball, Addo."

"This is blackmail."

"Business, like I said. Take it or leave it."

He knew what he was doing. And so did I. And at the end of the day, I knew what was up around here. I could agree to his demands, or else his uncle Steven, our publisher, would want to personally know why I wasn't being a team player.

"You are the most pompous pain in the—"

Lila chose that moment to walk in. "Ofosua, do you have the . . ." She straightened immediately and plastered a smile on her face as her gaze raked over Cole. Lila was in the wants-to-fuck-him category. "Cole! I had no idea you were here. I would love your opinion on some cover art for next season."

"I have a meeting, sorry. I was just stopping by to give Ofosua a quick budget update."

I knew he had me. I could fight him all I wanted, but I couldn't win. And certainly not in front of Lila, who would (rightly) ream me out for insubordination. I marshaled the control I needed. Zero emotion.

"Mr. Drake, I do appreciate you coming to address the matter with me and it seems that we'll figure something out. As we consider budgets, your suggestion to pair Evan Miles with my author was a—smart—business decision," I muttered through clenched teeth.

He flashed me a grin. He knew exactly what I was doing. "Ofosua, I've told you a thousand times, call me Cole. Mr. Drake is my uncle. And I appreciate you taking the time to work this out with me. You are really the future of this company, you know that?"

I smiled so hard he could see my molars. Such an asshole. "I appreciate you saying that, Mr.—I mean, *Cole*."

I really laid on the simpering-female thing thick. When he was gone, I had to force myself to take five deep breaths.

Lila watched me shrewdly. "Evan Miles? I thought we were done with him." She might want to get in Cole's pants, but she was smart, quick, and let nothing slip.

"Marketing strategy. At the right price, we publish him and pool his marketing budget with Allison Kent's."

Lila cursed under her breath. "Son of a bitch. Pretty *and* shrewd."

"Tell me about it." I hurried to add, "The shrewd part, not the pretty."

She just chuckled. "I suppose he's not your type. More of a Chris Evans than a Michael B. Jordan."

Michael B. Jordan? I knew she assumed that just because I was Black, I would only be interested in Michael B. Jordan. As if I couldn't appreciate beauty. "Actually? I'm an equal opportunity gorgeous man enthusiast. But it's unprofessional of me to notice men at work. Especially ones who like to irritate me."

"Well, you two certainly are actually *professional* with each other. You know in that way that there is some tension. You know, I've said this before, but you don't need to call him Mr. Drake. That antiquated office custom died with his grandfather. Even Steven doesn't require it."

"Yeah. I know. But boundaries are good." Boundaries. My life was complicated enough. It was just annoying that Cole Drake was the one who always brought my fire out.

COLE

Did I irritate her on purpose?

Yes.

Did I do it because I liked seeing the spark fire in her eyes? Also yes.

It wasn't like I invented a reason to go and talk to her. The Allison Kent budget did in fact need adjusting. But I also knew that Miles was a major pain in the ass. He hated being edited by women. He didn't think women understood his brand of hard-boiled detective fiction well.

Eventually, he'd been handed to Ofosua to see the book through because every other editor refused to work with him. And since she was only an associate editor at the time, she didn't really have the luxury of saying no. She'd heroically gotten the book out the door, but I remember it being a fight. And so shoving another Miles book on her in exchange for some piddling author events for Allison Kent wasn't playing fair. I knew it.

Did I care?

Too much.

I still had a job to do, didn't I?

Yes, but you could've sent her an email. You wanted to go talk to her.

I scowled at that as I rushed to grab the elevator to head down to accounts.

Usually, I could go days without seeing her. But seeing her at her church during yesterday's brunch had put her in the forefront of my mind. So even though I could've shot her an email, I'd deliberately chosen to go speak to her.

Because I was a fucking glutton for punishment.

Chad ran into the elevator just as the doors were closing. "Hey."

"Oh. Hey, man."

"What's wrong with you? You look like you're in a mood."

The short answer, yes. I was in a mood anytime I had to talk to him, but I didn't say that.

"Just had a meeting."

He laughed. "Ah, the only one who makes you look like that is the Addo bitch."

I clamped my jaw tight. "Didn't we already have this conversation about how you talk about her?"

He rolled his eyes. "Sorry. We're at work. 'Respect all employees' and that bullshit." He used air quotes.

I narrowed my gaze on him. "So we're clear, she's good at her job. We needed to negotiate a marketing budget. But she wasn't happy and made sure I knew it. Let me be clear, you don't talk about her, or anyone for that matter, like that. Not if you like your job."

He raised his hands in surrender. "Testy, testy. Why don't you just have her, like, transferred or demoted or fired or something?"

I studied him, wondering what the fuck his problem was.

"On what grounds?"

"You know, she was, like, an affirmative action hire or whatever, wasn't she? So I'm sure her work's not exactly up to par, even though you say it is. But beyond that, she irritates you, and you're the golden child. You can do what you want."

"Hey, douche canoe. You know she went to Columbia, right? Weren't you wait-listed there?"

He folded his arms. "It's all relative. I was wait-listed *because* they were letting in affirmative action cases. Besides, I went to Harvard, so it's fine."

Of course he'd explain that away. "Right. She's actually amazing at her job. Just because she irritates me isn't cause enough to fire her. After all, you're still here."

Chad guffawed. "Ah, funny man. Whatever. You know where your uncle is? I went to talk to him about some projections, and I could have sworn I saw Nazrin go into his office, but when I knocked, there was no answer."

I was too distracted to pay attention to him, so I grunted something noncommittal.

With a sigh, he said, "Look, fuck her or fire her. But you can't keep walking around with that look on your face every time you interact with her."

I blinked rapidly at him. "What did you say?"

"Fuck her or fire her. There's no anti-fraternization policy. Maybe she will stop irritating you so much once you get her out of your system one way or another."

CHAPTER 7

OFOSUA

ADINKRA SAYING:
(Kokuromotie) We don't bypass the thumb to tie a knot.

HELEN ADDO:
What can I tell you? Sometimes even the cleverest woman must work with fools.

SAMUEL ADDO:
When it comes to women . . . men are always fools.

Following Cole's infuriating visit that morning, I was in a hell of a mood, so when my phone vibrated in my hand and I saw who was calling, my stomach went into free fall.

Yofi.

I declined the call. I was not dealing with him right now. Seven months with no contact and then suddenly over the last month he wanted to reach out to me. There was a part of me that wanted to know why, but I wasn't giving up one of my nine lives to find out. The phone buzzed again. The name on the screen a taunting reminder that I could not outrun my past. He'd been calling since church yesterday, when he'd seen me essentially vanish in the crowd. But whatever he wanted, I did not care about it.

I'd read an article in some women's magazine that before you see an ex that hurt you, you needed to be the best version of yourself, and it didn't hurt if you had a new relationship either.

I knew most relationship advice was retro bullshit. Still, it would feel good to know I'd at least moved on. Right now I felt stuck.

My personal life was such a goddamn mess.

But as I traversed the wide hallways of Drake Publishing, I clung to the fact that my job was *not* a mess. Drake was my home.

When I started at Drake Publishing, I had been a lowly editorial intern until the senior Mr. Drake had unexpectedly given me his agented submissions to read. Interns and assistants were usually assigned to read the slush pile, meaning un-agented submissions. Drake was one of the last major publishers to accept them, because Grandfather Drake had always wanted the industry to be as "democratic as possible" for writers. And he was of the generation of publishers and editors who viewed agents as an "unnecessary layer." It was a different time. But also? His shining idea of democracy for writers mostly came in just one color.

My first stack of agented submissions was a trial by (incredibly dull) fire for the most part (and no doubt why Steven gave that particular set to me), but I'd found one manuscript that stood out from all the others. I couldn't put it down. The story was fresh, and the writing sparkled. I moved it to the top, added a note that this was the only manuscript worth reading in the whole pile, and that I couldn't wait to talk to him about it. I'd really been naïve in thinking he'd want to hear from me personally.

When his assistant had moved the manuscript, untouched, to the stack on his shelf that I knew *never* got read, I waited outside the building for him to come out for his lunch, and walked with him four blocks into the subway, pitching it.

He'd called me tenacious. Determined. Driven. And I had told him that he needed to stop complimenting me and read the book.

At the time, I was pretty sure I was going to be fired.

Instead, the next morning, Mr. Drake had come looking for me in the maze of cubicles where the interns and assistants toiled away while praying for a chance to make it onto the editorial teams one day.

I hadn't even noticed he'd been standing over me for five whole minutes, as I'd had my earbuds in, and I was busy editing a manuscript within an inch of its life. When he finally tapped me on the shoulder, I was so freaked out I spilled my entire water bottle all over my desk.

Way to make a great impression.

But Steven Drake laughed and said that I was clearly enjoying myself editing, and people like me were what he needed. And then, shockingly, he'd taken me to lunch and said I'd have a long future at Drake.

I'd made associate editor a year ago and had worked on some huge releases. I'd also been slowly pushing Drake toward bringing on more diverse authors as well as romance authors. I had the privilege of working alongside senior editors on books by major authors, and I hoped to sign my own star writers one day soon.

What they don't tell you in the movies about plucky young women working at publishing houses was that publishing didn't pay very well. Many of us in editorial, where the low-paying assistant years tended to stretch on and on, had parents with money or, in some cases, trust funds. I was lucky enough to have both, so I could really afford to say something as pretentious as, "I do it for the love of literature." Which was the God's honest truth.

The point was, that while my love life was up in flames, and my family life was stressful at best, at least I had work. I was busy telling myself that I loved everything about my job until I stopped in the doorway of the conference room and heard the deep chuckling.

Cole Drake.

He was holding court again, telling a story about his weekend.

I ignored the jolt of adrenaline-fueled awareness. My skin prickled, and I had to shake my head to keep the mellow timbre of his laugh from slipping past my defenses. God, I loathed him.

Is "loathe" the right word?

If anyone had asked me during my internship if Cole Drake would be on my *please don't make me talk to him* list, I'd have said no. Because I didn't know back then that a Cole *Drake* existed.

But that had all changed after his first day in the office and that horrible "introduction" in the hallway. I wanted to forget the way he'd forgotten me. I was desperate to know what had happened. But I had some pride. Now we tolerated each other. Barely. He spent his time trying to shoot down my ideas and cutting budgets for my favorite authors. And I spent my time outperforming his expectations, which wasn't hard.

There was no avoiding him, though. He was the heir apparent.

It was at the end of my intern year when Cole turned up as our new marketing director. Fresh out of his Yale graduate program. Full of smug Upper East Side upbringing and know-it-all privilege that rubbed me all the wrong ways.

Bet he'd rub you the right way too.

Another, more distant memory tickled my brain, and I shoved it aside.

I had to swallow hard at the unbidden thought. I was *not* hot for Cole.

Uh-huh, sure you're not.

I slid my gaze over him, quickly cataloging everything about him before I took my usual seat. If I was being generous, I noted that Cole was, in fact, handsome. He had that classic jaw of someone who could have been a movie star. Shrewd, deep-set, dark gray eyes that were fanned with ridiculously thick lashes. Cheekbones that gave me a run for my money, and the hair . . .

He had that perfectly disheveled look. Like someone else had run their fingers through it during sex. And it was all made worse by the fact that he insisted on coming to work in a suit. Every. Goddamn. Day. Sometimes the suit had a vest, and some kind of tie.

Always drool-worthy. Ugh, such a pompous ass. Why was he so easy on the eyes?

And now, his whiskey-laced voice was recounting some story about his weekend on the water on a friend's boat. I couldn't help it, I rolled my eyes so hard, one of them nearly got stuck. But I knew the rules. When I was making a face, I had to make sure to turn away from anyone who could see it, lest I get the "unfriendly" label.

Emory Briggs plopped onto the seat next to mine. She'd started with me as an intern and been promoted last year as well. As work friends went, she was pretty great, but I tried not to get too close.

Nothing against Emory; I didn't make a habit of getting close to anyone at work. It was easier that way.

She muttered under her breath. "Oh yes, the yachting story from the weekend. I feel like we've been here before. After *every* weekend."

My lips twitched, but I schooled my expression. Drake Publishing, while my first and only real job out of school, had taught me a lot about how I needed to present myself in these almost-all-white professional environments. First and foremost, I remembered to never look too enthusiastic, because then you are too passionate, too emotional in your decisions. I saved my enthusiasm for when it was *really* needed. The next rule was to never appear sad or upset or even mildly irritated, because then you are angry and unapproachable. Unprofessional.

Angry Black woman.

I knew that simple, everyday emotions could be read as anger. And I could afford many if not most things in this life, but I could not afford that perception in the workplace.

To avoid that label at all costs, I'd learned to form this mask. One that kept me right in the middle of *I am good at my job plus delighted to see you* and *I shall brook no arguments.* That tightrope was exhausting. And some days, I wanted to relax my shoulders and breathe.

To my surprise, Cole left his friends behind, plopped into his chair, and rolled it over to my seat at the table. In shock, I squared my shoulders and scooted back several inches.

"I saw you yesterday."

Immediately, my brows knit, but I forced them to smooth out. *Placid. Go for placid.*

"That seems rather unlikely. Is there something I can help you with, *Mr. Drake*?"

His brows furrowed at that. "Why do you call me that? It's weird. And I *did* see you. You must have been at a wedding or something. Everyone was really dressed up outside of a church."

Oh, hell, just what had he seen? "Well, *Mr. Drake*, shouldn't I be respectful to the future head of the company?"

My voice was saccharine, and it carried no edge to it. Anyone replaying this conversation couldn't say that I'd said anything wrong.

He ignored my barb. Instead, with a voice like smoky whiskey, he asked, "So, was it a wedding?" He leveled a gaze on me like he wanted me to give him a direct answer.

"Why do you ask?"

"You know," he said as he leaned forward, "I get the impression you don't like me."

"I don't know why you would have that impression. I don't think about you one way or the other."

He clutched a hand over his heart. "Oh, ouch. Look, you can keep pretending that you don't like me, but *everybody* likes me."

I cocked my head and stared at him. What was it like to assume that the whole world was on your side? "If you say so, *Mr. Drake.*" I kept my placid smile firmly in place, added some innocent doe eyes too for good measure. There was nothing better than the satisfaction of watching him narrow his gaze.

Before he could retort, the senior Mr. Drake strolled in with a wide smile and a bounce to his step. I expected Cole to roll his chair back toward his cronies, but he stayed put, right next to me.

On my right, Emory bumped my knee with hers and kind of nodded in Cole's direction. I shrugged in response. I didn't know what the hell he was up to, but I supposed I'd find out sooner or later.

The meeting went as it normally did—company business, company news—but then Mr. Drake said something I didn't expect. Actually, I think I can safely say that *nobody* expected what was coming.

He pushed to his feet, a beaming smile on his thin, over-Botoxed face. "I have an announcement. As you know, at Drake, we have some of the best young talent in the industry. And that talent is, among other things, forward-thinking. I like to think we reward such talent here. They are, after all, the future of the publishing industry."

In the corner of the room, I watched Fiona Bloom preen. She'd been after a senior editor job since I'd been here as an intern. But she was still an associate. A delusional one, given her first list, if you asked me. Which nobody did, of course.

Mr. Drake continued. "With that in mind, Drake will be launching a new imprint meant to better align us editorially with our social values as a company."

A new imprint? Social values? What social values? The hairs on my arm stood at attention. This could either be really good or really bad. Mr. Drake, while he'd always been mostly good to me, his token Black woman on staff, wasn't exactly what anyone would call woke or socially conscious.

But lately, all kinds of people were trying to "do the work" and "be better." I saw it all over social media, heard it on my favorite podcasts, and, yes, saw it happening in publishing houses. But it made me nervous. Why did people have to be forced to do what they should have done all along? And would they stay the course when things got hard? In my experience, the answer to that was "no."

"It's my honor to announce that Drake's new imprint, still to be named, will elevate new voices in commercial African American women's fiction. We'll publish in trade paper original, and the imprint will be headed editorially by none other than our own Ofosua Addo."

My world froze as my brain processed. Had he just said my name? And nearly correctly to boot? And he was giving me an imprint? *Me? Holy shitballs, Batman.*

I lifted my gaze, the knot of anxiety rising in my throat as I suddenly realized I couldn't hear. It wasn't until Emory started shaking my chair that the volume came back, accompanied by a tinny sound, like maybe I had lost part of my hearing from the anxiety.

I glanced around the room. Most people were smiling and clapping. Emory beamed and looked like she might hug me. Fiona looked murderous. Chad rolled his eyes and gave me a head nod, being the jackass that he was. And then there was Cole. While he clapped, his expression was neutral. Zero emotion.

Ouch.

Whatever. I didn't need his approval. But I did wish Mr. Drake had given me this news in private first. Wasn't that the way promotions usually went? Something felt very off. When Emory kicked me under the table, I cleared my throat. "Oh, wow, sir, thank you so much for believing in me. I won't let you down."

He beamed at me. "Of course you won't. My door is always open for any questions you might have. And I'll give you the best in-house support for your publicity, marketing, and sales."

My stomach flipped. "Really?"

"Yes, Nazrin Harimi has worked on some of the biggest publicity campaigns we've had; she'll be invaluable to you."

Nazrin had recently been promoted to associate director of publicity. She was one of the youngest people in the industry at that level and also one of the best book publicists in the business.

"Of course, for sales and marketing support, Cole will work hand in hand with you. In fact, think of him as your partner. Every step of the way."

And that was when the bottom fell out of my world. There was no way in hell Cole and I could peacefully work together.

Before this was over, one of us was going to die. I had to make sure it wouldn't be me.

—

COLE

I knocked at my uncle's door shortly after the meeting.

"Ah, Cole, come in. I was expecting you."

"Right." I stepped in. I'd always liked my uncle. Even though my aunt Ruby was the Drake, when they got married, he took her name. He said Drake had more gravitas than his name of Waincot. He'd come to Drake from a small, distinguished British publishing house where he had been the managing editor for years. After Grandpa died, he'd dutifully moved home to New York to take the helm without complaint, even though he'd loved the freedom of living in London and working in the family business but not *for* it. Which we'd all known couldn't last. Because Drake Publishing would always be in the Drake family, and my father was in no shape to take over for his generation.

I was still young when my grandfather died, but I was promised to join Drake as soon as I could. Steven and my aunt Ruby never had children of their own. So it was just the two of us Drakes for the foreseeable future at Drake Publishing. My uncle and I were equally determined that I'd learn this business from the ground up like he had. The last thing I ever wanted was for anyone to accuse me of being like my father and expecting the world on a silver platter.

"Close the door behind you."

I did as asked, and simply said, "Ofosua Addo and I can't work together."

My uncle lifted a brow. "Why?"

"Besides the fact that she's obstinate, picky, emotional, doesn't listen, thinks she knows everything and she's always right? Need I go on?" Fine, she wasn't really emotional, but not the point. I left out "gorgeous," "distracting," "brilliant," and all those other things that would've been telling. What was he even thinking? Associate editors didn't get their own imprints. That career plum was reserved for successful, mega-moneymaking editors with decades of experience under their belts.

"I'm well aware of the tensions between the two of you. However, this could still be a good partnership. She does have a specific kind of talent that Drake happens to need."

And I needed to make him hear me. "Listen, I know that she is one of your protégés. I get it. I've heard the story a thousand times of how she came running after you, forcing you to read a book."

"I like that kind of tenacity. You should too."

I knew my uncle. Something was off. No matter how tenacious Ofosua was, she was still a mostly green associate editor. She'd acquired all of one book on her own. "What gives? You can't possibly expect me to launch an imprint with her. My workload is already insane, and she hates me."

"She does not *hate* you. You're perfectly likable. It'll be good for you two to work together."

"In what universe would it be good for us to work together? Something is going on, Uncle Steven. It's almost like you want this division to fail. Because the two of us will be at each other's throats and one of us will end up dead. News flash, I'm not certain that it won't be me. There are other, better choices for this. Letty, for example. She's very good. Also a woman of color, which is perfect for the line. They know each other and worked together on a release last year. Letty is a better fit."

My uncle chuckled as he shrugged out of his suit jacket and laid it on the back of his chair before easing into his chair, Central Park acting as the tapestry behind him as he settled in for a lecture. "Cole. This is an easy ask. Just do your job. You might be the heir apparent, but let me remind you, nothing is guaranteed. Earn your place. Show me you can do this. It'll be easy. You'll see."

I took a seat opposite of him, folded my arms, and sat waiting. I was aware I was the only person in the building that could do this. Really push him to give me the true lay of the land. I'd seen the stats. Our numbers were down for the year. Now we were launching a new African American commercial fiction imprint? And he was forcing me to work with Ofosua? What was his plan? Was this a test?

Did my uncle even know what the term "African American" meant? There were venerable, Black-run publishers and imprints all over town, brand-new ones popping up alongside the handful of legacy imprints. Drake was known for pretty much the opposite.

We published a lot of great books, but they were mostly by old white literary types. Academics. And the Evan Mileses of the world. In recent years we'd begun to branch out to other categories of genre fiction aside from his kind of hard-boiled detective story, but that was as radical as we'd become, give or take a few titles. I was all for diversifying our list, but only if we knew what we were doing. And I was pretty damn sure we did not at Drake Publishing.

Uncle Steven sighed and leaned forward, planting his elbows on the massive oak desk. A large photograph of my grandfather at the very same desk, surrounded by books, stacks of paper, and mugs of coffee, was behind him. Not for the first time, I wished Grandpa were still here.

Uncle Steven hadn't changed much about the office. The heavy furniture, the dark colors and upholstery on the couch and accent chair, the wood. If I closed my eyes, I could smell the faint hint of wood polish and the sandalwood of the old man's cologne.

"Fine. We've only got two flagship authors. One of whom could die at any moment. It pains me greatly to say that about Colton Downs, but the man is seventy and still smokes three packs a day. And it doesn't look like the estate will want to publish new books under his brand by a collaborator, as we'd hoped. We needed the injection of new blood and new ideas. New authors. New readers. New revenue streams."

"I understand all that. But a new African American fiction imprint? While it potentially could be a smart move, is Drake the house that should be making that move?"

He shrugged. "Sure. Why not?"

"Uncle Steven, have you seen you? Have you seen most of our publicity, marketing, and sales staff? You're an old white man. Drake hasn't exactly been moving into the future with our acquisitions or with our employees. This just seems out of left field. While diversifying Drake's list is the right thing to do, I can't help but feel there's more going on here. And why am I only hearing about this now?"

He sighed. "It's supposed to be confidential and it's not a done deal, but Cosmos Film and Media wants to give us a massive investment. As you know, they've been very successful over the years with their adaptation of the *Queens of a Distant Galaxy* series we publish. They like working with us to co-promote the tie-in editions with the films. And Cosmos has always dreamed of having more of a hand in the book industry. There's a clear runway for that to happen here at Drake. We have the potential for a very healthy partnership. And we could certainly use the influx of money to take Drake into the future."

I nodded. This all made sense. The *Queens* series was our other flagship series. Not written by a seventy-year-old chain-smoker, thankfully. But it was still just one author and one series, and she could only write so fast.

"All right, so what does a new imprint run by Ofosua and me have to do with any of this?"

My uncle sat back and stroked his chin. "Brian Cosmos. You know he's Black."

I lifted my brow, wondering why that mattered.

My uncle continued. "He says he needs to see some color

at Drake, or we won't get the investment. He'll take his money elsewhere. He was very clear about that."

I blinked rapidly. "He said he needed to see more color at Drake? What does that mean?"

Uncle Steven rolled his eyes. "Okay, fine. How he put it was he had concerns about our lack of diversity and that we weren't socially conscious enough. He said that, as far as he could tell, Drake was making no moves to be more in line with modern publishing on the editorial side, on the author side, or on the executive management side, and it made him hesitate about investing in us. Even with the success of *Queens*."

I winced. He wasn't wrong. "All right, so all of this is a ploy to make Brian Cosmos happy?"

My uncle nodded. "Also, X and BookTok."

Was he serious? My uncle spent no time on either one.

I rolled my eyes. "There's no making *everyone* happy, Uncle Steven."

"Look, by pairing you with Ofosua, we look like we're *really* trying. A Drake himself will be taking this seriously. Of course, her picks probably won't perform like *Queens* or even some of the thrillers, so things might be a little quieter day-to-day than you're used to. She's not bad at picking mid-list gems, so you could have one or two that aren't complete write-offs. It's not personal. Just take one for the team while we get this investment, and then afterward, I'll move you back to the big guns like Colton Downs."

Was *this* how my uncle talked about a junior colleague who was, by his own estimation, one of his rising stars and the future of Drake? This didn't seem like the Uncle Steven I knew. Everything was just off today.

I blinked at him. "This is bullshit. For a lot of reasons."

"Don't get dramatic. This is good for the company. And it'll be good press."

"In case you've forgotten, Uncle Steven, I'm good at my job. Really fucking good at it. And I know you think Ofosua won't be able to make this imprint a smashing success, that this is just some tedious hoop you need to jump through to get the investment, but you're underestimating her. If I know anything about her, she'll succeed."

Why was I defending Ofosua Addo? Shut up, Cole.

"Well, then it'll be a win-win. You just do your job. And like I said, if she falls on her face, we'll quietly shuffle her away, but we'll have the investment by then. And then you get to go back to doing what you love most."

Wow. Shuffle away his protégé? I really, really didn't like what I was hearing. Ofosua may not have been my favorite colleague, but I was damn sure this was not the company culture I wanted at Drake. I had a lot to think about.

I stood to leave but asked one last question. "What did Nazrin want earlier?"

His brow furrowed. "What do you mean?"

"Chad said that she'd met with you earlier. Since she reports directly to me, and I didn't have anything for her to discuss with you, I was wondering what she wanted."

He shrugged. "I haven't the slightest. I haven't even been here half the day."

CHAPTER 8

OFOSUA

ADINKRA SAYING:
(Gye Nyame) Fear nothing except God.
HELEN ADDO:
And your mother. You should fear your mother small, small.

"Wait, so after he's basically tormented you for two years, you have to work directly with him? Like, on every project?" Cora asked me as she perched on the kitchen counter.

I bent over and pulled the garlic bread out of the oven as Megan leaned against the doorjamb. "Yeah, it would seem that way." I still couldn't process it all. On the one hand, I was so excited. My own imprint! It had to be a dream. On the other, I felt the albatross around my neck. "This is a huge opportunity, so I had to be really careful with what I said. I didn't want to look ungrateful."

"So, what are you going to do?"

"For now, I'm going to stack my team with people who will be just as passionate as I am and prepare for battle. I'm not going to let him ruin this for me."

Megan sauntered in and poured herself a very large glass of

wine. "Or maybe Cole will see the error of his ways. You know, realize that you are amazing and that you know what you're doing. This could be a good thing." She slid me a sly smile. "Or maybeeee . . ." She drew out the word. "He'll finally remember what happened between you two."

A hot flush of embarrassment crept up my neck as I transferred the garlic bread onto one of our fancier serving plates. Only Megan, Cora, and Kukua knew what had happened between us. They'd come to see me at the office one day, and the three of them had nearly tripped over themselves when they saw him with his *fuck me* hair, tailored suit, and cocky smile. So I'd had to explain the rules and the whys.

We did *not* drool over assholes who had ghosted and forgotten me.

That night felt like yesterday. My first publishing party. The hot guy on the balcony.

I could still remember—vividly, damn it—the first time I'd seen Cole. That kiss we shared and the promise of something I'd only ever dreamed of until then.

Growing up, my parents had been quite particular. "Boyfriend for what?" was my mother's favorite phrase. Yes, I'd been allowed to have dates for proms and things like that, usually with one of her Ghanaian friends' sons. But my parents had been old-school. No dating. And then suddenly, I entered college, and my mother acted like I needed to be on a husband hunt.

Sure, I'd been kissed before that night. In that sort of hurried, exploratory way of teenagers who knew their parents could be around the corner at any moment. Ethnic parents to boot. So that usually meant a beating was coming if you got caught.

My first kiss had been in Ghana, at Achimota Junior Secondary School, when I'd been in year nine, or what would be eighth grade in the US. Kwame Blankson and I had been caught by a prefect, and I'd had to do Eunice Quashie's laundry for two months as punishment for being a "bad girl," so she wouldn't tell the headmaster.

But the kiss with Cole was nothing like that. It had been a meandering, slow discovery.

That night had ended on such a high. And like a fool, I'd actually expected him to track me down and call. But he didn't. And I wasn't going to lie and say my feelings hadn't been hurt. They had been.

For days I'd been gutted, replaying the night over and over and wondering what I'd said or done wrong. Then I'd let it go and chalked it up to an experience every woman should have at least once: a swanky party complete with a hot mystery man and an even hotter unexpected kiss. A single-in-New-York story I could tell my friends over drinks.

Fast-forward eight months to when I started at Drake full-time, and my boss had introduced me to his nephew, Cole, who would be joining the team. My brows lifted in expectation of *some* kind of recognition, even a blush, but his face had been blank. He'd just sort of stared at me, but not in recognition, more like I wasn't worth his time. And that's when my heart truly, finally closed forever to Cole Drake. And when I decided my dating life needed to stay in a more traditional direction.

See how well that went?

Ghanaian guys were a known quantity. A few well-placed questions and you had everything. But Ghanaian men were notorious for their mistresses. Not just the older generations, but supposedly modern, enlightened men as well. It was some macho virility nonsense. Hell, many of them even cheated on mistresses with girlfriends. Culturally, having many women was supported by being able to have several traditional wives. As long as you could look after them financially, no problem.

But Yofi had been different.

Not different enough.

"Look, I know how this goes. I launch an amazing new imprint, then he takes credit as the Drake on the project. Or worse, he's been put on my team to keep an eye on me to make sure I don't screw up, but that is ludicrous given that (a) he is not an editor, and (b) he knows nothing about Black commercial fiction. I just have to figure out how to handle him without losing my shit. Because I cannot lose it at work. Ever."

The front door opened and closed, and I braced myself for my mother. But instead, it was Kukua. She held up a bottle of wine. "I heard you needed wine. I'm fresh from Brooklyn and I brought reinforcements. That chef I was seeing brought it to my place the last time he was over. But I figured you could use it more. Now, what's this about Hot Cole being assigned to you? Is this the start of a very sexy forbidden office romance where you pretend to hate each other, then bone on the conference room table? Because if it is, please, cuz, do not leave out a single detail. Please tell me that there's some kinky element to this."

I shook my head at her. "Hand me that wine." Chilled to perfection. She knew me well. I wasn't one of those girls who pretended I could tell you about hints of bougainvillea and leather or some sort of nonsense. I wanted my wine to taste good, and I wanted it to be cold.

"Have I told you lately that I love you?"

She immediately finished the song quote for me. Singing off-key about no one above me.

I rolled my eyes. "Ugh, God, why do you have to remind me?"

She gave me a chuckle. "Hey, like I keep telling you, this eight-month drought you have going is self-imposed. Now, about Hot Cole."

I scrunched my nose. "You know how I feel."

She scooted her ass up on the counter, grabbed a glass for herself, and poured some of the Barefoot wine. "I *know* you're still feeling it over Yofi. I say the fastest way to get over a guy is to get involved with someone else. And you and Hot Cole have tension. This is an opportunity in more ways than one."

Somewhere deep in my body, the forgotten remnants of my libido stirred to life just thinking about him. No. *No!* I was not going there. Hot conference room fantasy or not. "Right. Except, I don't need a guy. I'm perfectly happy." But, while I didn't *need* a man, it would be nice to not feel like this all the time. Like I was perpetually broken, somehow. Unlovable.

She laughed. "Sure, because you're the poster child for what happy looks like. All I'm saying is maybe you and Hot Cole can set aside your differences."

I had to choke out a laugh at that. "Oh, that is never ever going to happen."

"Never say never, love," she said with a wink.

"I think it's safe to say in this case. He's my archnemesis. I loathe him. He loathes me. We are not a match."

"But he's so pretty. Maybe you can muzzle him and still bang the hell out of him," Megan suggested hopefully.

"Like I said, *never* going to happen. This is just an opportunity." I took a sip of my wine and moaned at the bubbly sweetness. "But maybe you're not wrong entirely about my dating life."

Megan paused with a piece of garlic bread on the way to her

lips. Cora choked on her sip of wine. And as for my cousin, well, she stared at me agog.

Cora spoke softly as if she were approaching a spooked horse. "You might be interested in dating again?"

My cousin had less finesse. "Please revenge-date Hot Cole." She proceeded to make a crude gesture with her hand as she poked her tongue on the inside of her cheek.

"Gross," I said with a shudder. But that little flutter of butterflies in my belly would not be ignored. "We don't do smug white boys."

"He is smug," Cora agreed. "But the way he fights with you, he wants you."

"As exhibited by the fact that he seems to have forgotten that we kissed? Doubtful. But enough of Cole. I'm thinking maybe it's time I start dating again."

Cora clapped. "I have just the guy."

I lifted a brow. "Oh no. Don't get excited. I'm only *thinking* about dating. Not actually doing it. Baby steps."

"Auntie will be so pleased."

I shook my head vehemently. "No. You cannot tell her. You guys shut up. Not a word. I'll be inundated with doctors and lawyers."

Kukua snorted a laugh. "Only you would try to avoid a doctor."

Speak of the devil.

I heard the door open and saw my mother in the doorway, draped in a mustard-yellow bubu, cinched at the waist, the draped fabric giving her knockout curves. Only my mother could make a caftan-style dress look good.

I lowered my voice and hissed at them. "Promise me. Not a word to my mum." I met their gazes. "All of you."

They all put up three fingers for scout's honor. My mother

sauntered over to the kitchen. "What's this? Pasta? How is that dinner? You need proper food. I brought some things. I'm going to cook."

I'd already reheated the gnocchi, so I stared at my mother. "No, Mum, we're going to eat this."

"Ah, but your friends don't want this—"

I shook my head. "Today is not the day, Mum. I made this gnocchi, and we are all going to eat it." Okay fine, I'd heated it up. But still.

Cora and Megan looked back and forth like they didn't know what to do with us. My mother barging into the flat was a constant occurrence. So in instances like this, they didn't seem to know what they *could* actually do about it. She owned the place, after all.

Her living so close didn't help either. Twelve years ago, the unit next door had become available and my parents had snagged it, with the idea that they'd knock down the walls and make one giant unit.

But I'd been headed to college and Dad's travel schedule had been busy, and my mother's enthusiasm for construction had waned.

"Is this how you talk to your mother?"

"Mum, I've already cooked. You are welcome to join us, but we're not changing our plans to accommodate a late entry."

She huffed and placed down a pot of something that smelled like light soup, with its ginger, garlic, onions, and pepper. One sip was guaranteed to clear your sinuses.

Mom made it when I was depressed. Except I didn't want light soup. Actually, I quite hated it. Light soup was sort of a spicy-as-hell chicken soup.

She narrowed her gaze at me. "You watch your mouth."

I felt immediately guilty. I was in a mood, and she didn't

deserve to have me take it out on her. "Look, join us for dinner, why don't you?"

I didn't *really* want that, but she was my mum, and with my father working all the time, I knew she was lonely. "But we're still not having soup. We're having gnocchi."

"You're not having this garbage. That's unhealthy."

I forced myself to take a deep sigh. "Mum, please, you can join us or not. It's up to you."

She stared me down, and I knew this was a test. Because normally, to avoid an argument, I would give in to her, but I was tired of giving people their way. I was very tired of making myself small so everyone else could feel comfortable.

"This is it. Let me grab you a plate. We have garlic bread too."

"Garlic bread, what is this nonsense?"

"Actually, I made the bread myself. Watched it rise and everything."

She stared at me. "Heh, when did you start baking?"

I sighed. "I've baked for a while now, Mum."

Kukua jumped in and winked at me as she grabbed the goodies my mum brought. "Auntie, come and sit with me. I'll take some of that soup home. I hope that's okay."

Dinner was mostly fine, as everyone was preparing to watch *The Bachelor*. It was a train wreck waiting to happen, but none of us could look away. When the show started, my mother frowned. "What is this?"

"Mum, have you really never heard of this? It's called *The Bachelor*. It's like that South African dating show we were obsessed with on M-Net last summer when we went home. One guy dates all these women looking for love."

"I like the South African one better. The discarded women vote on who he should date next." She squinted at the screen for a moment. "Heh, it says here they're taking applications. Ofos, you should apply."

"Mum, I'm *not* going to be on *The Bachelor*. Once you see what these girls do, I'm pretty sure you'll have whiplash."

Kukua chuckled. "Hey, Auntie is not alone on this idea. We could do the application for you."

I glowered at her. "Don't you dare start."

My mother nodded enthusiastically. "Eh, tell your cousin. Because I'm trying to get her to meet people, but every time I bring someone to her, she makes a face. See, eh, that's the face right there." My mother pointed at my scowl.

"Well, maybe, Auntie, if you ask her what her type is, she'll make less of that face."

My mother waved her off. "Her type. Nonsense. I know what her type is."

I couldn't help it; my mother had poked the tiger. "Do tell, Mum, what is my type?"

"All right. Ghanaian, obviously. Ivy League–educated, of course. If not Ghanaian, at least African. Except Nigerians. How they will worry you. Black Americans are next. Then Europeans. Everyone else after. White Americans and white South Africans don't make the list, obviously."

I groaned. "Mum, this is *your* type for me. This isn't *my* type."

She ignored me and kept talking. "A lawyer, a doctor. Finance careers are good too, but like tech guys, they work too much."

I frowned. "And a lawyer or a doctor won't?"

"I'm saying the ideal match. Especially if you're not going to go and get your master's. You also know they'll look after you properly. You won't have to keep working this nonsense job."

Aaaaaand my roommates tapped out.

Megan bounced up. "Um, I'm going to get some more wine."

Cora suddenly had to take a very important phone call. "It's Travis. I have to let him into the building." Way to use her perfect boyfriend for escape.

Kukua was the only one who stood by me. "Um, look, Auntie." She put her hands on her hips. "Didn't you hear that Ofosua just got her very own imprint? She'll be curating the whole thing. It's a big deal."

My mother frowned at me. "What is this imprint?"

"African American women's fiction." I let a small smile peek out. I wasn't going to let on just how excited I was, though. "It's a pretty big deal that they are trusting me with this."

Her brow furrowed with her displeasure. "But you're *not* African American. Why couldn't they put you in charge of an African fiction line? That is work that needs to be highlighted. See, this is why you need to go and get that master's. Then you can work on more academic pursuits."

My teeth clamped down to force the bite of disappointment to the back of my throat. "I know that it bothers you I didn't get my master's, but you don't have to make me feel like shit about it every single time we talk."

She frowned. "Language."

"Mum, if you keep on doing this, I'm going to use the full breadth of my English-language vocabulary that you paid hand-somely for."

She sucked her teeth and waved me off, gathering her scarf and her purse. "Eh, one of these days you'll listen to me and realize it's important."

"Important for what, though? I really don't need a master's degree in my profession."

"Yes, but your prospects are limited if you don't have it."

"I don't think you're getting what I'm trying to say here. But anyway, you know, thanks for your congratulations and everything. I'm going to get another glass of wine."

"No need for dramatics. I'm going home."

"I'm telling you, there should be a show called *An African Mother*," I muttered under my breath to my cousin before I walked over and gave mine a kiss on the cheek. "Good night, Mum. I'll see you later."

She studied me. "You know I am proud of you. But I know you can do better."

And there it was. The resounding vote of confidence I needed. "Right. I can do better. Of course."

That seemed to be the motto of my entire life. I could do better.

When she left, Kukua wrapped her arms around me from behind. "I'm sorry, love."

"It's not your fault. You're not my mum."

"Yeah, but I know what it's like. The constant crushing disappointment and never feeling good enough. It sucks."

"Yeah, it does suck."

"But you're amazing. This promotion is exactly what you need to remind yourself. And I personally think you *should* enjoy working with Hot Cole. Use him. Well, not *use* him in a fun way, but *use* him. He has a shorthand with his uncle and the higher-ups that you obviously will never have. Use his shorthand while maintaining that you're in charge."

"Will you be happy and let this go if I tell you I will?"

"Yes, I will be. You see, unlike your mother, I'm easy to please."

She scooted out of the way as I went to swat her. But then she plopped back on the couch. "Cora! Megan! The coast is again clear!"

After reemerging, Cora glanced first at Megan and then at Kukua. And finally at me. "So you remember Travis's friend Omar?"

Oh God. Her boyfriend, Travis, had mentioned his friend, a

lawyer or something. They'd gone to Morehouse together. I was hoping it would take her a while to go into fix-up mode. "Oh no."

"Oh yes. You said you wanted to dive in. Why not now?"

The truth was I didn't have a very good reason for why not now. Except fear. Which, while valid, I wasn't going to use. "No. Thank you."

"You met him last year briefly at Travis's birthday. You guys would be perfect."

I lifted a brow skeptically. "Perfect?"

"No one's going to force you, honey, but Omar is a good first foray back into the pool. He's smart, sensitive, and kind. And Travis would murder him if he tried any funny business. And we'll do a casual meetup, so there's no pressure."

Except that's exactly what I felt. Pressure threatening to suffocate me. But I had said I wanted to go back out. I'd been hiding too long. "Okay, fine."

She beamed at me.

I did not beam back.

CHAPTER 9

OFOSUA

ADINKRA SAYING:
(Mako) All peppers on the same plant don't ripen at the
same time.

HELEN ADDO:
Not all husbands ripen the same. Be wise and choose correctly.

As it turned out, it wasn't *that* difficult to avoid Cole. Not that I had anything to market yet.

Not that I was *avoiding* him exactly, merely making it a strategic point to not be in the same room with him for longer than I had to be. Professional. It wasn't as impossible as I'd thought.

We'd managed to civilly discuss projections, independent booksellers we'd like to target, potentiality for tours, marketing strategy, all that. And although it did seem as if he was surprised that I'd given these things any thought, he also seemed confused that I'd come to him with my own numbers, particularly romance numbers.

I had my eye on a few authors and already had a couple of exciting prospects.

As soon as I'd been put in charge of the new imprint, I'd called every agent I'd ever worked with, asking for anyone who might fit the bill.

I wanted books with "magic," for lack of a better word.

We were selling fantasy and a story. We were selling escapism. Because for anywhere from three to eight hours of their lives, our readers were going to sit down, pick up these books, and live in someone else's shoes.

And God help me, but I was not falling into the trap and idea that Black women's stories had to be pain. I hated that narrative.

It was my biggest pet peeve in publishing. People always looked at Black women as if they were there to save a ho. We weren't doing that at my imprint. I wanted to publish compelling stories that at their core were full of joy. Though at our first acquisitions meeting, I could already tell that that was not Mr. Drake's vision.

More than once, I'd had to remind everyone that there was no unilateral Black experience. There was room for Nene Leakes, Kennedy Ryan, Jasmine Guillory, *and* Michelle Obama. Our readers were looking for genuine stories that made them feel something. And those stories should make them feel something other than pain. I'd even had to explain why we couldn't call this an African American imprint, that not all Black people fit into that category. *Including me.*

Of course, I looked around at the sea of white faces, and no one seemed to get it.

My first few weeks, coinciding with the warmer June weather, had gone smoothly. But, like the gorgeous weather, I should have known there was a catch. Just like how June came with allergies, my new job had gnats in the honey.

I knew it couldn't last.

Mr. Drake's old friend Greta Maples, an agent, had called last week to pitch me her client Aliza Mann's new novel, touting its frank portrayal of growing up a Black woman in America. I'd asked about Aliza's background, and Greta'd danced around the subject, returning again and again to the "rawness" of Aliza's "language." That told me something.

I told Greta I'd be happy to see the submission, hung up the phone, and called Emory into my office. Time for some detective work.

Aliza had no immediately obvious social media presence, which, in these days, was odd and would be counterintuitive to our marketing and sales efforts. She barely had a website.

But Emory, being the expert sleuth that she was, eventually found an old Facebook profile for Aliza Mann. Aliza Mann was a white woman. A white woman in her forties, with that whole pseudo-crunchy feminist vibe, which I would have dug if her manuscript wasn't rife with stereotypes and misrepresentation.

I had put her firmly on my "no" pile. It was my decision. At least it was supposed to be. I was the editorial director. But I'd already gotten an email from Steven that he expected the book in the "yes" pile. This whole thing was a mess. Yes, he was the publisher, but he wasn't supposed to insert himself. Pushing this book down my throat was a power play.

But I had a plan.

To: cdrake@drakepublishing.com
From: oaddo@drakepublishing.com

Your uncle wanted me to include a book on my list and I'm going to pass for this line. But I reviewed the manuscript and I can see the strong women's fiction thread. With my attached notes for tightening of the

storyline and a slight character adjustment, it would be
a great fit for Carol in women's fiction.

Thoughts?

Ofos

To: oaddo@drakepublishing.com
From: cdrake@drakepublishing.com

I see what you're doing. Can't say it's not smart.

Cole

To: cdrake@drakepublishing.com
From: oaddo@drakepublishing.com

You see that I am passionate about making this book the
best book it's capable of being?

Are you willing to help push this through with Mr. Drake
if necessary? I think women's fiction is the best possible
home for the book and would have the booksellers very
excited with a few strategic adjustments.

Ofos

To: oaddo@drakepublishing.com
From: cdrake@drakepublishing.com

I find it interesting that you didn't focus on the part
where I called it smart.

Cole

I narrowed my eyes at his email. Then practiced some deep breathing as I read it again . . . and again. What I was going to say was, *I'm not flattered by you telling me some shit I already know.* But I couldn't say that.

To: cdrake@drakepublishing.com
From: oaddo@drakepublishing.com

Yes, it is. I really believe in this book and its potential and want it to have the best opportunities it can.
So, do I have your support?

Ofos

To: oaddo@drakepublishing.com
From: cdrake@drakepublishing.com

I would pay a fortune to know what your actual verbal response was before you hit reply. And I'm leaning toward yes, but let's discuss after our meeting.

Cole

To: cdrake@drakepublishing.com
From: oaddo@drakepublishing.com

You'll never know. And thank you. It's great to have such supportive team members.

Ofos

You're flirting.
No. No, I was not. I was focused on my job. A job I was good

at. And this way, Steven would get what he wanted. And I would get her off my list. And surprise, surprise, Cole was willing to help.

The real question was, what was that warm fuzzy feeling in my chest just because he said he'd help me? And how did I get rid of it?

—

An hour later, I strolled into our biweekly meeting excited about the books I was pitching.

"My first pitch is Adriana Wright," I said. "She's got a huge following on social media, and her romance novels have been killing it in the indie market."

I paused to everyone's gaze.

"Her latest novel is an empowering story about her mother, defying stereotypes, and living life on her own terms. And it has a steamy love story woven in."

"I like where this is going," Mr. Drake said, raising his eyebrows.

"I'm thinking a Black *Eat, Pray, Love*," I continued, sensing that I had everyone's attention now.

My gaze met Cole's, and the corner of his lip lifted up. "Clever marketing angle," he said.

I gave him a beaming smile, a rarity at work. "Exactly!" He blinked at me in surprise, but his lips twitched as if he was holding back a smile.

When I gave Emory a nod, she put Adriana's file in our "yes" pile.

I eagerly grabbed the next manuscript, written by a trans woman named Sophia Jones. "This next book is my Black trans activist, Sophia Jones. It also has a glue-you-to-the-page love story woven into the plot. The heroine is a trans woman navigating the world of love and dating. Sophia calls it a fictionalized memoir. It's raw and emotional and hits just the right tone for women's fiction."

Nazrin leaned forward. "But why is it a good fit for this line?"

"For starters, the book takes place just outside of Atlanta. She talks about growing up in Atlanta in the early 2000s, her identity struggles and how she was viewed in the Black community. And for our purposes, it focuses on her growth and concludes happily."

Again, I looked at Cole, who, surprisingly, didn't object. He just took notes with his stylus. When he caught my eye, he shrugged. "Conservative booksellers in the South might be a struggle, but you let me worry about that."

Wait, was that another yes?

Keep going. Don't jinx yourself.

Steven didn't object to either acquisition. Nazrin had several questions about Adriana and looked displeased about Sophia, but she mostly kept her mouth shut. So far those were my only picks. I'd taken up ten minutes of our meeting.

Derrick Bowls, the senior editor for thrillers, spoke up then. "Those sound excellent, and I can't wait to read them. And while we're on the topic of your excellent eye, I'd love your take on this new African American writer, Boi Knowls. He's written this very smart, exciting thriller set in a gentrifying Harlem. I think you'll vibe with where he's coming from. And you can give me a gut check for authenticity."

I wonder why he thought I'd love it. Funny, he never asked me to weigh in on thrillers by white authors. Instead of asking those questions, though, I said, "I'd love to take a look."

The anxious flop sweat that had threatened at the beginning of the meeting had just started to dissipate when Mr. Drake said, "I have one more submission I want to discuss. Aliza Mann. Greta told me you passed, Ofosua."

Oh no. Not a clean getaway! I could do this. I would not die. "Aliza's manuscript, unfortunately, is not right for the new imprint."

Steven frowned, and I saw a flash of something that looked like irritation in his eyes.

"Greta is a personal friend. She felt slighted."

Slighted? What grown-ass agent felt slighted by a pass? Passes were part of the job. But I knew better than to say that out loud.

"I apologize. I'll take Greta to lunch and soothe any ruffled feathers, but Aliza is all wrong for this imprint. For starters, she's not Black or even a woman of color, so her writing Black women's fiction raises concerns for me."

Nazrin audibly scoffed. "That's reverse racism."

It was just on the tip of my tongue to say that wasn't a thing. But I bit that back. It wasn't my job to educate the ignorant.

Luckily, Emory jumped right in and leaned forward. "You should know reverse racism doesn't exist. Marginalized authors have a more difficult time in this industry, and you should check your privilege."

I winced. Nazrin was Persian. Yes, she had proximity to whiteness, but we were going to be in a whole icky gray spot if Emory kept talking. I put my hand up. "My point is, it's not a great look. We're a publishing house that is mostly known for its white male authors. We start a new line to tell Black women's stories, and we choose a Caucasian woman's objectively problematic novel as part of our debut list? Readers will notice."

Steven shook his head. "She stays. I've read it. She did her research."

I leaned back slightly, surprised by his stubbornness. "Her *research*? It might be worth asking Black women how they feel about Aliza's *research*. She's in essence taking a character that could be white and changed her race to Black. There are no cultural nods, no authenticity to the perspective she's writing from. It comes across as phony. Not to mention the side characters. She talks about how her side character, Na'quette's best friend, can't pay her hair bill at the salon. And then a fight over food stamps ensues. That's in chapter three. When did you read it?" Surely, he had to see the problem.

"Greta sent it to me months ago. She wanted me to read it as a personal favor, but I didn't see it on Drake's list. But now, for obvious reasons, I do. I told her to specifically submit it for your line."

I forced myself to take a deep breath and be even and placid. "And while I appreciate the opportunity to consider the novel, I think it's wrong for our imprint. Aliza Mann is telling the story of a Black woman from a perspective she's never lived before. Why is this story right for this imprint and not for any other we have at Drake? We said we wanted to highlight marginalized voices. Aliza's isn't a marginalized voice. Nor does it appear she's made the effort to get to know anyone in the community she wishes to represent in more than a two-dimensional aspect. Not to mention, she's cosplaying, which will be seen as offensive and profiteering. We cannot go to Black media with this book. They won't touch it."

I was floundering. I could feel it. But I had a plan B. I just needed to keep my cool long enough to implement it.

"And you're saying that can't happen? Don't Black writers write about white people all the time?"

One. Two. Three. Four. Alas, none of the digits were bringing calm. "Yes, but Caucasian is the assumed primary culture in this country. Aliza's writing from a perspective that's pejorative. I'm not saying that no white writer can write Black characters. Of course not. What I am saying is that it must be done with care and nuance."

"Greta said she's done all her research."

"And as a Black woman, I'm telling you readers will have no reason to trust us."

Steven leaned back, his gaze narrowing on mine. "She's a yes."

A voice from my left surprised me. "Actually, Ofosua has a point. This imprint is meant to bring Drake into the twenty-first century. We don't want any missteps. For starters, I'll have to tap-dance with the indie booksellers to get them to even consider buying this."

I suspected I wasn't going to win, but I hadn't expected anyone to bother siding with me. Let alone Cole.

But this is exactly what you need. An ally.

Steven shook his head. "No, you won't. We're simply not going to talk about the author's race because, in this instance, it doesn't matter. I've always said everyone should be color-blind. We aren't in the business of censoring authors. I shouldn't have to remind anyone at Drake of this foundational principle of our work."

Not for the first time, I wondered where he'd been these past few years. We all joked that Steven Drake didn't know what X was, that he'd be lost north of Seventy-Second Street and south of Fourteenth, and that Connecticut was as adventurous as he got, but maybe none of that was a joke at all.

My molars hurt from clamping them so tight. I knew I shouldn't. I knew how I would be perceived in this room. I knew how much I needed these people, this line, the ability to get the kinds of stories that I wanted to see published.

But I couldn't hold it in. "So you're banking on everyone responding to the story of a Black-washed white woman and her ghetto-struggling best friend with no joy in her life. That's the story you want to lean into and tell with the launch of Drake's Black imprint? Do you think that's a good idea? Or even accurate?

There are other stories to tell. Stories readers want. Brilliant ones right in front of us."

Steven put his phone down, steepled his fingers, and leveled a direct gaze at me. "We're acquiring this. Get on board. Also, in regard to your imprint name. I saw your suggestion for Sankofa Lit. No one will know what that means. Too foreign, so I'm going with Mahogany Prose."

My world tilted, and it felt like it was being shaken like a snow globe. I'd chosen Sankofa as it was a saying in Twi, one of my languages, meaning look to the past. It was my special tie to the imprint.

But that was personal. I could deal with that at home. Demanding I keep Aliza was something else.

Tears stung my eyes, making me blink rapidly. I had to keep fighting this. This book would hamstring my imprint. We'd be a joke. *I* would be the joke.

Easy does it. You know you can't fight this right now.

But I had to.

I held it together and shoved the panic and building rage back down. "How about we table the discussion about Aliza for next week? Emory and I will work together to see what we can do with the first few chapters that we have. We'll come up with something. If we can make it work, we'll try. But let's put her firmly in the 'maybe' pile."

At the moment, it was the best I could do.

"Ms. Addo, are you under the impression that I make mistakes?"

Steven's voice was quiet and calm, with an ice-cold hint of warning I'd never heard before. I'd crossed a line. *Shit.* I just wanted this meeting over.

"Sir, all I'm saying is—"

Nazrin chimed in then, her face prim, her brows lifted. "Ofosua, you're being a little aggressive here. Why don't you settle down?"

My hands started to tremble, and I had to plant my fingertips down on the glass, pressing them so that nobody would see them shaking. I angled my head toward her. "How am I being aggressive exactly?"

"You're practically yelling."

I *knew* I wasn't yelling. But I also knew what they were seeing. Or at least what Nazrin was choosing to see . . . an angry Black woman. As I opened my mouth to give her nothing but a saccharine slice of my silver tongue, Cole interrupted. "Nazrin, question. If I were the one fighting against this acquisition, would you tell me I was being aggressive?"

Nazrin blinked rapidly. "Well, I mean, it's just that she—"

Cole shook his head, his eyes hard. I don't think I'd ever seen him actually angry before. Sure, he was annoyed with me often enough, and I'd seen him irritated plenty of times. And he could be pushy when it came to the marketing teams or the major account reps sometimes. But I had never seen him *angry*.

But why was he angry on my behalf? That didn't make any sense.

"Answer the question, Nazrin. Would you have called me aggressive just now?"

"Well, no, but Ofosua is—"

He shook his head again. "This is Ofosua's imprint. *She* is in charge of it. *We* are the *support* team. Mr. Drake has made his opinions clear. But Ofosua is the *editorial director*. She'll make the final call as is customary, won't she?"

Cole stared down his uncle. Steven stared back. "I won't interfere with your other choices. But Aliza Mann's book will be published at Drake, so find a way to make it work. And I do appreciate your passion, Ofosua. This is why we gave this line to you."

I could hear the truth in his voice then. He hadn't given me my own imprint because he cared about Drake's diversity problem. Or because he believed in me. He needed this line for his own private reasons. I would surely discover them in time.

CHAPTER 10

COLE

ADINKRA SAYING:
(Fawohodie) Freedom walks with suffering.

HELEN ADDO:
Freedom comes with education and an advanced degree . . .
like a master's.

SAMUEL ADDO:
Freedom comes with your birthright. Your home.
Never forget your way.

That was a goddamn shit show.

It was a small miracle that no one got into an actual fistfight. True, emotions at acquisitions meetings could run high. Once, at my first intern gig after Princeton, at a small press, an editor lost his shit and threw a brick of Post-its at his director of sales.

That was years ago, though. And despite the fact that things hadn't quite gotten that far today, what had happened was ugly. We'd only been out of the meeting for twenty minutes, and I'd already heard whispers. The rumor mill could kill hopes and career aspirations in this place.

But Ofosua had handled it well. She'd kept her cool and her

poise. If my uncle had talked to me like that, I might have lost it. And I certainly would have told Nazrin where she could shove her comments.

If I wanted a shot at smoothing things over, I had two choices. Head for my uncle or Ofosua. And I was ninety-nine percent sure that neither was going to be receptive to my interference. But I thought maybe my uncle would be the easier of the two. I'd never seen him like that, waving his proverbial dick around. He was usually far more measured.

Yet he'd made it a point to shut Ofosua down, and publicly, over a book that frankly didn't seem worth the fight. What had just happened in that meeting and why? When I stuck my head into his office, Steven was already on the phone talking to Greta, letting her know that we'd be coming to her with an offer for Aliza Mann's manuscript within the next few days. Which was bullshit.

I lifted my brows as he hung up. "We need to talk."

"Later," he said.

And then he closed the door in my face.

All right. Ofosua, then.

As I made my way down the hall and to the right, where most of the editors sat, I managed to catch a glimpse of her back as she was headed in the opposite direction at a decent clip in her fuchsia-pink pencil skirt and sky-high heels that made her legs look a mile long.

As I rounded the corner to take the stairs behind her, Emory slid into my path. "What the hell was that? This imprint was your uncle's idea. And now it seems like he doesn't actually want Ofosua in charge. The vibe was way off. That was bad, Cole."

"You think I don't know that? Drake needs her."

You mean you need her.

I snapped my jaw shut so the errant thought wouldn't escape. I only meant she was good for Drake. And the only woman of color on our editing staff. We had Alejandro in thrillers. But they were the only brown people in upper-level positions. I knew the optics.

Also, you're worried about her.

Luckily, Emory wasn't privy to my inner thoughts.

I did not have time for this. "Emory, is this absolutely necessary right now? I need to talk to Ofosua before she gets too far. Like it or not, I've been assigned to her imprint. We're a team. And I'm trying to smooth things over before it gets bad."

When she'd left the conference room, she'd looked . . . hurt.

And that's your business because?

My inner voice was like going to fucking therapy. I didn't need to examine all these thoughts or feelings or whatever the fuck was going on. I just needed to get to her. What had happened in that meeting was fucked up. And at the end of the day, I wasn't my uncle. I knew she could do this job and do it well.

Twenty flights of stairs was a long fucking way down. How had she done it in heels? Had she slipped to another floor to use the elevators?

I scanned the street to the left and to the right. Central Park West was busy, cabs honking, pedestrians crowding the street. And then I saw her. A few tendrils of her curls had escaped her pinned-up style today, showcasing her long, elegant neck.

I took off in her direction, but she had over half a block on me. And as I wove my way through the crowd, I tried to figure out what the hell I was going to say to her.

If she had any indication I was following her, she didn't show it, though she eventually slowed her pace, allowing me to catch up. We'd gone several blocks north before she noticed me. She was looking at one of the store windows and then she hesitated and picked up her pace again.

"Ofosua. Don't run."

She didn't turn around.

"Ofosua. Wait."

"Stop following me, Cole," she called back.

"I just want to talk."

"I don't want to talk to you," she said before making a sharp right and hopping in a cab.

Shit.

I picked up my pace and slid into a taxi, stealing it from some guy in a suit. I gave him an apologetic look even as I asked the cabdriver to follow Ofos. I wasn't sure if I should thank the driver for sticking right on her tail or hold on for my life. Either way, when her taxi pulled over, so did mine. Not wanting to fuss with payment and lose her, I threw him a fifty and told him to keep the change.

I caught up to her easily. "Ofos. Please talk to me."

She turned on me. "Did you really just pull a *follow that cab* routine?"

I shrugged. "Maybe. Look." I applied a gentle pressure to her elbow and tugged her off the main walkway in front of a massive wrought-iron gate. The gate was open, exposing a street I'd never been on before. When I looked up, I didn't recognize where we were at all.

I looked for a sign and saw one. Pomander Walk. The stairs leading up provided a hidden quiet place to talk. "Look, I'm sorry that meeting was a shit show."

She was glancing up and around at our surroundings, which, to be fair, did look like something out of a Disney movie. It was a tiny, private, no-cars-possible street lined with two- and three-story Tudor-style single-family homes facing one another. Each home had colorful flowers planted in front of it, climbing vines, and brightly painted wooden doors and shutters in shades of cobalt, ruby, and hunter green. Were we even still in Manhattan?

"You think?"

"Look, I'm sorry. It shouldn't have gone like that."

"Did your uncle send you to find me? In case you haven't noticed, it's lunchtime, so I'm technically off the clock. I can do what I like."

"I know you can do what you like, and my uncle didn't send me. I just saw you leaving, and you looked . . . upset."

She pressed her lips together firmly. "I'm not *upset*. I'm not overly emotional. I'm not overly passionate, and I'm certainly not angry, Cole. I just wanted a brisk walk."

I'd seen this version of her before. The contained version. Her flat self. I'd seen it in meetings. When someone said something dumb or offensive, it was her zero-response face. Professional and detached.

But Ofosua's face was normally so expressive. When she smiled and was truly happy, she lit up a whole room. You couldn't help but watch her. When she was pitching a book she loved, it was impossible to tear your gaze away. The only choice was to sit there riveted until she released her hold on you. I also knew her sad face. It looked a lot like this one, except her eyes were more haunted.

I knew her pissed-off face too. That one I liked to think was reserved for me. She mostly kept that one locked away unless we were off-site. When we were butting heads in the office, she always stayed in the frosty, cool, contained zone with me. Which rankled.

"Oh, come on, don't give me this face. The cool, detached one. Get pissed off. That meeting was bullshit. *You* know it. *I* know it."

She gave me a tight smile then. "Pissed off? Because I didn't get my way? Because someone blasted microaggressions at me hot enough to melt my face off? Tell me what it's like to be you and pitch a tantrum whenever I like. Because I can't do that. I don't get to. What I *get to do* is take a fucking walk and make arguments to myself about why I have to go back to that office and keep fighting the good fight. So please tell me again how I should be acting."

"Jesus. That's not what I'm saying. I just . . ." Except that was what I was saying.

On her fingers, she recounted a few points to me. "I am good at my job. I handle bullshit like this all the time. I can handle hard conversations. What I don't handle well is the precious few minutes where I don't have to hold my shit together being eaten into by an entitled white guy." Her last point was punctuated with a finger to my chest.

Which was when I realized just how close I was standing to her. Close enough for the hint of her hibiscus shampoo to waft around me.

"This is not going how I imagined. I just—"

"What, Cole? Just what the hell do you need from me? I left all I had to give in that meeting. So I'm filling up my well again before I have to go back to pretending for everyone."

I hadn't realized it, but now we were pressed up against each other. Her eyes were fire as they sparked up at me. And suddenly my skin felt too hot, too tight, and I was all too aware of just how close she was standing. "You don't have to pretend for me. Would probably be easier if you didn't." My voice sounded like someone had put it through a cement mixer.

For a long moment, we stood like that. Too close for the distance to be professional. She had room to back up, but she didn't. I had room as well, but I was rooted to my spot, held in place by the fire in her eyes.

"You want me to thank you for your attempt to stand up for me."

I swallowed hard as I shook my head. "No."

"Because that didn't help, Cole. I know you think it did, but I need to fight my own battles."

"Everyone in there knows you can fight your own battles."

"Because I'm the aggressive one, right?"

I cursed under my breath. "Nazrin was out of order. And we are on the same team. I stand with my team, like it or not."

"Out of order or not—" Her voice broke, and I watched helplessly as she rapidly blinked her eyes, not meeting my gaze. "I've worked really hard to seem approachable, friendly, and a team player."

"You're not unapproachable."

Her teeth grazed her bottom lip, a soft frown marring her smooth forehead, the only crack in the armor she'd ever shown me. "Nazrin thinks I am. Now a lot of other people will too, because she's influential in the office. I didn't need you to come and give me a Band-Aid and kiss my boo-boos."

My gaze flickered to her lips. The overwhelming urge to kiss away a thousand hurts hit me like a wave. I cleared my throat. *Ofosua is your colleague.* "That's not why I came. I just wanted to see if you were okay."

Her eyes were large, dark pools that held me arrested in place when she looked up at me. One glance and she managed to hypnotize me.

"Why do you even care?"

I could at least be honest with my answer. "I have no idea. I just saw you and I ran after you. Because, like it or not, you and I are on the same team." I was standing close. Too close. But she didn't move back.

"You were put on that team. To keep me in check."

I shoved my hands in my pockets. "You know, when my uncle gave me this assignment, I think that's what he thought was going to happen. But he seems to forget that I'm my own person. I know you're good at your job. I might need to learn more about what we are doing with this new venture. It's the future. You embody what my grandfather wanted for Drake."

Her gaze searched mine, and then her tongue peeked out to swipe over her bottom lip. And all the blood in my body rushed south. *Fuck me.*

A new voice interrupted the moment. "I just had the best showing. Oh my God. It's small. I mean New York small. But it's perfect. And it's only two million." A woman in high heels came clattering out the door to the house closest to us, talking loudly on her phone about real estate. The noise she made broke the spell. Shattered that glass cocoon I'd started to build around us.

Ofosua cleared her throat, and then I stepped back. She blinked rapidly and smoothed down invisible wrinkles on the fuchsia-colored skirt she wore. "I should get back to the office."

I shook my head. "You don't have to do that. Maybe spend the rest of the day working from home or something."

She shook her head. "You should know by now that I don't run from a challenge. I'm going right back to work. I have five slots to fill."

She never said die. "Of course you do."

She tilted her chin up and gave me a fuller version of her smile, her full lips parting, showing straight, perfectly even, white teeth. The dazzle of it pulling me in. "Careful now, Cole Drake, someone might actually call you a decent guy."

"Oh, well, at least you'll always be there to remind them that I'm not."

CHAPTER 11

OFOSUA

ADINKRA SAYING:
(Hye Wo Nhye) Burn you won't burn.

HELEN ADDO:
Men are hardheaded. They will use all their gasoline before they realize you were born from fire.

To: ogthrillerwriter@yahoo.com
From: oaddo@drakepublishing.com
CC: dhodges@dwightagency.com,
   cdrake@drakepublishing.com

I'm glad to hear that you can have the manuscript ready in a short amount of time.

I was as polite and clear as possible as I typed out an email to Evan and his agent. All the while, I cursed Cole under my breath. This was all his fault. Despite having the new imprint, I still had to edit Evan Miles. But I could not help remembering how he had been helpful the day before.

My feelings toward him were such a jumbled mess now. It was easier to slide him into the annoying-nemesis role because that kept him at an arm's length. Kind and encouraging Cole, I didn't know what to do with.

But I would not concentrate on that. I had so much damn work to do, and of course, Evan was immediately uncooperative. Jackass didn't want to do an outline I could troubleshoot and was insisting on just delivering the completed manuscript in three months' time.

He was clearly testing me. So instead of getting out of the office by six, I was cutting into precious submission reading time. I'd had a whole plan for tonight; me, some reheated jollof, an Olivia Pope–sized wineglass, and manuscripts I actually wanted to read.

You're a wild one, aren't you?

Okay, fine, I probably did need a life, but damn.

I didn't want to waste my precious time on Evan. I had bigger fish to fry.

Just as I grabbed my purse and coat off the hanger, I heard the telltale ping of my email.

Shit. I was never leaving.

To: oaddo@drakepublishing.com
From: ogthrillerwriter@yahoo.com
CC: blank

No. It works better creatively if I don't do one. See you next week.

Evan

I forced myself to take a breath. And then another one. That little shit. I was never going to forgive Cole for saddling me with him.

But I had a strategy of my own.

To: ogthrillerwriter@yahoo.com
From: oaddo@drakepublishing.com
CC: dhodges@dwightagency.com,
    cdrake@drakepublishing.com,
    ajames@drakepublishing.com

To facilitate this process for you, Andrea James will be working with you on any editorial notes and questions you may have. She's brilliant, graduated from Yale, and worked on Tim Wandsworth's latest while at Brookfield Publishing.

 I look forward to seeing your outline.

Ofosua

I had handled him. Olivia Pope would be proud. I'd played him with all the things he couldn't resist.

Still, the blatant disrespect set my teeth grinding. "But at least now you can enjoy your wild and crazy night," I muttered to myself.

"You just played him, didn't you?" said a teasing voice.

Hot Cole.

I turned to frown at him. "This is your fault. I wouldn't have to play mind games if you hadn't blackmailed me."

He put his hands up. "I know, he's a dick. And I would hardly call it blackmail."

"What would you call it?"

He seemed to consider a moment. "Creative negotiating. Besides, you just fixed it. Expertly, I might add. Andrea is blonde and bubbly and he'll think she's hot, so he won't fight her as much. And then you played into his elitism, as he also went to Yale."

I shrugged. "Either way, he's locked in and will do what I need."

"See, I knew you'd have the answers."

"I wouldn't have needed to fix anything if you'd just—"

He held up his hand and interrupted me. "You're off the clock. We can fight tomorrow."

"Says the man who started this particular fracas."

"Guilty as charged. Let me make it up to you. Didn't you just say something about a wild night?"

"Not with you. What do you want, Drake?"

He gave me a teasing smile that lit up his dancing gray eyes. "You wound me. There's a happy hour tonight. You should come."

I hooked my Hermès Arcon bag on my shoulder and studied him. He looked impeccable in his Burberry charcoal vest and trousers. I could tell by the stitching that it had been expertly tailored to his tall, lean frame. He'd ditched his blue-and-gray Hermès tie at some point during the day. And he'd rolled up the sleeves of his crisp white shirt, showing off his forearms.

The whole deconstructed suit effect, combined with his artfully disheveled locks, and the dusting of stubble on his jaw, made the man look . . . good enough to eat. Which was wholly unfair. The sandalwood and leather of his cologne served as a reminder of just how close we'd been the other day.

And all week, he'd been borderline . . . nice. Or at least not nearly as annoying as usual.

And he came for you.

No one ever checked on me. I was the one who checked in on people. I was expected to hold it together. Be strong. But he had *come* for me.

I did my best to squash that pitch-and-dip thing my heart did thinking about him.

"I have a lot of work to do."

He stood staring at me for a long moment, and I could feel every prick of his scrutiny. "Look, what I'm saying is, you need to spend some time letting your colleagues and team get to know you personally. They need to see you as a little bit more of a person. Not some work robot."

"I am *not* a work robot."

He lifted a brow. "For starters, *I* didn't call you that. But since you seem sensitive about it, why don't you prove everyone wrong? Prove that you're not a robot. Come to happy hour tonight. I dare you."

He sauntered away, and my gaze slid after him. He thought I was no fun. My friends thought so too. When had this become my life? There was a time when I'd been fun and engaging. When I did things. Went out.

But being at home never set off my panic attacks. In the house, nothing could trigger me. But also, I didn't really live either.

Don't be a wuss.

I sent a text to Emory. It would be easier with a friend.

OFOSUA:

Are you at happy hour with the work peeps?

EMORY:

Yep. Do you need me for something?

Why was this so hard? All I had to do was stop obsessing over my emails and go have a little fun.

OFOSUA:

No. I was just going to join.

EMORY:

> Yay! Please come save me from dumbass Chad.

I guess it was settled. I was on my way to happy hour . . . with Hot Cole.

—

I was out of practice.

I had no idea what the hell to do at a happy hour anymore.

Whose fault is that?

There had been a time when I would be the one who attended at least one happy hour a week with my girlfriends. Objectively, I knew the rules of engagement. A strong drink, laugh the workday out of my system, home or on to dinner by seven p.m. But as I surveyed the rapidly filling bar, I simply had no idea what to do. I had planned on being married by now. That rising panic that told me that I was a social failure, that this was such a mistake, pricked at the back of my neck. I swallowed hard.

You can do this. Don't be a ballsack.

I was not going to lose it, goddamn it. This was nothing more than a work function. I'd done dozens of these without breaking a sweat.

Before Yofi.

Speaking of the asshole, he'd called again but hadn't left a message. What the hell did he want?

I walked straight up to the bar and ordered myself a tonic and lime. Even though a drink might help my anxiety, I rarely drank with workmates. But I knew that everyone expected you to drink at these things, so I had that tonic in my hand that I clutched like a lifeline, and that was how Emory found me.

"There you are. I grabbed a table over there. Join us."

"Who's 'us'?"

She took my hand, tugging me, and I froze.

She frowned at me. "Are you okay?"

"Uh-huh, yup, I'm fine. Everything is fine. Perfectly fine."

"You look like you're freaking out."

Well, damn. "Sorry, it's been a while."

She grinned. "Okay, we'll stay at the bar for a little bit. Drink your drink and then we'll go over, say our hellos, you buy them a round. See? Easy."

It didn't feel easy. As a matter of fact, it felt like a lot of steps.

After fifteen minutes of panic hovering at the bar, I followed her reluctantly to the tables and found Cole already sitting in one of the corner booths. Across from, of course, fuckwit Chad. Excellent. Exactly who I wanted to spend my evening with.

Emory maneuvered me over to Drea Louis from the accounting department. She gave me a bright smile and waved. She liked me because I always turned in my reports on time. "Hey, Drea, I haven't seen you in a while."

"Yeah, it's a shame. But hey, we're here now. Great shoes, by the way."

I glanced down at my pinky-nude Jimmy Choos. "Thanks."

I'd paired them with jeans and an African-print top from Christie Brown. And honestly, I mostly had the cute shoes off at work. Though I loved heels, I was *not* a masochist. Unless I was trying to impress someone, I didn't wear these shoes anywhere I was going to spend a significant amount of time standing.

Wait. Was I trying to impress someone tonight? I shook my head at the unbidden thought.

I forced myself to nod to Cole and Chad. Chad smiled at me, although with an equivocal expression. "Wow, look who came out. You never come out."

I smiled. A small one.

Chad had the distinct handicap of not knowing when to shut the fuck up, because he always had to go and say the wrong thing. "You know, we call you the robot because you're not like a real girl."

Did Cole put him up to this?

I blinked at Chad. Slow and steady, staring him down until he was the one to look away. "I think the word you're looking for is 'woman.' Not 'girl.'"

Cole looked like he was on the verge of a smile, his lips twitching at the corners.

What was that? He wasn't scowling at me like usual. "Glad to see you made it out, Addo."

"Well, you said to come, so I came, didn't I?"

"I am honestly surprised you listened to me at all."

For a good thirty minutes or so, it was easy. We all bantered about cats versus men then moved on to some lighthearted office chat. That tension knot that I'd felt between my shoulder blades eased. I did know how to do this. And I hated that it was Cole who'd reminded me.

When Drea got up to go to the bathroom, Chad took her spot. "So, Ofosua."

I lifted a brow and met his gaze. "Chad?"

"Weren't you supposed to be engaged or something?"

I felt like I'd been poleaxed right in the solar plexus, and for a long second, I couldn't speak. "Yeah, well, it didn't work out."

"Oh, he wasn't ready to settle down? Did the idea of fucking you forever scare him off?"

Cole's voice was tense and remarkably growly. "Chad, what the fuck is wrong with you?"

Fuckwit Chad lifted his brows. "What? I'm making conversation."

"Try not making conversation that proves to everyone what an asshole you are."

He shrugged at Cole, then at me. "I'm sorry. I didn't mean anything by it."

I knew I was expected to say it was okay, but it wasn't. "Yup, not your business."

He rolled his eyes. "All right, so how come you never come out? It's been a few months since you stopped blinding us with your ring. How come you're not on the prowl? I mean, if you need someone to break you back in . . ."

After I threw up a little in my mouth, I murmured, "You know this is sexual harassment, right?"

"All I'm saying is I can help you learn how to date again."

I lifted a brow. "Do you really think you're the guy I'd pick to help me start dating again? I'd be the one doing the charity work there."

He frowned. As if it had never occurred to him that he wouldn't be the kind of date women wanted. "What's wrong with me?"

Drea came back in time to save me from having to be the one to tell him, when she said, "You mean, besides you being an utter and complete asshole?"

Chad gave us a condescending laugh. "Yeah. Hit me."

Drea and Emory gave me an encouraging nod, egging me on to eviscerate him. Challenge accepted. "You think you're God's gift. No woman likes that. You're inherently selfish. Again, no woman likes that. And you're offensive. And guess what? No woman likes that. Yeah, it makes you not the best candidate, really."

Emory high-fived me. "What she said."

Chad rolled his eyes. "I'm trying to help Ofosua out."

"When I need your help, I'll ask for it."

He took his shot and slammed it down. "You'd be cute for a Black girl if you weren't so uptight."

The microaggression rolled off my back like I was a duck. "And I'm so concerned about what you think, why?"

He laughed. "Touché."

At that moment, my phone rang. I pulled it out of my purse, and pursed my lips when I saw who it was. *Yofi* . . . again. I immediately declined the call and shoved it back in my purse, my stomach pitching.

Cole leaned over, concern etched on his brow. "You look ashen. What's wrong?"

I stood up, ignoring him. I needed some air. Right away.

Before I knew it, Cole unfolded his long, lean body and took my hand. The sudden spark of electricity had me gasping, but he didn't seem to notice as he led us through the crowd.

My heartbeat started to echo in my head, and I could feel the panic of the walls closing around me. A busboy jostled me, making me trip over my feet. Damn these Jimmy Choos. Firm hands caught me quickly, pressing me against a solid, hard body.

Cole still held my hand, but had wrapped his free arm around me, his hand pressed firmly against my lower back, holding me steady.

I blinked up at him rapidly while, around us, the crowd grew. When his gaze dipped to my mouth, I licked my lips nervously. I watched in rapt fascination as his gaze narrowed and he muttered something I couldn't hear over the din in the bar. I wasn't a lip-reading expert, but it looked like he'd muttered, *Fuck me.*

Which obviously wasn't right.

But it wasn't until he leaned forward that my heart attempted a mutiny by trying to jump out of my chest and my lungs forgot how to function. And possibly the worst betrayal of all came from my brain, which promptly jumped on the *why, yes, it would be a delightful idea to kiss Hot Cole in the middle of a crowded bar* signal.

The closer he leaned, the tighter I held my body, lest my arms involuntarily wrap around him and pull him closer. *Much* closer.

But Hot Cole's proximity didn't hit the intended target of my lips; instead, he kept going and stopped at the shell of my ear. When he spoke, his words sent an involuntary shiver through me.

Christ. I was a mess. *Get it together, Addo. You don't even like him.*

"You good?" His words, while utterly innocuous, sent my body spiraling in a haze of need and uncertainty. He was going out of his way to be nice, and I was acting desperate and lust-crazed.

But to be fair, it wasn't my fault. His voice, pitched that low, should have been illegal. The husky quality, and the intimacy of his proximity, coupled with the musk of his cologne, would have sent anyone into a lust-fueled fog.

After I gave him a sharp nod, he pulled his hand away from my back, a move that had me missing the weight and the heat, and continued leading me outside to the back patio.

The cool fresh air instantly calmed me, helping my mind clear, and I dropped his hand when he found us a quiet spot in the corner. "Thank you."

"No problem. You looked like you needed a breather." His voice was soft when he spoke, and his gaze kept dropping to my lips.

I had to be imagining that, right?

"Careful: you keep being this nice, I might start to think we're *actually* partners."

He flashed a grin at me even as he flagged a waitress down. "Aren't we? 'Drake and Addo' has a nice sound to it."

"First of all, why did you assume you'd be first? My name starts with *A*. I should be first. But anyway, we're not partners, Cole.

That would imply we are equals." I guess with the new imprint, technically, I was his equal now, but the power dynamic hadn't quite shifted *that* much.

He sighed. "Look, I understand why you wouldn't want to work with me. But I still think we make a decent team. The authors are yours. You nurture them. But I can sell the shit out of them. And I'm actually going to do my job despite what you think. I'm not trying to screw you. And also, I speak rich dick."

The laugh burst out of my lips before I could stop it. "What?"

He shrugged. "Look, I know you think I'm a dick. And you would be right. Sometimes I am. But I really do speak the language." He rubbed the back of his neck. "About what you said . . . maybe my uncle isn't expecting much from your line. The fact that he paired me with you probably means he doesn't think much of me either, now that I think about it. But it's an opportunity to prove him wrong. Are you going to blow that?"

This imprint was never about me. Or about the work that I had done. This line was about looking good to outsiders. This line was about the *veneer* of moving forward as a company.

It stung but was no less than I expected. But it was an opportunity to show what I could do. And I *could* do something spectacular.

"Working together means you don't undermine me, Cole. No more bullshit tactics like Evan. No Aliza Manns. I'm getting her off my list. We have to *actually* be a team."

He shoved his hands in his pockets and rocked back on his heels. "Okay. Whatever you need. Also, give it another day. Evan will comply. If he doesn't, I will handle all his bullshit personally. As for Aliza, I agree with you. Do you think pawning her off is going to work?"

"I do. Taking another look at the book, it sort of feels like someone told her to make it edgier. She's not a bad writer, it just feels off. I'm going to send some notes to Carol about how to make the book shine. Top of that list, make it more authentic. No more literary blackface."

His eyes went wide. "Wow."

I shrugged. "That's what she did. If I can get Carol to see the diamond in the rough, my worries are over."

"Jesus, you're brilliant."

Did I preen at that? Yes. Was I proud of it? No. "Yes. In other news, water is wet."

His crack of laughter sent a wave of warmth through my chest. "Why didn't I know you were funny?"

"I'm only funny with people I like."

There it was: another flash of a grin. If the man kept smiling at me like that, I was going to have a problem. "I knew you liked me. Okay, so what can I do tomorrow to support you?"

I chewed my bottom lip as I pondered. "You can start by answering the emails I've already sent to him. I've trod softly; now you're my big stick." The immediate twist of his lips into a smirk had me shaking my head, panicked. "No! That's not what I meant."

The grin he flashed was wicked. "If you say so. How much time do you spend thinking about my big stick?"

"What? No!" I covered my face and despite myself, I laughed. *Laughed.* At the devil incarnate. The thing was, he was a colossal pain in the ass, but he was also right: I couldn't go at this alone. I hadn't handpicked half of my team, and the only person who was really in my corner rooting for me was Emory. It wouldn't kill me to have another ally. One who had power in the office. Even if it was Hot Cole.

But can you be friends with him?

That was the question of the century. Especially if I kept having these weird *I'd love to feel his lips on mine* flashbacks and vibes. I wasn't a fool.

At least not anymore.

I don't know what it was: the suddenly crisp, cool air, my ability to breathe, or my relief that I hadn't freaked out in front of everyone at the table. Whatever it was, I could hardly believe the words coming out of my own mouth.

"Fine. Partners," I muttered grudgingly.

He grinned at me. "I like how that sounds. Your skills, my big stick."

Heat crept up my neck. "Why do I regret this already?"

"That's not regret; that's excitement you're feeling." He nodded at someone he knew. "Give me one sec."

"Sure." When he was gone, I took the opportunity to check my phone.

There were several texts from Yofi asking me to please call him, one from Emory that she was on the dance floor, and one from Cora.

CORA:

> You, my love, have a date with Omar tomorrow. He'll pick you up at 7.

What the hell?

Sure, I'd said she could set me up, but this was so fast. I didn't even know the guy.

That's why it's called a blind date.

Oh God, was I this person? Could I say yes? Dare I say yes?

Or you could risk it all with Hot Cole.

Time to try new things.

OFOSUA:

That's great. I'm so excited. 😄

Had I used the right emoji to convey proper enthusiasm? Who knew, but the point was, I had a date. When Cole came back, my mood was lifted.

"You okay?" he asked.

"I'm good. Thanks." As the wind started to pick up, I inclined my head. "We'd better get back inside."

Cole let me go first. Which was probably for the best, so I didn't change my mind. I still felt lightheaded as my mind churned. What was Yofi *still* calling me for? I had nothing to say to him.

I hadn't expected the crush of people. "Wow, it's even more crowded in here now."

It was harder to maneuver as we traversed the bar. As we attempted to reach our group, we were stuck in the middle of the dance floor, and the music switched to Afrobeats. And there was Cole pressed up against me. All I could do was stand there stiffly.

Cole stared down at me, and I stared back at him, our bodies pressed together. To protect myself, I put my hands up, but that was almost worse, because then I could feel his chest muscles.

Where did he get those muscles from? His gaze stayed on me and mine on him. And there was this long beat of silence where I could almost see what my friends saw. He could be charming. And he was incredibly hot. I inhaled, the scent of sandalwood cologne wrapping me in a cocoon. A little musky, but mostly crisp. And then we were bumped again, creating space between us, and I could breathe. It was like someone had opened the window and let in the air.

"Hey, shithead, who's your friend?" The question came from

a tall, olive-skinned guy dressed in fancy jeans and a pullover, but by one of those designer brands where the fabric was so soft, it felt like butter on your skin.

When Cole didn't introduce us, he stuck out his hand. "I'm Tallon. Friend of Cole's. And you must be Ofosua Addo?"

My brows lifted. "Why do you know who I am?"

Tallon grinned. "Because you're the only one who can put that look on his face."

"You mean his *I'm going to commit murder* look?" I joked.

Tallon grinned. "Oh, buddy, I like her already."

I laughed despite myself. On the surface, he should be everything I loathed. Everything that reminded me of some of the kids I'd grown up with, who were more content to spend their father's money than actually do some work themselves. But there was something endearing about him. Like he might look the douchebag part, but there might be something nicer underneath.

"Are you sure you're his friend?"

Tallon laughed. "Sometimes I'm his worst enemy. But yeah, we're usually best friends."

"Do I have you to hold responsible for his behavior?"

Tallon held his hands up. "Oh no, not that. Listen, I barely know the guy. He turned up on my doorstep one day and begged me to be his friend. That's how I got here."

I laughed.

Cole ignored him. "Who wants a beer?"

It was the first time all night that I felt normal, a little bit lighter. I had to say, it was terrifying and exhilarating all at once.

CHAPTER 12

OFOSUA

ADINKRA SAYING:
(Kete Pa) It is when a woman enters a good marriage that she is
put on a good bed.

HELEN ADDO:
*A good bed should also come with children . . . and orgasms. Not
necessarily in that order.*

The next night, I got ready for my date with trepidation.

I wasn't a coward. I could do this.

It was just a date.

A date I *wanted* to go on. A date with a perfectly good man.
A man who was *not* Hot Cole. I would never ever in a million
years admit it, but my closeness with Cole had yielded some
unwanted results.

I'd been having dreams. *Inappropriate* dreams. About Cole.
Dirty, inappropriate dreams. Dream Cole was verbal and full of
praise. And very, very good with his tongue.

Which was all kinds of unacceptable, obvi, so this date couldn't
come soon enough. I needed to shift the focus away from him,
toward someone I could *actually* date.

It had been so long since I'd gone out. Last night I'd broken the seal. I was out of practice, so it had taken a moment to get ready. I'd gone with a simple red Diane von Furstenberg wrap dress.

The length was perfect, just above the knee. And it went perfectly with my satin Prada heels. I'd had it for years, but I felt like it was my lucky date outfit.

When was the last time I'd been on a date? Before Yofi, my last proper date was David Ayensu, a Ghanaian financier. We'd met in Ghana at an Achimota School alumni benefit. While I'd only attended for two years, both my parents were alumni.

David had done the whole sweep-me-off-my-feet thing, flying me from Accra to Capetown for our first date. But I'd been in my last year of school, and long distance was not in the cards.

Come to think of it, I hadn't dated all that much.

With a confidence I was faking for all I was worth, I strutted out of my building with a wide smile.

The moment I saw Omar's grin, I relaxed. He was good-looking. Medium-brown skin, smooth complexion. No beard. I hated beards. Decent jaw, slight divot in his chin, which I loved.

Cora knew me well. I was a sucker for a pretty boy. As I approached, I extended my hand. "Omar, hi. I'm Ofosua. It's lovely to meet you." He took my hand and immediately tugged me in for a hug.

He was strong. And admittedly, I was surprised by the hug, so I held myself stiffly for a moment. I didn't like people I didn't know touching me. And while he smelled fine, he smelled almost *too sweet*.

This was a date. He was going to touch me. I had to get used to it. "Oh, you're a hugger."

He pulled back and shook his head. "No, girl, but you look too good not to hug. True queen vibes."

I wasn't sure how I felt about that, but still, I held on to my Miu Miu clutch tightly and inclined my head toward the corner. "Shall we?"

As we walked toward the restaurant, we chatted amiably. Omar was clearly educated. He'd gone to Temple. He'd grown up in the suburbs of DC, and he was nice.

He did the door-opening thing when we arrived at the restaurant. Cubana was only a few short blocks from my apartment. It was new and a hot spot, and I'd needed Kukua to pull some strings to get a reservation as I'd chosen the location. She always seemed to have an in with the entertainment community, and the chef was a former Broadway star.

Luckily, we were right on time for our reservation.

As dates went, our conversation was easy. That was until our waitress came to the table. She was a beautiful biracial girl with her hair straightened within an inch of its life and elegantly clipped back with sparkly barrettes.

She had delicate tattoos lining her wrists and an eyebrow piercing. Those were her only real hints to being someone alternative. As she took our order, Omar spoke to her politely, he even asked me what my preferred choice of drink was. And since we were in a Cuban spot, of course I ordered a mojito.

I didn't miss the wrinkle of his nose, though. Was I not supposed to fortify myself with alcohol? It was a first date, and I was going to run out of topics eventually.

I tried to lighten the conversation. "Thank you for bringing me here. I've been meaning to come, but I just hadn't managed to make the time." He looked displeased, though, his gaze sliding back to our waitress. "Is there a problem?"

"Just I hate to see a young half sister ruin herself like that."

I glanced around. "Excuse me? Did you say 'half sister'?"

"The waitress. She's not really a sister. And you saw what she's done to her skin. And the piercings. If those markings were tribal, you know, from where she came from in Africa or at least where half of her came from, it would make sense. But those are the marks of the white man."

My breath caught. *Oh no, no, no, no.*

I had two choices here.

I could ask for elaboration, but I suspected the elaboration would come with verification of what I was dreading.

I was going to be locked in a dinner with him for the next hour and a half at least. Maybe I was overreacting. Maybe he was just very Afrocentric. Maybe there was a chance he wasn't a Hotep.

But it wasn't looking good. I mentally ran through my Hotep checklist.

Fringe of the culture—Not really; he was friends with Cora and her boyfriend. He had people to check him. And they'd vouched for him. Green flag so far.

A little carried away with Afrocentrism. There was down for the culture, then there was too down. Red flag number one.

Heavy dose of patriarchy, homophobia. He thankfully hadn't said anything homophobic. But the making judgments on our waitress and what she chose to look like was a red flag in itself.

The final nail in the coffin would be subscribing to conspiracy theories and pseudohistory with no real knowledge or education on the topic other than the internet. So far, no signs, but I was on edge already, just waiting for it.

There was no way I was overreacting. But I tried one more probe for clarity. "Well, I think she's beautiful."

He shook this head. "True beauty is in the soul. See, I can tell your soul is pure. You being from the motherland, the origin of the diaspora. But see, that waitress, I can tell everything I need to know about her just by looking."

Shit. Final red flag. Waving free. How could I extricate myself without making Cora look bad?

Technically, this is Cora's fault.

"You know what? I think—"

He cut me off. "I see a lot of young sisters doing that to themselves in my profession."

I lifted a brow, torn between seeing what depths of hell we were traveling to and telling him about himself. "I'm not sure what that means. You see a lot of waitresses as a lawyer?"

"Well, I'm not a lawyer yet. I'm a paralegal, but that's just for now, though. I plan to open a law practice that strictly serves the needs of Black men that this country has put in the school-to-prison pipeline."

I was *positive* Cora had said he was a lawyer, but he was doing something good, so maybe this was salvageable. "Noble pursuit."

"Right now, the only way to learn how the man works is to infiltrate. And then you get to figure out all their Illuminati bullshit."

Oh no. Conspiracy theorist. Check. The Hotep trifecta.

He had to be kidding. He was friends with Travis. Of course he was kidding. Travis was educated and liked to call out conspiracy theory freaks all the time. No way Omar had slipped through the cracks.

"Illuminati?" I asked as if I didn't understand.

He nodded enthusiastically. "Well, there certainly is a boys' club, a white boys' club, wherever you go."

Shit. This was bad. And I was trapped. *Maybe it's not as bad as you think.*

I would at least get my food. I'd been waiting to eat here for a month. He then turned the conversation to me, asked about publishing and what I was working on.

When I told him all about my work, he was actually enthusiastic.

And even though there was that niggling voice in the back of my mind, I ignored it. I was too closed off, and this was my first time out on a date in months. So I needed to try.

Suddenly, the voice of freedom beckoned. "Fancy seeing you here."

I was so caught in my reverie that, once again, I was surprised by the devil incarnate.

No, not the devil incarnate. Remember, you're allies now. Almost friends.

I turned my head. "Cole, hi."

His grin flashed bright, and his eyes danced. What was he up to? "I was at the bar with some friends. I just thought I'd come say hello. I didn't mean to interrupt your . . ." His voice trailed as he waited for me to complete his sentence.

I wasn't giving him the satisfaction. "Sorry. Cole Drake, this is Omar Matthews." I turned to Omar with a smile. "Omar, meet Cole Drake. Cole and I work together. He's one of my team members on that line I was just talking about."

They shook hands and did the pleasantry thing. I wasn't sure what it was about the exchange, but both of them were grinning at each other like idiots even though tension swirled between them.

"It was funny running into you here. I was just telling someone about the line and what a star you are. Audra Caplan. She's an agent and might have some authors you'll love."

What was he up to? My gaze flickered over to the bar. "That's great to hear."

"Would you want me to make an introduction?"

Oh, so he was going to try to press me. Typical Cole. "Off the clock and on a date, so why don't you be a dear and set up something for next week?"

There was no greater satisfaction than watching him try not to react to my treating him like my assistant. The tick in his jaw was prominent enough to give me pants feelings.

"Yeah, I can make that happen." His voice almost dropped to a whisper, forcing me to lean close to hear him. And that little forever spark that was between us that usually ignited into a fight hit me right in the lady parts. I could feel the tingles straight through my body just from the one glance.

What the hell? I was on a date. *With someone you have zero spark with.* And then Cole was here, interrupting my date, giving me sparks and making me clench my thighs together in order to appease the tight ache between my legs.

"I appreciate that."

"Of course. Sorry for interrupting. Matter of fact, I'm going to send a round of drinks to apologize. You two kids have fun."

Omar shook his head. "No, man, I can afford the lady's drinks."

I blinked rapidly. *What the hell?* "Cole, that's lovely but not necessary."

"Please, I insist. I interrupted. Good to meet you, man. Take care of her. She's one of our best and brightest," he said as he strolled away with enough swagger to make heads turn.

Asshole.

When I turned back to Omar, he was frowning. "How long ago did you two date?"

The bottom fell out of my stomach. "Cole?" I shuddered. "No. We've never dated. He's my coworker."

"I know how they operate, forever trying to take our women. Subjugate them. To make them submit to them all over again. I mean, granted, you don't carry any of that generational trauma. Since you're from Africa, you don't know. You think you can entertain them."

With the final grind of my molars, I lost my tenuous control on my temper. "Actually, there are fifty-four countries in Africa. I'm from *Ghana*. Born in the US, but raised in Ghana and all over the world. I'm not *entertaining* anyone. You know, I don't think this—"

He cut me off . . . again. "When Cora told me about you, she knew what I was looking for. A diamond in the rough. Last girl I tried to date was after me for my money. Cora assured me you were different."

I blinked slowly. "Excuse me?"

"Women out here want kings but refuse to be submissive. And then you all get confused and start mixing the blood, ruining yourselves."

Nope, this was my stop indeed. "Okay, I think I'm done." I pushed my hair back.

His eyes went wide. "What? Why?"

He couldn't be serious. "Besides your general Hotep fuckery? You've managed to insult our waitress, all Black women with tattoos, and women who speak their minds, and you've spouted no fewer than three disparate conspiracy theories and suggested that most women are after you for your money."

"Well, not you." He blinked at me owlishly. "You have a trust fund."

In desperation, I chugged the rest of my drink just as two more drinks arrived. When I glanced at the bar, Cole lifted his glass in salute. "I think we're done here."

Omar pulled out his calculator. "Well, let me figure out what you ordered."

And this was why I never left the house. "No worries. I have this," I said as I opened my Miu Miu clutch and pulled out two hundreds. Then I called the waitress over.

"Yes, how can I help you? I promise you, the food will be out shortly."

"Oh, it's not that," I reassured her. "This money will cover my portion and your tip. He's on his own for the rest of it."

She flushed and glanced back toward the bar. "I'm so sorry, but it's already been paid for. Everything. The guy at the bar said whatever you wanted tonight was yours."

I glanced back over, but couldn't see him. "Of course, he did. Well, in that case, this is all your tip. Thank you so much. And I'm sorry for him." I inclined my head toward Omar.

Omar frowned, the muscle in his jaw ticking. "I can pay for my own dates."

"Weren't you just complaining about women bleeding you dry?" I pushed to my feet. "This has been an experience. I'm going home."

"But why? Can I at least see you again?"

"What part of this has seemed like it was going well? I'm genuinely curious." I couldn't go on another date with him. I couldn't. There was no way. "I don't think we're compatible."

He wasn't listening, though. "I'll be at the Kukua Addo gallery opening in a few weeks. You'll be there, right? Cora said you were going."

I was going to kill Cora. "I'll be there." I ground my teeth and crossed my arms, trying to create a barrier between myself and his nonsense. "But I'll be quite busy helping out."

His grin flashed as if I hadn't just rejected him. "You won't be too busy for me. It's a date."

CHAPTER 13

OFOSUA

ADINKRA SAYING:
(Kuronti ne Akwamu) A symbol of democracy,
sharing ideas, taking counsel.

HELEN ADDO:
Who but your mother will give you the best advice?

I should have known my roommates and cousin would all be waiting up for me. There was no way on earth I could have a date without meddling. So, sure enough, when I walked inside the door at nine after taking a detour to Gray's Papaya for a hot dog, I found Cora and Megan—and my mother—all on the couch . . . with wine. Kukua was on the floor, hugging what looked like my Van der Hilst pillow.

Cora glanced at her watch. "A bit early, aren't you?"

I lifted a brow, but before I could answer her, Megan chimed in. "No, it's better this way: tempt them to distraction, then make it clear you have other plans and leave them wanting more."

And my mother was the closer. "No man wants to marry a woman who gives it up on the first date."

It had already been a long enough night, so I kept my retorts minimal as I stepped out of my Prada platforms, simply point-ing to them in order as I said, "He's a Hotep, he's toxic, and the patriarchy still has him in its clutches." I lifted my brow at my cousin. "Is that my pillow?"

Kukua gave me a sheepish grin. "Sorry. It's just so comfy."

My mother and Megan asked in unison, "Hotep?"

I lifted my brow at Cora, and she winced before answering them. "Well, a Hotep is a Black man who is really Afrocentric and into his roots. I thought he'd be a great fit. And to be fair, I didn't *know* he was a Hotep."

I shook my head. "No. Don't sugarcoat. You left out the *really* into his roots, but only in ancient Egypt and hasn't actually done any of the legitimate research into his 'roots.' So he spouts off about how things are taking us away from 'our culture' when he has no clue."

Another wince. "Well, I'm sure he'd be willing to learn," she added hopefully.

I lifted a brow. "You also forgot about the conspiracy theories and underlying bigotry, misogyny, homophobia, and transphobia. How he was calling Black women queens one minute but was quick to say how we bleed men for their funds the next. And, oh, wait, then he was quick to say at least he knew I wouldn't try to bleed him out because of my trust fund."

My mother gasped. Megan started coughing around her sip of wine, and Cora flailed on the couch.

"He did not!" Kukua, bless her, had rolled over and was laugh-ing into the pillow.

"Oh, but he did. And then asked me for a second date. Which I tried to say no to, but he asked me to Kukua's gallery opening with you and Travis. Once I said I was already going, he said, 'It's a date,' completely ignoring that I already told him we weren't compatible. So now I'll have to spend the entire opening trying to avoid him."

All the while I was ranting, I didn't realize the others had started laughing too. Especially my mother. Howling actually.

Mum recovered quickly. "And so, girls, who wants to help me get her a new date? Someone more suitable."

"Mum."

She ignored me. "Eh, what? You're ready now. You just went out. Now we can take this seriously. Are we pretending that you don't need a good man? What did Kukua say about it yesterday? You're dusty and will atrophy. It's been long enough. This boy wasn't the one. I have several more we can set up."

I knew where this was going. "You know what's weird? Yofi's been calling."

"Why?"

"Dunno. Didn't answer. I don't really have anything to say to him."

Kukua pursed her full lips as she scooped up her long auburn-and-blonde faux locs and secured them on top of her head. "Next time he calls, give me the phone."

While my staunchest supporter, my cousin was known for having a distinct lack of chill. If you fucked with her people, she would have a lot to say about it. And your ears would ring for the next month. "No, it's all right. I am not answering it."

My mother watched me anxiously. "Well, maybe he has rethought everything."

"Mum, even if he came back and said I was the love of his life, I would never, *ever* get back with him."

She sighed as if she thought that was the wrong tactic. "Hm, you're a hard woman, you know? Of course we don't want him, but his family is influential. Your 'no' should come with some small, small honey. Don't you want to be married?"

"I'm not hard, Mum. I have self-respect." I sighed. "What's left of it, anyway."

"Eh, fine. Self-respect. But it's not a dick in your bed, is it?"

Silence descended upon the room, and then Kukua fell over again, holding her sides as she howled in laughter. Megan and Cora were no better, giggling as they took swigs of wine.

"Mum, please stop saying things like that."

"Okay, fine, fine. I found a dating app, okay? It's for Africans seeking Africans. And you see, the qualifications are all here. It's everything you'd want to know. Whether or not someone has been to university, and if they have a mustache, and even better, an advanced degree."

I sighed. "You're kidding me."

"No, I'm not kidding, why would I kid? This is your future." She pulled up her phone. "See, I think we should create your profile."

I stared at her. "You can't be serious."

My friends, although I didn't think I could call them that anymore if they were taking her side, crowded around her, staring at the app while they drank.

My mother talked to herself as she tapped away on the phone screen.

"Objective: Marriage and several children."

Did she have to say "several"?

She continued on. "What's your family like: Good Christian, professional home."

"Mum, I hardly think—"

One flick of her gaze at me over her phone and I shut up. She was going to do what she wanted. At least the girls would correct her if she went too wild.

My mother continued to mumble to herself: "Profession and Education: Graduate school for finance. Senior editor at a major publishing house."

I stared at her. "Now we're just lying?" I reached for the phone. "Give me that."

Megan had already proven to be of no help. "Leave her be. I promise you, these men will embellish. They'll tell you they're six feet and they turn up missing five inches. This sounds great. At the very least, it will get you out of the house more."

I glowered at my roommate. "What do you mean, get me out of the house? I leave the house plenty. You know, for work and things. Hell, I just had a date."

They all laughed. It was Megan who said, "No, not for work functions. We're talking for pussy functions. And obviously this date didn't count."

My mother stared at them. "Heh, you girls are naughty." She turned to me. "But they're right."

"Mum, you can't really expect me to create a profile and to date some of the people on this thing."

"Eh, look, I'm saying, you don't have to *marry* anybody. You have to start trying small, small."

"I did try *small, small*. Even Kukua can testify to that."

"Cuz, please, you know I love you, but one date is *not* trying."

I gasped. *The betrayal.*

My mother kept typing. "Heh, your father better watch out. There weren't dating apps for my age. But now, now the world could be my oyster."

"Mum, you're going to make me throw up in my mouth," I muttered.

"Auntie, there are so many options now. You could find the exact kind of relationship you want. You could even get someone who's a sugar daddy. Someone who wants you to be a dominatrix."

"Heh, a domina-what?!" my mother shouted.

I laughed. "Kukua . . ."

"I'm saying if financial stability is your main criteria, there are lots of transactional relationships."

My mum stared at her. "You're suggesting my daughter become a prostitute?!"

She laughed. "No, Auntie. That's not what I'm saying. I'm saying that there are different kinds of relationships, all depending on exactly what Ofos is looking for."

I waved a hand. "It would be great if you guys were, you know, talking about me like I was *here*, present, asking me what I wanted, if I even *wanted* to do a dating app."

They ignored me as they enumerated the benefits of a dating app.

Cora leaned over. "Honey, it's time. Omar was a dud. Travis has other friends. Black love can still happen."

Megan sat back. "Or maybe you're batting for the wrong team. I think double-dipping is excellent. It gives me that connectedness I sometimes look for, plus, you know, dick."

I coughed with a quick glance to my mother. She had no idea Megan was bisexual. It was one of those things in Ghana that people tried to pretend wasn't real or that "happened" to other, "non-Christian people." I never understood how she could live with her dichotomy of thought. On the one hand, she believed in equality, and everyone being treated with respect. She would and had put her safety and job on the line before to defend queer patients and their right to quality care when she was at the hospital.

On the other hand, she believed being queer was something God didn't want. It was baffling bullshit.

"I don't think I'm ready for anyone. And I really am not in the mood for it. Big things could be happening at work, and I want to focus on me."

Cora sat back and took a long sip. "That's some shit women say when their pussies are dried up."

I sighed. "Oh my God, you guys, what happened to feminism? Finding ourselves. Falling in love with *ourselves*."

All four of them, including my mother, looked up at me and said, "Bullshit."

And before the end of that night, I had a dating app profile on AfricaMatch.com.

—

COLE

After my run-in with Ofosua and her date, I headed to Wessex House to meet a friend.

As I left Cubana, I told myself I was not searching the restaurant for Ofosua. Not that she'd be happy to see me again.

Maybe because you interrupted her date.

I'd just gone over to her table to say hi. We were friends now, weren't we? And that guy was a tool. He'd tried to out squeeze me on our handshake when I'd genuinely been saying hello.

Liar.

Who was that guy? Clearly, once her engagement ring vanished about eight months ago, it hadn't shown up again. And given her body language, I was sure that it was a first date.

Like you're going to get the balls to ask her out?

The working-together thing was tricky, but it wasn't against the rules. But while I had certainly felt a vibe between us at happy hour, she still wasn't my biggest fan.

Or maybe that vibe was one-way?

No. I hadn't imagined that. We'd almost kissed. That hadn't been one-sided. But whatever attraction was there, she didn't want to acknowledge.

Patience.

I tried to drag myself out of my reverie as I approached Wessex House. I was so lost in my thoughts, I didn't sense the shift in the Force.

"Cole?"

The sharp tone, the slight derision, had my head snapping up. I knew that voice.

"Dad?"

Sure enough, there was my father, stumbling out of Wessex House, drunk with some bimbo that looked about eighteen. A bimbo that was *not* my stepmother.

My father had a type, though. Young, plastic, blonde. When I was a kid, I thought all the mom replacements were because he missed her, that he couldn't bear to have anyone who didn't look like her.

But no. My father was as susceptible to bullshit as the rest of us. He thought the young blonde ones conveyed to the world that he was still young or, at the very least, powerful. He was neither. He was your garden-variety middle-aged dickhead.

The blonde eyed me up and down and gave me an appraising smile. I slid my eyes away and ignored her. What was he doing here? I'd had his membership revoked when they'd had to rush him to the hospital eight months ago after he'd cut himself smashing a glass table and then punching the bartender for refusing to serve him after that.

"Candy, this is my son, Cole."

She grinned. "Wow, Cole. You two don't look like you're related."

And that was because I looked like my mother.

"Dad, what are you doing here?"

"Well, as it turned out, Candy knows someone who knows someone and got us in."

I sighed and made a mental note to send the owner a box of cigars for any trouble Dad might have caused.

"What's up, Dad?"

"I hoped we'd run into you, actually. I thought we could have dinner or something." He licked his lips nervously. "Cole, we need to talk about what happened that night in the hospital. I didn't mean it . . ."

As if we could pretend that needing eight stiches in his hand was nothing. As if we could pretend he hadn't screamed vitriol at me when I'd arrived. We lived in that land of pretend most of the time.

Dinner usually meant he wanted a favor. And that favor usually involved getting my aunt and uncle to release his trust allowance early. "Been busy with work, Dad."

He rolled his eyes. "Cole. Who talks about work on a beautiful night in front of a beautiful girl?"

I shoved my hands in my pockets and rolled back on my heels. "You sure dislike the word, Dad."

He laughed. "My son thinks he's clever. No one actually likes work, Cole. And you don't have to work."

That wouldn't be the case for him much longer. If he kept burning through his money, soon he'd have nothing. But you couldn't tell my father that because he was still operating on the idea that he was Miles Drake and nothing could touch him. Most especially not reality.

"Listen, the reason I wanted to see you was that matter we discussed last time."

Here we go.

"I'm sorry, but I already told you I can't help you. You know that."

I tried to move aside, but he stopped me. "Cole, I'm your father. Do you know how many times I bailed you out?"

And that was true. He'd bailed me out a lot in my teenage years when I had pulled some idiotic prank or nearly gotten myself expelled. When I'd run my mouth and gotten my ass kicked by some Russian oligarch's kid. The pattern was always the same.

I'd been a dick when I was a kid. I was told that everything was open and available for me. And I had acted like it. Until I'd gone to college and done a volunteer trip.

Yes, it was cliché. Yes, I'd gone in like the great white hope, but hopefully I'd done some good, though I knew enough now to know that was doubtful. Truthfully, I should simply hope I'd done no harm. My perspective on my place in the world was forever changed, and I'd come home a little different. At least less of a prick . . . maybe. And he had never had to bail me out since.

Thinking about that kid I'd been was enough to give me a cold shiver down my back.

"I'm sorry, Dad. I can't help you in that way."

Now his face turned ugly.

"What? You think that your fucking uncle and aunt are going to somehow magically see you as some kind of do-gooder work-hard type and reward you? They won't. You're not good enough. Do you still think you're going to earn the old man's crown? I was his fucking son, and he cut me off."

People were starting to stare, and I shifted on my feet. "Dad, we'll talk another time. Not like this."

Candy shifted on her feet before trying to pull him away.

"Let me go. This is none of your business," he slurred at her.

Her face pinched in disgust before she dropped his arm abruptly. I gave her an apologetic look.

"Dad, I have to go."

"I'm not done talking to you, Cole." Dad grabbed my arm.

I jerked my arm away. "Sober up, and we can have a conversation. Maybe I can talk to Aunt Ruby for you about a place."

He scowled at me. "What? So I can come and work for her buffoon of a husband who's not even a Drake? Fuck you."

Then he tore away from me and stormed off with Candy tottering on her heels after him. My stomach churned. He was the ghost of my Christmas future. I had always known if I didn't keep my shit together, I'd end up like him.

Because of how bad news traveled fast, I called my aunt immediately. The night was unusually warm for spring, and people milled about on the streets, taking full advantage of the warmer spring weather.

I leaned against a stone pillar of a clothing boutique as the phone rang. When she finally answered on the third ring, I expelled a breath of relief.

"Cole, my darling boy, tell me something amazing."

Just hearing her voice was enough to bring my anxiety down several notches. "Sorry, Aunt Ruby. I'm fresh out of amazing, But I'll raise you one asshole," I muttered under my breath.

"Damn it. Your dad? How bad?"

"I'm not sure. I ran into him with some woman outside of Wessex House. He's toasted and on his way to belligerent."

"I swear my brother lives to disappoint. How are you doing? You okay? I know how hurtful he can be when he's sober, let alone . . ."

My aunt was the only one who'd really paid attention to how my father treated me. The things he said, the way he could withhold love. She made certain I'd always had someone to talk to growing up. "I'm good. I'm just worried he'll end up in the hospital again."

"You should never have had to deal with that on your own. I put a little fail-safe into place after the last incident. I'm tracking his phone and will have my people pick him up so he can dry out."

"What would I do without you?"

"You'll never have to find out. No, go and do what young people do. I've got this. Do your aunt a favor and go meet up with friends or perhaps a girlfriend?" she asked hopefully.

"No girlfriend."

But why on earth was Ofosua Addo the first person I thought of?

CHAPTER 14

OFOSUA

ADINKRA SAYING:
(Boa Me Na Me Mmoa Wo) Help me and let me help you.
HELEN ADDO:
Marriage is helping a man to learn how to help himself.

A couple of weeks after my Hotep adventures, when my May hay fever had given way to warm days and nights in the city, I could feel the energy in the air as I got ready to head to my event.

I had been looking forward to this Aurora St. James reading for a month. Even before I had my own imprint, she'd been on my list of authors to watch. She was a romance author, so she wasn't previously on Drake's radar. But I knew for a fact her books could read like the best book club fiction. Not to mention her agent had sent me her latest manuscript, and I'd fallen in love all over again.

Then her agent had sent me an invite to a reading she was doing to benefit the Library Hope Charity, and I'd jumped at the chance and dragged Emory with me.

Dead Darlings was a staple for me. I'd been coming to readings here at Judson Memorial Church since I was a sullen teenager.

Authors read bits that had been cut from their published works. It was a brilliant series.

Just as Emory grabbed us two seats, I glanced up and froze. "What the hell is he doing here?" Cole sat in one of the seats at the back of the balcony and grinned at me like an idiot.

Emory winced. "We can't pretend we don't see him."

Reluctantly, we moved our things and joined his small round table. "Ladies, I'm so glad to see that you could attend. I'd worried you were going to be late."

"What the hell are you doing here?" I asked.

He held his hands up in surrender. "You're always talking about signing up authors who can make the reader feel connected. So I figured I should take the opportunity to see one of your favorites in person. It'll help me hone my pitch to the major accounts."

"How did you find me? You weren't even supposed to know I was coming here."

He laughed. "I'm not a rookie. You keep your calendar private, but *she* does not." His finger pointed directly at Emory.

The two of us just sighed. He was really determined that we were going to do this together.

"I meant to ask, how was your date last night? You look far too rested for it to have been a long night."

Keeping my voice low, I muttered, "My dating life is none of your business."

His Cheshire cat grin remained in place. "Oh, that good, huh?"

I was still contemplating the best places to bury a body when Aurora took the stage.

Once she started reading, I couldn't help but grin. And of course, I couldn't help but cast a quick glance over at Cole, who was sitting forward, elbows on the table, gaze riveted on Aurora. He was into this. Good.

I laughed and he turned to me. "What's so funny?"

"The way you're staring at Aurora like she is the second coming."

He gave me a sheepish grin, dimple peeking out from where stubble dusted his jaw. He obviously had no idea how sexy he looked.

So you think he's sexy.

"Aurora is kicking ass."

I nodded. "I know, right? She's got such a great story. And an amazing way of delivering. I love it."

Emory's phone buzzed, and she excused herself to go take it outside.

Cole leaned over. "My uncle should hear her read. She's riveting. Brilliant on delivery. On a book tour with maybe a television spot, she would kill."

I blinked rapidly. "You're thinking a book tour for her?"

He pointed toward the stage. "She's the kind of author that's an easy sell. She's funny and can capture an audience, which makes her great for outlets like NPR and major podcasts. Her words have the juice. Her deleted scene is funny, sure, but it's also lyrical and fluid and almost heartbreaking as she talks about lost love."

I listened to him, completely transfixed. He wasn't kidding. "You're serious about this? This isn't a joke to you?"

I watched as he lifted a hand to the back of his neck. "Can I be honest with you?"

I shrugged. "Honesty is preferred."

"I've been a bit of a prick."

I couldn't help but break out in a laugh. "A bit?"

"Okay, fine. I've been *a lot* of a prick. All this time you've been talking about publishing a wider range of fiction than what we've typically done at Drake, and I have dismissed you and spouted all the nonsense I've heard over the years about certain urban genres

GOLD COAST DILEMMA • 169

being 'over.' It's bullshit. The point is, I can *see* the potential in Aurora. Probably in a way I've never seen it for another author before. We could go a long way with her."

A smile spread over my lips before I could really stop it. "Told you so."

His deep, rumbling chuckle made my heart trip. "Yes, yes, you have an eye for talent. So let's find a way to actually give her the money she deserves and make this happen."

I laughed. "You're serious?"

"Like I said before, it would be a mistake to underestimate either one of us."

"Okay, then. Her book needs work. I'm not saying it doesn't. But she has the touch."

"You have some more authors for me to check out?"

I nodded. "Yeah, I have three more. A Latinx author who wrote a really beautiful memoir about her time as a dominatrix. She's a total badass. Then there is Seun Akewele. I think she's Nigerian. She's written this funny commercial novel about the women in her family and the secrets they keep. And then there is Christina Pratt, a biracial woman. Hers starts out as the standard sort of women's fiction, divorced-and-trying-to-find-themselves sort of fare, but then it takes a brilliant turn no reader would guess. I couldn't put it down."

Something happened then: the world washed away and suddenly it was just the two of us locked in a bubble talking prospects and books and potential. It was the buzz. That feeling when you're really vibing with someone and you just know they are going to be your best friend. Or something else entirely.

You've been here before, though.

Yes, I had.

In the end it was Emory who broke the spell. But then she

abandoned us. There was a flood in her apartment, and she had to go.

"You want to get some food?" Cole asked.

I blinked at him. It was close to six, so I would have headed home anyway. "Sure, we can grab a bite."

"They're doing Around the World in Bryant Park. Do you want to check it out?"

That sounded like a lot of people and uncontrollable situations. And, hell, I was already so close to home. There was no reason to say yes. Also, it was Cole.

But when I opened my mouth to beg off, instead of no, I said, "Sure."

Around the World in Bryant Park was an event that had started two years ago. Local vendors from all over the city set up their food trucks along the edge of the park, and world cuisine was at your fingertips. We took the subway uptown, and I noticed Cole fidgeting. "When was the last time you took the subway?" I asked as I clung onto one of the railings.

He frowned. "I took it this week."

"But you don't take it often, do you?"

He shook his head. "No, not really. Does it show?"

I laughed. "Yeah, it does."

"Why are you so comfortable on the subway? You give off a high-maintenance vibe."

I shrugged. "Honestly, my mother would be appalled to see me on this train."

Cole laughed. "She sounds like my mother."

"They might get along."

He chuckled. "Maybe. My mom is a pill, though, so possibly not."

"Well, you haven't lived until you've met a Ghanaian mother

like Helen Addo. I like to equate being her daughter to a true running of the gauntlet. No occasion is ever complete unless you had to spend several hours in her presence and endure her telling you everything about you, from your hair to your clothes, to your demeanor and your college degree, is all wrong."

He chuckled. "We might have the same mother."

It was easy talking to him now for some reason. I couldn't explain when it shifted between us, but maybe he wasn't quite what I'd thought he was. And I probably wasn't anywhere near what he'd thought I was.

When we reached Bryant Park and walked through the throngs of people, the spring air made me smile. The scent of flowers, the people, the food. "Okay, I know you've been around the world. What's your favorite thing to eat?"

"Ah, you're putting me on the spot," he said, looking pensive. "Well, there's a place here that has the best Kobe beef burgers I've ever had."

I blinked at him. "Wait, so you have the opportunity to eat from anywhere in the world, food truck vendors from all kinds of places, and somehow you *still* pick burgers."

"What? Technically, it's from Japan."

"Okay. How about we meet under the clock in ten minutes?"

He looked like he didn't want to agree with that. "The clock, right."

"I promise, I'm not going to ditch you."

He laughed. "You know, I'm hard to ditch."

"Yes, I have noticed. You're persistent when you want something."

His grin was so wicked, again, butterflies were mobilizing in my belly.

My favorite Ghanaian food truck had kelewele, and the vendor served me a heaping mound of it. The ginger mixed with the pepper and the onions seasoning the plantain made my stomach growl. It conjured instant memories of my favorite kelewele seller at Labone Junction, near my parents' compound in the Cantonments area of Accra. First thing I did every time I went home was head there straight from the airport.

I did a little happy dance as they added a side of jollof, the reddish-orange color of the rice making me smile.

Ghanaian food I didn't cook and that didn't come with mom strings? Brilliant.

We found a seat in the middle of the park with one of the borrowed blankets from the event organizers. I sat down immediately, unable to wait. I couldn't deny it, his Kobe beef did smell good. But not as good as my food.

With a curious glance at my plate, he asked, "Okay, explain to me, what is all that?"

"You've got your own food."

He took a bite of his Kobe beef burger. "Let me guess, you know how to make all of this?"

I laughed. "Of course. My mother would insult me for days if I didn't. Granted she insults me anyway."

"So it's a big deal that you know how to cook?"

"Every Ghanaian mother sees it as her stock in trade that her *daughter* knows how to cook. If her son doesn't know how to cook, it doesn't matter."

"Sexist."

"My mother would tell you it's *traditional*."

As we were munching in companionable silence, I turned my head slightly, enjoying the setting sun and the twilight of the city. But when I turned my head back to my food, Cole was stealing a piece of plantain off my plate. "Hey." I slapped his hand.

He popped it in his mouth and then groaned as he nodded, looking happy as a clam. "Oh my God," he said around a mouthful of food. "That's amazing."

"I know. Which is why I got it. Try that again and you're going to lose a limb."

He laughed. "You didn't tell me it was going to be that good."

"*You* didn't tell me you were a food thief."

He grinned. "I'm a food thief. I admit it. So get ready to share, because I can't let that go."

"Cole Drake, if you take another piece of my food—"

I didn't get to finish. He stole another plantain and then worked his fork around to take some jollof. I tried to stab him with my fork. Sadly, it was plastic, so not that damaging.

"Ow, worth it, though," he said around a mouthful of jollof.

"If this were Ghana, you'd be beaten for your insolence."

He laughed as he merrily chewed. "Okay, my bad. Next time, I'll let you make all the food choices."

"What makes you think there is going to be a *next time*?"

"Because you like me now. So there's definitely going to be a next time."

Heat suffused my face. "You know this isn't a date, right? I work with you."

He grinned. "Pretty sure this is a better date than your last one."

I was never going to tell him how right he was.

COLE

I hated it when Ofos was right. I liked her. I knew I liked her. Hell, it was probably written all over my face that I liked her.

She was easy to hang around with. Fun. Entertaining. Energetic. And if she kept smiling at me like that, I was going to say something stupid.

As if you haven't already.

We'd eventually gone off to get me my own plate of Ghanaian food, which we shared because that was only fair. I'd even managed to snag a recently occupied bench so she didn't have to sit back in the grass in her Gucci A-line skirt. I recognized it from Fashion Week last season.

Honestly, I hadn't thought about what I was doing when I suggested we get some dinner. I thought we'd talk shop or something.

Or you wanted to spend time with her.

I'd take time with her any way I could get it. Though trying to date her might be tricky. She worked for my uncle's company. Hopefully, someday *my* company, assuming I didn't screw up. And there was the fact that up until today she wasn't my biggest fan.

Is that what you're really worried about? With her new imprint she's on your level. She's not in your direct reporting structure.

She leaned over. "You have this look of consternation on your face. What's wrong?"

"Nothing." I shrugged. "This afternoon just highlighted that maybe Drake Publishing has been going about things all wrong for too long. I am trying to figure out how to show that to my uncle and prove to him that trusting me isn't a wasted endeavor."

She watched me closely. "Do you think that he thinks that?"

"I don't know. But given my father's performance, I'm always aware he might."

"Yeah, I've heard a few things here and there."

I laughed. "Let me guess, you've read about my father?"

She shrugged. "Can't really believe everything you read online."

"Unfortunately, if it's about my dad, you probably can. All those tales of him with actual Playboy bunnies running around, all accurate. My dad is that guy who can't let go of a bygone era, or whatever the hell you want to call it. He still thinks he has the power, influence, and money to bend the world to his will. He doesn't. His whole life, everything has been handed to him. And then there's my mother, who's embarrassed by him, so she was always drilling into my head that I was *not* going to turn out like him."

"You don't want to be anything like him?"

I shook my head. "No, I don't."

Then she asked, "Is that why your uncle is running Drake Publishing instead of your dad?"

Ah, she didn't know my *aunt* was the Drake. Well, not many publishing people in our generation did. "Dad is a fuckup. My aunt is not. She loves the business but she wants nothing to do with the day-to-day of publishing, but her husband, Uncle Steven, did. He worked for a major UK publisher before he met her."

"Oh, wow. But his last name is Drake."

I chuckled at that. "He said he wanted to look progressive to my aunt. And that it was an honor to take such a famous literary name. He'll never admit it, but I think my grandfather twisted his arm. This is Drake Publishing, and at the time I was too young to take the helm. The old man needed a Drake in the big seat. It's dumb, but it made sense to them."

"No man in Ghana would *ever* take a woman's name. Too much ego."

"Let's just say Uncle Steven is *more* than happy to run Drake until I hit my thirtieth birthday."

"Is that when you'll take over?"

"That's the plan, I guess. If that's what I want. If I step out of line, though, the board can choose to make the position in name only and hire a CEO."

"Well, good to know the timeline. I'll have moved on by then."

The fuck? "Why?"

"I'm pretty sure I wouldn't be allowed to cuss out the CEO, and I have to tell you, that's one of the best parts of my day."

Her smile was bright, and her eyes danced. I was so mesmerized that I forgot I wasn't supposed to get sucked in.

"You've never once cussed me out and you know it. You are so professional it's infuriating. Especially when I'm trying to rile you. Your eyes, though. They say *I will murder you* at least once a day."

"Violence is beneath me," she said with a haughty sniffle, then added, "My murder-Cole fantasies usually involve you having a horrifyingly embarrassing incident where you perish from humiliation."

"Well, I would miss our daily battles if you weren't here. I'd probably still message you daily with *per my last email* emails just to make your day."

Her laugh trilled, and just like that I was caught in her snare, unable to look away or breathe or think about anything other than kissing her.

I'd been so locked on her laugh, I had to catch up to what she was saying. ". . . There are some moments when I can step back and see the struggle my parents went through when they arrived here. Even though I know that struggle is relative. Dad came for school at Dartmouth, and Mum followed after—Oxford medical school. I grew up mostly here, and I still struggle to navigate. I can't imagine what it was like for them. Still, the pressure to perform to their expectations is actually astronomical."

"Do you also feel like you're always a bit of a disappointment?"

"Most days. I was a good student. And I've always loved books. I graduated with honors. But don't ask my mother about the fact that I did not get a master's degree."

I laughed. "But does she not know that you don't need one for the career you chose?"

"Who's to say what she knows? She's humiliated that her only daughter doesn't have a master's degree."

"What do your parents do?"

"My father is in tech, got his PhD in computer science. He gives lots of talks about bridging the digital divide around the world. He's built quite a name for himself."

"That's amazing. What about your mom?"

"Well, she was a doctor, then a hospital administrator. She retired a few years ago, and something tells me she's bored out of her skull, because now *I'm* her project. And the woman sure knows how to argue her case."

"It sucks to think you haven't lived up to expectations, doesn't it?"

"Especially when I know I never will."

"You know, growing up, I always thought it was just me."

"Nah. Everyone's parents put pressure on their kids somehow."

I nodded. "You're different than I thought you were."

She laughed then. "Oh, am I?"

"Yeah, you are. Not nearly as uptight." *Way to be smooth there.*

"Is this your way of calling for a truce? You waving the white flag, Drake?"

"I think we're a good team. *And*, God help me, if we work together and stop fighting each other, we can get a lot done."

She bumped my shoulder with a wide grin. "Go ahead and say it. In our nemesis war, I'm the winner."

My gaze searched hers for a long moment before dropping to

her lips. All my blood rushed south, leaving me dizzy and incapable of thinking correctly. My voice was husky when I spoke. "Fine. You're the winner. What do you demand as your reward?"

When my gaze lifted to hers again, her pupils were dilated and she licked her lips nervously, but she didn't move away. My heart thundered behind my ribs as I took the leap and inched closer. The longer she held eye contact, the dizzier I felt.

I inched closer and this time, her gaze dipped down to my mouth. Blood rushed and pumped in my head, and I would give everything I had to taste her.

Then something caught the periphery of my gaze. A man with two hands overloaded with plates and a drink. A little boy jumped enthusiastically around his feet.

Automatically, I reached for her shoulder, pulling her to my side of the bench so she was practically sitting on my lap. Her eyes went wide, but her body didn't stiffen. If anything, she took one long breath, and relaxed into the hold, her eyes glued on my lips.

Only vaguely aware of the chaos around us as the father argued with his son to stay still, I held her tight, trying to tamp down the spike of need in my blood. All it took was one peek of her tongue to moisten her lip to drown out everything, freezing us in time. Or maybe that was the roaring of my blood.

Sliding my hand up, I traced fingertips along the back of her neck and inched forward. Her lids fluttered closed and—

"Shit!" Unable to get a handle on his plates and the kid, the man dropped his food on the bench.

Ofos whipped her head around as if she'd finally understood what had just happened.

On her side of the bench, there was a plate of a gumbo-like stew and another red stew made with what looked like black-eyed peas splattered on what would have been her Gucci skirt. "I guess you just saved me from a wardrobe disaster. Thank you," she said as she pushed away from me and shoved to her feet, the moment severed now.

Yeah. Sure. That's what I was doing. "No problem," I muttered, trying to cool that spike of need in my blood.

The harried dad tried to calm his son down. "Damn, I'm sorry. Everyone okay?"

She turned a warm smile on the man. "Yep. Everything's fine." Turning to the kid, she knelt, then handed over her dessert tickets that we picked up when we got our plates of food. "Here you go. I think there's a bofrot stand right over there. It should keep you a little bit full till your dad gets you a new plate."

The kid took off for the donut-like dessert with a hastily muttered thank-you, while his father tried to grab what remained of his tower of plates.

One look at Ofos told me the moment was long since over. But that didn't stop me from trying to reach for that connection again. "You okay? Nothing got on you? I can't imagine that red oil would be easy to get out of clothes."

"You're right. Palm oil is a bitch, but you were the ultimate superhero. Is there anything you can't do?"

She was taking us back to a light place, backing off from the intensity of before. Fine, I could do that for now. Whatever made her more comfortable. "I'm sure you already have that running list, but we're not going to let you off the hook. You were telling me all your secrets."

"No," she said with a laugh, "you were about to tell me what I won in your surrender."

I had to chuckle at that. "You don't let anything slide, do you?"

"You sound like my cousin. She's the one always telling me to loosen up."

I laughed. "Why does she think you need to loosen up?"

Ofosua shrugged. "All my friends and family think I've become this shell version of myself. Very straight. No fun."

I met her gaze. That dark gaze pulling me in, making me want to know more and be closer to her. "Are they right?"

"I'm not sure. I had a vision for my life, you know? But then everything changed, and suddenly I couldn't function. So now I have to figure out a new life for myself. I'm still in the process of licking my wounds, I guess."

I nodded. "That makes sense. Not that I'm butting into your business."

She laughed. "Yeah, but you actually *are* butting into my business."

I grinned. "Since I'm already butting in, tell me what happened. One day, you walked in with a big old smile on your face and a flashy-ass ring. And then that ring was gone. And you seemed"—I shrugged as I tried to find the right word—"distant."

She took umbrage at that. "My ring was *not* flashy."

I laughed. "It was a three-carat stunner, with emeralds and rubies around it. It was flashy."

She flushed. "Okay, fine, it was a little flashy. As to what happened, I caught him cheating on me during our traditional wedding, and I walked out. Consequently, I passed out after a panic attack. That's when you saw me in the hospital."

Who the hell would do that to her? "Fuck. I'm so sorry. He's a dick."

Her brow furrowed as she considered. "I know. And I appreciate it. Just have to figure out who I am now and try to put it all behind me. I've been doing that for nearly nine months."

I nodded, thinking about my conversation with my father. "You'll get there."

She laughed. "Are you sure? Because some days I fantasize about the best places to bury a body in New York."

I met her gaze then. "Just call me if you need some muscle."

The corner of her lips tipped up in a hint of a smile. "Careful now, Cole Drake. I might actually start to like you."

"News flash, you more than like me," I said with a wink.

CHAPTER 15

OFOSUA

ADINKRA SAYING:
(Fofo) A symbol of warning against jealousy and covetousness.
HELEN ADDO:
Fofo is a constant companion for most.
Try not to marry a man who holds his against you.

Two weeks after the near-kiss incident in the park, I still didn't know what to quite make of Cole. That day in the park was like having a layer peeled off of our interactions for the last few years.

But then . . . nothing. As if that night had never happened. What did it *mean*? Did he remember? Should we talk about it? So far, we hadn't, and I was fine with going back to pretending. *Liar.*

Didn't matter. I had bigger fish to fry. I was sweating, and my nerves were going haywire.

When Cole strolled by my shoebox of an office, his brow fell the moment he saw me.

"What's wrong?"

"After the acquisitions meeting a couple of weeks ago, I feel like I'm gearing up for battle every time I have a meeting with Steven."

He gave me a sardonic lift of his brow. "I'm here. What do you need to hear, that you have this, that this is in the bag, fuck them? Which pep talk version do you need?"

I leaned back in my chair and eyed him up and down. I knew he was trying to help, but he had a totally different perspective. "What is it like to be you and think everything can be resolved with a pep talk?"

His brow furrowed. "I've seen movies, Black people get pep talks too."

"Yeah, but I'm *not* Black American. I'm *African*. It's different. Even though we have some shared experiences, there's other cultural differences. There's no such thing as a pep talk with African parents. Especially abroad. You are an immigrant first, African second. So the idea is there's no room for failure. The pep talk is more like, do you know how lucky you are to even have an opportunity? No room for feelings. Usually it's 'waje mɔr he',' which, translated, is basically 'harden yourself' or 'toughen up.' And then you get knocked on the back of the head and are expected to perform."

He shoved his hands in his pockets and gave me a sheepish smile. "I can tell you to harden yourself if it helps."

God, his smile, it warmed something in the middle of my chest. "As pep talks go, that is severely lacking."

He shrugged. "I know. It's what I've got. But maybe it helps that I know you'll be fine."

I pushed to my feet and grabbed my laptop and my tablet. Cole gave me a gentle pat on the shoulder. The contact made me suck in a sharp breath and focus on the electricity coursing through my veins.

On the plus side, it gave me something else to think about besides the last shit show of an acquisitions meeting.

For the love of Christ, haven't you learned anything?

Had I learned? The thing was, ever since Bryant Park, I'd found him *less* annoying than usual.

Every now and again he'd bring lunch and we'd talk about new submissions. Marketing plans and ideas. He'd even brought me a prospect. Some girl he saw busking on the subway reading her work. Yes, he'd gotten back on the subway. He needed to get to a meeting and a cab wasn't going to cut it. He'd given her his card and taken her information. So of course I'd been stalking the poor girl online.

And he'd even managed to drag me out to one more happy hour. That one had gone far more smoothly. I'd managed to mingle and chitchat just fine before ducking out after an hour.

Not that I was falling back into that sinkhole of the starry-eyed girl who thought this guy could be totally into her. Although, let's face it, I was probably the most fabulous woman he'd ever met in his entire life, but more like, actual friends. Which was new.

"Okay." He put both hands on my shoulders and leveled a gaze on me. "We have this. Your lineup is great. We can sell every single one of the books you've acquired."

"Why are you helping me?"

His smile was soft as he released me. "I may be a dick sometimes, but I like you."

"Since when?"

"I've *always* liked you. You're just a pain in the ass."

"*I'm* the pain in the ass?" I asked him incredulously.

"No, you're not a pain in the ass to everyone. You're professional, courteous, gracious. Easy to work with for most other people. You're just a pain in the ass to me, specifically. But now that we're friends, that's all over."

"I don't know. Now I sort of have the faint urge to be a pain in the ass again."

He rolled his eyes. "Come on, Addo. Game face on. Let's go get Aurora St. James on our list."

"Right. I've got this."

Steven, as was the case more and more these days, was late.

I sat back and forced myself to take a deep breath. There was no starting a meeting at Drake without him. And I knew from experience he'd be the first one to complain if we ran over at the end.

When he strolled in a full fifteen minutes late, without apology or explanation, I was certain I'd cracked a molar from clenching my teeth. If *I* had so disrespected my colleagues' time even just once . . . I'd be done for.

Heat suffused my face. Steven sat down and smiled as if he had not a care in the world. Across from me, though, I took in the set of Cole's shoulders. They were rigid, and I noted the muscle ticking in his jaw. He was pissed too.

I decided to begin as if everything was going perfectly.

"Let's get started, shall we? I wanted to start with the current authors and where we are on development. At the sales conference last week, we discussed Aurora St. James. Here's why she's amazing. You've all already seen the first few chapters of the book she submitted, plus her backlist sales, and I hope you've had an opportunity to review the material. If not, let me give you the highlights."

I slid my gaze over to Cole, who gave me a quick wink that hit me directly in the lady parts. Which was inconvenient. But it also gave me a boost.

For once, I wasn't alone.

Cole and I were like a bookselling dynamic duo. While I described everything that was transformative about Aurora's work, Cole jumped in immediately to talk about how easy she would be to sell into major accounts at a higher level than she currently was and all the things he loved about seeing her reading with Emory and me.

And of course Emory was there to give the social media hot take. Aurora already had a substantial platform. She didn't even need us for the socials. In truth, we needed *her*.

The three of us made a hell of a case and ended with zero objections from the acquisitions board to Aurora. I was elated. We could do this. We *were* doing it. That feeling made the sting of what I had to report next to my team hurt a little less.

"As for Kenya Jones, the actress and activist with that wildly successful indie romance hit last year, she's currently declined through her agent to submit her new novel to us, but I follow her Substack and she had posted some early snippets. I think she would be a great addition to the line. I'll reach out to her agent and see if I can keep the conversation going." I was leaving Aliza Mann out of the conversation for now. Carol was still reviewing the material I'd sent her.

Steven's chuckle was without mirth. "*She* doesn't want to submit to *Drake*? That's ridiculous."

Of course he'd see it that way. I thought I could and should explain, that it would be helpful. "Kenya has good reason. We aren't exactly known for publishing diverse voices, and she wants a house that has a track record already. I think our new imprint is perfect for her, so I'll keep pushing. We might get lucky."

Steven became very red in the face and looked like he had plenty to say about *all* of that (none of which was likely to be good). *Oh no.* I shouldn't have said lucky. I should have reminded myself that I would never be in the clear to speak freely in a room like this one. I braced myself for what was coming.

But again Cole was right there for the one-two punch, persuasively redirecting his uncle to focus on the very promising debut list we had so far. Somehow, it worked. Steven seemed to lose all interest in Kenya Jones, his face placid again within seconds.

You're doing that thing again.

I was not doing the thing.

Yeah, you are. You're starting to believe in him. You're starting to like it.

I had to forget about him immediately. Besides, I had lunch with my mother in exactly twenty minutes, and I needed to grab my purse and get the hell out of there.

After the meeting, Cole beat me to my office. I found him with an arm raised. "What, no high five?"

"I'm not really a high-fiver."

"This deserves a high five. Come on. We kicked ass in there. Whatever my uncle's motivations for starting the line, you're far exceeding his expectations. Or was I in a different meeting?"

I laughed. "Yes, Cole, we kicked ass."

"What do you say we go to lunch to celebrate?"

"I would actually die to take you up on that right now. But I have lunch with my mother. So I might as well enjoy the happy endorphins while I can. Because those will be gone by one thirty."

He wrinkled his nose. "That bad?"

"Yeah, well, she's about to dive in on what a barren wasteland my love life is, so not ideal, but thank you, though, and thank you for the assist in there. I really appreciate it."

The smile he gave lit his eyes up, making them crinkle at the corners. Jesus Christ, any woman he turned that full grin on was done for.

Might as well sacrifice your panties on the altar of Cole Drake's smile.

Nope. No thank you. I wasn't going there with him. Not again. "Well, you have a great lunch. But after-work drinks are on me."

"I can't drink every night after work, Cole."

"Fine, dinner?"

Ugh, this man was on a mission to force me out of my house. *And isn't that exactly what you need?*

"Happy hour. How's that?"

"I'll take what I can get. My treat. I'll see you later." He turned to leave but then stopped abruptly. "Oh, I almost forgot." He pulled out an envelope of heavy stock from his suit. "This is for you."

I glanced at the envelope warily. "What is it?

"Why don't you open it and find out?"

I took the envelope from him, careful not to touch him. When I pulled out the black card stock with silver writing, I gasped. "The McMillan Gala for the Arts! Are you kidding me?" The McMillans were New York billionaire royalty and had a massive endowment for the arts. Every year in early June, they had a massive gala to support the visual, performing, and literary arts. I'd never gotten to go. Of course not. Most publishing houses invited only a very short list of the most senior staff if they were going to attend. Tickets were expensive.

There was no hiding my grin or containing my little wiggle of excitement. That's when I made the mistake. One I would take back if I could, but I was so damn excited that I hugged him.

It was brief and exuberant, and I immediately backed away, but the damage was done. The memories, sweet and sharp, hit me like a truck. His arms around me, his hand cupping my face, the little growl he made as he deepened our kiss. He barely had time to register my hug and hug me back.

But my mind and body were flooded with the kind of endorphins I didn't need. My brain cells had immediately vacated the premises, and there was a dull ache in my lower belly now that reminded me it had been nearly a year since I'd gotten laid.

Fantastic.

He didn't help me either when he flashed me his grin, clearly happy with himself. "Drake has a table every year. My aunt didn't want to go, and my uncle never goes, so I got the tickets. I figured they make a good congratulations gift."

I chewed my bottom lip, reconsidering. "Are you sure this is okay?" There were editors at Drake who would literally kill to attend.

"Yes, of course. And, bonus, Kenya Jones will be there."

"What?" I smacked his arm. "Way to bury the lede. When did you find out?"

"I know her manager from Princeton. He confirmed while we were in the meeting."

"Cole, this is . . ." Riding the wave of serotonin, I couldn't hide my smile. "Thank you."

"Don't thank me yet. You'll still need to make the pitch. But we have an in. I'll see you tonight." As he backed out of my office, I tried not to watch him go. But it was a hell of a view.

"You like him."

I squeaked in alarm when Emory popped into my office. "Who? What? I have to go."

"No, not until you tell me what is going on with Cole. It's like you were speaking your own language in there. Are you two . . ."

"No! Absolutely not, never."

Emory blinked slowly at me. "Okay. Something tells me there's a story there."

"Nope, no story. I don't bone people I work with. I'm not messy." She sighed. "No one thinks you're messy."

"Trust me, I'm sure Nazrin would love, love, love to think I'm messy. And I'm sure someone thinks I fucked somebody to get this imprint. You know how the other editors can be."

She winced. "Yeah, but honestly, no one thinks you fucked your way into this imprint. They're jealous as hell and kind of pissed off. And maybe some of them think it's some bullshit affirmative action nonsense, but they can go fuck themselves. No one thinks you fucked Steven Drake."

"Well, thank God, because ew."

She shuddered on my behalf. "Exactly. I came to pump you for gossip, but since you don't have any, you may go."

"I promise you, Emory, if I have gossip, you'll be the first one to know."

And as I went to go meet my executioner, I prayed to God I never had any gossip to give her or anyone else at the office.

CHAPTER 16

OFOSUA

ADINKRA SAYING:
(Akoben) War horn. A symbol of a call to action,
readiness to be called to action, readiness, and voluntarism.

HELEN ADDO:
*Love is a game of war. With strategies and tactics. To gather the
right tools for war, you must first pick the right partner.*

An hour later, with my bag in the crook of my elbow, I marched
into the restaurant. It was around the corner from the office. At
least this way, I made lunch convenient for me. And it was nice
enough that I was hoping my mother wouldn't complain inces-
santly. Her complaints were so legendary, I'd almost given up on
taking her anywhere. It was embarrassing.

Mom had a very specific way she liked things. *Her way.* And
the thing was, almost nobody could do things her way exactly. It
was exhausting. She would shake her head and smile sweetly but
complain as she ate and then leave a generous tip. It was no better
in Ghana. God help anyone who thought they could surpass *her*
cooking. The only exception was our housekeeper, Estela. I think

it was because my mother had trained Estela from the time she was twelve.

When I walked into the restaurant, she was already seated. Today's outfit was an all-white Givenchy suit, which I, no doubt, would have already spilled something on. "Eh, there you are."

"Sorry, Mum. I am coming from work, and I had a meeting."

"As if lunch with your mother isn't also important."

Cool it—she's trying to get your ire up. You are not going to lose your shit today. Coast on those endorphins.

I wasn't going to let her steal my happy high.

"Did you already order?"

"You know I don't really like the food in these oyibo places."

And we were off to the races. She was lying. She liked Western food just fine. She just enjoyed the theater of being picky. That pursed lip I knew so well had already taken up residence on her beautiful face as she perused the menu.

"Mum, please, not today. Let's just have a nice lunch."

"So, everything okay?"

She gave her unenthusiastic order by changing the fish to sole and explaining that they needed to add ginger to the sauce and how not to overcook her vegetables. "You know I've been busy with the foundation."

I'd never known how she'd managed to be at the hospital and do all that charity work and be around for me so often. As a kid, I had no idea that she was superwoman.

I'd been in Ghana with my grandparents when she was doing her fellowship in London. Dad had been in the States starting his company. I'd seen Mum about once a month and my father once every three months until finally, we'd all moved to the States once Mum was offered a job in New York.

It had been hard for her, especially when I was little, having to navigate the schools, and the moms, and the PTA, and the disdain on the faces when we would walk in.

Whenever I thought about those kinds of things, I was always proud of her. And then there were moments like this, when she said, "Oh, good, you're settled in. Now I can bring him over."

My eyes went wide. "'Him'?"

I saw the shadow before I felt the heat and turned. My first impression was the shiny oxfords, bespoke plaid suit, and trim figure, obviously in shape. No jacket, but a vest.

Nice touch.

The pattern was a very fine plaid, green and blue over gray. Crisp white shirt, silver-and-diamond cuff links, beautiful dark onyx skin with a close-trimmed beard.

So close.

I *hated* beards. But he had a wide smile, shrewd deep-set dark eyes, and the lashes . . . Hell, they were thicker than mine. This man was fine with a capital *F*.

"Uh, hello?"

"Hello, I'm Jacob. Your mother has told me everything about you."

I darted a glance at my mother, who was giving me a wide grin and nodding encouragingly.

Every. Single. Time.

It was like she carried around successful dick in Tupperware containers, just waiting to offer you one.

When he took a seat next to me, I tried to stay calm and not be irritated he hadn't asked to sit. I turned to face him. "Um, Jacob, is it?"

His grin flashed. "Yes."

"What is it that you do, Jacob?"

"I'm a doctor."

Ironically, I do know my mother as well as she thinks she knows me. "Oh, right, a doctor. Let me guess, a surgeon?"

He grinned. "Of course."

I turned to my mother, who was starting to stand and take her purse. "Where are you going?" I nearly shrieked in panic. There was no way I was doing this forced date alone.

"Well, I'm going to leave you and Jacob to get to know each other better. Jacob, dear, I ordered you the sole."

Jacob grinned and placed his arm around the back of my chair. "Auntie, thank you. Did you also tell them my schedule? I can't stay long. There is that Black Doctors under Thirty photo spread I need to get to." He winked at me as he said it.

Lord save me from the arrogance.

His fingers grazed my shoulder, and I know he thought that was sexy, but his fingers were ice-cold and sent a shiver down my spine in a bad way. I turned slowly to him.

Surely, at some point, my mother would run out of wealthy, eligible Ghanaian men in New York. "Jacob, I know this isn't your fault, so pardon my rudeness. But maybe, before you touch someone, you ask for their consent. Because as my mother should have told you, I really, really, *really* don't like to be touched. Second, I didn't agree to this date. My mother did. So she really is the one who should stay."

My mother gawked. "Ofosua, behave yourself. He's nice."

"I'm sure he thinks he is." I shifted my chair over so his hand was forced to fall down.

Jacob's brows lifted, and then, in filtered his Ghanaian accent. "Eh, Auntie, you didn't tell me she was so opinionated. This one is a *hard* woman."

My mother sighed. "You're telling me?"

I laughed as I started to stand up. "You know what? Since the two of you are of the same opinion, you can enjoy your lunch. I'm going back to the office."

I was in such a hurry to get out of there that I wasn't looking where I was going. I bumped into a brick wall. In slow motion, I skittered backward, my heels unable to manage the tilt and my weight. The floor ever-so-obligingly rose to meet my ass. In front of the whole restaurant.

"Fuck me."

A strong hand reached for me. But then instead of pulling me up, he leaned down. "While that is a tempting proposition, I think you would probably kill me."

I lifted my gaze to find myself sprawled in front of none other than Cole Drake. "What are the chances you'll forget you ever saw this?" I muttered.

"Change happy hour to actual dinner tonight, and it's forgotten. I want to hear all about your date."

"I'm going to kill you."

"So you keep promising."

COLE

Since Ofos declined my invitation, I thought it would be a good idea to catch up with my uncle, as I often did after acquisitions meetings. Today it seemed especially important, as something was especially off with him in that meeting. The atmosphere at Busca was as boisterous as ever.

After bumping into Ofos running away from what looked like a very awkward date, I spotted my uncle at his usual table by the west window. It wasn't until I rounded the corner that I saw

Nazrin was seated with him. I pulled up short with a smile when I saw them. "Hey, Nazrin. What are you doing here?"

When she saw me, she gave me a wan smile. "Just giving your uncle the rundown on a project he asked me to coordinate. I'm done now, though," she said, taking her bag off the hook under the table.

"Don't let me run you off. What project? Am I missing something?"

"I'm sure he'll explain. I'll be late for my appointment."

As she left, my uncle spoke. "I'm considering hiring outside PR for our larger releases. I asked Nazrin to investigate our options."

"Maybe we should have discussed that? I would have liked to know that was the plan, since Nazrin is part of my department."

He rolled his eyes. "Don't get territorial. You have your hands full, remember?"

I studied him carefully. "I'm just curious about what my direct reports are up to."

"When it is something important, you'll know. Do you care to explain just what the fuck it is you think you're doing?" he asked, changing the subject.

He looked legitimately angry. But I'd dealt with far worse when it came to angry Drakes. It was time to find out what was truly going on.

I took a seat and signaled for the waiter. "What are you talking about, Uncle Steven? We just left an acquisitions meeting any publisher would consider a success."

"I didn't think that you were going to lose sight of what's important here."

"And what is that?"

"You openly took her side. On everything. When you should have explained to a very green editor why we don't waste valuable time. Experience counts for something, you know. People seem to forget that."

"Waste time? Are you talking about Kenya Jones? She has a huge platform and thousands of loyal readers. We're going to have to agree to disagree on her."

"Am I hearing you correctly, Cole?"

I lowered my chin and leveled a hard look at my uncle. "Yes. I have a job to do and you shouldn't be worried. What you said about me being able to sell just about anything, was that bullshit? You either want me to do my job or you don't."

He scowled at me. "Oh, Cole, don't be ridiculous. You were supposed to guide her into making some good choices, that's all."

"Did you even read the manuscripts or glance at the authors' platforms, Uncle Steven? Because they're actually great."

"What's really going on with you and Ofosua?"

"I don't know what you mean." I stared at him.

He backed down. "Fine. Have it your way."

"We want the same thing, Uncle Steven: for Drake to be a success. We've struggled over the last few years. Cosmos is offering an infusion of cash. And his requirements are reasonable ones. Up until now, you've been a fan of Ofosua, and she's doing a good job, so what's the problem?"

"You and I know full well the reason she's helming a line before she's ready. In my day, people had to work for these things. I'm worried about what this is doing to morale."

There it was again, that knot. The underlying thing that he wasn't saying outright that sat uneasily with me.

If it sits uneasy with you, say something. For once in your life, fucking do something about it.

"What would that reason be, Uncle Steven? And by the way, morale is fine."

"None of it matters as long as Cosmos gives us the money."

He really wasn't going to say it.

"Fine. Then if it doesn't matter, let her do her job. Succeed or fail, let it at least be on her merit, instead of trying to make it harder for her at every turn."

"Have you forgotten I'm the CEO? When they say 'publisher,' they do mean me."

"*Until* they mean me. It's like you're deliberately trying to sabotage her. Which doesn't make any sense at all. Do you think Cosmos is going to just hand over the money without you making any real changes?"

He narrowed his gaze at me, and I saw the truth. That was exactly what he intended. He didn't want his world to change.

"Uncle Steven, Cosmos is not that foolish. Sure, we might get a little infusion of cash. But if he's smart, which he seems to be, he'll put it on a schedule. We have to show a real commitment. You can't just pull something or not support it."

"One day, she'll make a fine editor. And I'm for progress. I believe in diversity. But how much so-called change are we pushing through right now just for optics? Nobody wants to say this, but I will. I'm not going to be forced to publish subpar books just because the author is Black and we need to be more woke or whatever your generation calls it, so we don't get canceled. I don't care about being canceled. I care about finding the next Dan Brown, and so should you, because that's what readers want. If we were smart, we'd just ask Evan or Colton to create a new series with a Black detective as the lead. We could be just as successful, even more so, actually."

A year ago I probably would've thought that was something you could do: just commission a seasoned author with a known brand to write about an experience that wasn't their own, that wasn't authentic. And I would've equated it to authors of color writing white characters. But now I was starting to know better, and I was horrified that my uncle couldn't see it. Or, actually, he *wouldn't* see.

"Evan would never fly with Cosmos."

He scoffed and waved a hand. "Practicability politics. Ofosua's writers are unproven."

"Once again, I direct you to the audience deck we created for Aurora James. But also, have you thought that maybe some of these authors just haven't been given a chance yet, Uncle Steven? And it's our job to do that?"

"You've been drinking the Kool-Aid."

I narrowed my gaze. I couldn't believe the shit that was coming out of his mouth. "What's that even supposed to mean?"

"You heard me."

There was nothing like realizing the man you thought you knew was someone else entirely. "Uncle Steven. I just feel like you're trying to say something without saying it. It's just us, so you might as well say it."

"Fine. You and Ofos need more books on your list that will appeal to *all* readers. I'm not letting a bunch of teenagers on the internet dictate what Drake publishes."

"You do realize you sound out of touch, right? At best."

He lifted a brow. "Careful. I need at least one more unquestionably commercial author."

"Please read the books Ofosua pitched. Also, Uncle Steven? You can't fire me, if that's what you are hinting at."

"We need people who are known."

"Uncle Steven, Aurora James has more followers on social media than Drake Publishing as a whole does."

"Followers? I loathe that word. A publishing house leads."

"Then kill the line and tell Cosmos we don't want his money, or let Ofosua do her job. Those are the two options as I see it. What's it going to—"

"Gentlemen, this is a surprise." Brian Cosmos had a wide smile for the both of us, seemingly unaware of the tension he'd just shattered.

My uncle's countenance changed immediately. "Cosmos, great to see you."

"I'm just in town for a few meetings. I was going to come by the office tomorrow, but since you're here, I'd love to sit down and see how things are going at Drake."

I'd always liked Cosmos. He was smart. Shrewd. The *Queens of a Distant Galaxy* series had made quite a bit of money due to our collaboration.

"Cole, it's been a minute. How are you?"

"Can't complain. Good to see you." I didn't wait for my uncle to speak before adding, "Join us, please, if you have time."

Cosmos pulled up a chair, folding his long body into it as he and my uncle exchanged pleasantries and I called the waiter over.

We chatted for a minute, and then Cosmos brought up the inevitable. "I understand you've started work on your new Black women's fiction imprint. Cole, your uncle says you're on that team."

I refrained from smirking at my uncle. "I am. We've got a brilliant editor too. Ofosua Addo. Her taste is incredible. We've already acquired some very solid projects."

Cosmos frowned. "Addo? Is she from Ghana by chance?"

Was Addo a common name in Ghana? Why didn't I know that?

"Yeah. Actually, she is."

"A good friend of mine from college is from Ghana. He's a fraternity brother."

My uncle looked lost at our exchange, as if it had never occurred to him to ask if Ofosua was from anywhere else but here.

Cosmos sat forward. "I have to tell you, I was very excited to hear that the new imprint is in progress. Hiring a woman of color to helm it was the right call."

Uncle Steven chimed in, "At Drake, we look to the future." This was the same man who had basically just told me to add white authors to our new Black imprint. I had to work hard to keep the frown off my brow and keep my lip from curling. He was lying.

"I'm happy to hear it. I want a long-term partnership and investment."

I slid my uncle a glance. He was going to have to get on board.

"Will I get the opportunity to meet your editor?"

Uncle Steven pressed his lips together. "Eventually. As you can imagine, she's got her hands full."

Cosmos nodded. "I like that, a go-getter."

My uncle looked displeased, but what the hell could he say? "That she is."

"You're off to an impressive start. No shortcuts, no cheat codes. Which is critical. I don't have time for publicity nightmares."

My uncle nodded. "Brian, Drake believes that it is our responsibility to lead necessary change, which is why we promoted a woman of color from within. It's why we're painstakingly combing over each and every submission for underrepresented voices."

And little did my uncle know how true that was. He was playing games, but Ofos had already outmaneuvered him. We'd gotten an email from Carol as I was walking over. Thanks to the notes Ofos had given and the sales and marketing package I had laid out, our commercial women's fiction line was getting a new addition.

The question was, what was my uncle going to do once he found out?

CHAPTER 17

OFOSUA

ADINKRA SAYING:
(Mmere Danc) Time changes.
A symbol of things changing with time.

HELEN ADDO:
Men do not change.
Only their tactics for getting in your trousers.

SAMUEL ADDO:
Don't waste your time trying to change anybody's mind.
Instead, make yourself happy.

The thing with becoming friends with Cole was there had been this current between me and Cole, like we were circling each other, trying to ascertain if our friendship or whatever was real. The more time I spent with him, the more real things between us felt. And he was in my dreams . . . still.

My *sex* dreams.

Sure, he'd become my partner at work and sort of my friend. Though that was insane. Sure, his friend Tallon seemed okay, but guys like Cole were friends with people like Chad. The Chads were the norm. *Not* the Tallons. I'd grown up with guys like that.

There would always be a comment here, a whisper there. A casual microaggression chipping away at my soul.

Cole and I could never be friends. *And certainly not more than that.*

I swallowed hard as I grabbed the pillow and shoved it over my head. Maybe if I tried hard enough, I could make these feelings go away.

Except the more I closed my eyes, the more I pictured Cole and that look he'd been giving me that night in Bryant Park, the one that said he wanted to kiss me.

I hadn't been interested in anyone in nine months. Cole was all wrong. I'd learned that lesson years ago. Also, he wasn't Ghanaian. Not African. Not Black.

It would be complicated at best. Not to mention we worked together. Wasn't there someone more appropriate?

And you know better.

Was it time to let my mother actually pick my dates for me? Never a good option.

I had to get over this niggling Cole feeling. I couldn't go there.

Which was what I told myself later that evening. It was nearly six thirty before I made it out of my last meeting of the day and headed back to my office, with Emory on my heels. "Any big plans for tonight? Did that guy ever call you? What was his name? Omar?"

I choked a cough. "The last thing I want is for him to call me. One date was enough. Nope. Just work and hanging out with the roommates, trying to exhaust myself into a dreamless sleep." The Cole dreams had, unfortunately, continued.

"Why dreamless?"

Shit. "I haven't been sleeping much. Weird dreams lately." We stopped just outside of my office.

"What kind of dreams are we talking about? The kind where

you haven't gone to class all semester, or the kind that everyone has about Henry Cavill?"

I blew a wisp of hair out of my face. What had possessed me to straighten it? I always missed my curls when I did. "The Henry Cavill kind. Except not about him," I whispered. The halls were practically empty, but the last thing I wanted was for anyone to overhear me.

Emory laughed. "Then who . . ." She caught herself, her eyes going wide, then she glanced furtively around. "Oh my God. Did you have a dream about C—"

I placed a finger over my lips to shush her. "Do not speak his name. God, it's bad enough I had the stupid dream. I don't need to hear you say it out loud."

Emory laughed. "Well, I mean, is that so bad?"

"What? This is terrible. First of all, he's our sort-of future boss. Not to mention, we've seen the women he likes. Very much *not* me."

"So why the dreams?"

"If I knew, I'd make them stop."

"Or," she emphasized, "maybe your dreams are trying to tell you something."

I shook my head to clear it. "Nope. Not going there. Why did I even tell you?"

"Because you know I will sympathize. I know just how hot he is. And also how much of a pain in the ass he is. If you won't let me tease you, just look at this as a sign that you are ready to be out there again."

"Now you sound like my roommates and my cousin."

"Well, they're right. Okay, look, take this stack of notes. I'll go grab the mail and packages. You pack up. Don't let me find you hunched over your laptop."

"I'm on it." I turned into my office and I stopped short at the scent of spicy Chinese food. I was dead on my feet. My stomach grumbled, and I realized I had skipped lunch. Goddamn it. Something else I'd been too distracted to remember. And the object of my distraction was sitting at my desk holding takeout.

"Wow, someone's hungry. Good thing I brought food."

Cole was in here all along? How much had he just heard? *Oh no. No. No. No.* Maybe he hadn't heard anything. Which I hoped to God was true.

"Is that from Lin's?"

Cole grinned. "Yeah, I remembered when you were talking to Emory the other day about the best Chinese in the city. So I went to Chinatown. You know they don't deliver this far uptown."

I frowned. "But that's all the way downtown."

"I know, but I figured if we were going to be working, you would need fuel, right?"

He went all the way across downtown. In traffic.

No wonder you're having sex dreams about him.

I cleared my throat. "Ah, right. Thanks."

He studied me closely. His gaze searching my face. "So, Henry Cavill dreams?"

Heat bloomed up my neck and I covered my face. "Oh my God."

He started opening up all the boxes, and ginger and garlic scents filled the air.

I needed to get Dream Cole out of my mind before I said something insane.

He lifted a brow and smirked. "Who's the hot *not* Henry Cavill? Not that guy you were on a date with. Doesn't seem like your type." His laugh was rich and clear and made my stomach do this little flip-flop thing that was wholly inappropriate.

I glowered at him. "We are not doing this."

"Oh, relax. We're friends now. We can talk about stuff."

"The jury is still out." A smile tugged at the corner of my lips. What was my libido thinking?

With mischief in his eyes, he cocked his head and studied me. "Anyone I know?" The teasing note in his voice melted my resolve and made me giggle.

My brows knitted. "We are not having this conversation."

He plopped down onto one of the office chairs. "That's okay. I overheard it all anyway. Don't worry about it."

A laugh bubbled out before I could stop it. "I swear to God"—I waved a fork at him—"I will gut you, hide the body, and no one will ever find it if you ever mention this again."

His wink and grin were positively wicked. "That tells me that this dream was *excellent*."

The laughter was hard to control. "Nope. It was . . . adequate."

That wiped the smug grin off his face. "Adequate?" He stood ramrod straight. "That's bullshit. I think I can do better than adequate."

This was the moment when I was supposed to make some quip that would have cut through the tension. When I could have said something funny and light. But my brain-to-mouth connection was clearly on the fritz, because I said, "I'm sure you could." Like a dare.

The tension that permanently swirled around us ratcheted up from an ever-present hum to a full-blown lightning storm.

The corner of his lip quirked into a smile, and that hint of dimple had a direct line to my vagina. "You feel it too? The tension between us?"

I swallowed hard and nodded.

It's more than that and you know it.

"It's just chemistry. We can ignore it."

He took a step forward. "I don't think I can." His voice was all smoke and gravel.

I held my ground, refusing to back away from the wildly terrifying thrill of wanting something I shouldn't want. "It's complicated with us working together."

He was close enough that the delicious, crisp scent of his cologne wrapped around me. I was strong enough to resist, wasn't I?

Why are we resisting?

"I really want to kiss you. But if you don't want me to, tell me to stop and I will. We can go right back to being just friends."

That was my out. My get-out-of-pussy-jail card. Because I'd been down this road before. With *him*. I knew better. Or at least I should. But I couldn't find the one word that would put an end to this. I could say "no" in ten languages, but there was not a "nein," "nyet," "non," or "daa-bi" to be found.

And when he reached for me, closing the gap between our bodies, his firm chest pressed against my breasts and I couldn't breathe. I couldn't think. I was dickmatized. Completely enthralled. As he leaned down, my lashes fluttered closed and my breath caught. I wanted this. I wanted hi—

Emory rushed in, leading with her voice. The two of us jumped apart. Emory hesitated for a moment, narrowing her gaze at me. "H-heeey, sorry. Ofos, I grabbed your mail for you from downstairs. I'm just heading out. Do you need anything else?"

I cleared my throat. "Nope. All good here."

I watched as the smile tugged at her lips. "You sure?"

No. I was not sure. Matter of fact, I might never be sure about anything else in my lifetime. But lying was more prudent. "Yep. All good. Have a good night."

She left with a smirk, calling out, "Don't work too hard."

When she was gone, Cole chuckled. "We are so busted."

"Wide open," I muttered as I sat down. My stack of mail fell off the table. Cole leaned close to help me pick it up, our earlier tension swirling again. My gaze caught on something much too familiar. The ivory lettering of a wedding invitation . . . *my* wedding invitation. The exact same very expensive, very custom ones Yofi and I were meant to send out. Before he fucked someone in a closet at our traditional wedding. I could see the delicate lace etching around the edges of the envelope.

"Ofosua? What's wrong?" Cole asked, but I could barely hear him.

I stared at the envelope. It was addressed to me, postmarked two days ago. How was that possible?

I could hear my heartbeat thudding in my ears, and I couldn't breathe.

"Oh my God."

Cole was at my side. "Hey, what is it?"

I stared down at the envelope, words not forming as the dizziness tried to take over me. Nausea made my stomach roil.

He took it from my fingers. "Looks like an invitation of some sort. What's the matter?"

I shook my head even as I blinked back the tears and pulled out the card stock. It was all too familiar. Heavy black stock with silver and rose-gold writing. *The Honorable Kweku Ade and his wife Ema Ade would like to humbly invite you to the wedding of their daughter Pamela Ade to one Yofi Tutu on the date,* blah, blah, blah, bullshit, asshole, bullshit fuckery. My brain started to fill in the words as I went.

Pamela? I knew her. She was a year or so younger than I was. Her mother was a friend of my parents. Had *she* been the one in the closet with Yofi?

"Oh my God. Oh my God. Oh my God."

It took me a moment to realize I'd been speaking out loud because Cole was kneeling right in front of me. "What does it say?"

I shook my head, dropping the card from my fingers. I needed air. I needed to breathe.

I was going to be ill, and I did not want to throw up in here. Not in front of him.

I ran. I wasn't even sure where I was going. All I knew was that I had to leave that room. Away from that fucking invitation.

Behind me, I could hear him calling out to me, telling me to wait. I made it to the stairs, and I went up.

Another wave of dizziness hit me, and I wanted it to stop. I wanted to collapse and cry, but I was not going to do that. Behind me, I could still hear Cole, so I ran all the way to the roof. Another ten flights. When I shoved the heavy fire doors open, I staggered out onto the cement and inhaled a deep breath.

I went to the railing and held on tight, dragging in more air, remembering what that long-ago therapist that I'd only seen that one time had told me: breathe deeply.

Somewhere behind me I heard the door open, and Cole's voice tentatively called out my name. "Ofosua, what's wrong?"

"I had to get out of there. I couldn't breathe."

I could hear his footsteps making their slow approach. "You're okay. I've got you."

"No, you don't have me. He told me he didn't want to get married. That he wasn't ready. Apparently, he just didn't want to get married to *me*. What did I do wrong?"

Before I knew it, Cole's arms were around me, holding me tight. "You didn't do anything wrong. He is a twat. That's the end of it. Why would he even invite you? God, that's so fucked up."

I didn't want to be in his arms. I didn't.

Lies.

But he was so strong. And he smelled good. With his arms around me, I felt safe. I felt seen. But the anxiety hovered in the back of my mind. All the self-doubt, the worry, the anxiety, all of it was going to come seeping out if I couldn't hold it together until I could get home and cry like a normal person. But oh no, even as I held on to the outer seams, I started leaking from the eyes. Fucking tears in front of Cole Drake. Jesus.

But he didn't run. He didn't admonish me to toughen up. All he did was hold me tight against his chest, offering me the kind of comfort that I hadn't anticipated but was exactly what I needed.

—

COLE

Holding her was the easy part. Watching her body curl in on itself and hearing her sobs tore me in two. I didn't know what else to do except hold her. I wasn't even sure that was helping. But I could feel her body, the shaking, the coughing, and all I could do was stroke my hand through her hair and hush her. "You're going to be okay, I promise."

"I don't feel okay. I feel like I'm losing it."

"Why?" I pulled back and slid a finger under her chin so that she had to meet my gaze. Her eyes were brimming with tears. "Fuck, I'm so sorry. And the fact he expects that you would come, or that he should invite you, that's bullshit."

"It's . . . It's what you do. His parents were humiliated by the breakup, and they're probably trying to save face. And you know what the worst part of it is?" She swiped at her nose.

I hunted my pockets for a tissue but couldn't find one.

She continued. "Those are *my* wedding invitations. I came up with all of that, *by myself*, because he couldn't be bothered. He didn't care. Which, in retrospect, should have been a red flag, but I was dumb. I wasn't listening to my emotions, to my mind, and that thing where women know when something is bad for us. We know, and still, we do it, like we pretend and lie to ourselves that it can't possibly be that bad, that we must be imagining it."

I sighed. "I wish I had some kind of an answer that might even be a little bit of what you need to hear, but I don't, other than he's a dick."

She pulled back a little to wipe her tears, and then she dropped her forehead back to my chest. And that swell of pride that she could lean on me was even better than finding out she'd maybe had a sex dream about me.

God, how in the world had this happened? A month ago, yes, I was mildly obsessed with her. But I hadn't *known* her. Now I knew her better, and the feeling was worse somehow. That need to make her feel better, happier. That was a problem.

Don't worry about it right now. Deal with her crying now.

"Is there something I can do?"

She shook her head. "No, I have already embarrassed myself too much, and God, fuck my life. I'm so sorry. You brought dinner too."

Fuck dinner. I'd completely forgotten because I'd only been worried about taking care of her. "Listen, come on downstairs. We're not going to work. We are going to pull up something awful on Netflix. Something hilarious to take your mind off it. And then we'll eat Chinese food. You know, like friends."

"Careful, Cole, someone is going to start to think that you care."

"I do care. Don't tell anyone, of course. It would ruin my reputation."

And there it was, a snort giggle. It seemed like it was against her will, but I would take it. Any kind of smile from her would be better than her not smiling at all right now.

"You know what we're going to watch? That matchmaking show. I've heard it's a hot mess and I'm here for it. Come on. If anything is going to make you feel better about the shitty night, it'll be that. Okay?"

She gave me a small nod. "Thank you."

"For what? Telling you the truth you already knew? Your ex is a douche. You're smarter than I am, so, of course, you know that, right?"

She bit the inside of her cheek. "Yeah, I know that."

"See. I knew you were smart. He's a dick, and you don't have to deal with him."

She sniffled and wiped the tears from her cheeks. "Actually, I'll have to go to the wedding."

I stopped short. "You're kidding."

"I am not kidding. It'll be expected."

"No, no, no. That's bullshit. There's no way. You broke up. There's no way you'll have to go to that wedding." I don't know why, but the idea of her being around that guy made me want to tear through something.

You know what it is. It's jealousy.

Fine, it was jealousy. But this was worse than that. This was torture.

"You know you can't go by yourself."

She laughed. "What, you're going to be my date?"

My skin flushed hot, and I was grateful for the waning moonlight. "Yeah, why not?" I was probably crimson right now. "Think about it. You and I will go, and we'll eat a lot. You will show me more Ghanaian food. I will refrain from hitting on any of the bridesmaids because you are my date, and that's the proper thing to do. And we'll dance."

That earned me a second laugh. "I know you *think* you can dance, but I don't think it's a good idea."

"Fine, you're going to show me how to dance. How is that?"

"That's really sweet, Cole. I never thought I'd say that to you, but I will figure it out, okay? I appreciate your concern."

"That's what friends are for." Which was bullshit because fifteen minutes ago, we were a breath away from being more than friends.

She laughed then. "Who would have ever thought we would be friends?"

I couldn't help but laugh too. "Yeah, you know, you were not on the top of my friends list."

"Well, you were annoying. And you deliberately tried to make me hate you."

I opened the door to let her into the stairwell. Then the best thing happened.

Ofosua reached down and took my hand. She gave me two simple squeezes, sending a wave of warmth through my chest. I knew what it was. It was a thank-you. But still, that one motion was something I wouldn't be able to let go of. I wanted her. But for now, she needed me. So whatever she needed, I'd give it to her.

You have got it so bad.

Didn't I know it.

CHAPTER 18

OFOSUA

ADINKRA SAYING:
(Akokonan) Mercy, nurturing.
HELEN ADDO:
Waje mɔr he'. Harden yourself. Life can be hard.
You're an Addo. Nobody brings you to your knees.

In the office, with the twinkling lights of the Manhattan skyline watching, Cole had insisted I eat, so we'd finished the Chinese takeout on the floor of my office. There had also been copious amounts of wine. Thanks to BevMo. I'd even brought a bottle home so I could keep the pity party up.

I also owed him a thank-you for putting me in a car.

He had been surprisingly sweet. Even when I'd eaten more than half the Chinese, drunk most of the wine, and spent the rest of the night cursing people out, he'd let me.

Rest of the night? You were home by nine.

I couldn't even wallow and drink properly.

"Hey, honey, what is going on?" Cora stepped out and eyed me as I entered the apartment and flopped onto the couch.

Oh, nothing . . . just my life imploding. "I got a wedding invitation. And there was wine."

Right then, Megan came strutting in. "Did you tell her?"

Cora gave her a sharp shake of the head.

I grinned sloppily at my best friends and pulled my wine from my bag. If I was going to be hit with bad news, I didn't want my buzz to wear off. Luckily for me, it was a twist-off cap.

Cole had said if I wanted to get blitz drunk, I shouldn't do it on the good stuff.

"Tell me what? Forget it. I want to lie here and be shitty, and feel shitty, and insult people shittily." I lifted my head. "But you know who I can't even be shitty about? Fucking Hot Cole. Nope, not the white boy." I lowered my voice and then whispered loudly, "I had a sex dream about him. And guess what, dream Cole knows how to fuck dirty. And he's very good with his mouth. It's not fair. He's so . . . ugh."

Megan's brows lifted into her hairline. Then she turned to Cora. "The fuck?"

"I don't know. Something about a wedding and a sex dream about Hot Cole."

I sat up. "Cora, you need to pay better attention. My ex-husband sent me a wedding invitation."

I started to stand as I waved my bottle of wine around like a crazy person. "First, he cheats on me at our wedding. And then nine months later, I get an invitation. Looks like he wanted to be married after all, just not to *me*." I took a swig of wine. "And worse, he sent me *my* wedding invitation. The one I picked out and designed myself."

Both of them winced.

I pointed to myself. "I'm awesome. I'm amazing. I'm accomplished. I'm educated. Funny. Witty." Okay, I might have sprayed a little spittle on that last one.

Both of them looked strangled. As if they wanted to stop me from speaking. But I was not going to be deterred. I had things to say. Things I'd been holding in. "Do you know how long it's been since I've had sex?"

Megan stumbled forward, trying to stop me, but I waved her off. "No! We are not going to shut me up, because I'm going to talk about it. It's been nine months. You know, Yofi used to say that he was tired all the time, but I guess he was tired from fucking *other* people," I whisper-shouted.

Megan's gaze darted toward the kitchen.

I was too busy with my tirade to even pay attention to what she was looking at. "Yeah, that's him. A cheater. And I'm the idiot who fell for it. Who gets married at twenty-five? Me. Because I was being a good Ghanaian girl to make up for disappointing my parents by not going to grad school. How dare he cheat on me then tell me he's marrying her?" Then suddenly it dawned on me. "What if he's not even marrying that chick? Maybe this is a different chick?"

Both of them continued to stare. "Why are you both looking that way? You look weird. Why are you making weird faces?"

Cora stepped forward. "Honey, I need you to put that bottle down because you have—"

I hugged the bottle to my chest. "No, this bottle is my friend."

And then that voice dropped like an anvil.

"Ofosua Addo. What in the world?"

My head whipped around to find a good-looking man in my kitchen. Six feet tall, dark brown eyes, and a set of lashes prettier than mine. He looked horrified. *Excellent.* That was the way he should look when looking at me. My mother stood by his side, hands on her hips. "I have brought you a guest and is this how you talk?"

I knew my roommates had been telling me to shut the fuck up and say nothing. Meanwhile, I was gearing up for the fight of my lifetime as I took an unsteady step toward my mum. "Another one?"

My mother opened her mouth and then closed it, studying me closely. "What is wrong with you? This is not how I raised you."

"*Me?* After this afternoon, when you surprised me with a strange man at lunch without my permission, you think it was a good idea to bring *another* one? Are you delusional?"

Oh, shit. You have really screwed the pooch this time.

Somewhere in Ghana, my ancestors were rolling around in graves and calling the spirits to torment me.

You did not call your parents crazy if you were Ghanaian. *Ever.*

Anything to imply mental illness or that they were fools were the quickest ways to meet God.

My mother's mouth hung open. Next to her, the man's mouth hung open too as he blinked.

My roommates, ever unhelpful, stared at me like I had lost my mind. And then I realized I had spilled my cheap bottle of wine all over our cream-colored rug.

Fuck. "Mum, I told you this afternoon, I don't need your help dating. Whatever the heck your name is, I'm sure you are very nice. Let me guess, a doctor, a lawyer, or in finance?"

He nodded. "Well, actually, I'm a medical researcher, and I—"

I put up my hand. "I don't care," I slurred. "See, I know me talking to you indicated that maybe I give a shit, but I don't. I'm sure whatever you are, you are extremely accomplished. I. Don't. Care. Because right now, my world is falling apart. I am not interested. Except to have *sex* dreams about an obroni boy. Clearly, I'm fucked in the head. You don't want me."

His jaw dropped. Then he looked at my mother, nodded, and walked out my front door.

"Eh, what is wrong with you? Why can't you be meek, *small*?"

I stared at my mother. I knew that to her, my being meek and being quiet and accepting the status quo would fix so many things. But *she* wasn't like that. She wasn't meek. She didn't accept things. So why did she think I should?

Well, maybe she thinks that's all you deserve.

I tucked away those feelings because I could not afford to be in any more pain today.

"I'm trying to help you, Ofosua. You may think this is all nonsense, but family and community mean something in our culture. They aren't just words you toss around. I'm trying to help you secure your future."

I shook my head. "Mum, no. I know you're not used to hearing that word from me, but you're about to start hearing it a lot more. No. I don't care what you say to Daddy. I don't care what you tell your friends. I'm not doing this. I got an invitation to Yofi's wedding."

She shrugged her shoulders. "Yes, we got ours two days ago."

What the fuck? "So instead of telling me that this was happening, you let me find out on my own and turned up with men for me?"

"Well, you need a date for the wedding. You can't go by yourself. So I was hoping you'd like one of them."

"Instead of *talking* to me, instead of communicating, this is what you did?"

"I know what's best for you. And what's best for you is not showing up at that wedding by yourself. Why can't you see I want you taken care of? Is that so wrong?"

I stared at her and then turned my face to my roommates. "You know what, I'm going to bed. Well, first I'm going to clean up that wine, then I'm going to bed. Mum, I love you, but I can't talk to you for a bit. When I can talk to you, I'll call you."

I staggered to my room with dignity . . . if you call "dignity" bumping into the wall, then the hall table, spilling even more wine, and tripping on the runner.

Yep. Super classy.

—

By the time Sunday rolled around, I was still reeling.

My mother hadn't broken down and come over.

Under normal circumstances, I'd be ecstatic. Dancing in the aisle even. But the guilt was eating away at me. Guilt was a useless emotion, and worse, I knew that she was going to use that guilt to her advantage. It didn't stop me from feeling it, though.

I was blessedly, blissfully alone when one of the doormen buzzed me from downstairs about what I thought was a food delivery. But when I checked our security screen, I realized it wasn't a delivery guy, but none other than Cole Drake in the flesh.

I opened the door but didn't let him in. I tugged my ancient DVF tan cardigan tighter around me. The color did nothing for me, and I probably looked like death. "How do you even know where I live?"

"You gave me your address on Friday when I ordered the car service. And maybe I verified in employee records," he added sheepishly. He glanced past me and whistled at my view. "You can see all of downtown from here."

"Yes, I know. What are you doing here?"

"You going to invite me in?"

"No. When you show up unannounced, you don't get to come in."

He lifted a brow. I knew that look. He would stay right there until I let him in. "Fine." I stepped aside. "Come in. Now what do you want?"

Marching past me, he started to explore my apartment. "Kitchen? I'll put this in the fridge. You can eat it later."

I pointed him in the right direction, and he made himself at home. "I appreciate the gesture, but it's not necessary. I have a mother, and I find her irritating. I don't need another."

"You need something. Something happened on Friday. Anxiety, a panic attack. I don't know. You shut down."

Oh, so that was the thing he wanted to talk about. I swallowed hard. "I'm fine."

He coughed a laugh. "Fine? Are you kidding me right now?"

"No, I am not, in fact, kidding you. I am fine. I feel great."

He laughed. "Bullshit. You have so much tension you vibrate with it. And never once have I seen you in beige. Or so tired. You had a rough blow, and I want to help. I think you need to get out of here for a bit."

"I'm sorry, Friday was shitty and I'm wallowing, okay? I don't mean to be short or snappy, or anything."

He watched me warily. "You have every right to wallow. Panic attacks are no joke. And clearly, you had one. I'm worried about you. If you won't talk to me, you need to talk to *someone*."

I rolled my eyes. "Listen, therapy is some white people shit. I don't need to talk to anyone."

He shook his head in exasperation. "Since when is therapy for white people?"

I laughed. "Are you serious?"

"Yes, I'd like to know."

I stared him down. "Black people don't have the luxury of whining about their problems, especially not Black women. If we don't fix them, we won't survive. And let's be clear on how difficult it can be to find someone culturally sensitive, who gets it, isn't racist, and won't dismiss how you feel."

I had tried therapy. In the weeks following the wedding. I'd needed something to help me get out of bed every day. She'd told me my family was toxic and I should go no contact. She'd also been trying to dig out a reason from me as to how I could be responsible for what Yofi had done.

It was a disaster.

He stood silent for a moment. "I honestly have no idea what to even say to that. I'm sure there is some truth in that idea somewhere, but it wouldn't hurt to talk to someone."

"Yes, it would. If I show a moment of weakness, I will lose everything. *I* have to hold myself together. I don't get to take a break from my life while I process it. And it never stops. There's always something new. My mother lost her mind when I told her I was done with her nonstop attempts to control and manipulate me. She stormed out. I mean after she brought me another date, of course. *Then* she stormed out."

His brows lifted. "What do you mean, *another* date?"

"My parents evidently got their wedding invitation before me. She's been frantically trying to find me a date ever since, and when I tell you that frantic and my mother are a dangerous combination, I'm not exaggerating."

He rolled his eyes. "That's bullshit. I already told you I'll be your date."

He didn't get it. "And I already told you that won't work out."

"Why, because I'm white?" he asked with a lifted brow.

I laughed. "Well, yes. I'll already be under scrutiny because Yofi is my ex, and I don't need an extra level."

"Is it the dancing? I promise you I can clap on the one and the four," he said with an expression so serious I almost believed him.

Despite myself, a chuckle escaped. How did he do that? I definitely did not want to laugh.

"I get why you don't want to take me. I really do get it. But you need a date, and wouldn't I be better than some strange guy you don't know at all?"

"*Do* I know you at all, Cole?"

He nodded. "You do. Right now, I think you even know more about me than my mother does."

"You're not close?"

He shrugged. "We don't have anything in common. Nothing to talk about. You and I are at least talking about some real shit. Shit that matters to you and to me now. Now that I'm seeing things, I can't unsee them. That's real."

And right in that moment, I knew I was in trouble. I could take his sexiness, and his outrageousness, and that pretty smile of his. But this, him really seeing me . . . I could fall for him. Even though I knew better.

I was capable of falling head over heels with this guy, and that was far too dangerous.

"Now, go and shower," he said. "We're going out."

CHAPTER 19

OFOSUA

ADINKRA SAYING:
(*Akoma*) Patience, nurturing

HELEN ADDO:
*Love is patient, love is kind. No one is more patient
than a mother trying to get her daughter married.*

SAMUEL ADDO:
*Patience is letting your wife talk to her heart's content.
It will bring peace.*

Cole was right. I did feel better after a shower. As it turned out, smelling like stale wine messed with your head.

Instead of thanking him, I blurted out, "Is this a date?"

Cole laughed. "You are really out of practice, aren't you?"

"I guess a little. I'm sorry. I feel like I should know."

"How about we say this is two friends headed out to do something fun, and we'll see about it being a date later? Besides, I don't think you're exactly ready to date."

What the hell was that supposed to mean? "I am ready to date . . . sort of. Okay, maybe not really."

"See? So, this is not a date. Come on. Are you ready to go? You look great, by the way."

I glanced down. I'd worn an African-print skirt and a plain white T-shirt tied in a knot at the back, showing a hint of skin. "Am I dressed appropriately for wherever we're going?"

He laughed. "Like I said, you look great, and you'll be fine with that. Come on."

He'd worn dark jeans and a casual button-down shirt with the sleeves rolled up to the elbows, so it couldn't be that fancy.

"Okay, let me grab a blazer or something first."

"Yeah. I mean, it's warm now, but it could be chilly later."

"You're really not telling me where we're going?"

He shook his head. "Nope."

"So, you grew up here?" he asked.

I nodded. "Yup, down the hall is the same room I grew up in. Humiliating, I know."

He laughed. "Hardly, this is Charles Street, in the heart of Greenwich Village, with a view of the Hudson. You have views of the whole damn neighborhood. If I could stand my father at all, I'd still be in the same place I grew up in too."

"Where did you grow up?"

"Upper East Side. It was my grandfather's place." Not that surprising.

"I see. So where do you live now?"

He shrugged. "I've got a place in Tribeca. I love it. I get to feel like I'm my own person without all the bullshit." Tribeca suited him. Trendy, hip, alive. He'd want to be in the heart of nightlife and restaurants.

"Yeah, that was kind of the plan I had for the whole, you know, run-off-and-get-married thing."

He laughed. "Well, you can still have that plan without the marriage."

I reached into the closet and pulled out a blazer. "Oh, that is the plan. Saving some money so I can be on my own."

"I'm sure you could probably live somewhere on your own *now*."

"I could, but you haven't met my mother. There will be a lot of string-pulling to control me if I go anywhere near my trust fund. And I'd like to be financially independent before I pull that trigger."

We made the escape without any of my roommates or, God forbid, my mother coming home and seeing Hot Cole.

We even made it down the hall and into the elevator without seeing anyone, not even any of our neighbors. As luck went, mine was looking up.

It was only after he opened the car door for me and slid in beside me that I saw the flyer and laughed. "You're taking me to a Republic Day Festival?"

"Oh, damn it, I wanted to surprise you."

"I *am* surprised."

"It's not lame, is it?"

I shook my head. "No, it's perfect. I'm not going to the Ghana Association dinner tonight, so this way I can still celebrate."

"There's a Ghana Association in New York?"

"Oh yes. Complete with society boards and charity boards, and all those kinds of things that I don't care about."

"Well, okay, then. But do you like Republic Day celebrations?"

"What's not to love? It's not as big as Independence Day, but there is food, and dancing, and drinks. I do love it. Thank you. This was thoughtful of you."

He grinned. "I know. So all you have to do is relax, kick back, have fun, and of course, tell me what the hell I'm eating. I was reading a review in the *Times*, and they said that you should literally go on an empty stomach. Matter of fact, they said don't eat for two days beforehand because you will be stuffed. They have to roll you home."

As I laughed, I said, "You know, that's actually quite accurate. If I'd known where we were going, I wouldn't have eaten breakfast."

I was glad he'd used a car service. Something told me the struggle to find parking would have ruined the mood.

The streets teemed around us, and we enjoyed a companionable silence in the car. Next to me on the seat, his hand was mere inches from mine. And all I could think about was what if he wrapped it around mine like he'd done the other night, would I pull my hand free?

The more time I spent with Cole, the more I looked forward to spending time with him. Because somehow, in working so closely with him, I'd grown to like the person that he was. And then somewhere along the way it had become more than that. The way he'd held me on that roof, the way he'd comforted me, I couldn't remember the last time someone had taken care of me like that, taken care of my feelings. He made it a point to make sure I was okay.

But then there was that little problem of how he'd completely forgotten me. It was years ago, and I should let it go, but I just couldn't forget that feeling. The way my stomach had dropped. The embarrassment I felt.

You could just ask him about it.

I wasn't sure I wanted to hear his answer.

"You're quiet. Are you not up to this?"

I smiled at him. "No, I am. And this is actually perfect. I get to enjoy all the parts of home and my culture without actually having to deal with my mother, so it's a bonus really."

He laughed. "Your mom can't be that bad."

"You have no idea."

Once we arrived at the Republic Day festival out in Queens, Cole had gotten so pumped up that he looked like a kid on Christmas Day. He was smiling harder than I was. Oh, my smile was pretty big too. I couldn't help it.

Ghanaians from all over New York and New England gathered in one place, loving life. There was music, and food, and screaming children. Cole took my hand then. Easily, as if we'd been holding hands forever.

As we walked into the crowd, I introduced him to bofrot, which he'd never had. But the moment he took a bite, he moaned. It was basically an air-filled fried pastry, but he likened it to an orgasm in edible form.

I scoffed. "I mean, it's good, but I'm sure there's something much better."

"There's something better than this?"

I laughed. "Yes."

"What's your favorite, then?"

"Plantain. Always plantain. It doesn't matter how you make it. Baked, fried, however. That's how I want it."

"Let's find you a stand, then."

When we found the kelewele stand, my stomach grumbled.

Cole bought me a bunch wrapped in newspaper, and I ate merrily. "This is so good."

As we shared it, our fingers were becoming sticky from the sweetness and the oil. All around us, there was hiplife music and kids doing traditional dances. Cole stopped me. "Can you do that?"

I explained they were doing an adowa, which is a dance by the Akans, one of the tribes in Ghana. But then I found my people, the Ga-Adangmes, doing a kpatsa dance on the other side. "Over there, those are my people."

He laughed. "Can you do any of those?"

"Yeah, I mean a little."

He took my hand. Many bystanders had started joining in the dances, trying to do them. Mostly obroni, because of course, the white folks couldn't help themselves the first time they heard real deep bass.

But even as Cole tugged my hand and joined in the dance and I watched him wind his waist and try and find the rhythm and get into it, I laughed. Real, genuine laughter that felt so good it seeped into my bones.

He was so carefree. He didn't seem to give a shit if I was laughing with him or at him. He was having fun. And I realized that was what I had always both admired and hated about him. He could make anything sound fun and inviting, and I wanted to be like that. I wished I could be. There was a part of me that longed to be like that. And he came by it so easily, while it was a source of contention for me.

At one point he looked over and grabbed me by the waist and twirled me around. "Having fun?"

I nodded with a laugh. "Yeah, thank you for this. It was exactly what I needed."

And by the way he was looking at me as we danced, our hips moving in time with the music together, his body pressed against mine, leaning in with his muscles and his scent, I wanted him to kiss me.

I wanted to ignore every single rule I had told myself I needed and be lost in the moment with him, lost in his kiss. I knew he would taste sweet like bofrot and kelewele, and that's how I would taste to him too. I wanted to matter to him as someone more than a friend.

He was looking at me like he might kiss me. Like if we stayed together like this any longer, it would happen. That fear was strong. Strong enough to back me up. So I planted my hands on his shoulders and stepped back, still dancing, but the spell was broken.

I had to watch myself, because if I wasn't careful, I was going to fall for him. Hard. And at some point soon, we would be adversaries again. Or worse, I was going to care about him for real. And I was going to be brokenhearted when he eventually chose someone else. Like Yofi did.

Because guys like Cole Drake didn't go out with girls like me. He'd already proven that once.

———

COLE

I'd almost kissed her . . . again.

The sweet ache of desire coursed through me, and I tamped it down. It had seemed like she wanted me to. But given the way she'd backed up from me, she knew I'd almost kissed her and was giving me *back off* signals, so I was going to respect those.

Something *was* happening here, and I was patient. I had nothing but time. After all, she'd almost married some dude.

You are so into her.

There was really no point denying it. I had never intended on saying anything today. Today she'd been truly happy.

We'd opted for the subway home. Traffic would have been gnarly coming back, and we needed some sleep.

After being crammed in the subway car for twenty minutes, we exited the station. I was walking close enough to her to take her hand. And more than once, our fingers brushed and all I wanted to do was slip her hand into mine and hold on to it. She was chatting animatedly about travel and her favorite places. Talking about how nothing felt quite the same as Accra or New York, which I imagined to be true because those were both home for her.

Her enthusiasm alone made me want to go to all these places. Not just go, but go *with* her. We had been to some of the same places and the same cities. Mostly, I'd kept it to Europe, Australia, and Japan. She'd gone to all the other places. You name it, chances were she'd been or wanted to go or was curious about it.

"Cole, is that you?"

I froze. For a moment I was unwilling to believe I recognized the voice calling me. "Shit."

Ofosua glanced up at me, a smile still playing on her lips. "What's the matter?"

"Nothing. Um, I just want to apologize in advance for anything she might say."

She glanced around. "Who?"

"My mom. That's her."

Ofosua's eyes went wide. "Oh, I should just—I can just walk home from here."

I glowered down at her. "I picked you up, and I'll take you home. That's how this works."

She opened her mouth and then closed it. And I could see her fighting a smile.

"Like I said, if she says something stupid, that's on her." *Except is it?*

"Cole, she's your mother. How bad can it be?"

I lifted my brows. My mother liked to pretend she was liberal and believed in all the good things she should. But she wore her biases on her sleeve. And Ofos shouldn't have to be exposed.

And what if you'd kissed her like you wanted to? What if it became something? Would you avoid your mother?

That was a question I didn't want to brood over just yet. I waved to my mom and placed my hand on Ofosua's lower back. When we jogged across the street, my mother's gaze was mostly on me but flickered occasionally to Ofosua.

"Cole, sweetheart, what are you doing here? I thought you only left Tribeca to come home."

I rolled my eyes. "If I want to see you, I do have to leave Tribeca. But other neighborhoods are good too. Glad to see you're testing out other parts of Manhattan."

She laughed. "Are you kidding? Tower Grand is the latest fusion spot. The chef has three Michelin stars. It's impossible to get in, but of course I was able to get a table. And who is this?"

The way she said it lacked her usual bite, so I was hopeful. "This is Ofosua Addo. She's a friend of mine. She works at Drake with me."

That was the safest way to introduce her, right? We *were* friends.

Ofosua stepped forward. "Mrs. Drake, it's a pleasure to meet you."

"Oh, lovely to meet you too. You work at Drake, you say? As what?"

"I'm an editor."

"Not just an editor. She's being modest. She has her own imprint."

My mother's brows lifted. "Good for you, dear. My brother-in-law is well-known for giving opportunities to, you know, *all* his employees." She dipped her chin as if they were in on a delicious little secret.

Ofosua's smile faltered the tiniest bit. I wondered if my mother caught that. "Well, Mr. Drake has been great, and I love the company."

My mother chuckled and whispered conspiratorially, "You know, dear, I voted for Obama. His energy was truly inspiring to me."

Ofosua's brows lifted. "Uhm, that's great to know."

"And naturally we were very happy to support his campaign."

I groaned. "Mom, is there a specific reason you're bringing up President Obama?"

She shook her head. "Well, I simply thought your *friend* would be interested to know that about our family."

I shook my head.

"Wait, sweetheart, something brilliant just occurred to me. As you know, I sit on the board for Women Empowering Women. Wonderful organization. But we've had a ghastly time of recruiting minority members. I wonder if I could pick your friend's brain to help me try and figure out why that might be. We could have lunch someplace marvelous. My treat, of course. I know how those assistant salaries can be." My mother smiled delightedly as she looked at Ofosua, sure of her reply.

Ofosua's brow furrowed. "I, ah, I d-d-don't . . . ," she stammered.

"Mom. Why don't we get back to you. It's a busy time right now at Drake. And Ofosua's not an assistant."

Ofosua touched my arm. "It's okay, Cole. I'll be happy to have a conversation. I don't really know anything about charity boards, though."

"But you know your people. We would *so* love to help the underprivileged. But every time we try and approach organizations, it never quite comes together in the end. Can you imagine how frustrating that is for us?"

Ofosua stiffened. "Um, ma'am—"

I stepped between them, hoping my body provided some cover. "Mom, enough. I'm going to get Ofosua home. And then, if she wants, I'll put you two in touch."

She frowned and then immediately brightened, because nothing could ever truly be wrong in my mother's world. "Thank you, Cole. It would certainly be a coup to have someone like Ofosua advising us, because we've been struggling for a while. Carolyn Melter will lose her mind when she finds out I actually have someone who can give us real direction as to what Black women need from groups like ours."

I shook my head. There weren't enough apologies. "Goodbye, Mom."

Ofosua gave her a small nod. "Goodbye, Mrs. Drake."

My mother beamed. "Since we're going to be such close friends, please call me Rebecca. I would love to mentor a young woman such as yourself on the finer parts of society, really build you up a network."

Fucking hell. "Enough, Mom. Ofos doesn't need your network. She has her own. She also doesn't need you to save her. She's not a project to be taken on to assuage your guilt for the shitty things you just said. And before you start, you know full well they were shitty. I suggest you look up the Doctors Addo. I'll send you a couple of articles. We're leaving."

I turned Ofos back toward her building and tugged her along. "Fuck, I'm so sorry for that."

She released a long sigh. "You're not the one who needs to apologize."

"Every time I introduce you to anyone, I just get more and more embarrassed."

"Like I said before, *you* are trying to be different. *You* checked her. That's a start. Most people would pretend that I was overreacting. Don't worry about your mom."

She was letting me off easy, and I understood why. It cut the awkwardness. And holy hell, having to fight a constant barrage of that daily, I could imagine sometimes she just wanted to crawl in on herself and take a break from people.

"Yeah, whether you blame me for her or not, I blame *her* for her. So I'm going to apologize anyway."

She took my hand and squeezed it, and a shiver went up my arm. "I already said don't worry about it. I know she wants help on her charity thing or whatever, and I can give you some pointers to give to her. Or point her toward all the society things that my mom is a part of with plenty of minority members."

"Or she can Google."

Ofosua shrugged. "True. But she won't. She's a product of her privilege. She hasn't seen anything else. I mean, it's a chain. Look, she's got that casual bias thing going where she votes for all the 'right' people and all the right policies, but she still harbors all these ideas that her skin and her money make her better than other people. That's all she's known. Sometimes people who mean well are almost the worst. I can't hold you responsible for her. That's not fair. But you can help educate her."

"So I will be her Google?"

"You are very cute for a search engine. Not like that Bing I've heard millennials moan about."

I stared down at her again, and for the second time today, I was desperate to kiss her. Instead, I behaved myself and squeezed her hand. "What do you say we get you home?"

She gave me a bright smile. And while I appreciated the effort, I could tell it was forced. I'd wanted to give her a perfect day, but somehow that day already had some tarnish on it.

CHAPTER 20

OFOSUA

ADINKRA SAYING:
(Denkyem) Adaptability and cleverness.
SAMUEL ADDO:
Spend less time listening to what you should do and more time listening to your instincts and you'll be fine.

Two weeks later and I was going to the wedding alone.

I could do this. I could. I wasn't scared. It was just a wedding. I'd done how many of these? God, hundreds now.

Ghanaians loved a party. Surrounding birth of a new baby, funerals, and getting married. The funniest thing was that people didn't really celebrate birthdays like that. That was a strictly Western kind of thing. So our birthdays were ignored as merely the ordinary passing of a year, with a small token celebration, but the big things got celebrated like nobody's business.

When I knocked on my parents' door, they weren't ready to leave on time, and my mother was pulling her usual shenanigans of "Eh, why are you people rushing me?" And because I didn't want everyone to see me being late, I headed off to the wedding venue on my own. I texted ahead to Kukua, telling her to meet me at the door so at least I wouldn't walk in by myself.

I felt good about the decision to attend Yofi's wedding alone, and Cole was a large part of that. Bolstered by an outfit that was so shockingly expensive, it was a status symbol more than fashion, I felt strong and powerful. Well, at least that's what I told myself.

All day I'd been feeling that prelude to a racing heartbeat. But I had been practicing my breathing, following all the things I knew would lower my stress and my anxiety. My phone buzzed.

COLE:

You're going to do great.

I typed back a quick response.

OFOSUA:

Thanks. I got this. No big deal. Attending my ex's wedding, by myself.

He sent back a crazy face emoji and it made me laugh. I tucked my phone back into my bag and sat back against the seat in the car. I could do this. The one thing I had learned over the last nine months was that I could survive anything. And that I had to learn to embrace the unexpected, because if I hadn't, I would not have an imprint. Cole and I wouldn't be friends now. We wouldn't be working together. I wouldn't have this warm, gushy feeling every time I thought about him. Or my own imprint.

When the car pulled up to the church, I inhaled deeply. What was the worst that could happen?

I stepped out, knowing I looked like a million dollars. Today

I'd chosen vermilion red. My favorite color. No matter what, I would stand out in this sea of white. For weddings and all sorts of celebrations, everybody liked to wear white lace. Not the Western kind of lace, but a larger, broader, sturdier pattern of lace.

Beyond the expected white, there was a sea of periwinkle, black, and ivory. Mainly in the decorations, balloons, ribbons, and the lettering on the programs. And of course the family and wedding party had dressed to impress in the same colors. Some with custom dyes and traditional cloth. Periwinkle. Black. Ivory. Those were the *exact* same colors I had chosen for my white wedding to Yofi. This Pamela woman had taken my entire wedding design—groom included—for her own. I knew her only a little, but I was surprised she didn't want to plan her own wedding. But congratulations to her: she'd gotten a bargain on wedding planning.

Kukua stood at the top of the stairs, grinning like an idiot as I marched up toward her, loving the way my vermilion-red Giambattista Valli high-low skirt flowed in the back. It only came to mid-thigh in the front, fluttering a little with every step and showing off my mile-long legs. The bodice of my Christie Brown corset was fitted tight, the sleeves poofed out at the shoulders, and tiny adinkra symbols adorned it. Kukua gave me a slow clap as I approached.

"Oh my God. You are a vision. Is that Valli I see?"

"Good eye. The top is one of ours. Christie Brown. The skirt is off the Valli runway, and the shoes are Blahniks, as you do." The bodice had embroidery on it with some balls stamped all over it in a shade that was one off from the vermilion. So you had to get up very close to notice each of the adinkra symbols.

Kukua took my hand and we started to march into the back of the church. But as we approached, I could feel that familiar feeling beginning to take hold as the bottom fell out of my stomach. "Um, you go on in, pick a seat in the back, and I'll join you in a minute."

"Hey, you're doing great. Look at me."

My stomach roiled. "I need a minute."

All around us, guests stepped in, eager to find a seat right away. There were a few curious glances at me. Some whispers. I really didn't want to be here. Why was I doing this to myself? For what purpose, to save face? Prove something to Yofi? Prove I'd survived the humiliation?

"Do you want to get out of here?"

I frowned at her. "I can't run."

"Sure you can. We turn right back around and hightail our asses out. Valli and Blahniks and all."

I shook my head. "No, I'm not going to run."

"Hey, I don't think you know what you look like. You look ill. Really, really ill."

"I feel fine. I just need a minute."

"Okay, come on, why don't we use the bathroom? You can freak out in there."

I laughed as I let her pull me into the bathroom. "What would I do without you?"

"Good thing for you, you'll never have to find out. Now tell me what's happening."

"I don't know. I saw the aisle, and I imagined seeing Yofi walking down it, and I sort of felt like my world was tilting a little, I guess." The more I spoke words to it, the more I could own *all* the feelings. "It feels like everything is spinning and spinning, and I can't get off this ride, and I want everything to stop for a minute."

"That's how it goes sometimes. You're going to be okay. You're amazing. I couldn't do this."

I stared at my cousin as I eased onto the settee in the bathroom. "That might make two of us. But let me just catch my breath."

Suddenly, the tight rein of control I'd been using to hold my emotions in all day snapped, and the dam finally broke. "I don't think I *can* do this. I can't. I absolutely cannot. I'm sorry."

I *was* sorry. I shouldn't have come here on my own, ruining my cousin's night.

She put a soft hand down to the intricate braids on my head that led into an Afro. It was a style similar to the one I'd worn for my traditional wedding. "When are you going to learn? You have nothing to be sorry about. Emotions are normal and good. No one expects you to be perfect all the time. You're allowed to have a bad day. And just so you know, I bet you anything he'd come."

"Who?" As if I didn't know.

"You know who," she said gently.

"No, please don't text Cole."

She already had my phone in her hand. "Yeah, well, it's too late. I've already texted him. And something tells me he cares that you need him, and he's going to come running. *That's* the kind of man you need in your life. Are you finally going to accept some help?"

I could feel my heart racing. It was either run or go out there and face the music. And facing the music alone, despite what I told my mother, was not an option.

"Okay. I need someone. Maybe him."

CHAPTER 21

OFOSUA

ADINKRA SAYING:
(Akoma Ntoso) Understanding, agreement.
HELEN ADDO:
There is only one rule when dealing with your ex.
Make sure you have somebody on your arm.

I was still hiding out in the bathroom when there was a knock. I glanced at my watch. There were only fifteen minutes left until the wedding. If I didn't hurry up and get it together, I'd be that person sneaking in the back of the church. Then *everyone* would notice.

My heart was still doing that gallop that made me unsure I wouldn't faint if I tried walking.

Kukua left me on the settee, and I tried to clutch her hand. "No, don't open it. Let them go to another one."

"Relax, I'll be right back."

When she opened the door, she sighed. "Ah, there you are. I was starting to worry."

"I said I'd be here." The deep voice, which reminded me of smoked whiskey, relaxed me. In walked Cole in all his tuxedoed splendor.

He smiled at me. "You know, this would have been a lot easier if you'd just asked me to be your date like I suggested. I could have picked you up in a nice car, but now I'm picking you up from a bathroom. I mean, it's a stunning bathroom, but still."

I laughed. He always knew how to distract me. Exactly what to say to calm me down. Even as I thought it, my heart rate was slowing and my stomach was settling.

Kukua lifted a brow. "Now can we go inside so I can enjoy watching everyone see you look this fly with your date on your arm?"

Cole held out his hand. "I'm here for you, whatever you need. We can go in and I can make every man in the room jealous of my date. If you want to sneak out of here, I can make the rest of the city jealous instead. I think I win either way."

I laughed through a sniffle. "We're not sneaking out of here. I spent hours getting ready."

"And you look fantastic." His voice dropped an octave. "Good enough to eat. So let's go show you off."

I could stay in there and cry, and he would hold my hand. I could tell him that I wanted to go, and he would take me home. And whichever choice I made, he'd tell me it was exactly right.

I lifted my chin and met his gaze. His gray stare was steady. Unwavering. "What do you say?"

When I took his hand, it was firm and warm and sent tingles up my arm as he laced his fingers with mine. "Now, I'm going to need you to forgive me if I embarrass you on the dance floor."

I laughed. "We don't have to dance. It's fine."

"I'm looking forward to it. I've been practicing since before I even got the call. You know, in case I got the chance to have you put me in, Coach."

I laughed. "When have you ever *not* been put into a game?"

He chuckled. "That's a very good point. I'm an excellent athlete. Basketball, actually."

I blinked owlishly at him. "They let white boys play basketball?"

"Sometimes. Let's go have some fun."

And with that, he led me out of the bathroom. We followed Kukua down the marble corridor with the priceless paintings on the walls. Part of me wanted to stop and gaze at them. It didn't even faze me now that this was supposed to be *my* wedding venue. That *I* was supposed to be the one getting married. I felt no sadness. No envy. Nothing, really.

At the entrance to the nave, Cole squeezed my hand. "Are you sure about this?"

I nodded. "Yeah. And Cole?" He leaned into me. To any observer, it just looked like we were having a quiet, intimate conversation. "Thank you."

"Anytime."

We walked in and took our seats next to Kukua. At first, no one seemed to notice. And then a low murmur started to spread through the church. I noticed one or two people casually pass a look and then a quick secondary glance over at Cole.

The whole time, Cole held my hand. His thumb stroked over my fingers, and he sat there as if not noticing that we were on display, the objects of scrutiny and gossip.

It was my mother's reaction that took the cake.

Of course she arrived just a hair before the bride did. Kukua had to wave her and my father down. When they joined us, my mother gave me a cursory glance and I stiffened, ready for the criticism.

"Eh, you look good. You tried for once."

Not exactly a compliment. Nonetheless, I breathed a sigh of relief, the tension started to roll out of my shoulders, and then she said loudly enough for the people in the front pew to hear, "Eh, but who is this? You look familiar."

I gave her a tight smile and whispered. "Mum, this is Cole Drake. You met him some time ago at the hospital. Cole, this is my mother, Helen Addo."

Cole smiled and reached over me to shake her hand. "Dr. Addo, Dr. Addo, it's a pleasure to meet you."

He shook my father's hand, and my father stared at him as if ascertaining what to do with the white man holding his daughter's hand so blatantly. But when I started to shake off Cole's hand, he only held on tighter.

My mother blinked, took his hand, and then stared at me as if to ask, *What the fuck?* But I wasn't dealing with her questions right now. Besides, he wasn't the only white guy in the church. Right now, I was focused on keeping my head held high while someone else had my wedding.

I couldn't let one single crack show, or everyone would talk and exaggerate.

I heard the familiar notes of "Ave Maria" and bit the inside of my mouth. *Really? My* song *too?*

Cole noticed the tension in my hand, and so his thumb started working overtime. Soothe, soothe, stroke.

I knew my mother was fuming. She wanted to know all the details. She wanted to ask me all the questions. But she was going to have to wait.

The ceremony was mostly painless, but it was surreal. The one thing that wasn't mine from the ceremony was the vows. At least I hadn't left those notes around anywhere.

The bride, Pamela, looked so young. She also looked happy. But somehow, Yofi looked bored, like always.

Like he didn't want to be there. That was not the face of a man in love.

That got my attention.

Maybe this was all his parents' doing, a *you can't humiliate us* scenario. I hoped he finally got what he wanted, because as I sat there watching him marry another woman, I realized what I had wanted was the wedding, not the man.

And then all I felt was sweet relief.

Throughout the rest of the ceremony, while rings were exchanged and the attendees were diverted to the plaza for the reception, Cole was right by my side. And then when he saw the layout for dinner, he grinned. "Oh, I cannot wait to eat everything in sight." I watched him as he clapped his hands gleefully.

He and my father had found something to discuss. Cole actually liked to watch football, as the rest of the world knew it. He and my dad chatted about teams while my mother scowled at them both.

Kukua leaned into me. "If you don't fuck that white boy tonight, I will have to take one for the team. Jesus, he's amazing."

"Seriously?"

"Yes. Don't you see how he's looking at you? Like you put a hurt on him and he doesn't know how he got here, but he never wants to leave."

I snorted a laugh. "Stop."

"I'm serious, cuz. He's giving you the heart eyes."

I slid my glance back to Cole. He was having fun, or at least looked like it. None of this intimidated him. Not the whispers or the stares, none of it.

He had no shame. He could get out there in the middle of the dance floor among three hundred people he didn't know and hang. Even Kukua was tired from dancing with him, and she was *never* tired. When it came time to bust out the handkerchief and really cut loose, she hung with him as long as she could, but then she was exhausted.

At one point she even came to me and said, "Please come and take your obroni boyfriend. He's making us all look bad. What he lacks in rhythm, he makes up for in *enthusiasm*. I beg you, go and collect him."

He was having a plain old good time. And maybe it was time I followed suit.

How was Cole Drake, of all people, the perfect date?

I took him out on the balcony for a rest. His smile was impish and childlike. "Are you having fun?"

"I am, actually. And you look like you're having fun too."

"Well, when in Rome, let your hair down." He started winding his hips again, and I giggled. Halfway through dinner, it was clear people were more interested in my date than me. Which was a blessing if I was honest. Anyone who did stop by to speak was instantly charmed. It was so easy for him.

He's doing it for you.

"You're smiling at me. Does that mean you're not down in the dumps about your ex getting married so soon and using your wedding blueprint?"

I even smiled at that. "You know, thinking about it, all of this wouldn't have made me happy. Not in the long run. Yes, it's what my parents wanted. It's what his parents wanted. It was the expectation. But if you're asking me if I feel the pang of loss of him getting married today . . ." I shook my head and then glanced out at the city lights before us. "At first, I thought maybe I was numb from the shock, but I don't actually feel *disappointed*. I feel embarrassed, yes. But sad? No."

"I'm glad to hear it." He laughed and added, "Did you see how he almost forgot her name, though? Like he had to work really hard not to say your name?"

I brought my hands up to my face, covering my cheeks. "Oh my God, I had such secondhand embarrassment for both of them."

Cole laughed. "That's what he gets for hurting my Ofosua."

"Oh, I'm *your* Ofosua now, am I?" I asked with a raised brow.

He licked his bottom lip. "Well, it seems I've been thinking of you that way for a while now."

My heart raced and my breathing went shallower as I asked, "Did you ever plan on telling me?"

He rubbed a hand along the back of his neck. "I wanted to give you space in case you were still hung up on him."

I didn't know what to say. He was right. He could feel it the same way that I could. It was one thing for us to laugh, and joke, and tease at other times. But now, now it felt real.

His gaze met mine. "You are on my mind all the time. It's complicated, obviously. And this is probably a really bad idea, but I don't give a shit. From the moment I saw you, you have been plaguing my mind, and I can't walk away. I can't pretend that I don't feel this anymore."

I swallowed hard. "Cole."

"I never hated you, Ofosua. That first day when we met, I was stunned stupid. Like an idiot, I couldn't talk."

I held my breath.

Just tell him. But I couldn't.

He started to pace. "You were so put together and collected. Even my uncle spoke about you like you walked on water or some shit, and there you were, seriously the most stunning creature

I'd ever seen in my life, and I couldn't find the words. Your face was delightful and open, and you were on the verge of a smile. And then I waited too long to say something as simple as 'hello' and made you feel . . . I don't know how I made you feel, but it couldn't have been good, because you never looked at me the same way again. And I did that, so I own it. But I wanted you to know why. You have been on my mind since that moment."

I watched him. "Why didn't you say something before?"

"Well, we work together, for one. But mostly, I figured I blew it."

He stepped closer and I backed up against the stone balcony. "Not quite."

Our breath comingled. All I could do was breathe in his scent. He smelled like mint and sin and bad decisions. Except those wouldn't *really* be bad decisions. Scary ones, yes. Because whatever this was, it wasn't casual.

"I come with a mess, Cole."

"I see your mess, and I'll raise you an even bigger mess that you will hopefully never see."

And in that moment, I made my choice. I didn't give a damn about consequences. For once, I was going to do something Ofosua Addo never did: make the same mistake twice.

"Hey, Cole."

"Yes, Ofosua?"

"Will you hurry up and kiss me already?"

A slow smile spread over his lips. "Bossy."

I grinned at him. "Assertive."

He chuckled then, his hands wrapped around my waist. "I like assertive." And then his lips were on mine.

A slow slide like that moment where you hold your breath before you sink into the kiss and relax, inhaling the other person.

I wanted to hold on to this one moment forever. Because as I already knew, Cole Drake could *kiss*.

His tongue slid around mine in a dance that we'd already been dancing for weeks now. My hands slid up his chest and into his hair, and Cole angled his head. His moan was throaty as his hands gripped me tighter and slid around my waist and over my ass.

In the twilight of New York City, Cole Drake kissed me like I was the breath he'd been searching for, and I kissed him back like he was the answer I'd been looking for.

Cole broke the kiss and dropped his forehead to mine, his eyes mournful. "I've kissed you before, haven't I?"

He knew.

I lifted my gaze to meet his. My voice was a hoarse whisper. "Yes. We met once when I was an intern at a party your uncle had for one of the authors, at his penthouse." There, I'd said it.

"Fuck."

"It was my first book party. The Jason Moyner launch. The balcony of your uncle's penthouse." My hands shook as I recounted the story of him erasing me. Humiliation seeping through my pores. It was so dumb that it still mattered so much to me.

"Fuuuuck." I could see as the memory fully dawned. His wide eyes, the way his hands rubbed over his face. "Ofosua. I'm so, so sorry." He licked his lips and started talking fast. "God, I'm such a fuckup. Now I know why you hated me. *I* hate me. You know that even bigger mess I mentioned a few minutes ago? The one I said you'd hopefully never see? You already saw it. That night at the party. My dad was lurking outside of my aunt and uncle's building, waiting for me to arrive. We had a hell of an argument. He asked me to intervene with my aunt to unlock the remainder of his trust fund, like I could even do that. When I said no, the fucker took a swing at me and said that I was no longer his son.

Which gutted me. I know it's hard to believe, but my dad and I were a team growing up, two fun guys against the world. Until we weren't. When I went upstairs to the party, I started drinking immediately. The champagne I shared with you was not the beginning of my, ah, binge. Or the end. I spent the rest of the night with Tallon, drinking even more to cover up the stink of my father's rejection. I don't remember most of that night. Just the argument with my dad and then dim bits and pieces. Turns out the fastest way to a wake-up call is to employ the same coping mechanisms as your fucked-up parents. It's why I rarely drink now, and if I'm drinking it's just a beer. As in, one. I'm afraid I'll turn out just like them. That night was proof I'm not wrong to be afraid. I don't know if you've heard the term 'blackout drunk,' but that's what I was that night. It's super embarrassing and it's the truth. It's also not who I want to be."

I stared at him. *Was* he telling the truth? He hadn't been drinking anything but seltzer at the wedding just now. And I'd only ever seen him clutch a beer at happy hour. But never actually drink that beer, now that I thought about it.

Deep down I wanted to believe him. It was his eyes. There was real fear and worry in them. He desperately wanted me to believe him. "God, that really happened, didn't it? That's why I never heard from you."

"Tallon will tell you."

I had held on to that balcony scene for years, thinking Cole had forgotten me. "That's horrible. I thought . . ." I let my voice trail. The tears pricked my eyes, and I blinked rapidly.

"I—I thought I dreamed you. When I met you again and started having these vivid dreams about how you tasted . . . it was disconcerting. I'm sorry, Ofos." He reached for my hand. "Please. Can you ever forgive me?"

I knew what it would mean if I took it. The threshold I would be crossing, what we would mean to each other. And it wasn't even a choice.

I slipped my hand into his and let him pull me inside onto the dance floor.

CHAPTER 22

OFOSUA

ADINKRA SAYING:
(Mpatapo) Peacemaking, reconciliation.

SAMUEL ADDO:
There is nothing more special than finding love again.

On my doorstep, Cole's thumb rubbed over my knuckles. "You made an absolutely stunning date. Thank you for letting me escort you."

"Flattery looks good on you, Mr. Drake."

His grin was all mischief when he said, "It's so sexy when you call me Mr. Drake."

"Cole—"

"I'm available for outdoorings too. I love the idea of a baby naming day. I like kids. Although I don't know exactly what I'm supposed to do at one of —"

"Cole—"

"What?"

"You talk too much," I whispered as I looped my arms around his neck, stood on tiptoe, and kissed him.

The contact was a soft brush of our lips. Barely a kiss. The next brush of our lips was a tease. Then Cole made this low growly sound and snapped his arms around me, caging me in and deepening the kiss.

I couldn't help but gasp and part my lips as a shudder ran through me, and Cole dragged me closer. His tongue slid over mine.

When I threaded my hands through his hair, he growled low before sucking on my bottom lip, making me moan and meet his tongue with mine. It didn't take long for the cyclone of need and lust and pent-up emotion from the last month—hell, *years*—to spill over.

Quickly, our kisses became a desperate attempt to fuse ourselves together as Cole backed me up against my door, bracketing me with his big body.

Cole scooped his hand down my back and made contact with my ass, drawing me closer to him, bending his knees slightly and angling me just how he wanted, and eventually picking me up.

With our bodies melded together, there was no mistaking the hard ridge of his erection, which throbbed against my abdomen. As it turned out, Cole was carrying around a cannon in his tuxedo trousers.

Dropping his forehead to mine, he ran a hand up my bodice. I drew in a shuddering breath and arched my back into him, waiting for him to touch me where I'd been imagining him touching me for weeks.

Gently, his thumbs traced where the material met flesh. The stinging ache was almost too much to bear. I pulled him closer, but he was hell-bent on torturing me with his fingers.

"Better than any fantasy," he whispered.

"Cole."

When he traced his thumb over my nipple, my grip tightened in his hair as I rocked my hips.

"We need to go inside now. We've put on a hell of a show, but I plan on spending the majority of my time licking every inch of you, which calls for privacy."

Heat snaked down my spine, making my skin tight and itchy. I fumbled with my keys to unlock the door, but Cole took them from me and still managed the door without breaking our kiss.

I pointed the way to my bedroom and delighted in his kisses as his fingers dug into my ass while he carried me in the general direction.

In my room, he set me down gently before turning me around. My breath came out in ragged pants.

The zippers for the two-piece outfit were a cinch for him, and the tight bodice and skirt fell away from my body, leaving me in my strapless bra and thong. When I turned slowly to face him, his eyes were dark and heavy-lidded. "Absolutely incredible," he whispered before reaching for me again.

He slid a hand into my Afro, his kiss reverent as he licked into my mouth, coaxing me into sin. In an effort to get closer, I clung to him, and his cock jerked against my stomach. I gave an automatic rotation of my hips in response.

I was teetering on a cliff's edge, and he knew it. He slid a hand between my legs, searching for my center, his fingers playing with the edge of my panties.

"Cole," I moaned.

When he shoved the flimsy scrap of material to the side and dipped a finger into my slick heat, my knees gave way. His muttered curse against my neck was part epithet and part exultation. Desperate, clawing need threatened to tear me apart. I bucked as he withdrew his finger then slowly slid in again, this time with a second finger. He buried his lips in my neck, kissing me. "You feel so fucking good, Ofos."

I couldn't string any kind of coherent phrase together. Even as I dug my nails into his shoulders and whimpered, he took his time. Never mind that I was on the verge of spontaneously combusting. He kept up the slow, lazy retreat and entry. I started to quiver, my sex pulsing around his fingers as he slowly pulled out.

He lifted his head and met my gaze with an intense one of his own. Then, with his free hand, he wound his fingers around the edge of my panties and gave a sharp tug.

The tear could be heard over our ragged breathing.

My eyes flew open. "Hey!"

"Sorry. I'll buy you a dozen new pairs."

"Cole, oh my God."

"Look at me." I wasn't even aware my eyes had drifted shut, but opening them was a distinct effort as all I wanted to do was sink into bliss. "Do you have any idea how much I've wanted this? How many times I've *dreamed* of this?"

I bit my bottom lip but didn't break eye contact. I watched with rapt attention as he dragged his teeth over his bottom lip, fighting for control. The knowledge that I was making him crazy was so heady, and I wanted more of it. When he slid his thumb over my clit, molten lava coursed through my whole body.

He was going to be the death of me.

With a smirk, he brushed away one of the intricate braids that had fallen free of my style. "On the bed. I want to take that bra off with my teeth."

As I scooted backward on the bed, Cole made quick work of his tux, toeing off his shoes as he quickly stripped. When he was down to just his boxer briefs he tossed a strip of condoms on my nightstand, and I licked my lips in anticipation. "Hurry."

"Are you always this impatient?" he teased. Then he hooked his thumbs in his waistband and tugged his boxer briefs down.

I ogled him openly. "Wow, you are . . . wow. 'Cocky' has a whole other meaning now."

His chuckle was soft. "I'm glad you like what you see."

His hands traversed a path from my ass to my waist to my breasts, never quite reaching the tips. I moaned and rocked against him trying to get him closer, urging him to take my breasts in his hands.

He took the hint and hitched me higher. Dipping his head, he grazed first one nipple, then the other, with his five-o'clock shadow. He followed up with his tongue and with playful tugs with his teeth. Each tug had me pulling him closer.

The tip of his cock nudged my slick folds, and my eyes fluttered closed. I made one small rotation of my hips, and for the barest moment we were skin to skin and it felt divine.

Cole cursed under his breath, but found the strength to reach for a condom on the nightstand. Sheathing himself quickly, he rolled back between my thighs. With his hand wrapped around the base of his cock he teased my entrance, nice and slow. When I whimpered, his gaze lifted to mine as he employed tilting motions of his hips and slid in to the hilt. When I threw my head back, he muttered, "Holy shit," as he seated himself.

All I could manage were whimpering moans as he wrapped a hand in my hair and tugged backward, forcing my back to arch. He took that opportunity to graze my nipple with his teeth, all the while working on that deep, soul-bending grind. With every deep stroke, my eyes rolled into the back of my head as that sensation of bone-deep bliss danced within reach.

"Cole, I—"

Reaching between us, he stroked my clit with his thumb in slow circles, even as he picked up the pace, his body coated in sweat. "Ofos, God, you feel so good."

My body clamped down tighter around his thick length as he drove me higher and higher. With a shuddering breath, my legs tightened around him, and my fingers twined into his hair, pulling him close as we fought for control.

But it was too late for me. I was only putting off the inevitable. My gaze locked on his, I whispered his name, and my body clamped tight around his just before breaking apart in his arms.

It seemed that was what he'd been waiting for, because he picked up his pace. His hands pushed open my legs, giving him a clear view of what was happening. With his thumb, he stroked my clit, his concentration pinpointed on only me as the freight train of my orgasm threatened again.

"Fuck me." His growling shout had him dropping forward, his body more determined than ever to bring me over the edge with him.

When he buried his face in my neck even as he drove home over and over again, he used his teeth until he finally let go, making me his. With one more hip swivel, he ground his hips right where I needed, and I fractured yet again.

All around me, he quaked from the force of his release.

—

COLE

I woke to the scent of coconut and hibiscus on the soft satin pillow and a warm, curvy female beside me. With a moan, I snuggled in further.

Ofosua.

I relaxed then, enjoying the feel of her curves pressed up against my bare skin. She was so damn beautiful. And she smelled good.

When she'd texted last night, it hadn't even been a question of if I'd come for her.

You have it bad.

Last night had been . . . I was exhausted. I had no idea what time we'd actually gone to bed, but I didn't want to wake up. If I could just live in this space, I could be happy forever.

How are you going to figure out the work thing?

Goddamn it. I didn't need rational thought intruding right now. Ofosua snuggled back. I rolled my thumb over her nipple, and she gasped. "Oh God, Cole."

When I spoke, my voice was rumbly. "Good morning, beautiful."

"Jesus, you can go again?"

"If you don't want me to be quite so eager, then stop being so sexy."

She stretched and then rolled into me, and I loved every little movement, the curve of her back, the way her tits sat up and paid attention as she arched. The way her smooth thigh lifted over mine.

"I don't know if I'm going to be able to let you out of bed ever again."

Her eyes lowered for a moment before she lifted those dark pools to meet mine. "I don't know how to do this."

I grinned down at her. "You're severely underselling yourself, because I'm pretty sure you tried to kill me several times last night. God. And that thing that you can do with your tongue, that was . . . wow. I'm having a hard time thinking about anything other than your tits brushing against my chest right now. I really want to take one into my mouth."

She bit her bottom lip and her hips rocked ever so slightly into mine. "Cole, I'm being serious."

I dropped my voice an octave. "So am I. Maybe one more

time, before we have to get up and find food. Or you know what, food is overrated. Twice more. Twice and we can get up. Do you want to hit up that breakfast spot on the corner?"

Her gaze met mine. "You want to go to breakfast?"

I watched her carefully. "You thought that I was Mr. Hit It and Quit It?"

She wrinkled her nose. "That doesn't even sound right coming out of your mouth."

I laughed. "No, it doesn't. And in case you missed it, I'm into you. Like *really* into you. I actually *like* you, Ofosua. So yes, I want to have breakfast. Well, if I'm looking at the time right, it's nine forty-five. By the time I get home and change, and—well, let's be frank—by the time we get out of the shower, it's going to be eleven, so we're going to make it brunch."

She laughed. "Yeah, probably brunch. And PS, you *are* very insistent against my thigh." It was my turn to roll my hips, and she laughed. "Cole, time to be serious here."

I pulled her closer, and the tip of my head was notched against her slick entrance. "Now, I need you to explain to me what the fuck we're going to do about condoms because we don't have any more. We can play. There's a lot of playing to be done. We have a million places to christen now. Like my place. Probably the office too."

Her jaw unhinged. "We are not having sex at the office!"

I laughed. "Are you sure?"

"Yes, I'm *sure*. I'm a *professional*, Cole. Besides, sure, you'll get spared from the gossip, but me, I'd lose my job and any shred of respect I've earned."

I frowned. "You wouldn't lose your job."

She lifted a brow and I realized I'd done that thing again where my privilege was massively on display. I winced. "Sorry, you're right. Generally, not a good look. Okay, no condoms at the office, then. I will keep some in my wallet, though, you know, in case we make an outside-the-office excursion." I grinned cheekily at her.

"Oh my God, are we negotiating the terms of where we're going to screw now?"

I didn't like the way she said that. "Hey, we're not *screwing*. We're making sweet, sweet love." I winked at her, and she giggled.

Even though that feeling, that niggling voice at the back of my head told me that to her, this was temporary.

"Okay, let's go. You need to get clothes, and I want to see your place."

I smiled down at her. "Excellent. Come on. You will love Tribeca. There are some great cafés near my place too. And if you want, we can call Tallon and maybe meet his new girlfriend, Carmen."

"Oh, so I'm meeting girlfriends of friends now?"

I nodded. "Yes, you are."

She reached down and wrapped her soft fingers around me, and I coughed. "Oh, fuck. Fuck. Fuck. Fuck."

"Do you need a hand with this? I think maybe in the shower we could do something with him."

"Jesus, you're going to kill me."

"Well, in that case, let me—" A loud clattering noise came from the kitchen.

"What have you people done with the big pan?" came Helen Addo's voice.

I held my breath. "Is that your—"

Ofosua sprang out of bed so fast it made everything bounce. I could only appreciate the view for a quick second before she threw my clothes at me. "You have to go."

"What? We were going to go and have breakfast."

She pointed at the door. "My *mother* is here, and she's going to make both of our lives a living hell. So you have to go, right now!"

"Where? Where am I going to go?"

"I'll sneak you out."

I had to laugh as I stalked over and wrapped my arms around her. "Hey, you're freaking out. I get it. You freak out. I'll be calm for the both of us. I will get my clothes and I will get out of here, and then I'll text you when I'm ready to go, and you can meet me somewhere. How's that?"

She relaxed against me as she nodded. My dick, well, he couldn't be controlled. It wasn't his fault. Her ass was pressed up against me, and he pulsed.

She moaned and dropped her head forward as I continued to kiss at her neck.

"See, Ofosua, you moaning and rubbing your ass against me makes me think you don't *want* me to go."

"I don't. I mean, I do. I don't. But I do. You have to go." She chuckled a little.

"All right, all right, I'm going. But he's going to want a proper reintroduction when I see you."

"Okay, go."

I tossed my clothes on quickly, leaving the jacket slung over my shoulder. "Where am I going?"

She glanced at the window, and I shook my head. "If you want to use my dick again, me dying is going to seriously hinder your plans."

"No, there's a fire escape."

I lifted my brows. "A fire escape?"

Her brow furrowed. "My mother is in the kitchen. Your options are out the window or down the hall."

I eyed the window dubiously. "Down the hall."

She nodded. "Let me put some underwear on."

I shook my head. "No. If you're going to sneak me out of here, I want to know that you're at least naked under your robe."

She rolled her eyes at me. "Fine, this way."

"One more thing, this is the last time I sneak out. You're going to have to find a way to deal with that."

CHAPTER 23

COLE

ADINKRA SAYING:
(Nea Onnim No Sua A, Ohu) Lifelong knowledge.

HELEN ADDO:
When dealing with men, don't repeat your mistakes.

I knew the rules.

We would not take any of this into the office.

None of it. Except as we were squished into the back of the elevator with the usual morning crowd heading to work on Monday morning, I couldn't help but latch my pinky with hers.

I was acting like a lovesick puppy. I knew it. But, fuck, I was having a good time. I couldn't help it.

I had never been like this with anyone about anything.

When was the last time you cared about someone?

I couldn't remember.

I'd never been friends with a woman first before. I already knew my favorite smile of hers. What made her laugh. What made her sad. What irritated her.

And the more surprising part was I felt like she could see clear into my soul. And it didn't terrify me.

What happens when everyone finds out?

I frowned at the thought and tried to banish it. We'd be fine. No one would find out. *Are you sure?*

Even if they did, she wasn't a direct report. We would be fine.

You *will be fine. But what about her? What will people say? How will it affect her?*

A sense of dread prickled my gut. She'd kept me at arm's length for a long time. Was this the reason?

After more people stepped out of the elevator, she unhooked her pinky from mine and gripped tightly onto the rail. I could see how she slipped her work mask back on.

Gone was the soft, sweet Ofos. Now she was in badass mode.

When we hit the fourteenth floor, one other person got out. Two others stayed as they were going up higher. I nodded to one of the guys I knew from finance. I also noted the way his eyes chased over Ofosua's ass as she walked by both of us.

I scowled at him, and he shrugged as if asking what my problem was.

I needed to cool it. Ofosua was concerned about the fallout from anyone finding out about us. So tamping down the possessiveness was a good idea.

I followed Ofosua down the hall. "Lunch later?"

She turned over her shoulder, the mustard-yellow pants she'd worn today hugging her hips the way I liked. She'd paired them with a graphic tee that had some kind of unicorn on it. A long Neil Lane diamond chain hung between her breasts, and I wanted to see her wearing nothing but that chain.

"Maybe. There is a lot to do, and some idiot chained me with a legacy author, Evan Miles."

I grinned, leaning in close to catch a hint of her YSL perfume.

"Who did that to you? You should punish them immediately. I have some ideas on just how to do that."

She smiled. "I am sure you do, but it'll have to wait."

This was going to be harder than I thought. I wanted to see her. I wanted to be with her. I basically wanted to spend all of my lunch hours holed up in some dark corner of a restaurant where I could stick my hand up her skirt if she was wearing one.

She grinned and winked at me as I followed her along the same path, possibly too close. Her perfume drew me in like a beacon, and I almost took another sniff when Jess Langley, one of the associate editors for crime fiction, barreled out of her office.

She stopped short when she saw Ofos. "Hey, girl!"

Ofosua's step faltered. "Hi, Jess."

Jess reached up for her hair and smoothed a finger over one springing curl. "Oh my God, I love what you're doing with this. What is that, a braid-out situation?"

And then I watched in horror as Jess put her fingers through Ofosua's curls, tugging softly. Ofosua stepped out of the way to escape most of the brunt of it, her jaw tight as she muttered, "Gotta run, Jess."

What the fuck had I just watched? Had she really reached out and touched Ofosua like that? When Ofosua went to her office, I followed. Her brows lifted in surprise. "What's up? What's wrong?"

"What the hell happened with Jess?"

She shrugged. "She's trying to be extra sister-girl and down since I got the imprint. Just the usual bullshit. Why?"

I blinked at her incredulously. "She stuck her hands in your *hair*."

She sighed. "Notice how I tried to duck and weave out of the way? Jess has a problem. I've asked her not to touch me, but she still can't seem to help herself and her commentary all the time. 'Oh my God, I love your curls. I can't make my hair do this. God, I love the Afro texture,'" Ofosua mimicked.

"That's bullshit. She put her hands on you."

She sighed and slowly blinked at me as if preparing for a lecture. "Yes, Cole, it's called a microaggression. I'm pretty used to them happening all day, every day. She's done this before."

Why was she so calm? "Are you fucking serious? Why would you put up with that?"

She blinked at me slowly. "Put up with that? Tell me something. You remember how Nazrin called me aggressive for simply voicing my opinion? Every time I bring up that we need diversity in the workplace, everyone nods along, but in the end, they are resistant. Half the people here think I got my promotion by banging your uncle. How do you think it will be perceived if I properly tell off Jess? Really let her know?"

"Surely, you can go to human resources. Or—"

"You're not *listening*, Cole. Who says I haven't already? But there is no way to anonymously lodge a complaint. I'm the only Black woman here. Then I become the angry one again, putting an even tighter strain on me. And for fuck's sake, some days I'm just exhausted from having to deal, so for survival's sake, I duck and avoid so that I can get on with my day. Some days I fight, but all I can do is put it in my little notebook, for if I ever need it, and move on. We talk about inclusion and respect here, but it's a joke. I stay because this is my dream job. And if I can effect change one book at a time, I'll do that. I can put up with the Jesses of the world for *that*."

The flame of shame hit my body at once. Had I really been that fucking blind? "But she touched you. In the *workplace*. Like it was normal." I understood what she was saying, but I was having a hard time letting it go.

Ofos eased herself into her chair. "Before you and I started talking, how often did you see microaggressions?"

I swallowed hard. "I guess I wasn't looking."

"You're programmed not to. And everything in the world is set up for you. I will always have to put up with shit you will never see. And while I appreciate the indignance on my behalf, I can't fight every battle. I need to be strategic."

"That's fucked."

She huffed out an exasperated breath. "I know. There's nothing I can do about it. When it gets wild, I go to HR. Not that anything gets done other than people telling me I'm too emotional."

My skin flushed hot. "I'm sure I've said something stupid before."

She chewed her bottom lip then. "Oh, you have."

My stomach knotted. "Fuck me. I'm so sorry."

She put up a hand. "Don't bother. You're seeing things now. *Be* better. Fix them. Don't wait for me to tell you. Now that you see, do something about it."

I wouldn't be able to fix everything today, but this I could fucking fix. "You're right."

"I know. I love my job and, for the most part, the people I work with. Not everyone is a Jess, and not everyone is a Chad. Most people fall somewhere on the spectrum of *not knowing better* to *forgetting to do better*. And when they fuck up, I tell them. Hopefully, they listen."

Hearing someone walking toward her office, I straightened up immediately and took a step backward. "All right, I'll send you those marketing suggestions I have for Aurora St. James, and I will touch base with you later."

It wasn't just anyone, though. It was my uncle.

"I need both of you in my office. Right now."

—

OFOSUA

When we walked in, Steven made quick introductions. "Cosmos, you obviously know my nephew. This is Ofosua Addo. She's the editor on our new African American women's fiction line. She's the one you have all the questions for."

I froze. I was supposed to give a presentation now? *Fuck my life.*

Cosmos was tall and well-built, and his three-piece Tom Ford cream-colored suit complemented his light brown skin perfectly. He took my hand, and while his handshake was firm, it was also gentle, though he held on for a moment too long. "Ms. Addo. You are the one I've heard so much about."

"All good things, I hope, sir," I said as Cole and I took seats across from each other.

"Please call me Brian." He turned to Cole and gave him a bracing handshake. "Cole, good to see you again. I know you and I have already caught up. But I did want to speak to Ofosua about some of the packaging, since she's heading up this imprint that I think is vital for the growth of Drake Publishing."

Wait, they'd caught up? About Mahogany Prose? When? How? Why hadn't Cole told me?

I cleared my throat, suddenly apprehensive. "Well, hopefully I can answer any questions you have."

"I was looking at the initial lineup, and I have to say it's very exciting. I like your choice of authors and the kind of books you're trying to publish."

Okay, so nothing to worry about. "Wow, thank you. We're excited about the whole imprint, but there are some authors who are just special. And we can't wait to dig in with them."

"Yes. I was reading about Aurora St. James. She's brilliant. Enthusiastic. You can feel her zest for life in her work. I've been following her newsletter."

"Oh, I know. She's one of my favorites." I couldn't help it. The fact that he'd actually read the books was exciting. Knowing that someone outside of our little bubble was just as enthusiastic about our picks thrilled me. I leaned forward. "She's fresh and innovative, and her words are beautiful."

Cole sat forward too. "Yes, like I was telling you the last time we met, she's a marketer's dream. She'll perform well. She's worth putting budget behind."

Cosmos rubbed at his chin. "It seems, Ms. Addo, that you've managed to make everyone around you just as enthusiastic as you are."

"Oh, it's a team effort." I gave Cole and then his uncle a big smile.

Cosmos sat forward. "Right. Before we get ahead of ourselves, Miss Addo, when I saw your initial list, there was one book on the list that doesn't seem like it fits with the others, that I can't quite understand. And Steven suggested I talk to you about it since you're the acquiring editor."

Shit. My stomach sank. He'd thrown me under the bus? He knew full well we'd moved that book to women's fiction. God save me.

Cole's eyes went wide. He sat forward and started to speak, but I didn't need him to save me. Clearing my throat, I said, "While Steven made a strong push for that book, after much discussing as a team, and diving further into the book, we decided that Aliza

Mann's *Hood Rat Beginnings*, with some changes, would make a great addition to our women's fiction list. Meanwhile we can focus on Mahogany Prose and the great authors we've got lined up."

My skin heated as I flickered my gaze toward Steven, who categorically refused to look back. *Jackass.* Funny how the man who had shoved Aliza Mann down my throat was now leaving me with my ass hanging out. At least Cosmos would understand that she had been Steven's pick and that I hadn't lost my mind.

It figured. I'd learned long ago that the only person I could truly count on in the office was myself. I didn't bother looking at Cole. He knew what had happened in that acquisitions meeting. But I had no expectation for him to cover me, regardless of the state of our relationship.

But he sat forward. "The books Ofosua has cultivated are all amazing. She's an amazing editor. We're very excited about them."

I ground my molars together. Not a word about how I'd been put in a tight spot?

You know he can't say she was shoved down your throat. You know that.

But knowing it and feeling the sting were two different things. He had a company reputation to protect.

What about a girlfriend to protect?

I knew I was being irrational. This was business. I knew the reason why, but I still felt like I was left twisting in the wind. I forced a smile on my face. "You have nothing to worry about, Brian. We have a cohesive vision for this imprint." *Liar.*

Cosmos sat back, but he didn't smile. "It's your imprint, and you're the one to watch. I'm interested to see what you do."

I had a damn target on my back, and Cole had left me to float or sink on my own in shark-infested waters.

CHAPTER 24

COLE

ADINKRA SAYING:
(Sankofa) Learn from the past.

HELEN ADDO:
What is an apology? I do not understand the question.

That meeting hadn't gone well. We'd both been blindsided. But at the end of that meeting, I knew one thing. I'd fucked up. I could see it on Ofosua's face when she looked at me.

But we hadn't had time to talk after—she'd made sure of that—so I wasn't certain *where* I'd fucked up. I could only assume she was mad I'd met with Cosmos even though she was named the imprint's editor. Or maybe my reaction after Jess had tugged her hair wasn't what she'd hoped for. Not my finest moment.

I'd been pissed off, and hadn't handled the Jess situation well when it happened. But I thought I could fix it. So I went to HR at lunch and told them exactly what I'd witnessed. I knew there was a chance Ofosua might not appreciate it, but I had to do *something*.

All we needed to do was talk. I'd tell her about the step I'd taken, show her I was serious about change at Drake. And serious about her.

I'd texted her through the day, but she hadn't replied. Not even when I asked if our date was still on for tonight.

As I paced my apartment, I watched the clock. I'd texted her twice more, but she hadn't responded.

At ten minutes past eight, when my buzzer sounded, I rushed to the door. "Ofosua?"

There were traffic sounds, cars honking, someone shouting, music, and then finally Ofosua's voice. "Yeah, it's me. Can you buzz me up?"

My gut knotted into a tight ball.

Calm the fuck down. It's fine. Just explain.

Would it be fine, though?

When she knocked at the door, I rushed to open it, and she looked tired but still as beautiful as she did at the beginning of the day, when everything was fresh and amazing. "Hey," I said.

"Hey, yourself."

I stepped aside. "Come on in."

When she stepped in, I closed the door behind her. "I'll be right back." I put her things in the bedroom deliberately so she couldn't just pick them up and leave. Look, it was a little manipulative, I admit, but I needed to work every angle I had here.

I started with the groveling right away. "I fucked up. I'm sorry."

"Cole—"

"Look, before you start, I know I should have handled that bullshit with Jess better. And I know that this, with us, is going to be hard, but I *want* to do this, and please don't give up on me. You and I are just getting started."

I dragged a hand through my hair and watched as she tucked herself into the corner of my couch, making herself small, before sliding her gaze toward me.

"Jess? No. Cole, I'm annoyed about that meeting. You met with

Cosmos about *my* imprint, for starters. And you didn't communicate that. I was surprised. Then when he asked about Aliza, you and Steven sat there, mute. As if I made that choice. You *know* the real reason Aliza Mann was ever on the roster. But you and your uncle left me to explain to Cosmos. And I know you have to protect Drake's reputation. I know you have to think about your position as well, but I felt unsupported. It sucked."

Shit. "I—I told him that you were a fantastic editor, and you were going to make it shine."

She searched my gaze, as if willing me to understand. "Cole, I needed you to say Aliza wasn't my choice. Back me up and say it was my fast thinking that got Aliza moved to women's fiction. *Something.* I needed you to *back* me." She sniffed as I watched her lips quiver. "I knew Steven was going to leave me out there, but I hated that it felt like you left me hanging too."

"Shit." I knelt in front of her. "I'm so sorry. I thought I was helping." I cleared a tear with my thumb. She rarely cried. She never let herself break down. I hated being the one who'd made her cry. "I'll fix it. I'll call Cosmos myself."

"I don't want you to do that. I don't *need* saving. It just sucked. I'm allowed to just be sad."

She was wrong. I did need to fix this. "You don't *need* saving, but you deserve having someone who looks out for you. Hold on."

I pushed to my feet and grabbed my phone off the coffee table. She watched me with wide eyes as I quickly scrolled through my contacts. I found the number I was looking for and made the call.

Cosmos answered on the second ring. "Cole? What's going on?"

"Sorry to call this evening. I hope I haven't interrupted dinner or something."

"I was just getting ready to grab a drink. Would you like to join me? I'm meeting the actress Markella Walsh."

"Thank you, but no. I just wanted to clarify something."

"Sure, what's up?"

"This morning, there was something I didn't say that my uncle should have mentioned."

"Oh yeah?"

"Aliza Mann was not Ofosua Addo's choice. In our acquisitions meeting, Ofosua fought against her. *Hard.* My uncle forced her hand. It was Ofosua's quick thinking that got her moved to a different imprint."

"Why didn't she say something?"

My gaze flickered to her. Her eyes were wide and concerned. I knew Drake needed this investment. My legacy depended on it. Maybe that's why I didn't speak up at the meeting. But I had to speak the truth. "She's a professional, and this imprint is everything to her. She would never do or say anything to jeopardize the authors on it, who matter to her. But I felt it was important for you to know."

"I got the feeling. I worried when I made this proposal to Steven that he might try to just pay lip service, but Ofosua is the real deal. That's why Aliza Mann's inclusion was a red flag for me."

"Ofosua Addo *is* the real deal, I promise you that. She's one of our best editors."

"I can see why. She seems very talented. I appreciate your honesty."

"Thank you. Have a good night."

"You too, Cole."

When I hung up, Ofos stared at me. "I cannot believe you did that. Your uncle is going to kill you. That call might hurt this deal."

"*I* hurt you. I needed to fix it. You aren't alone anymore."

"Thank you, but you didn't *need* to fix it."

I lifted her chin so she met my gaze. "Yes, I did."

She watched me warily. "Why do you look nervous? You're doing that thing that you always do when you're nervous, chewing the corner of your mouth."

I frowned. "I do not."

She nodded. "Yes, you do too. It's very cute. But I want to know why you're nervous."

"Come with me." I stood and took her hand and tugged her to her feet.

"All right, all right. I'm coming."

We stepped into my room, and her eyes went wide when I turned on the lights. "Jesus, your room really is huge."

"Yeah. I love the light that comes in, and it's got an awesome view of the city."

She laughed when I let her go. "You're not going to kiss me?"

"Patience is a virtue."

"I think we've already established it's not one of mine."

"Come on, I'm going to show you. I hope I got the right one. I wasn't sure."

Reluctantly, she followed, and I pulled back the covers from her side of the bed. "Did I get the right thing?"

She glanced down. "What are you talking about?"

"Well, I—"

It took her a second, but then she saw it. The set of pillow-cases. She was quiet long enough to make me worry I'd fucked up, gotten the exact *wrong* thing. When she turned to me, her eyes were shiny with tears again. "Cole."

She'd told me at her place, when I asked about her satin pillowcases, that cotton strips Black hair of much-needed moisture, but satin protects it. But maybe I'd fucked this up. "I can fix it. Just tell me what you need."

She didn't say anything. Instead, she launched herself at me.

She planted her hands on my shoulders and jumped up. When she slammed her lips on mine, I staggered back before righting myself. The kiss she gave me was deep. Her tongue sliding over my lips into my mouth, claiming me. The tension I'd been carrying around loosened even more. When she pulled back, she smiled at me. "Thank you."

"So you like it?"

"Yeah, I like it," she whispered.

And she proceeded to show me how much. Between the sliding of her tongue over mine and her hands sliding up under my shirt to tug it off, I was ready to combust.

The tension from today had made us impatient. As we fumbled with our clothes, there was some ripping, a lot of tugging, some cramping muscles. But finally, I had her naked.

Fuck, she was so sexy. When she lay sprawled on the bed, I stared down at her, trying to decide where I was going to feast first.

But it seemed Ofos had other plans, and she reached for my belt. She made quick work of the buckle, yanking it furiously and then throwing it somewhere behind us. I heard a series of thuds and could picture it hitting the wall and then falling down to the hardwood. Did I give a fuck about that? Nope, sure did not.

My gaze was entirely focused on her hands pulling down my zipper. "Ofos . . ." I groaned out.

But she paid me no mind, reaching into my boxer briefs and pulling out my thick erection. My eyes were on her; her gaze was on my dick. She licked her lips before sliding down and taking me into her hot, wet mouth.

I was done for.

All thought ceased the moment she wrapped her lips around me. I threw my head back, pleasure coursing through my body as she bobbed her head up and down on my cock.

"Oh, fuck," I moaned, the feel of her warm, wet mouth the most intense feeling, like someone had plugged me into a power outlet. I wrapped a hand in her thick curls, groaning as she began to bob her head up and down slowly.

She flicked her tongue as she moved over me. She stopped for a moment to kiss her way along my abs, and then back up, before wrapping her lips around me again and taking my whole length down her throat.

"Baby . . . I'm about to come," I gasped out as the pleasure overpowered me.

"Mmm-hmmmm," she purred in response. And then she squeezed my balls, leaned forward, and sucked me off like nothing I'd ever experienced.

She took me deep, her mouth so wet and warm my knees started to give as a wave of need hit me, making me weak. Fuck, she felt amazing.

When she gave me a gentle squeeze my head snapped up as I felt the orgasm coming for me. As much as I wanted nothing more than to lose full control, to give her everything, I wasn't nearly done with her yet.

She gave me a petulant whine when I caressed her cheek and pulled her off my dick.

"Oh no you don't. I haven't even started. I have a hundred ways to apologize. I plan to use every single one."

"Cole . . ."

"I'm so glad you're familiar with my name. I plan on making you scream it a lot." And I did. I apologized in a million different ways. With soft kisses, with deep ones. With my tongue inside her pussy and my mouth on her clit, fingers teasing her ass. And finally, the most important way to apologize.

I met her gaze with mine as I lined my dick up with her slick heat and kept it on her as I slid all the way home. When I was buried inside her to the hilt, her inner muscles gripping me, I tucked my face into her neck and whispered so she could hear me, "I'm sorry."

I didn't stop whispering it until I'd wrung yet another orgasm out of her.

CHAPTER 25

OFOSUA

ADINKRA SAYING:
(Bese Saka) Affluence.

HELEN ADDO:
The fastest way to affluence is to marry well . . .
and get your master's.

SAMUEL ADDO:
Trust no one, get a prenup.

This was too good to be true.

I had gone exactly two weeks without an ambush from Steven or anyone at work. I had settled into a steady flow. Well, I still had to edit that idiot Evan Miles. Cole had warned him to be on his best behavior, and I kept most of my communication through his agent, so it was mostly painless.

My time had been spent trying to figure out production schedules for each of the books. I obviously wanted to lead with our strongest contenders, which were Kenya and Aurora. But Kenya's book needed more work.

All in all, though, I was happy.

Cole had really heard me when I'd told him how it felt when

he hadn't backed me with Brian Cosmos. Now, any meeting with Cosmos on the calendar, he made sure I was there.

And in the evenings, Cole was mine. All mine. We stayed most nights at his place, since he didn't have roommates or an overbearing mother. But I had taken him to meet my friends. And Cole had been perfect date material. Fun and funny and teasing my friends. Super attentive with me. A girl could get used to the constant attention and flirting. And then, of course, we went back to his place. Where he did deliciously dirty things to me with his tongue.

It was my own fault. I should have been expecting the ambush at home. Things had been too quiet since Yofi's wedding, and I'd grown complacent. My mother still did her usual *come to church with me* demands and her usual appearances in my apartment out of nowhere, but there hadn't been a single blind date attempt on her part since the wedding.

I knew at some point I was going to have to acknowledge that Cole and I were together to my family, but it was so much nicer to pretend I didn't have to worry about saying anything to my mother.

That was the main reason I had chosen to sneak into my own apartment on Sunday evening.

Coward.

When the elevator let me off at my floor, I sighed with relief when I didn't see my parents. A glance down the hall pricked at my conscience. I really should go over there, say hi, and check in with my dad later.

Feeling resolute and like I had an actual action plan, I opened my door, far too happy and relaxed, because I was not expecting my mother to be waiting for me.

As soon as I walked into my apartment, Cora pointed toward the kitchen and then made herself scarce.

I glowered in her direction, and she grinned as she backed away. "Mum?"

She came out of the kitchen, carrying a large pot of jollof. "Eh, as for you, you don't have any food in your house. Did you know that?"

I sighed. "Hi to you too, Mum." I went around her into the kitchen, grabbed a soda from the fridge, and then made a mental note that I *should* do some grocery shopping. We had a group shopping list that got ordered weekly, and paid for out of a joint fund, but for my personal things, I was running low.

I sighed. I needed to make nice. "So, Mum, how is it going?"

She was standing in the dining room, hands on her hips, next to the table, where she'd placed the jollof. "Where is Megan? It's Sunday. I usually come and cook on Sunday. Where did everyone go?"

I pursed my lips and tried to find some calm. "Mum, did you let anyone know you were coming? Because then people might not have made other plans."

She frowned. "But where would anyone be going?"

"I don't know. But even I have work to do."

She frowned. "Is that where you have been? Eh, you're always working. If you would only focus on getting married instead of work all the time."

I frowned at her. "Mum, remember when I was in school? You insisted that I didn't need a boyfriend and that boys only caused pregnancy and syphilis. Do you recall saying that to me?"

Her eyes went wide. "I would never have said any such thing."

"I'm pretty sure I have a recording of it somewhere."

Then she pulled her specialty. When she wasn't getting the response she wanted from me, she changed the subject. "So this thing with the obroni boy, you can't be serious with him, can you?"

I sputtered my sip of soda. "What are you talking about?"
When in doubt, deny, deny, deny.

"Don't play stupid with me. You brought him to the wedding, where everyone has seen. Are you keeping him?"

What did that even mean? We were figuring it out. "I like him, so I will keep him for now."

It sounded like a nice neutral answer.

"Keep him for now? Nonsense. If you're bringing him to family things, where everyone can see you, then you think you're keeping him." She watched me shrewdly. "These boys, they're fun. Sure. But they're not serious. He will never understand you, or what you stand for, so you have your fun. But be sensible. And for the love of God, do not get pregnant. Lord Jesus."

I rolled my eyes. "Okay, first, he's a man. Second, who says I'm serious? I ran to get married, and it blew up in my face. Right now, he's cool. And I like him. For the first time in months, I'm feeling again. So I'll keep him for the moment. And, again, that's my choice. Not yours."

"But he's an obroni! Who *are* his people even?"

I knew that was going to come up eventually. Who are his people? What's his family like? "Mum, you don't need to do this. His family is good, well-to-do. As a matter of fact, I work for his uncle."

She frowned. "What do you mean, you work for his uncle?"

"Mum, Cole's last name is Drake. His family owns Drake Publishing."

Her eyes went wide. "You're dating the boy who owns the company? Heh, aren't you worried people are going to say you slept your way to the top? But not my daughter, because you know better than to sleep with that boy."

"*Man*, and that's none of your business, Mum."

She blinked at me owlishly. "That's not how I raised you."

I pinched the bridge of my nose. "I don't even know what to say to you. I am twenty-five years old. Almost twenty-six. I was married for a whole four hours. I *lived* with Yofi. I've had sex before."

She harrumphed. "If you're going to have sex with him, we should meet him. Bring that boy to Kukua's exhibit. I bought a table."

"I don't think—"

"My dear, that is not a suggestion."

"You spring this on me now? Maybe we're not at the-turn-up-at-family-events level yet. Maybe Cole has something going on with his own family?"

"If he wants to see my daughter, he'll come."

"Except you don't control me, right?"

She laughed. "If that's what you need to believe to get up every day, then feel free. Next Saturday, I'm telling you now. And repent." She added, more loudly, "I am praying for you and for Megan!"

As she took the rice back into the kitchen, I frowned at her back. This was going to be a disaster.

CHAPTER 26

COLE

ADINKRA SAYING:
(Ese Na Tekrama) Friendship.

HELEN ADDO:
Do you have a husband? No?
Then why waste your time with these obroni boyfriends?

It was a beautiful night. Clear and balmy. While the moon shone bright, the stars were nowhere to be seen, so we'd have to make do with the skyline. I told myself it was going to be okay. After all, I'd already met her parents at the wedding. This was an exhibit and dinner. I could survive dinner.

The exhibit for her cousin Kukua was being held at the Lestin Center for the Arts, in SoHo. All through the night you could bid on Kukua's paintings. I'd already bought a piece for my apartment, *Village Shores*. It was bright and vibrant and so colorful. It reminded me of how Ofosua talked about home.

Next to me, I could practically feel Ofosua vibrating. "Would you stop?" I said. "You're making me nervous."

She turned to face me, hands grazing my shoulders and down my arms on my suit jacket. I watched as her pupils dilated, and then I smirked down at her. "We probably should have done *that* before you got dressed. I'm likely to rip your dress if you keep looking at me like that."

She lifted a brow and bit back a smile. "Look, no sex eyes, okay?"

"What are sex eyes?"

"The ones you're looking at me with right now. Also, no touching. Don't touch me in front of my parents."

"Okay, so I'm not supposed to look at you like I normally look at you or touch you."

"Yes. No. Show interest, but not *too much* interest."

"Okay, relax. It's going to be fine. And I'll show as much interest as I like, thank you very much."

"My parents will eviscerate you. Well, really my mother."

"Look, your dad and I already talked about soccer. I can bring that up again. As for your mother . . . Well, everyone finds me charming, so don't worry about it."

She blinked at me. "This isn't funny."

"Look, I got this. Let me impress them. Give me a chance. I'm a good boyfriend."

She softened then. I could see it in the small uptick at the corners of her mouth. Her shoulders loosened, and gently, I brushed my thumb over her bottom lip. "Ah, there we go. There's my Ofos. We'll go inside, we'll eat, and I'll buy another one of Kukua's paintings for my office at work."

"You don't have to do that."

"You let me spend my trust fund how I like, okay?"

Even as she shook her head, she whispered, "Cole, are you sure about this?"

The elevator pulled to a stop, and I tugged her close, kissing her forehead. "I'm sure. I'm not worried. I don't want you to worry either. No matter what happens tonight, I walk out of here with you. No one is chasing me off."

"Are you sure? That's pretty much my mother's specialty."

"Leave it to me."

The exhibit floor was exquisitely decorated. Long chandeliers hung from the ceiling, electronic ones that changed light levels and shapes by remote control. The lights within them reflected adinkra symbols along the ceiling. They were exquisite. Obviously custom-made by someone.

All along the walls were paintings in varying sizes. I hadn't realized Kukua was so prolific. When Ofos told me her cousin was an artist, sure, I'd looked her up. She'd had some gallery openings in New York and Los Angeles. Atlanta too. But I hadn't realized she'd also exhibited all around the world. A lot in various parts of Africa, but Paris and London as well. Kukua Addo was a wunderkind.

Kukua ran up to us with a squeak, gave Ofos a tight hug, and then enveloped me in one as well. For someone so tiny, she was surprisingly strong.

I hugged her back. "This is amazing. I've already got something for my apartment, but I think I need something else."

She shook her head. "No. Don't buy from here. The gallery tacks on an exorbitant price. Tell me something you like, and I'll have something similar in storage. This shit on the walls is for rich pricks who I don't mind fleecing."

I leaned forward conspiratorially. "News flash, I *am* a rich prick. Let me buy it from here, give the gallery their commission, and they'll be excited to have you again."

"In that case, buy away."

The three of us chatted amicably until we heard the faint chime leading us toward the dining tables. So far, I hadn't seen Ofosua's parents, and, despite what I'd told her earlier, I was a little nervous.

I wanted her to be happy. For once in my life, I needed to actually impress with real shit. Not just the surface nonsense. This time it mattered.

We found her father, and he shook my hand amiably as we made small talk. Helen finally joined us, giving her daughter an appraising glance before narrowing her eyes at her clutch. "Oh, that isn't the one I would have chosen for this outfit."

When Helen turned her gaze on me, I could feel her careful assessment. I looked impeccable. She knew it and I knew it, and she couldn't find anything wrong with me. Instead, she pursed her lips and said, "Oh, Colten, good to see you again."

And so we began. "Mrs. Addo, I'm thrilled to see you again. It's Cole, actually." I handed her the Persian lilies that I'd brought for her. "These are for you. Thank you so much for inviting me tonight."

She lifted her brow at the flowers and gave me a polite smile. "I'm so sorry. Sometimes these obroni names are hard for me to remember." She did, however, pause and sniff the flowers, and I could see the corners of her lips tip up for real. She may be tough, but I had just scored a point. I would take them wherever I could find them.

She was playing for keeps, and I had better learn to keep up. Still, though, I found her amusing. Ofos just looked mortified.

Kukua went to greet more of her guests, and I found our names at the table. I realized I was seated next to Helen and someone named Emanuel was sitting next to Ofos.

She frowned at the name card and deliberately switched them as I pulled out her chair for her. "Are you sure that's a good idea?"

"I don't know who Emanuel is, but I have a feeling it's not going to be good."

When Helen sat down, she frowned at the switched name

cards. A guy about my age strolled up to the table, dark skin, trim beard, killer suit. I would have to ask who his tailor was.

"Did I hear my name?" he said.

Next to me Ofos ground out, "Cole. I'm so sorry. My mother has—"

Emanuel took a seat next to Helen, then lifted a brow at me as if he knew he was meant to sit next to my girlfriend. To add insult to good-looking injury, he looked like he liked to work out too.

I frowned at him. Maybe he was a brother I didn't know about?

The hell he is. That, you dim fuck, is the competition. Ofosua's mother was playing to win. So I did the only thing I could. I marked my damn territory like a caveman. "Hello, I'm Cole, Ofosua's boyfriend."

Emanuel's brows lifted. "Boyfriend? Ofosua, your mother didn't say anything about you having an obroni boyfriend. I wish you had mentioned it when I met you that night at your place."

I lifted my brow and Ofos leaned in. "Mum surprised me with him the night I got the invitation."

Oh, I remembered that night. I was beginning to see that Ofosua hadn't exaggerated a bit about her mother. The woman was impressively devious. "What does 'obroni' mean?"

She winced. "It means 'white person.'"

Emanuel gave me a smile that was all teeth. "It's not a nice way of saying it."

I nodded. "Okay, then."

Ofosua turned to me. "I am so sorry."

I shrugged. "If I can't survive this discomfort, I don't deserve you."

Once we were seated and dinner was served, I recognized almost everything on the table because Ofosua had been teaching me the ways of Ghanaian cuisine.

When the bowl was passed around for us to wash our hands, I even knew what to do because Ofosua had taken me to Gold Coast, a West African restaurant in Queens. Her mother stared at me when I washed my hands and then dried them on the handy little towel provided after passing on the bowl.

Her father raised his brows at his wife. Ofosua squeezed my knee, and what I really wanted to do was drag her off to the bathroom for a kiss or something so I could feel connected to her and reassure her that I wasn't going to embarrass her.

Dinner was upscale kenkey, jollof, gari, or plantain. There was also a red stew I didn't recognize, but would try. There was tilapia with what looked like fresh shito on top. Ofos had given me shito to try before. There was the black shito, which was made of dried shrimp, onions, and scotch bonnet peppers. The fresh shito was onions and scotch bonnets and tomato.

All foods I'd seen so far and knew how to eat. If I made any other choice but the kenkey I felt like I'd fail some kind of test. Her mother wanted to see if I knew how and if I was willing to eat with my hands.

It might not be pretty, but I did, in fact, know how to do that.

When I dove in, her father hooted. "Heh, this obroni has been taught our ways. Ofosua, well done. Well done."

I could feel Ofosua breathing in through her nose, out through her mouth. She was practicing her exercises, and I prayed to God she was not in the midst of a panic attack.

Emanuel was not thrilled by my presence. I thought the toughest questions would be from Ofosua's parents, but of course, I hadn't even considered that there might be a backup boyfriend at the table as well.

"So, where do you work again, Cole?"

I opened my mouth to address him, but Ofosua rode in.

"Emanuel, why are you even here? This routine is not impressive to me. In case I wasn't clear when we met, I'm not interested."

Helen Addo was not having it. "Ofosua, I didn't teach you to be rude to our guests."

"Oh, really? You could have fooled me. You're being rude to Cole by inviting . . . What is he supposed to be? A spare date?"

Helen eyed me levelly. "Well, I know your dating history, and in case something didn't work out, I invited Emanuel."

I could feel Ofosua vibrating beside me. "Did it occur to you—I'm sure it didn't—that I don't *want* to get to know him?"

Helen looked like she wasn't sure what to do. I could have jumped in and done my charming act, smoothed things over, but this was Ofosua's play. All I could do was not let Emanuel rattle me.

—

OFOSUA

I clenched my jaw trying to determine the best way to commit matricide and not go to jail.

Emanuel tried to get my attention once again. "So, Ofosua, what is it you do?"

I was sure my mother would have already told him, but still, I was polite. "I'm in publishing. Much to my parents' horror."

Mum sucked her teeth. "Why can't you do things like your cousins do? Your cousin Miriam, she's now getting her PhD."

Cole rushed to smooth things over before they got out of hand. "Dr. Addo, has Ofos updated you on her imprint? She's managed to put together a fantastic debut list. She's amazing at what she does. She has a real eye for literary talent."

"An eye for talent. What does that even mean?" she scoffed.

I clenched my jaw so hard it hurt. "This is not a conversation to have with guests. This is Kukua's night."

Cole's hand was warm and firm on my knee. The firm squeeze told me he was there for me, whatever I needed.

"Emanuel, I'm sorry. You've been dragged into some kind of family situation here. I'm not single. As you can see, I have a boyfriend."

Emanuel perked up. "I see your boyfriend, but I mean, honestly, this obroni? He'll get bored eventually."

"Wow, I see you think very highly of me."

Emanuel instantly saw his error. "Oh, I don't mean you are boring. How could you be? I'm saying—"

"Yes, I heard what you were saying." Cole was helping himself to all the dishes. The shito on the tilapia would be hot. When he reached for it, I shook my head. "Ah, no, I don't think you should have that one."

He ignored me. And when he tucked in, I could see him turn red. The sweat started to bead on his forehead. He was not at all ready for that level of heat.

But instead of grabbing for his water and bitching out, nope, Cole kept eating.

Eventually, my mother and I were at a stalemate.

She knew she would finally have to talk to Cole. "So, obroni boy, what are your intentions?"

Cole stopped eating. "Toward Ofosua? Well, we're seeing where it goes. But your daughter is incredibly talented and beautiful and smart, and I'm very much appreciating the fact that she chooses to spend time with me."

My mother rolled her eyes. "I don't know why you white people are always saying people are talented. Sometimes it's not about being talented. It's about putting in the work ethic. Talent. That's such a white people notion."

I tensed. But again, there was Cole's hand. Nice, steady, calming pressure. His voice was even. "Yes. You're right. It is. Not only is she talented, but she has the best work ethic I've ever seen. I've never seen anyone work harder. She deserves all the accolades."

Every curveball she threw him to try and get him to slip up, or say something wrong, or have some kind of average reaction, he ignored, sidestepped, and deflected.

Through the whole dinner, my mother looked irritated. As if she had truly expected that her setup would work.

By the time the dessert of Ghana pancakes with Nutella and ice cream, topped with edible gold flakes, was carted out, I was grinding my teeth so hard I was in danger of cracking a molar.

But Cole remained affable through it all. Easy to talk to. And as we all stood and washed our hands again, he ignored my rule. He wrapped his arm around me, making it perfectly clear that we were together.

And all it did was make my mother raise her brows. But I knew she would hate everything about this.

Public displays of affection, his claiming of me, my rejection of her choice for me, it was all going to haunt me for years, I could already tell. And the funny thing was, I wasn't upset about it at all.

By the time we walked out of the exhibit three hours later, my nerves were shot, Cole's stomach was full, and I had dashed Emanuel's hopes.

Before we left, my father stopped me and gave me a hug. "Your mother loves you. She's only trying to do what's best."

"Then maybe she should learn to let me make my own choices."

He laughed. "You know that she's a Ghanaian mother. She's

physically incapable. But as choices go, your obroni boy isn't so bad."

I searched my father's dark brown eyes. "Thanks, Daddy."

"Besides, I know that you're not doing the same thing you did before. Rushing to marry someone to get away from your mother."

"Daddy, that's not what I did."

"You're my daughter. You think I don't know you?"

I laughed. "Yeah, good point."

All along, he'd known. Which made me wonder if he also knew that Yofi wasn't right for me all along.

CHAPTER 27

COLE

ADINKRA SAYING:
(Nyansapo) Wisdom.
HELEN ADDO:
With age comes hard truths.
Love does not conquer all.

After the gallery opening, we went to Tribeca. Ofosua had said everything was fine, but she was off. She'd tossed and turned all night. And she hadn't wanted to talk about it. Sunday, she'd been quiet and had gone home early citing work. I'd taken her dinner in the evening and her mood had seemed to improve, but she'd still been quiet.

This morning, as I'd done my level best to distract her with mind-shattering orgasms in the shower, she'd held on to me tight like she was afraid I was going to run away. Sure, the gallery night had been less than ideal, but I'd made it clear I wasn't running. Nothing was going to send me packing.

I was returning from a breakfast meeting with my mind focused on maybe taking her to grab coffee before my next round of calls, but I stopped short when I saw someone familiar in the lobby.

"Dr. Addo, have you been helped? Did someone let Ofos know you were here?"

Helen Addo was dressed to the nines. I saw where Ofosua got her elegance from. Not a hair out of place, a full-on, no-bullshit, *I eat idiots like you for dinner* pristine air about her. She wore her blue-and-white African print like a badge of grace. And I had to say it—she was stunning.

She smiled as the receptionist looked up. "Oh, there you are, Cole. I just pinged your office. Dr. Addo said she's here to see you?"

I turned back to the woman, who looked every bit the regal queen seated in our plush reception furniture. "You're here to see me?"

She gave me a sharp nod. "I am."

My stomach sank. There was no way this was good. Her wanting to speak with me could only end in disaster.

Maybe she wants to apologize.

No way. Ofos told me African parents don't apologize. She was here to eviscerate me. "Okay. Right this way. We can go to my office."

"I appreciate this. I took the chance that you might be available."

I held my door open for her. "I'm glad I was here. And, ah, I'm honored to see you."

Once I had her seated and closed the door, she laid it on me. "I've been wanting to speak to you."

I sat next to her. "What about?"

"This is awkward," she said as she smoothed down her skirt.

I sighed. "You can say that again. I get the distinct impression you are not, uh, very impressed with me?"

"That would be accurate. I'm not."

I raised my brows, irritation bubbling to the surface. "Well, tell me how you really feel."

With pursed lips and then a sigh, she said, "Well, for starters, you can stop playing with my daughter."

I swallowed hard before I spoke. "I assure you, Dr. Addo, I am doing no such thing. The last few weeks with her have been some of the best in my life. She's very important to me."

"Listen, you are not the first obroni boy who thinks he's taking some kind of walk on the wild side. I will not have my daughter be your dating experiment."

I frowned at that. "That's not what this is. I care about her."

"I know you *think* you do. And you seem like a nice boy. But this thing you're doing with my daughter, she's going to get hurt."

"I understand your concern, Dr. Addo, but I'm not going to hurt her. She's the best person I know. Just being with her pushes me to strive to be the kind of man she deserves."

"You should come to her fully formed. She is not here to *fix* you. Or to prop you up. You care about her right now because it's convenient for you."

My gut twisted. "That's not the case." Except part of what she'd said was true. Ofos had been fixing me, brick by brick. The blade of shame sliced deep. Emanuel or whoever would never need a primer on microaggressions. His mother would treat Ofos with respect.

"Look, no one ever wants to hear the hard truth. You and my daughter, nothing is coming out of this. Dating her is a fun detour for you, but this is her *life*. Ofosua has worked too hard and had too many disappointments. You would be another one. When you get bored, you're going to marry the appropriate girl from the Upper East Side and live your bland boring life. My daughter needs community. Support. Family. All things that you can't provide."

I ground my teeth at that. She had no idea what I could

provide. "I can and I will give her those things. All due respect, Dr. Addo, you don't even know me."

She frowned. "No, I don't. But I know your type. You're the type to get bored, like Emanuel said last night. I know you think that you care about my daughter, and that you want to be with her, and you love her and all her 'talent.' Obroni-type things. But let me explain to you, when things get difficult, when your family doesn't approve, when they insist that you give her up to remain in the family fold, when your so-called friends shun her, *she* is the one who will get hurt."

I swallowed hard. "I keep telling you, I won't hurt her."

"You won't mean to hurt her, but you will. So let's save everyone the time and energy and pain, shall we?"

"You think so little of your daughter?"

"No. I think the *world* of my daughter. I've spent my life nurturing her for something *better* than you. She deserves to find someone ready for the road ahead. You are ill-equipped for the realities of the world she has to live in, Mr. Drake."

I frowned at that. "Have you told Ofosua any of this?"

She smiled. "You know my daughter; she won't listen. She will happily tell me that she is seeing where this goes, whatever the hell that means. But you and I both know how this works. Imagine taking her home to your family. What will your mother say? What will your father say? And I know you want to go ahead and condemn me because, yes, I'm doing all those things as well. But this is my *daughter* we're talking about. See, Cole, Ofosua is not pretending. She truly likes you. And because she likes you, it's my job to see that she makes the right choice, not just for herself, but for her family, her community. She will be shunned by our community if she one day chooses a life with you. Always an outsider. Do you want that for her?"

I pursed my lips at that.

"And if you think about it, you will see she deserves a life with someone who is not going to break her. Who understands all parts of her. Not just the comfortable parts."

My heart was beating too fast, pulsing against the confines of my ribs. I didn't want to hear this bullshit. But what if she was right? "Oh yeah, like Yofi?"

You know she's right.

"Yofi was a problem. He wanted to be too American. We can do better."

I sighed. "I'm not sure what you want. I expect that you want me to stop seeing her, right?"

"Yes, it would be helpful. She'll get over it like she got over Yofi. Think it through, and then you'll see that I'm right. Don't take this personally. I'm sure you're a very nice boy. But not for my Ofosua."

And then she stood to walk out as if she hadn't tried to rip apart my world. I still couldn't believe it. Was I supposed to just accept it? What kind of bullshit was that?

"You know I'm not going to walk away," I said stubbornly.

"Think about your next move very carefully, obroni. One day, one of your friends, or perhaps your mother, is going to say something to my daughter, something that aims to dim her light or to make her feel small, so they can feel powerful. And you won't see it. You'll tell yourself that you will. You tell yourself that you'll believe her, but you won't. And when you don't protect her, you will break her just a little. If that's not enough to sway you, then think about your mother's circles. How she will take the news of your supposed girlfriend. You think you won't quit? I can see it. And I would hate to have to make a polite call to Rebecca Drake to let her know what her son has been up to. Just because our social circles don't overlap doesn't mean our paths might not cross."

She'd looked up my mother. She wouldn't.

She would.

"Have a good afternoon. I really do wish I could trust you with my daughter's heart. But the life that would make her truly happy is one of familiarity, culture, food, ease. You cannot give her that, no matter how many Ghanaian dances you learn." And then she was gone.

Ofosua's mother was out the door, taking my heart with her. I didn't want to believe her, didn't want to think that any of what she said made any kind of sense. Until she spoke the simple truth, I'd never been afraid that maybe our worlds were too different.

CHAPTER 28

OFOSUA

ADINKRA SAYING:
(Adwo) Calmness. A symbol for peace, tranquility, and quiet.

SAMUEL ADDO:
You are stronger than you think. Know yourself.

"I was thinking we should try that new Peruvian spot. I know since Bryant Park you've been trying to one-up me on the restaurant selections, but this one is the winner. They have this hot up-and-coming chef. I know that you're always trying to discover the best restaurant, but finally, I think I have one that's going to kick your ass."

Cole nodded absently. His face was stuck in his phone, much like it had been for the past twenty minutes since we left the office.

"Everything okay?" I asked.

"Yeah, sorry. Just some things I have to deal with."

"Um, okay. So, Peruvian?"

He nodded absently. "Sure, sounds great."

"Or do you want to save it for tomorrow night, when we're supposed to meet Carmen and Tallon?" The muscle in his jaw ticked. "Okay, what gives? You're acting weird."

He shook his head. "Nothing gives. Sure, tomorrow night. Tallon and Carmen."

"What's going on?"

He shook his head. "I told you, I'm dealing with something. My mind is on the marketing and sales conference meeting, that's all."

"Do you want to talk about it?" He looked worried. If he was worried, I should be worried. After all, I was doing the pitch.

He shook his head. "No, it's nothing you have to worry about."

I tried to ignore the sting of pain on that one. "Okay, well, if you want to talk, I'm here."

He nodded and squeezed my hand. I knew it was meant to be reassuring, but there was something about it that felt dismissive. Maybe I'd be able to get him to open up at dinner after this.

When we arrived at Aurora's event, I found her in the corner slinging slam poetry to some kids.

She saw us and grinned wide. "Ah, if it isn't my favorite people here to tell me how I'm going to be the next big thing."

I gave her a squeeze. "Well, I mean, you are. We're happy to support you."

"I know. You guys are the best. The notes you sent were spot-on. I've already started to dive into them."

As she and I chatted, my thoughts kept drifting back to the fact that something was definitely off with Cole. When he only nodded, I tried to ignore the gnawing in my stomach. If something was going on with him, he would tell me. Right? He'd made love to me in the shower that morning like a man on a mission. Like multiple orgasms would chase the gray away.

They had been a great start. That and being at work and digging into edits had me shaking off the melancholy. Even if my parents didn't understand me, at least I had this. How many other women my age had their own publishing lines? I needed to try and enjoy my life and my very sexy boyfriend.

Who was so distracted he wasn't even paying attention to Aurora.

Maybe he's upset that the two of you are still sneaking around at the office.

Maybe, but he hadn't said anything this week. He got it. There would be very different perceptions for the two of us once we went public.

Aurora shrugged. "Well, okay, I'll be ready to talk shop after the performance. In the meantime, I'm gonna go give these tickets away to some kids."

Cole said, "You don't need me today, do you?"

What? He was ditching work?

"Aren't we going to talk marketing strategy with Aurora?" I asked.

He sighed. "Maybe we can reschedule for later this week. I have something to deal with."

He gave Emory a wave and then squeezed my hand before striding out, leaving me speechless and wondering what the hell happened.

I wished he would talk to me so we could deal with whatever was bothering him together.

Or maybe it's not something that you can do anything about.

That idea worried me even more.

—

Three hours later, I turned up at Cole's doorstep, overnight bag in tow. Though the usual excitement I felt at staying over at his place was dampened because I knew something was wrong. And unlike before, I was unwilling to stick my head in the sand and pretend that it didn't exist.

We were off, so we were going to talk about it and get back on track. If I could fix it, I would.

Or maybe it has nothing to do with you.

Which was entirely possible. But if I *had* done something, I wanted to know.

My stomach twisted and knotted as if trying to warn me. *Danger, Will Robinson, danger.*

But still, I marched on. I took the elevator up, and when I reached his penthouse apartment, he opened the door, looked at my bag with surprise, and said, "Oh, you're staying?"

Wow, so it was like that. "I don't know what's going on with you, but we're going to talk about this, because I can't do the eggshell thing. Whatever I did, I'm sorry. Give me a chance to apologize and make sure it doesn't happen again. But this whole thing where you cold-shoulder me, I'm not doing that. We promised to communicate with each other."

He ran his hands through his hair. "You know what, can we just not right now? You're doing a lot. It's been a long day. I can't do some moralistic lesson right now."

I blinked at him slowly. "Sure, I'll go. But before I do, you *will* tell me what the hell is up with you. We go from everything being great this morning to everything being utter shit. In like twelve hours! You're distracted. You won't speak to me. If I have done something or said something, be a grown-up and fucking tell me. But this, where you act like I have somehow wronged you and are distant and cold, I'm not doing this again."

He groaned. "For the last time, I'm not *him*!"

I flinched as if he'd slapped me. "You know what's funny? You're sure acting like him."

He winced and softened his voice. "I just have a lot on my

plate right now between work and my family shit. You wouldn't understand."

"Right. Everyone has problems, Cole. Adults discuss them, work them out. Hell, adults even say, I'm not ready to talk right now. You are having a mini mental tantrum about something. As for moralistic lessons—I'm sorry I've tried to open your eyes to a world outside of your own rarified privilege. Do you even understand how lucky you are? How many people would kill for your problems?"

He turned at me and growled. "You know, I'm getting real sick and tired of you shoving the world's problems on my shoulders. Can we just have one damn night where we're not talking my *supposed* privilege? A normal night where all the world's bullshit isn't at the center of every fucking thing? I would kill for one night where we're just Cole and Ofosua. And let's not forget that you are just as rich as I am. You are *dripping* with the same privilege."

That sliced deep, and I lifted my chin, ready to challenge him. "The difference is, *I* at least recognize that I have privilege. Not to mention you have a whole other privilege I'll never attain. You're acting like a petulant child. You could talk to me like a grown-up, tell me if I have done something wrong, give me the chance to apologize and rectify the mistake. But instead, you're not talking to me. You're distant. If you're breaking up with me, just bloody break up with me."

Then he did the one thing I didn't expect. Stalking toward me with grim determination in his eyes, he dug his hands into my hair at my nape and dragged me to him. And when he kissed me, his tongue was equal parts harsh and coaxing. When he growled low, pouring all his need and frustration into me, my world tilted upside down.

My body begged me to give in to the tempest. Every cell wanted to relinquish control. But I could still feel the errant thread I needed to tug on, and when I shoved him away, he released me.

He swallowed hard, his gaze flickering back to my lips.

"What is going on? I'm not leaving here until you at least tell me what the hell it is, and then I'm going to take my bag and get the hell out of your hair. But you will damn well tell me what is bothering you. Look at it as a chance to finally tell me what you really think of me. Go on, let loose."

There was this breadth of a moment where he winced, and I could tell he didn't want to do this. He knew he was hurting me, and he didn't want to.

I softened my voice. "Look, I don't know what's up. Is it your family? Work stuff? Just tell me. Maybe I can help."

He ran a hand through his hair. "Ofosua, I just . . ." His voice trailed. When his gaze met mine, his eyes were glassy with unshed tears. "This is all moving too fast."

I jerked back as if he'd slapped me. "What?"

"I can't do this. We're moving fast and not thinking about the consequences. I feel like I'm being pushed into making this real when what's right in front of me is this: You work for Drake. And Drake is my legacy. I can't fuck that up."

He was *not* doing this to me. "*You* insisted that you didn't care how fast it was moving, *you* promised that us working together wasn't a problem that couldn't be solved, but now you're telling me that *I* moved this too fast? God, you actually do sound just like Yofi. I can't believe this. Am I cursed?"

"For fuck's sake, I'm not him!" he roared.

"Sure you're not." I couldn't help the sadness and disappointment, and the words slipped out before I could stop them. "Jesus, what is wrong with me?"

In the far recesses of my gut, I could feel the rising panic, but

I bit it back. I was going to face whatever this was. I wasn't going to cower and hide and cry. I could stand on my own two feet.

I hadn't actually loved Yofi, I knew that now, but Cole? This was going to hurt. It was going to be a soul-crushing pain, but I was going to survive it because at least this wasn't going to be a public situation where everyone in my life knew and was judging me on it. But, Jesus, I just wanted to understand. "Why are you doing this?"

"Look, she's right, okay? She's right. We *are* different. We have seen it with my friends and your family. My mom. God, your mother *hates* me. And there's nothing I can do about the fact that I'm white. I don't know what it's going to be like if we one day get married, have kids, and all that. We're just really different, and it's better if we just call it."

I stared at him. "Who's right?"

His face flamed. He shook his head and tried to move past me toward the foyer to open the door for me. "It doesn't matter. I'm sorry. I didn't want to hurt you."

"But you did."

He whirled around. "You think it's fucking easy for me? I've wanted you so bad for so long, and then when I finally think it's going to happen, I can't have you."

"You can't or you *won't*?"

"I *can't*."

"Wow. I didn't peg you for a coward."

He flinched. "What the fuck did you say to me?"

"You heard me. A *cowaaard*," I emphasized slowly. "I knew you were going to do this. I knew it."

He blinked and stared at me. "Ofosua."

"No, don't you dare 'Ofosua' me. *You* are doing this to me. I knew you weren't ready to handle this. I knew that this was going to be work. But that's typical. The moment that you had to work for something, off you go running." I landed my hit and I wasn't even sorry. All I could feel was the fury pumping through my veins.

"Wow," he whispered.

He had the nerve to "wow" me? "Yeah, wow."

"I can't believe you would say that to me."

"Well, it's true. And instead of telling me what's crawled up your ass, you make me pry it out of you. You couldn't just suck it up and tell me?"

"I was trying not to *hurt* you!" he shouted.

"Bullshit. You're being a coward."

We were facing each other in a heated grudge match. At any point we were either going to start angry fucking, which, given my vow to kill him, was highly unlikely, or we were going to start throwing things.

"It was your *fucking* mother who came and told me that I couldn't have you. That I was not the first white boy who'd thought he liked you. Do you know how humiliating that was?"

I staggered backward. "What?"

He grabbed his hair with both fists. "Fuck me, Ofosua. Look, I'm sorry. But she's right. My family would be complete assholes. You've met my mother, and Dad's a thousand times worse. You have already seen what my friends are like, and I just—I don't want to subject you to that."

"What?" I shook my head, trying to clear it. "Y-you talked to my mother?"

He started to pace in front of the door. "Look, she came to the office, and I thought she was there to see you, but she was there to see me. And she had a lot to say. Reminding me that I'm not good for you and if I care about you, I should let you go."

"*My mother* told you that you're not good for me?" I pointed to myself, back at him then back at myself. I tried to make sure

I understood. "She told you that you're not good for me, and you listened and decided that was it? You're just not even going to bother to try?"

"Ofosua, I'm trying to do the right thing for you here. You have no fucking idea how much I care about you."

"Shut up. You're a liar. When you care about someone, you don't do this to them. You fight. Instead of fighting, instead of actually putting in the work, you caved. You know what? It's better that I know that's who you really are now rather than later. I'm gone."

The tears were already filling my eyes; they would choke me if I stayed. I had to get out.

I'd taken a risk, and it had not paid off. And once again, I was left all alone.

You're not at fault here. But lucky for you, you know who is.

COLE

I had carved out my heart with a rusty blade. After she left, I ran to the door. I even had a hand on the knob because my immediate response was to fix it, to get her back, to show her that I wasn't a complete tool.

But I knew she deserved better than me, so I slid down to the floor, bracing my back against the door and wallowing in the pile of shit that was my life now.

She had called me a coward. And the worst part of it was, of course, she wasn't wrong. I'd done the right thing, but I *was* a coward. She deserved better than me. If I were the guy she deserved, I would have fought. If I were the guy she deserved, I would have stuck it out.

And hurt her?

Every time my mother made a comment, or my father, or, hell, my uncle, it would have hurt her. Every time a member of my family underestimated her or made her feel like anything less than the absolute queen she was, would I have taken the arrows for her? Every single time?

You already fucked up once. This is for the best.

—

My morning did not bring improvement. When my mother called, my brain was still foggy. At some point last night, the tears and self-pity had led to scotch.

I knew drinking wasn't going to make me forget, and now I was paying for it.

"What do you want, Mom?"

My mother tsked in my ear. "Cole, is that how you speak to your mother? What's wrong with you? Why do you sound like your father?"

That was the first jab. And as jabs went, it had enough bite to make me wince. She was right. I did sound like my father. And I probably felt like him too. *Fuck.* How did he walk around in a constant stupor like this?

"None of your business. What do you want?"

"Well, if you're going to be like this, Cole, perhaps we should speak at another time."

I cursed under my breath. "Sorry, Mom."

I forced myself to sit up in bed and scrubbed my hand over my face before I pushed myself onto my feet and into the bathroom. I made the mistake of glancing in the mirror.

Jesus, I looked like shit. "Sorry, I'm here. I'm wide awake." I ran the water and splashed it on my face to try and make that a true statement. It didn't help.

"What is wrong with you?"

Was this the time when I finally caved in and started talking to my mother about feelings and shit? Pretended that she was a real mother? One who cared more about me than her friends, tennis matches, and nonprofit boards?

Nope. Twenty-five was too late for that shit. "Nothing. What do you need?"

"Well, I was talking to Carolyn and the topic of diverse members came up. I was wondering if I could speak to that friend of yours. You know, the *Black* one. The one your uncle just up and gave a whole imprint to. Which I suppose *is* the smart thing to do in these times. Steven has always been a big supporter of affirmative action."

I clenched my jaw so hard I got a cramp. "'The *Black* one'?"

"The one I met a few weeks ago. And don't think I don't know you're sleeping with her. Because I know you, Cole. Just be careful. You're a level up, and women are aware of that, believe me. Anyway, I'd like to speak to your *friend*. Can you bring her to lunch?"

Wow. It kept getting worse. "Do you even hear yourself, Mom?"

"What now, Cole? What could I have possibly said to offend you?"

"Well, for starters, you didn't bother to remember Ofosua's name. Someone whose help it sounds like you need. And then there's the small matter of you just referring to her as 'the Black one.' As if she doesn't have an identity outside of her being Black. You could have said, 'Oh, the girl you work with, the one I met that night a few weeks ago. The beautiful one. The really smart one.' You could have said *any* of those things, but you chose to boil her down to her skin color. And then you suggested that the only way she would get her current job was affirmative action. Ofosua doesn't need it. You didn't look up her parents, did you? They own two penthouse units in the 150 Charles Street building. Ofosua hardly needs your connections. And before you get on that high and mighty horse of 'Oh, I voted for Obama,' you voted for Obama because it was the cool thing to do, not because you actually believed in what he stood for, which makes you just as bad as the racists."

She gasped. "Cole. How dare you?"

"Okay, then why did you refer to Ofosua as my Black friend? If you can answer that, I'm happy to let this go."

"What has gotten into you? You've never spoken like this before."

"But I've always felt like this. Things you say and do make me uncomfortable, and no, I have never said anything before, which is on me. But please start educating yourself on what to change, or I will be saying a lot of things all the time, publicly, in front of *your* friends. And that's going to get really embarrassing for you."

She sucked in a sharp breath. "You don't have the right to speak to your mother like that."

"I have the right when it's the truth. And for your information, Ofosua and I broke up."

"How . . . unfortunate. There's no way you can get her to do this small favor?"

I pinched the bridge of my nose. "No. Glad to see you're so worried about me."

"Well, that's a shame. Now Carolyn will think that I lied."

Just when I'd thought she was starting to listen. "Mom, you really are just inherently selfish, aren't you?"

"Cole, why you have taken this tiresome attitude is a mystery."

"I haven't taken any attitude, Mom. I'm just sad. And, frankly, disappointed."

She sighed. "Surely, you recognize you and this girl never would have worked? You're from two different worlds, darling. It's good to think the world is postracial this, and woke that, but that's not how it works. Fundamentally, *they're* different."

"What the fuck did you just say?"

My mother gasped. "Don't use that language with me, I just meant that culturally they're different. That's all I meant, Cole. I'm not an entirely horrible person, and one day you'll realize that. Do you seriously think that her people would accept you at their family gatherings? What about your circles? Think about Ofosua in Kennebunkport. Would she be comfortable? And if she wasn't, how would you enjoy your summer? It's better you end up with someone more like you. Someone who understands your life, your standing in the world. Someone who can help you achieve your dreams. Relationships are hard enough without swimming upstream."

"Mom, I can't talk about this anymore."

"Cole, stop being dramatic. It's unbecoming. It's not like you're in love with her."

Her words speared me. "I'll call you later, Mom."

"Don't forget to send me her email."

I shook my head. My mother had said the exact same things as Ofosua's mother. Two different worlds. That there was no way forward for Ofosua and me. But people made it work all the time. Granted, not without some difficulty, but they did. I'd stood up to my mother but folded when it came to Helen Addo. Maybe it was the messenger. Talking about all of this was much harder with Helen.

Or maybe you're a fool.

I told myself I'd caved *for* Ofosua. Because of what was best for her, what was right.

But I was lying to myself.

I was the one who was scared.

CHAPTER 29

OFOSUA

ADINKRA SAYING:
(Aban) A symbol of strength.

HELEN ADDO:
Hmm, next time too, go and bring another obroni boy.
This should be a lesson to never do that again.

For three days I hadn't slept. It didn't matter that the summer weather beckoned with summer fun and weekend Hamptons trips or Central Park concerts.

I was numb.

I had walked away from Cole knowing he'd chosen the easy way out. He didn't believe in me, in *us*, enough to try. And worse, it was my own mother who'd forced him into that realization.

But the cold truth was that he would have made the decision on his own in the long run. You couldn't make someone love you more, after all.

I'd said all those things to myself. But that did nothing to soothe the deep, dark, empty pit in my gut. I was numb and broken. I'd so stupidly let myself start to fall in love with him. I had forgotten the basics. Again. Guys like Cole didn't fall in love with women like me. They weren't ever going to stick around.

I needed to focus on what I did have. Work.

I had an imprint to launch, and I was not going to throw it away because some fuck boy had dumped me.

Kukua's friend had an empty flat, so I'd stayed there for the last few nights. I didn't want to run the risk of running into my mother. I wasn't ready to face her yet.

It had actually been peaceful. During the day, I'd work on my presentations for launch. Launch was the meeting where I'd present my whole debut list to the heads of sales, marketing, and publicity. It was the big meeting for editors, and we spent weeks preparing. I'd also unveil the name of the imprint, which made the meeting feel even bigger. I still didn't love the name. It didn't feel like me. But there was nothing to be done about it.

At night? Well, I'd been drinking. A lot. Not my finest set of hours, but it helped numb the pain I felt.

Thinking about Cole hurt too much.

Focus on work. You've got this.

My hands were sweaty as I stood up in the conference room. I'd known most of these people during my whole career at Drake. Hell, ever since Cole—my stomach cramped, just thinking of his name—but ever since he-who-shall-not-be-named started forcing me out to happy hours, I'd even gotten closer to some of them. I could do this.

Also in the conference room was Brian Cosmos, who gave me a warm smile. And Steven, who was, well, being Steven.

I just couldn't understand how he could smile to my face all the time and not realize that I knew he didn't have my career or this imprint's best interest at heart. That he didn't truly believe the books on my list were necessary to readers or to Drake.

He's not your friend. He's the boss.

I knew that. I did. But it still hurt. Because for so long, I had looked at Drake as my home. And that had been my mistake. Drake wasn't my home; it was my job. A job I loved, yes, but it was still a job. One I could replace if I needed to.

You are not running. He's not going to run you out of a job that you love.

As I took my spot, Emory gave me a sweet smile and two big thumbs-ups. "Good luck."

"I don't need luck. I'm prepared."

She grinned. "Same old Ofos."

Yep, cool, calm, and in control.

At least until Cole walked in.

I could feel him, his gaze, the heat of it, and I wanted to run, I wanted to crawl in a dark hole and hide. But I didn't. Instead, I squared my shoulders, turned, and leveled a glance on him, one of nothing but derision. At least I hoped that's what it was. Because I was concerned that it was one of pleading and longing.

And this is why we don't fuck colleagues.

Watching him swallow hard and then shift his gaze, I knew I'd hit my target. But focusing on Cole wasn't going to make this meeting go any easier. So instead, I focused on Brian Cosmos and started my presentation.

I was sweating by the time I finished, and I was pretty sure I could smell myself. But Emory was clapping her hands, and even Steven looked pleased. I did not spare even one glance at Cole. He didn't deserve any of my attention. The one person I did pay attention to was Brian Cosmos, who approached with a grin. "My goodness, I knew when I met you a few weeks ago that you were something special. Well done."

"Thank you. I'm really proud of our debut list. I'm excited

about what we can do, and Mahogany Prose is everything I dreamed of as a young editor getting into this business. I have you to thank for the opportunity."

He laughed. "We can look out for each other. Because from the looks of it, you'll be bringing major opportunities my way too. And you don't have to pretend to love *all* the books with me. I know the one I was concerned about was shoved down your throat."

I sighed. "I can't really speak to that right now."

"I understand. Actually, do you think I could borrow you for a few minutes? I have something I want to run by you."

Alone in my office, Brian gave me a warm smile. Something in his gaze held on for just a moment. And if I were anything other than dead inside, I would've seen it as interest. But I shut that off immediately.

It didn't matter that he might be interested. Or that he was good-looking and brilliant. I couldn't even think about anything to do with relationships again. I needed more time by myself. Eight months hadn't been enough. Hell, according to all the smartest researchers, the happiest demographic was single women without children. Maybe that needed to be my life. My mother would die, but I at least would be happy.

"I know I said it before, but I'm impressed by what you've done with Mahogany Prose. The launch was perfect, full of passion and excitement, and you actually care about the stories being told."

"Yeah. I mean, I come from a long line of storytellers. Everyone in Ghana is a storyteller. From the market to the elders to church, there's always a story being told. I'm truly passionate about it. I want to tell love stories, especially those that center Black women. I want to tell stories of joy. Black people living joyfully, wouldn't that be a shocker? Black women especially."

"And that is specifically why I wanted to talk to you in private.

We have an emerging stories arm at Cosmos Film and Media that focuses on marginalized stories."

"Yes. That was your first division, right?"

"The young lady has done her research."

"Well, when there are conversations being had about an investment possibility, you do your research."

"I'm happy to hear that. And while I'm excited about what you can do with this imprint, what I'm most excited about is *you*. I'd love to see your passion and drive at Cosmos Film and Media."

I stared at him. "What?"

"I know you are just getting your career in swing here at Drake. But your talents are being wasted. And I don't think you necessarily have the support here someone like you needs."

I swallowed hard. "Um, I'm not a film producer."

"I don't need you to be, but I do need you to be able to pitch a movie. From what I saw today, you can do that. I want someone to work with me who knows story, who can spot the diamonds and help develop them. Your eye is a large part of what makes you so valuable to a company like mine. And I want to remind you that we are Black-owned. Black-led."

"You've caught me completely off guard. I'm not sure I can just abandon my authors. I don't know what to say."

"Say you will think about it. I don't head back to LA for another couple of days. We can talk more, maybe over dinner. I will try and convince you to come to LA. And maybe you come out for a week and see how you like it. I'm sure it'll work."

"You're serious about this."

"Very. I believe—"

Steven barged into my office without knocking just then, his face red. "Ofosua, I wanted to talk with you immediately after the launch, because that's the best time to debrief, and then you disappear." He lifted a brow at Brian. "Everything all right?"

Brian gave him a wide, confident grin. "Relax, Steven. I'm just having a conversation with your bright young star here."

"Or were you trying to poach her?" Steven laughed as if that couldn't possibly be what was happening.

Brian's easy expression didn't change. "Can you blame me?"

"*I* was just joking, Brian. Let's be serious now. After everything I've done for her, she wouldn't dare run off to Hollywood, would you, Ofosua?"

"Mr. Drake. I haven't made any decisions yet."

"I see. Well. Hmph. Well." He straightened up in my doorway as a look of distaste settled on his face. "Don't think you'll be able to come running back to Drake when you discover that television is not the same as books."

My stomach fell. "Sir, I wouldn't . . . I'm not . . . This is not that."

Brian Cosmos did me no favors by laughing out loud. "First and foremost, Ofosua hasn't said yes. And this was my idea, not hers."

Steven turned to glower at me. "Normally, I'd save this for a private discussion, but as that's not possible now, I hope you'll still hear me. Mahogany Prose was specifically built for you. No editor would throw that opportunity away, least of all one so young. Your publishing career is all but made."

I had to laugh then. "Was Mahogany Prose built *for me*? Really? And here I thought we were diversifying at Drake because you needed Cosmos to invest. Did I miss something?"

Steven glared. "That's called business, Ofosua."

"Of course it is. Look, I haven't said yes to anything."

"If you take some nonsense job in Hollywood, you'll be seriously damaging your future career prospects in book publishing. I hope you realize that."

My breath caught. Was Steven Drake threatening me? "Thank you, sir. I appreciate your honesty." I turned to Brian. "And thank you for giving me the opportunity to see the truth about my employment here for myself. I'm more than happy to accept your offer."

Brian's eyes went wide. "What?"

"Yeah." I grabbed one of the Post-its on top of my stack of presentation materials, put my number on it, and handed it over. "I think I just quit my job, so you'll want to call me on my cell to make arrangements."

Cosmos gave me a beaming smile, his almost-too-white teeth setting off his sandy brown skin. "Ofosua, you are not going to regret this."

I glanced at Steven, who glowered. "Thank you for everything you've done for me, Mr. Drake. It's been an education."

And with that, I walked away from Drake Publishing.

CHAPTER 30

COLE

ADINKRA SAYING:
(Abe Dua) A symbol of wealth.

SAMUEL ADDO:
What good is the wealth without a wife to nag you for it?

Gray. My entire world was damn gray. Never mind the scorcher of a day blazing outside.

The depression clawed at me . . . as did my raging hangover. I was my father's son, after all.

It had been three days since I had blown up my life, and I was wallowing in a self-pitying spiral. It had gotten so bad, last night Tallon had even come by to check on me and ended up crashing on the couch because apparently I was too pathetic to be left alone.

My mind kept replaying the brokenhearted look on Ofos's face. Instead of standing up for her, I had let myself be talked out of us. By her own mother, nonetheless. And then *my* mother. Talking to my own mother had only cemented what Ofosua had said. I was a coward. I'd told myself I was doing what was best for her, but I'd caved and I'd hurt her.

In the worst way possible. You abandoned her.

Fuck. I didn't deserve her. I was a goddamn mess. I needed to talk to her. Hell, I didn't even know if I could get her to agree to see me, let alone let me apologize.

Seeing her at the office over the last several days had been the purest kind of torture. I thought if I could go to work and ignore the pain, it wouldn't hurt as bad. Rookie mistake. I knew there would be no recovering from her.

When I stepped out on my terrace, I found Tallon with a cup of coffee. "You know, the espresso machine is broken. So I brought you coffee because I know you're—Jesus, you look like shit."

"Wow, thanks. That's good to hear from you, my best friend, of all people."

He shrugged. "I'm telling you the truth, man, you look like hell."

"Thanks, you're pretty awesome too."

"You weren't exactly chatty last night. But I assume your current state of dishevelment is about Ofos?"

I was truly embarrassed to say it out loud, to tell Tallon what an idiot I'd been.

"Her mother came to see me. She gave me an earful about how I couldn't possibly understand what it's like to date someone like Ofosua, and about how my family would never accept her, and hers would never accept me, and that the kinder thing to do was to break it off now."

He cursed under his breath. "And you listened to that bullshit?"

"It made sense. It was the easier thing to do, I guess. And then Mom called. I got another earful about how Ofosua would never fit in with our world. How everyone we knew would look at her and treat her. And that wasn't what I wanted for her."

He blinked at me and then he leaned forward. "Okay, you and I have been friends since we were kids. But you are the dumbest son of a bitch I have ever met."

I blinked. "Well, I can't argue with that."

"Shut up and I'll finish. You fucked up bad. Isn't this what she's always telling you, not to take the fucking easy route? You sat there as her mother echoed the things that maybe you're a little bit afraid of, and you fell right into her trap." He threw his hands up. "Then Rebecca turned it up a notch."

I pinched the bridge of my nose. He was right. I knew what I wanted out of my life, how I planned to get there, and that I wanted Ofosua to be by my side. So essentially, I'd pushed away one of the few truly good relationships I'd ever actually had. She made me a better person, and I had walked away from her.

"Anything else you want to say?"

He nodded. "Fucking fix this. You love her. You're just too dumb to see it yet."

Tallon left me alone with a lot to think about. Which was good because my mind was spinning, but he kind of gave me the bit of clarity I needed. I decided to go to Ofosua right then and there to talk this out. Maybe we wouldn't resolve it, but I had to start proving I wanted to.

But when I went to the office, she wasn't at her desk.

Then my uncle called me into his office.

"Hey, what's up?"

"The pitch went well yesterday. You were terrific."

"Ofosua was, that's for sure. Have you seen her this morning?"

"Take the compliment."

"Thank you, I guess."

My uncle smiled. "Your marketing plans were perfect."

"Thanks. A lot of thought went into positioning. We have a solid plan."

And then he said, "Your grandfather would have been proud."

Those fucking words nearly made me choke.

"I appreciate it, but Ofosua was really the reason it all came together."

He smiled briefly. "If you insist. So, were you going to tell me that you and she were, ah, fraternizing in some way, or you were going to hope I didn't notice?"

I blinked at him. "Excuse me?"

He leaned forward and planted his hands on his desk. "I've seen the way you look at each other."

I groaned. *Fuck.* Was I that obvious? "You're not pissed?"

He laughed. "Hopefully, you were smart about it so we don't end up with a Me Too situation. Or worse."

I winced. "Just when I think you can't be any more out of touch. If we're finished here, I'm going to go find Ofosua. We need to talk."

My uncle chuckled low. "I'm surprised she didn't tell you since you're so chummy."

I frowned at him. "Tell me what?"

"She took a job with Brian Cosmos. Her last day was yesterday."

I blinked at him slowly. "What?"

I had to find her.

Hauling ass, I made it to Greenwich Village in less than twenty minutes. It seemed she hadn't removed me from the automatic entry list, which was a gift from the heavens. I didn't bother with the elevator. It would take too long. I raced up the stairs to her apartment and then banged on it like the sound alone was going to get her to answer. Granted, if she knew it was me, she probably wouldn't, but it was worth a shot.

One of her roommates came to the door. She was pretty, with medium-brown skin and long braids. We'd met before. If I remembered right, her name was Cora.

"Hi, I'm sorry to interrupt. I'm looking for Ofosua."

She glared. "You know, Hot Cole, I had high hopes for you."

I winced. "I'm here to fix it."

She shook her head. "I'm sorry, you're too late."

"Fuck, I'll call her."

She shook her head. "Nope, she left this behind."

I stared at the silver iPhone in her hand. "When is she coming back?"

She hesitated. "She's not. She leaves tonight for LA, and right now, she's out with Kukua."

"Do you have Kukua's number?"

She winced again, fiddling her fingers on the phone. "Yeah, she figured Auntie Helen would be calling Kukua when she couldn't reach Ofos, so she left it behind too."

Fuck me. I had no way of getting to her before she left tonight. I was completely screwed.

"Thanks. I appreciate it."

She sighed. "For what it's worth, she's broken up. Like, honestly, a wreck. She cares about you. So whatever you did, you can probably fix it, but you might have to wait until she gets back from LA in a few weeks. From what I understand, the job is bicoastal."

The easy thing to do would have been to wait, but that would mean weeks to resolve this. I'd be losing precious time. Besides, I really wasn't doing things the easy way anymore. That's what had gotten me into this situation. And I had zero interest in going backward. I needed to go to LA, but I was going to need some reinforcements.

OFOSUA

Maybe it was a little bit of homesickness, something that the excitement of the huge leap forward I'd just taken couldn't stamp out. LA was great, but it was an adjustment getting used to driving everywhere. And the traffic. Don't get me started.

I'd been in LA for exactly two weeks. Only Cora, Megan, and Kukua had my new number. Each of them could be trusted not to give that number to Cole or my mum.

Brian walked into the office for our weekly Monday meeting with a smile. "Good weekend?"

"Yeah, I explored a little bit. Got settled into my place some more, which is beautiful, by the way. I still can't believe that's a company apartment."

"I wanted to make sure that you were comfortable. And I think that you must be, given the way you've hit the ground running. I love it when my instincts are proven right. Which, gotta say, they usually are." He winked.

What I liked about Brian was that when he said things like this, it wasn't ever with typical male self-important puffery. No jackass alerts went off in my head. Here was a man who was comfortable with himself. And with me.

He asked about a few scripts I'd read, wanting my take on them. There was so much to learn. I loved it so far. Mostly. Then he asked about Aurora St. James.

"I need to get back to her. She's hosting a major literacy event tomorrow. I'll call since I can't be there in person to show her support. To be honest, handing her off to another editor at Drake still doesn't feel quite right, but it is what it is. I'll stay involved any way I can."

As we worked for the rest of the hour, I thought to myself that I could settle in here, do my work, and be happy. Wasn't that what I'd always wanted? Still, there were these constant and persistent things that kept weighing at the back of my mind.

Every now and again, I'd thought of my mother. I hated to admit it, but I missed her, even her nagging about how I should be dating the right African man or how to improve my cooking.

The truth of it was, I had never really lived in a possibly permanent way on my own. I'd briefly traveled abroad after college, and then come back and spent six months at home in Ghana at my parents' house before connecting with Yofi and moving in with him. It had all been so quick. Having this time on my own was freeing but actually a little lonely too.

Not that I would tell my mother anything of the sort.

I would never tell her I missed my old life.

The feeling was worse at night because then I missed something altogether different. I could still see Cole's smiling face as he danced at Republic Day, laughing his ass off, doing his best to find the beat.

And that was what made the nights unbearable. Missing him, constantly. I wanted the pain to stop, but no distraction lessened it.

That's because you fucked up and fell in love when you really should have known better.

CHAPTER 31

COLE

ADINKRA SAYING:
(Anyi Me Aye A) A symbol of ingratitude.

HELEN ADDO:
Why would you spite your whole self when given good advice?

My palms were sweaty. I was actually nervous. I didn't know if this was going to work, but I had to try.

Which was why I was standing at her mother's door, twenty feet away from Ofosua's old apartment.

I wiped my hands on my jeans and knocked. As I waited, I tried not to focus too much on the fact that without her mother's approval, there would always be this tension constantly hovering over our heads, this note of uncertainty about whether or not we would be accepted as a couple by our families. This was where I'd fucked up, and I had to make it right. Also, I knew her mother needed to make amends to Ofosua too. Like me, she'd done her wrong by meddling too much in her daughter's life. Or at least I hoped she also saw it that way. We'd both fucked up bad. And we both needed to go beg for her forgiveness.

When Helen Addo opened the door, her brows immediately dipped. "You. What are you doing here?"

"Dr. Addo, do you have a moment? I'd like to talk to you."

She stared at me. "I've already said everything I have to say to you. Because of you, Ofosua has run off."

I lifted my brows then. "Because of *me*? Is that accurate?"

Her eyes went wide. "How dare you question me in my own house? What kind of foolish nonsense—"

I put my hands up. "Dr. Addo, I only want to tell you something about Ofosua. I know where she is, and you and I both need to go see her and apologize because we both messed up."

She stared at me. "Apologize for what? All I ever did was protect her best interest. But she can't see that, so eh, it's not my problem."

I sighed. "Okay, if that's the way you want to look at it, I can't make you see it any other way. But maybe if you look at this from Ofosua's perspective, I'm not the only one who did her wrong here. She told you she was happy. And yet you deliberately interfered."

Her mother's eyes went wide. "You're suggesting that I'm the reason she's unhappy?"

I was going to screw this up if I wasn't careful. "Let me try again. I made a huge mistake. We both messed up. If you have a problem with me, fine, have a problem with me. It's her I need to prove my worthiness to right now. But you also did the wrong thing by going around her. So you and I need to form some kind of truce to get her back. It's the only chance we have. Since we messed up together, we should fix it together."

For a moment, I thought she would tell me no and to mind my own business. But then I noticed her eyes were misty. "Do you really know where she is? Is she safe?"

I nodded. "I do know where she is, and you can either come with me, or you can stay here. If you don't come, you lose the chance to talk to her. And trust me, I won't give you her new phone number or her new address unless she tells me I can."

She stared at me. "You're blackmailing me."

"Yes, if you want access to your daughter, you need me. It's your choice."

She pointed a finger at my face. "That pretty face of yours, it's giving you so much trouble, but you're not too big for me to beat you senseless."

I bit the inside of my cheek. "Yes, ma'am. Now, are you coming with me or not?"

"Where are we going?"

"Bring a bag. This could be an overnight situation."

"Overnight? With a white man? This is how Black people end up dead. You're going to tell me where we're going."

I laughed. "You think I'm a serial killer?"

"Ah, you're a wise man, aren't you? This is a lesson all Black girls should learn. If you have a white boyfriend, you could end up in a freezer. This is true. Everybody knows this."

I had to laugh, because she did have a solid point; statistically speaking, white guys were more likely to be serial killers.

"Okay, noted. Can we go now? We have a flight to catch."

Her eyes went wide. "A flight? Where are we going?"

"Your daughter is in Los Angeles. So that's where we need to go if we're going to go beg for her forgiveness."

She sniffed. "Hm, me? I don't beg. You beg."

"Whatever your version of apology looks like, bring it with you. Let's go."

She grumbled, but meanwhile, she was moving. Albeit slowly.

When she had her bag and her keys and what looked like a fur stole, I smiled. "Are you ready? The car is waiting."

"Car waiting? Don't you have your own car?"

"I do, but we're going to the airport, so best not to drive ourselves."

She sniffed. "It better be a private car, not an Uber. That's nonsense."

I coughed. As it turned out, my suspicions were correct; Helen Addo had a lot in common with my own mother.

—

So far, I'd been lucky. Helen had been satisfied with first class. She had a mimosa that she deemed acceptable and mostly kept her opinions to herself.

I didn't need her to like me—yet. I needed her to apologize to her daughter because that's what would make Ofosua happier. Or feel better, at least. Fuck, I didn't know. I knew that I had to see her because I was in serious danger of losing my sanity without her in my life.

We went to Brian's office. I'd actually been there before on a trip out to LA nine months before. At the time, I'd been really excited to see how the operations went on their movie development side. Now I was anxious, looking for Ofosua around every corner.

I found Brian first.

I gave him a nod and a smile. "Brian, it's good to see you again. I'm actually looking for Ofosua Addo. This is Dr. Helen Addo, her mother."

He smiled warmly. "Dr. Addo, it's nice to meet you. Ofosua has spoken of you often."

Helen wasn't charmed in the slightest, and she had no time for niceties. She was on a mission. "Eh, where's my daughter? Running away from home like a teenager."

Brian's lip twitched. As if, yes, he'd heard about Helen, but he hadn't quite believed until now. He suddenly slipped me a sympathetic look. "I am sorry, you've missed Ofosua. She's actually back in New York. She is pitching Aurora St. James's novel to some of our favorite producing partners tomorrow."

My heart stopped. Ofosua was back in New York for Aurora. And I had come here for her.

Brian frowned. "I hope nothing is wrong."

No way was I giving him the satisfaction of admitting I was here because I was in love and I'd fucked up. Dr. Addo, on the other hand, had no such compunction about spilling my private business. "This obroni boy thinks he's in love or some such nonsense. He dragged me all the way here to apologize to somebody who doesn't even want an apology."

It was then that he shook his head. "So it's you?"

I lifted my brows. "What?"

"The one she's been homesick for."

I swallowed hard. "Let's hope so."

"Good luck and safe travels."

Ofosua's mother said, "Travels? Look, if I'm here, I'm going to enjoy the time I have in Los Angeles, since my daughter isn't willing to speak to me."

I sighed. "She didn't know we were coming. That's the nature of a surprise."

"Nonsense. Surprises, grand gestures. You know this is some obroni nonsense."

Suddenly, she eyed Brian. "Are you single?"

He grinned. "Oh, Ofosua wasn't kidding."

"What is that supposed to mean?"

"She said that you are extremely invested in her romantic life."

"Extremely invested? Nonsense. I have a job to do. A mother's job. This child, you know she has always been difficult."

I laughed at that. I couldn't help it. "Somehow, something tells me she'd say the same about you."

I swear I thought I was going to get smacked. Ofosua had told me about how her mother once chased her around the whole house with a wooden spoon. But instead, she laughed too. "Eh, look who has a backbone?"

I glowered at her. "My understanding was you didn't want anyone with a backbone."

"Ah, but I have to see if you're good enough for my daughter. The jury is still out."

I nodded. "Right. Jury is still out. I get you."

She laughed. "But so far, you're doing a little better. Small, small."

"Thanks for the vote of confidence. Are you ready to go back to New York?"

"Another commercial flight. I'm an old woman. I need to rest."

Brian turned around and said, "Dr. Addo, let me offer you one of our corporate suites so you can rest, recuperate, and then return tomorrow."

"Eh, are we going to be on a private plane back? Because this boy, he made me fly commercial. Can you believe such obroni nonsense?"

Brian frowned and turned to me. "Obroni?"

I shrugged. "White person. And not in a nice way."

He coughed a laugh. "I'll see what we can arrange. Until then, we will keep you entirely comfortable."

She patted his arm. "And you're single, eh? You know, I have a niece, an artist. I know, not the best thing, but since you're sort of an artist yourself and you work with artists, it's okay. You should meet her next time you're in New York."

He grinned. "What about your daughter, Dr. Addo?"

She shook her head then. "Eh, she's a lost cause. She thinks she loves this one."

She pointed at me, and my heart squeezed. If even her mother thought she loved me, then maybe I still had a chance.

Brian checked his watch. "You better go, Cole. If you catch the red-eye, you might make it in time for Aurora's show tomorrow."

I gave him a nod of thanks. "You're being awfully decent. Why?"

"Because her mother is right. She thinks she's in love with you."

"Yeah. I think I'm in love with her too."

CHAPTER 32

OFOSUA

ADINKRA SAYING:
(Asase Ye Duru) A symbol of providence.
SAMUEL ADDO:
What is meant to be will be. Don't tell your mother,
but it's rarely ever that hard to find your fate.

I wasn't sure why, but I was nervous. Hell, it didn't make any sense. It wasn't like I was presenting *my* stories to a roomful of producers.

These guys were people Brian had worked with in the past. And they were looking for some love stories featuring Black joy. Aurora and I could deliver that in spades. It hadn't been easy to convince her agent to let us co-rep her on the film side. She and Aurora were still disappointed about my move from Drake. The books I'd toiled over for months were now in limbo because once Steven found out Cosmos was having second thoughts about investing, he saw no reason to keep Mahogany Prose, and instead he'd reassigned my authors to other editors, dissolving my imprint. That was standard procedure when an editor left a house, and it usually worked out okay in the end. But I knew the real score:

Steven had never seen these books' true worth in the first place. I just had to hope my former colleagues did.

At least I had an opportunity to help Aurora and the rest of my authors tell their stories in different ways. I stared back up at the Cosmos Film and Media offices, shielding my eyes from the sun and hoping I'd done enough.

"She's going to do great, you know?"

I whipped around on the sidewalk, the familiar voice burning me deep in my womb. Seeing him standing there, looking as gorgeous as always, had my stomach in knots, and all the air whooshed out of my lungs.

"Cole."

"Yes, that is my name."

It hurt to look at him. Why did he look like that? Completely unaffected by anything that had happened. And I, well, I felt like a wreck. I had to turn away. "Yup, she's always great."

There was a pause, and I thought maybe he'd walked away. Somehow, that made me disappointed. But when I turned, he was right behind me. "Do you have to stand so close?"

"There was a time when you liked me standing close."

"Well, you know, that was before you dumped me unceremoniously, so I'm not exactly too keen on you standing this close right now."

"I was a dick."

I laughed. "That's accurate."

"I miss you."

I blinked rapidly. "What?"

"You heard me. I miss you."

He thought he could just come back? After what he'd done? "No, Cole. You don't get to do this. You don't get to cut me out of your life then turn up randomly—on the sidewalk, no less—in my new one and tell me things like you miss me. That's not how this works."

"I know. I completely understand. I fucked up."

"You think?"

"I let go of the one person who believed in me even when she shouldn't. I was terrified of hurting you, of getting it wrong. So I fucked it up. I have no right to ask anything of you. No right to turn back up in your life. But if you maybe thought you wanted to give me some time to apologize, you know where to find me."

I couldn't breathe.

This wasn't fair; he was supposed to be gone. Away.

"This is about Aurora. Why are you even here?"

"Her work means as much to me as it does to you. Mahogany Prose was *ours*. We built it together."

"Don't do this, Cole. Don't do this thing where you act like you care, because I want to believe you. And I can't afford to do that right now."

"I know. You have no reason to believe me. No reason to count on me. No reason to trust my word. I fucked up bad. And I want nothing more than to fall at your feet and tell you that I'm sorry, but I know I need to do more than say the words, which you won't trust anyway. So I'm going to show you."

I turned and blinked at him. "What?"

"All I need is time to show you." And with that he started backing up through the crowd. Soon the pedestrians swallowed him up and I was left standing on the sidewalk staring after him. What the hell was he talking about? He had to be delusional. There was no way I was getting sucked back in by Cole Drake for a third time.

I was still confused and in a daze when I met Emory for coffee. She squeezed me hard and said, "God, I miss you. Everything has been a shit show of turmoil since you left. Now, what's up with you and Cole?"

"Nothing. We're . . . nothing."

"Ugh, God, I thought for sure once you heard that he'd been looking for you . . ."

I frowned. "He's been looking for me?"

She laughed. "Yeah. He about lost it in the office when he discovered you were gone. When I was talking to Cora about it, she said he also went there looking for you."

"He went to my house?"

She nodded. "None of us were giving out your number. All he knew was Cosmos had given you a job. That's how he found you in LA. I thought he saw you."

My skin went clammy and cold. He'd gone to LA? "Wait, what?"

Her eyes went wide. "Oh my God, you don't know? You have no idea what he's been doing?"

I shook my head. My heart suddenly racing. What had he been doing?

"Oh my God, Ofosua." She sighed. "You didn't know he went to LA? Or that he took your mother with him?"

My mother? I needed something stronger than coffee for this. I couldn't comprehend the words that she was saying. But what struck me dumb was the fact that Cole and my mother went to LA. *Together.* And he was still alive.

"I can't believe he didn't tell you."

I shook my head. "He didn't tell me anything except that he would show me he's sorry, or something like that."

"Yeah, as he should. And I presume you also didn't how he's fighting to keep the imprint. Things have been really tense with him and Steven."

"Cole's trying to keep Mahogany Prose? I thought he scrapped it."

"*Steven* tried. But Cole's been looking for an editor to replace you, and in the meantime he's making sure your books land with just the right editors in-house until the new you arrives. He and Steven have daily fights. It's pretty intense. Steven is pissed, but Cole is holding firm."

"He's trying to keep all of my books?" I still couldn't believe it. "He's done all of that for me?"

Cole had come for me. He'd come for me, and he hadn't even said so.

I was going to find out why.

COLE

The Mandrake was every bit the opulent hotel the name suggested. Brian had helped me out again and told me where she'd be after her meetings.

Though she'd been less than thrilled to find me on her hotel doorstep.

"Ofosua—"

She put up her hand, and that simple gesture was breaking my heart all over again. She looked beautiful.

"You hurt me."

"I know, and I don't deserve your forgiveness, but I'm going to ask for it anyway."

But she was ready for me as she shook her head. "Why did you go to LA?"

I shook my head. "It doesn't matter. What matters is that it was my fault you ended up in LA at all. You were right when you told me that I was a coward."

"I am so afraid of you hurting me again, Cole."

"Ofosua, you know why I went to LA, why I had to see you."

"No, I don't. Why would you do any of this?"

I ran my hands through my hair. "Can't you see it?"

"See what, Cole? You told me you didn't want me."

"That's not what I said. I said that it wasn't a good idea. I was terrified, Ofosua. I know this sounds like an excuse, but I somehow came to the conclusion that our relationship would only hurt you in the end, especially with our families involved, and then I chickened out. I shouldn't have let your mother run me off. But she said all the things that I had been afraid of out loud, including that I wasn't good enough for you. I should have told her that I would fight for you every step of the way. Every minute away from you was like a void that sucked the essence of my very existence. It's like the air was pulled out of me, and I couldn't breathe. So I made a promise to myself to do anything possible to get you back at my side."

Her eyes burned with tears. "I can't."

"And you shouldn't have to. I know I have a lot of work to do to prove to you what I actually mean. I'm trying. So I'm going to keep doing the things I should have done since the night I first met you on my uncle's balcony until you take me back. I'm going to keep turning up for you. I'm going to keep showing you that even though I don't deserve you, I am sorry for making you feel like this was the Yofi situation all over again. I thought I was doing the right thing, but I clearly wasn't, and I'm fucking miserable because of it."

She laughed softly. "I can't believe you actually went to LA and back in one day. For me."

I shrugged. "Well, that's where I thought you were."

"That's insane. You even took my mother with you?"

"How did you know?" I shrugged. "Doesn't matter. She is, um . . . You know what, I think I've grown on her."

She rolled her eyes. "Oh my God, I'm sorry you had to go through the ordeal of being trapped on a plane with my mum."

"Hey, it's part of the penance I have to pay."

She was still staring at me, and her wide eyes were brimming with tears. "I don't know what to do with you."

I shrugged. "Well, then why don't you allow me to prove to you how much I want and need you? I love you."

She stared at me.

"Oh, did I not mention that before? I love you. I love you with all of me, Ofosua. I won't ever get tired of saying those words to you, even when you get tired of hearing me say them. I love you, Ofosua Addo."

The first tears spilled, and I palmed her cheek. "I probably should have been saying that a lot sooner, since I've been in love with you for God knows how long."

"What? Really?"

I nodded. "I know it's going to take you a while to warm up to the idea. But like I said, I'm not going anywhere."

"What am I supposed to do with you?"

"Well, I have an idea or two, but you tell me what you want, and I'll do it."

"You. I want you, Cole. I've always wanted you, but all the same obstacles are still in our way."

She wasn't wrong, but I didn't care. "I know. And it won't be easy. But two weeks without you and I felt like I was dying inside. We belong together because that's what we want, and fuck anyone who has anything to say about it. I will never leave your side again. I can't breathe without you." I swiped away another tear on her cheek as I spoke. "I'm going to kiss you now, okay?"

More tears followed as she laughed and cried. As I slid my lips over hers, I knew that I was the luckiest, happiest person alive. I would do whatever it took for her to give me a second chance. I was going to fight like hell to hold on tight. No one was going to stop me from winning her trust.

Not her mother, and certainly not myself.

CHAPTER 33

COLE

ADINKRA SAYING:
(Dono Ntoaso) A symbol of united action.

HELEN ADDO:
Since when is your own mother expected to apologize?

I had been waiting for this moment.

I had known from the moment he assigned me the imprint with Ofosua that at some point things were going to come to a head. And today was that day.

I was a Drake. Drake Publishing was my legacy. And if my uncle was allowed to stay at that helm, I would have no legacy left.

I still had almost five years before I'd be able to take over. So I had to take drastic action.

My uncle had insisted the meeting with Brian Cosmos to try to lock down the investment happen in his office. It was certainly large enough, and the views of Central Park were unbelievable.

But it was a power move. In this office, my uncle was in charge. And all his dark oak furniture and paneling made the room look extremely masculine and traditional. He hadn't updated it to be bright, open, and modern like the rest of the office.

But it had always struck me as odd that there were no Drake books on the bookshelves in here. Instead, the shelves were filled with books from his London days. What kind of publisher didn't have his own books on display?

I wondered how I hadn't been able to see it before.

My uncle hadn't grown up with my grandfather. He didn't understand his values. Instead, he'd had his own agenda this whole time. And he'd thought we were all going to pay for it.

I kept watching the clock, waiting for the Cosmos team to arrive. Five minutes before they did, Ofos sent me a text.

OFOS:

See you in five.

A smile tugged at my lips. We still had work to do, but we were working on us. She was starting to forgive me. Not that I deserved it, but I wasn't wasting this opportunity.

My uncle frowned at me. "What's that look on your face? What is wrong with you? Cosmos is about to hand us a massive check."

I cleared my throat and put my phone away. "Well, let's hope so. After what happened, I'm not so certain."

He frowned at me. "That was an employee stepping out of line. He understands business."

"Sure, he understands business, but you recognize she works for him now? And she went voluntarily and made it very clear that you were the reason why. You really think he's going to hand *us* a check?"

He scoffed. "He'll see our way of thinking."

"This might not go the way you think."

"He has nowhere else to go. Drake is the ideal partnership for him. Cosmos is an upstart. I'll make it clear that other companies won't work with him. Not after what he pulled here."

I shook my head. "You can't just toss your weight around."

"This is how things get done, Cole."

"I really hope not."

"You're a Drake. You'll come to realize how these things happen."

Cosmos walked in with Ofos behind him, swathed in a Stella McCartney electric-blue wrap dress and black Manolo Blahnik pumps. I knew the shoes well. She'd been wearing nothing but those shoes when I'd made love to her this morning.

Her gaze flickered to me, and the corners of her lips twitched.

Warmth bloomed in my chest, threatening to expand until I fully exploded into a supernova.

Cosmos shook my uncle's hand, then mine. Ofos gave me a smile and nodded at my uncle before taking a seat next to Brian.

Uncle Steven was less gracious. "This is a surprise. We were expecting only you, Brian."

"Ofosua is a key part of my team, Steven. I'll keep this brief. Obviously, we've been in negotiations for some time, and we've had a good partnership until very recently. And that's what I want to discuss. I'm reconsidering the investment with you."

My uncle sat back and toyed with his fountain pen while glowering at Cosmos. "Is this because of her? You're making a gut decision based on a low-level employee you've known for a couple of months. Despite what Ofosua may have told you, Drake has done nothing but support her."

Brian held up a hand. "Steven, I'm going to stop you there. You wanted my money, and I can understand that, but Drake very obviously still has a lot of work to do. The imprint was a strong step in the right direction, but instead of moving forward from an authentic place, you were only making your money grab. Do you think I don't know that you've been trying to shut the imprint down these past few weeks, and not only that but you are blaming it on Ofosua's departure? The deals and partnerships we make at Cosmos aren't just about money. They're about making an impact. And Drake, as it currently stands, is the wrong kind of partner."

My uncle leaned forward. "We had an agreement. And I'm still publishing the books you wanted me to publish. I'm going to have Drake's lawyers on this immediately."

"I don't think you'll have the right to make those kinds of decisions for very much longer."

My uncle laughed. "In case you haven't noticed, I *am* Drake Publishing. Our lawyers do what I tell them to."

And that was where I sat forward. "Actually, Uncle Steven, about that."

I glanced up at the glass door of the office in time to see my aunt Ruby breeze past my uncle's panicked executive assistant.

Clad in understated Burberry elegance, Aunt Ruby looked every bit the Upper East Side Manhattan socialite of a certain age that she was. "Darling. I'm so sorry to interrupt." Then she paused and smiled brightly. "Actually, that's not true. I'm not sorry at all."

My uncle looked shocked. "Ruby, what are you doing here? I'm in the middle of a meeting."

"Actually, you no longer are in the middle of a meeting. Well, not the meeting you think you are in, anyway."

He coughed a laugh and practically fell back in his chair. "Excuse me?"

She shifted her gaze to me and winked. "You see, while you've been so busy underestimating my nephew, he's been filling me in on your, ah, exploits here at Drake."

Uncle Steven turned his gaze to me. "Cole? He's nothing but a spoiled malcontent. I'd had such hopes for him. But he's just like his father. Unfit to run this company."

"Well, the good news is that it isn't actually up to you to determine this company's successor. It never was up to you. Your malcontent nephew also informed me that you and one of your publicists—Nazrin, is it?—have been carrying on a secret affair. Sometimes you even carry it on in the office. Which was not very smart, Steven. Did you forget that there are cameras in the elevator? You must have. Did you also forget that the Drake family owns this building, pays the security teams, and can review the tapes at will? I've been content all these years to let you run around doing what you needed to do. I thought that no matter what, at least you cared about books and Drake Publishing the same way my father did. I can't tell you how many times I've told myself that over the years. But you almost losing the deal we need to ensure that my family's legacy survives made me see the truth. It's over, Steven. All of it. I have the power to fire you, another thing you seem to have forgotten."

She turned her gaze to Ofosua. "It was a shame to lose you. You started something important with Mahogany Prose. I read all the manuscripts, and Cole is right—you have an incredible eye. Also, I love a love story."

Ofos sat up straighter. "Oh, thank you."

Ruby turned back to my uncle. "So, as per the agreement in our prenup, my lawyers are waiting right outside this office to deliver the really bad news to you. The board will meet this afternoon, and I'll name Cole as interim co-CEO, with me. In five years, I'll hand Drake fully over. Cole and I are very excited about our new partnership with Mr. Cosmos."

Brian grinned at my uncle. "You see, I have no intention of working with *you*, Steven, but Cole and your soon-to-be ex-wife have made me an offer I can't refuse. It's been great watching your face through this whole little thing." He turned to Ofos. "Thank you for convincing me to come here in person and not just make the phone call."

"My pleasure."

For a moment, I thought my uncle was going to lunge at my aunt, so I pushed to my feet and stepped directly between the two of them. "Uncle Steven, don't do this. I watched you squander the opportunity we had. I didn't see it at first, maybe because I didn't want to, but at every turn you have dug this company into a hole it didn't need to be in because you refuse to change."

I turned to Ofos. "I know that you are very happy at Cosmos Film and Media. But if you could do Drake one more favor and help us find an editor who's worthy of the imprint, I would be grateful."

I could see the tears in her eyes as she said, "I'm happy to lend my services."

"Excellent. I think my uncle Steven and aunt Ruby have a lot to discuss. So, Brian, if you will, maybe I can take you and Ofos to lunch?"

He grinned. "Sounds good. Let's make sure it includes a champagne toast."

I gave my uncle a nod. "See you around, Uncle Steven. I told you not to underestimate us."

I didn't bother with a glance back at him.

—

OFOSUA

As we lay in bed, the sunlight streamed into Cole's bedroom while he fingered my hair. "I really love your curls, you know."

My fingers played with the dusting of hair on his chest. "I love that you love them."

I tried to sit up, but he pulled me back into his arms, tucking me close to his chest. "Try to get up again, and I'll have to put you back into a sex-drunk stupor."

I muffled a giggle against his chest. "Oh no, anything but that." He was so very good at the stupor. Truth be told, after last night I wasn't sure I'd be able to walk properly. He hadn't let me rest.

He kissed my forehead softly before asking, "How long are you staying before you go back to LA?"

I wrinkled my nose. "I don't have any meetings for the next two weeks or so, and honestly my position is technically remote. So most of it can also be done from here."

He pressed my hand over his chest. "So I have you for two weeks before you have to go back?"

I nodded. "Then I've got a couple of meetings to take care of, but afterward I'll come back."

"We really have to sync our schedules."

I lifted my head and studied him. "Don't worry. There is always phone sex."

"We can practice." He lowered his voice an octave before whispering, "I can still taste you from last night. I love the way you ride my tongue. I'm hungry again."

Automatically, my skin flushed hot, and that pulsing heat between my thighs became impossible to ignore. "You're trying to kill me, Cole."

I laughed as he nipped my shoulder. He played with the skin of my collarbone as he whispered, "No, I'm trying to make you eager to come back."

I raised my head to meet his gaze at the slight seriousness in his voice. "It's only two weeks. I'll be back."

"I know. I'll just miss you." He kissed me softly before adding, "There is the other tiny elephant in the room."

"Tiny elephant?"

"Your mother. I don't think she'd take it kindly if she heard that I called her an elephant."

I frowned. "Right. I'd been trying not to think about her."

"I know, but she did travel all the way to Los Angeles with me. I mean, she complained the whole way, but she misses you too."

"Let me guess, then she tried to convince Brian that he needs to date me?"

He shook his head. "Kukua. Actually, she said *you* were in love with me."

I laughed. "She's not wrong. I *am* in love with you."

It was the first time I'd said the words out loud, and I made a point to meet his gaze when I said them.

The slow smile that spread over his lips warmed my heart and healed all those little fissures and cracks that had been formed when he broke me.

"Well, that's good. Because if I continued to love you and you didn't love me back, that would have been awkward. Though I would have persevered."

I laughed. "You're ridiculous."

"Maybe a little." He shrugged.

"I still can't believe you brought my mum with you to LA."

"She really does miss you, you know."

"Yeah, well, it's not as easy to forget what she did to me. To *us*. And saying she misses me isn't going to erase that."

"Look, be mad at her all you want. But I had an equal part in it, and I own it. For all it's worth, I think you guys should try to find your common ground."

"Oh, look at you, waxing poetic."

"It's been known to happen." He pulled me down for another kiss. "Either way, I think you should talk to her. I'm not going to tell you what to do, obviously. But if you talk to her, you might actually feel better."

"I'm not sure I will. I've never been this angry with her before."

"If you can forgive me, I'm pretty sure you can find a way to forgive her."

"It's more complicated than that. She's interfered with *all* of my relationships. It's like she's incapable of being cured."

"Maybe she's just desperate to be involved in your life."

"And that needs to end. Literally. I've had enough of it."

"You're right. But wouldn't it be better if you're on good terms with your mum? You might feel better then."

I scowled at him. "I hate it when you talk sense."

"Come here, I'll show you how good me talking sense can be."

Once we were showered and headed out for breakfast, he grabbed me by the waist, twirling me around as we waited for the elevator in his building. When the doors dinged and slid apart, we both froze. Inside the elevator stood my mother, her angry gaze pinned to Cole's face. "Eh, of course. You left me in Los Angeles so you could, what, come and *enjoy* her yourself?"

"Hi, Dr. Addo."

I frowned at them both. "Did you set me up?"

Cole's face went ashen. "No, I didn't know she was coming."

My mother, in her typical way, stormed forward. "He would have run away. Worried I was going to give him the beating of a lifetime."

And sure enough, with her handkerchief in hand, she aimed for him.

He ducked easily. "Dr. Addo, I needed to get to Ofosua. *You* opted to stay in LA."

"That Brian boy, he's nice. He's cute." She turned to me, looking me up and down. "He's single."

"Not going to happen, Mum."

"Mm-hmm. Of course not. But Kukua is single. It could happen with her."

I sighed. "You will never stop, will you?"

She turned on me. "You. I've been traveling across the country and back again looking for you."

I frowned. I was looking for the remorse in her eyes, but I knew I wouldn't find it. Cole was right. Running away from my mother wasn't going to solve things for me.

Cole watched me warily. "I'm going to make myself scarce. Why don't you two use my apartment for this conversation?"

"Hm, the way he turned up on my doorstep, insisting that I had to come and chase you down. What kind of child makes her own mother chase her?"

When Cole left the two of us alone, she turned to face me. "Do you even understand that something could have happened to me and you wouldn't have even known?"

"I would have known. Dad knew how to reach me."

She pursed her lips. "Your *father* knew how to reach you? But I did not?"

"Is this about being left out, or what? I'm having a hard time following."

She watched me. "Do you not even care that you hurt me with your antics?"

"All right, Mum. I love you very much. But you still can't have my number. Not until you learn some boundaries."

"What boundaries? You know, these obroni things that you have picked up, I don't like them. Not one bit."

"You didn't stop to think that there was a reason that *you*, of all people, didn't have my number? You don't listen. You only want to hear what you want to hear."

She sniffed as she started a stroll around Cole's apartment. "Is that what you think?"

"It's what I have seen. You know, after thinking about it, I'm not even sure I wanted to marry Yofi. I wanted to be away and not have you constantly in my head. 'When are you going to get married, Ofosua? Why won't you go get your master's, Ofosua? My friend's son is available, Ofosua.' I was exhausted and worn down. I know I'm your only child. And I know you're worried that I will be alone. But the constant harping turned me into a twenty-five-year-old divorcée."

"I don't care about you being alone. As your father says, you're quite capable. I'm worried about you continuing your culture. Having a connection to your people. You don't seem to care."

Clasping a hand to my chest, I stepped in her path in an effort to make her truly see me. "I care, Mum. I have a different way of caring, and my ways are also valid. No matter where I am or who I love, I am an African. I am Ghanaian. I am a *Ga*. But I have to do that my way."

"Your way. You young people, you think you're the only ones who ever invented a need for freedom? You're not. Dare I say, me and my generation, we did it better."

"Look, Mum, I don't want to do this. I don't want to fight with you. I'm so tired, and you hurt me."

She rolled her lips inward. "Look, maybe Yofi was a mistake. But—"

"Yofi was *maybe* a mistake? Was he the only way for you to be proud of me?"

"What nonsense are you speaking? Your father and I are *very* proud of you."

"Really? How come I've never heard you say it before?"

She frowned. "Oh, I've said it before. Why?"

"Okay, say it now." I just wanted the words.

"Say what?" She used that voice I was so accustomed to.

"That you're *proud* of me." How could she not see what I was saying?

She frowned. "Why do you need such sentiments? It's not what *we* do. We're Ghanaian."

I sighed. This was exhausting. Honestly, maybe this was how she did it with my father all these years. I'd always wondered if all this really wore him down. Maybe that was why he traveled so much.

"So you're not even sorry about Cole, are you?"

She frowned at me. "What happened was in your best interest."

I had always known that a Ghanaian parent would rather bite off their left arm than issue an apology. Yet still, somehow, I was surprised at my own mother's reluctance to offer anything even resembling one.

"So what now? Mum, I'm not going to fight this fight with you. I love you, and you're my mother. I respect you. I know our culture. You and Daddy gave me a strong foundation. I'm so impressed and honored that you're my mother, but to sit back and let you continue to meddle in my life? I don't have to subject myself to this. If you call me and you need something, I'll come. But if you never let me be an adult, I will never act like an adult. If you want to cut me off, that's fine. I understand. And that's okay because I have been saving money, and I actually earn enough to support myself."

She watched me warily in stony silence. When I hitched my purse higher on my shoulder, she mumbled something.

I frowned. "What was that?" Her gaze was downcast, and I couldn't quite hear what she was saying. "Mum, I can't hear you."

"Fine. I'm sorry, okay? Now will you come home?"

I shook my head. "No, you're not listening. I'm not coming home. I moved out."

"But this is nonsense. I said sorry."

"But did you say it because you meant it or because you thought it would shut me up?"

She bit her bottom lip. "Fine, okay? I'm sorry. I didn't mean to hurt you. Perhaps, sometimes my zealousness to do right by you causes problems."

I laughed. "Sometimes you're overzealous? Wow, this apology, be still my heart."

She scowled at me. "Stop talking and let me finish."

I bit the inside of my cheek.

"Sometimes I don't see. I know that you had stress in this country. I know in Ghana things would have been so much easier for you. You could have met some boy whose family we knew, and you could have done your own thing. But we raised you here, so I have to try harder."

"And I can *survive* here, Mum. You and Dad have made me strong. I'm pretty badass if you let me be."

She sniffed. "I'm sorry. Yofi, hm, that boy, he's lucky I have such a calm temperament that I barely considered killing him. You know, I might still beat him for the way he tried to humiliate you."

My mother had been threatening to beat people since I was a child. To my knowledge, she'd never actually beaten anyone. It was that Ga way of being all talk.

"And Cole?"

She sighed. "He's—he's so white."

I coughed a laugh. "Hey, he didn't embarrass me on the dance floor."

"It's true. But, ah, still so white."

"Yeah. He is. He's not Ghanaian, and he's not a lawyer, or

a doctor, or in finance. But he's a good man. And he'll run the publishing company soon, Mum. I could do worse."

She sighed. "Publisher. It's almost as bad as being a professor. Eh, he's your choice. He's your choice."

"Great, then I might even tell you where I live now."

"I'm ready to bring you jollof. Did you ever learn how to make it like me?"

And then she walked me through the jollof recipe, and I had to take down notes. I smiled because I *had* missed her. Psycho antics and all. She was my mum, after all.

It was then that Cole walked in. "Ah, how are my girls?"

My mother looked him up and down. "I'm not your girl."

He laughed and strode forward and gave her a big hug. "You might as well get used to me. I'm going to be here a long time."

My mother tried to wiggle out of his hug, but at the corner of her mouth, I could see she was smiling.

—

COLE

My hands were sweating.

Maybe that's because you had to avoid a wooden spoon.

"Obroni, pay attention, or else you'll burn the jollof."

"Yes, Auntie," I murmured.

Over the last month or so, I'd gotten used to the auntie custom. And I had to make a mental note of all the ingredients that she'd used so I could replicate this whole thing for Ofos.

When I'd arrived to the Addos' to ask Ofos's parents to marry her, Helen had just given me a stiff nod and then insisted that the best way to propose was through food.

I just didn't realize that the instruction would come first-hand . . . from her. Complete with wooden spoon.

It had been worth it, though. Because I knew that Ofosua would be much happier with her parents on board.

When I thanked Helen for her help, she sniffed and then rapidly blinked her eyes. "Eh, if I don't teach you, who will? Otherwise you people would cook poorly all the time."

That had been weeks ago. I'd been planning this for weeks and getting lessons. I was pretty sure Ofos was suspicious. Every time she called me from Los Angeles, I had to call her back because I was at her parents' house. And I couldn't risk her hearing her father screaming at the television or her mother screaming at me.

But today was the day, and I hoped to God I was ready.

When Ofos arrived at my apartment, I had everything prepped. I'd left work at noon to make sure I had everything. It had taken that long to prep. But I was clean, freshly shaven, and had made jollof, chicken, a side stew, and a whole heap of Ghana pancakes. That one I had slightly cheated on because I'd made the batter yesterday. And the ring was in my jacket pocket.

For the band, I'd sourced gold from Ghana. Helen had helped me. I'd gotten a braided band with yellow gold, white gold, and rose gold intertwined with each other and studded with diamonds. And a five-carat marquis cut on top.

Helen had accompanied me as I designed the ring. She'd had *many* opinions, but I could tell she liked to be involved.

I knew exactly what I was going to say about how I wanted to braid our lives and our cultures and our families together. I was so nervous, though, my stomach twisting and pitching every time I practiced. When the buzzer went off, I took a deep breath and let her up.

There was a rapid series of knocks on my door, and when I

opened it with a grin, Ofosua pushed past me, her rollaway bag in tow. I smiled at her. "Hello, gorgeous."

Ofos had her hair in slim, beautiful braids in an ombré brown color from her roots all the way past her ass. She looked good in braids. Somehow, they made her look younger, though. Like I was about to get engaged to a college student. She lifted a brow at me and marched straight to the bedroom, searching for something. "Where is she?"

"Who?"

"My mother. I smell her cooking."

That made me grin. "So I got it right?"

"Got what right? Mom. She was here."

I shook my head. "No, she wasn't."

"Where's my mother?"

I cupped her face. "Stop worrying about your mother. I cooked."

She blinked once, her brow furrowing. "*You* cooked?"

"Yes. I can cook."

"I know. But I've never seen you make anything other than, you know, pasta or chicken."

"Doesn't mean I can't cook anything else."

"That smells like seasoning, Cole."

"I certainly hope so. Your mother would kill me if I got the recipe wrong."

Her brows shot up. "You asked my mother for her recipe?"

I shook my head. "No. I had her teach me how to make things."

Ofos's mouth fell open, and I grinned as I ran my thumb over her bottom lip. Then I sank to my knee, pulling the box from my pocket.

"Oh my God. What are you doing?"

I grinned up at her. "I'm going to need you to be quiet now, my love. I have something important to ask you."

The waterworks started before I even started to talk. And she was shaking her head back and forth. "Ofosua Abena Addo, I love you. I've loved you from the moment we met. I've loved you from the moment you decided you hated me. I've loved you from the moment that you decided that you might like me. I've loved you through it all, and I will continue to love you until my dying day. I promise to always strive to be better, to do better, to learn more. To be a man worthy of you. Will you marry me?"

I watched as the tears moved freely down her cheeks now. "Oh my God, Cole."

She wasn't saying yes. Why wasn't she saying yes? I started to sweat. "Anything you want. I will bend the heavens to give it to you. Just say yes. Give me a chance."

She blinked rapidly. "Oh my God, yes. I said it in my head."

I laughed as I slid the ring on her finger.

She stared at it and blinked. "We're going to need to get something smaller for me to wear every day."

I laughed. "Not on your life. I'll probably upgrade the stone for every year we're married."

"You upgrade the stone, and I won't be able to wear it in public without someone trying to rob me."

"Great, then I'll give you an armed guard. I don't care. We belong to each other. And I want everyone to know that your husband will move heaven and earth to give you the best."

She stared at the ring, and her gaze lifted to mine. "Oh my God. Are you sure about this?"

I wrapped my arms around her, pulling her close, inhaling her scent and instantly relaxing. "I let your mother teach me to cook. I'm sure. PS, she really does whack you with a wooden spoon."

She laughed through her tears. "I told you! You didn't duck out of the way?"

"She's shockingly fast for such a small woman."

"Are you going to feed me now?"

"Yes, I am. And I have one request."

She tilted her chin up as she nuzzled into my chest. "What's your request, besides that I marry you?"

"Don't be jealous that I'm a better cook than you."

Predictably, her brow lifted and she pursed her lips. And then she said the sweetest words other than the "yes" that she'd just given me a few moments ago. "I smell a challenge coming on."

CHAPTER 34

OFOSUA

ADINKRA SAYING:
(Odo Nnyew Fie Kwan) Love does not lose its way home.

SAMUEL ADDO:
Nobody can tell you who or how to love.
You have to fumble in the dark like the rest of us.

My mother was in her element. She loved nothing more than cooking for a large brood. She really should have been a caterer. As we packed my old apartment full of friends, old and new, colleagues, and family, I gently tapped my fork against my flute of champagne. "I just wanted to thank everyone for coming tonight." That felt amazing to say. Cole grinned at me as I continued the toast. "And this is sort of off topic, but I want to say congratulations to my fiancé, the new co-CEO of Drake Publishing. You really were the best one for the job."

"Only because you took off to work for someone else," he groused, and everyone laughed.

Cole's aunt Ruby took a heaping plateful of food from my mother, and I watched as she delicately chewed on a piece of kelewele. "This is incredible. What is this? Can your caterer do an office function?"

My mother laughed. "Caterer? Heh. I would never use a caterer in my own home. Who does that? But I do have some people I can call for you. Keep in mind, I'll tell them to up their prices since you people can afford it."

I laughed. "Mum!"

"What? It's true." She shrugged.

Ruby, however didn't even bat an eye. "Helen, I'd love the contact."

My father looked like he was trying to extricate himself from a conversation with Megan, who was chatting animatedly about *The Bachelor*. When he caught my gaze, he gave me the *help me* eyes, but it didn't happen. He'd survived my mother, and besides, he didn't spend much time rescuing *me* from uncomfortable conversations.

Kukua was flirting shamelessly with Brian, and my mother looked on approvingly.

Cole wrapped his arm around my waist. "I love you."

I grinned at him. "I love you too."

"I wanted to say that to you before I brought *my* mother into the mix."

My stomach twisted. "Your mother decided to come after all?" They'd had a strained relationship since our breakup. Still, I had invited her. I just hadn't thought she would show up.

He nodded. "Aunt Ruby convinced her to make an effort."

"I really do love your aunt. She's actually great. I just wish I'd had more time to prepare." I swallowed hard and smoothed a hand down my African-print pants, which had stamped adinkra symbols all over them. Maybe I should have worn something else. His mother was a piece of work. I needed better armor. I should have worn couture.

"You look just as stunning as you always do. And Aunt Ruby

loves you too. She's the only one in my family besides my grandfather I've ever really connected to," he murmured into my hair, then took my hand and leaned forward to kiss my forehead. "No matter what happens, I love you, and no matter what she says, it doesn't mean anything to us, right? Remember that, love, please."

I smoothed a thumb over his cheek. "It's fine, Cole. As long as I have you, that's all I care about. Nothing can dampen that."

He nodded. "Okay, then let's go say hi."

He worked us through the crowd until we found her near the opening to the balcony. "Mrs. Drake, it's nice to see you again."

She wore a crisp white Stella McCartney jumpsuit and had her hair up in a chignon. She studied me with a shrewd eye. "It seems I underestimated your resilience."

"You probably shouldn't do that again. Underestimate me, I mean."

She chuckled at that. "I don't make the same mistake twice."

I turned to meet Cole's gaze and squeezed his hand. "That's good to hear. I can't wait to get to know you better, Mom."

Her eyes went wide, and her lips parted in surprise. I could tell she didn't like it, but that only made me more determined to use it. I was her new daughter now. She was going to have to get used to it. "I see. Well, if you two are insistent on doing this, then we must at least do it correctly. I'll have to get on the phone with the Plaza. This, of course, will have to be a long engagement. They won't have anything decent available for the next two years."

It felt like a dig. It didn't necessarily sound like one, but it felt like one. And next to me, Cole tensed. "Actually, the entire wedding will take place in Accra. We won't be doing a ceremony here, just a reception, eventually."

She sputtered, "You can't be serious. Drakes don't run off to third-world nations and elope."

Cole opened his mouth, and I knew it was going to be bad, so I stopped him. "Actually, they're called developing nations now. And we're not eloping. Everything you want to do at the Plaza, we'll do in Ghana. I encourage you to do your research about venues. You and my mother can certainly entertain yourselves."

I pointed her in the direction of my parents, who were now on the floor dancing. Any moment now, I felt like my father was going to bust out his James Brown split, and we'd have to get a paramedic watch for that. He was old and couldn't quite do it the same way he used to.

"Well, *this* is certainly nicer than I expected."

I lifted a brow. The second blow. "What did you expect?"

"I don't know. When you hear 'Africans,' you assume poor, like *from* Africa."

And another one. She said that with her fingers in quotes, and Cole stepped forward. "That is enough, Mom. You need to apologize right now or you can——"

I tugged him back. I could handle this. "Well, that's one story people have been told. Can you believe people are dumb enough to believe everything they see in the media? I mean, I went to Dalton, then Columbia like my father. I've lived all over the world. And my parents' home in Ghana makes this place look like the shabby summer house. Don't believe media portrayals of a place that those in power have a vested interest in keeping you ignorant about."

Her brows narrowed by degrees, eventually dipping down. "Well, aren't you a different one. I mean, you're the first girl that stuck around this long."

I was determined to be cool about it, so I snuggled up to Cole, who was stiff beside me. "Well, it's not to say we haven't had our bumps and bruises, but I think we make a great team."

She nodded. "Of course you do. You know, however, that we will ask you to sign a prenup, right?"

I blinked. Oh, this had to be the final blow.

Cole leaned forward then, vibrating beside me. "Have you considered that I'm the one who needs to sign a prenup? Turns out her net worth is higher than mine." He turned to me. "PS, I will totally sign, by the way."

I squeezed Cole's hand. "I'll sign one too, to love you forever."

He grinned. "It hadn't occurred to me we could write our own clauses. Maybe this could work after all."

"Are you two being serious?" she asked in shock. It was as if she couldn't believe it. "Wow." She turned to me and gave me a tight smile. "Well, at least there's champagne." Then she drifted away and made for the door.

Cole pulled me in and gave me a kiss. "If that were a Gatling gun, I wouldn't know where to run."

"I'm sorry she lived up to your expectations."

"It's fine." Then he took my hand. "Come on, follow me to the dance floor."

I smiled up at him. "Let's show them old folks how it's done."

And from the corner of my eye, I saw my mother coming for me. "Eh, you, small girl, who are you calling old?"

I could only laugh as Cole pulled me into his arms. "You knew full well she was going to hear that."

I grinned. "Yes, I did. As you know, my mother is really the happiest when she's busy complaining about something. So never let it be said I didn't give her anything."

He laughed. "I love you, Ofosua Addo."

"I love you too, Cole Drake."

OFOSUA

ACCRA

"Cole, stop it."

But Cole was having none of it and slid a hand over my ass. Up ahead, my mother chatted rapid-fire over the wedding coordinator as she gave the tour of La Palm Royal Beach Hotel. The hotel was beautiful and had been recently updated. But we were, as my mother said, only there because one of her friends was the director of events and she had to make a show.

She had other plans for where she wanted us to get married: the Ado Lane Resort, two hours away in Cape Coast and brand-spanking-new. Off in the distance, you could see Elmina Castle. Cape Coast had some of the most stunning beaches, far less crowded than Accra. Either way, we walked hand in hand behind my mother as she rattled off requests for catering and space. I was bored. My feet hurt. Cole was incorrigible as always. "Hey, come on. Let's leave your mom to it. She obviously doesn't need us. None of this wedding is about us at all."

I laughed. "I told you. The moment you slid this ring on my finger, it gave her carte blanche to be the motherzilla of the bride."

He laughed. "Well, it makes her happy. And at the end of the day, I get you, and that's all I care about."

I squeezed his hand. "Agreed. I will let her do whatever she wants, plan whatever she wants, invite whomever she wants, because honestly, I'm exhausted. And I would rather just get to show you Ghana."

Thus far, we'd had quite the adventure. The day after we arrived, I'd dragged him off to Wli Waterfalls. We'd done the six-hour hike, stayed overnight and everything. Despite the treacherous hike where we almost died more than once, the greenery and view of Togo from the top was truly awe-inspiring. And the view had sight lines straight into Togo.

I couldn't believe that I'd never done it before. I was, at the core, a city girl. The city was comforting to me. The sounds. The sights. The people. But there was so much more to Ghana than Accra. So much more to be seen. So much more to be felt. So much more to experience. And I was glad I was able to show Cole some of it.

But the moment we'd returned from the falls and that treacherous drive, my mother had gone full-on wedding planning ballistic. If there was time, I wanted to sneak off and take Cole to Peduase. There was a beautiful resort there where we'd get to unwind and chill out. But we'd have to sneak away. Mum was busy filling our days.

She didn't seem to care that we were only here for two weeks, which I knew wasn't long enough to be in Ghana, but at least it was a start. And Cole and I had started talking about vacation homes and the best areas to live in.

He tugged my hand, and I laughed. "What are you doing?"

"I am sneaking off with my wife-to-be."

I laughed as my shoes made a clopping sound on the terrazzo floors of the hotel. "Where are we going?"

"I have no idea." But he took my hand, squeezed it tightly, and then he was off running with me in tow, and we were giggling like schoolkids off to be naughty. My mother didn't even seem to notice.

When we stopped, he tugged open a door, pulling me in. I squeaked. "What are you doing?"

He laughed. "Shh, you ask a lot of questions."

We were in a small supply closet, given the small amount of light sneaking in from under the doorway. "Cole, we can't be in here."

"Nonsense." He leaned in and kissed my neck. "You're my wife. Or at least you will be soon."

His hands slid to my waist, squeezing slightly and then lifting me on top of something. "You see, staying in your parents' house has put a damper on sexy times with my stunning fiancée. You know full well I love seeing you wear nothing except that beautiful smile and that rock on your finger."

I laughed. "You know full well I shouldn't be wearing this thing. It's five freaking carats, Cole. It belongs in a safe. I am happy to wear a replica. This is terrifying. What if it slides off?"

He shook his head. "It's not going to slide off. Besides, I want people to see that thing from space." He nuzzled into my neck and whispered, "Just be happy, Ofosua."

"I am happy, baby."

He laughed. "You still haven't settled on an endearment? I personally would prefer Hot Cole."

I rolled my eyes. "I will never forgive Kukua for telling you that we call you Hot Cole."

He grinned. "Oh, you will call me Hot Cole, woman. Especially when I show you just how hot I am."

He nipped at my neck, and I groaned. "What are you doing?"

He whispered against the shell of my ear. "I'm showing my wife-to-be what she does to me. I don't think I can wait until we get home."

"Cole," I breathed.

His hands slid to the hem of my skirt, pushing it up as I spread my thighs farther apart, allowing him room. "You are a temptress, walking around looking like that. How am I supposed to concentrate?"

"Who said you're supposed to concentrate?"

As he chuckled, he kissed along my jaw and then finally made it to my lips. I parted mine on a gasp, because as always, kissing Cole was like coming home and riding a tornado all at once. There was no taking a breath.

When Cole slid his tongue between my lips, it was all plunder. All need and excitement and urgency. In seconds, I was grasping at his short sleeves, grabbing his shirt, going for the buttons. He was shoving my skirt even farther up, and along the edges of the fabulous brown, white, and green Christie Brown creation, his fingers made contact with my sex.

"Fuck, Ofosua." He breathed into my mouth. He kissed me again. Slower this time, as if trying to get himself under control.

His fingers teased the hem, his knuckles brushing over my clit, making me groan. When he slid his fingers beneath the lace trim of my panties, I shivered. "Cole."

I ran my hands through his hair, tugging, and he hissed. "Fuck, Ofosua." And then we were in a flurry. Me tugging at his shirt and belt, pulling it through the loops and snapping open his shorts.

Cole dragged his lips from mine, kissing along the column of my neck, down to the bodice of my blouse, which he'd pushed open. His groan was muffled as he nuzzled into my breasts. "So fucking perfect."

With one large hand on my ass, he scooted me to the edge of whatever I was sitting on, and he was right there. Thick and full and very, very erect, pressing against me, wrapping strong fingers around the base of his dick. When he lifted his gaze and met mine, he smirked. "Every time. I can't fucking believe—"

I leaned in and bit his bottom lip, murmuring, "You talk too much."

And he sank in. His lips dragged from mine and his head fell back as he muttered very loudly, "Oh, shit."

I hissed at the fullness. "Cole, oh my God."

"Next time, we need to find some time alone so we can take our time. But oh my God, Ofosua . . ."

And then we were a murmur of lips and kisses and hushed, "Right there," and "Don't stop." And of course, the ever-present "Fuck. Fuck. Oh, fuck."

The adrenaline spiked in my blood, mixed with desire and longing and pure joy. Our climaxes hit us hard, leaving the two of us shaking, breathing heavy, gazes locked, and he grinned that shit-eating grin that told me everything I needed to know about him as he said, "You are a menace."

I laughed. "Me? I was minding my business."

"You have to do something about this sexiness, or I'm going to have a hard time controlling myself."

"And who's the menace?"

Our kisses and touches in the dark were soft as we righted our clothes. And, true to form, he couldn't keep his hands off me. Being loved by Cole made me feel sinful and sexy and loved.

When he tried to help me fix my hair, we laughed together. He was only making it worse.

I caught him watching me intently in the low light. "What?"

"You are absolutely incredible. I'm so lucky."

I grinned up at him. "I love you, Hot Cole."

"I love you, Ofosua Addo, soon-to-be Drake."

"Addo-Drake, please."

He looked serious. "How about we both go hyphenated? That way, our kids have the hyphen."

I quickly blinked away tears. "You're on. How did I get lucky enough to find you?"

He grinned. "I was right under your nose all along."

He opened the door and we tumbled out, giggling as we fixed each other's clothes and hair. Cole just shook his head as he looked at mine.

I gave him a major side-eye as we turned to find two presumably Ghanaian men engaged in a very intense conversation at the end of the hallway. There was no one else in the hall except the four of us, and they hadn't seen us yet. One of them reached out to the other, almost cupping his face as he held on, bringing their noses within an inch of each other. They looked like they were about to either fight or fuck.

It wasn't until we took another step forward and I could see the other man better that I realized I knew that profile. I knew it well.

When I froze, Cole looked at me. "What's wrong? You know them?"

"It's Yofi," I breathed.

Cole frowned, and then recognition dawned. "Oh my God."

Our hushed tones had made the other two aware that we were there, and they sprang apart. Yofi's eyes met mine, and he stumbled forward. "Ofosua, this isn't wha—"

I put a hand up. "No, stop. It's none of my business."

His eyes went wide with panic. "No, wait." We heard the other man scoff and run off. Yofi turned around to look. "Thomas, fuck."

He turned back to me. "Any chance that you will pretend you never saw that?"

Suddenly, all the puzzle pieces my brain had been working on in the background fit together. The distance, the indifference. And I knew everything that happened had never been about me. Only about him and his attempt at survival. "Already forgotten. I saw nothing."

He sighed. "Ofosua, I—"

Cole squeezed my hand, letting me know he was going to take the lead, and I squeezed back. "No, Yofi, you're fine. You have nothing to fear from us."

His whole body sagged as if he was letting go of something. "I'm sorry."

I shook my head. "You should be for what you did and for how you did it, but you should never be sorry for who you love."

"Yeah, well, I'm already locked in, aren't I?"

Pamela.

I nodded. "You should talk to her. Don't hurt her like you hurt me, okay?"

He shook his head. "I don't know if she's going to understand."

"Maybe she won't, and maybe she leaves. But don't hurt her. It's not fair. She didn't do anything wrong."

He nodded. "It's an impossible situation."

I shook my head. "I can't pretend to know what you're feeling or what you think you would lose, but I know living a half life can't be what you want. Especially if you have someone who really loves you. You have to try."

He held my gaze for a long beat, and then his gaze flicked to Cole. "You were at my wedding."

Cole grinned. "You recognized me for my dance moves, huh?"

Yofi laughed. "Looks like you two figured it out."

Cole wrapped his arms around my shoulders and I snuggled in, tilting my gaze up to meet his. "I think we did."

And with that, Cole and I scooted around Yofi and tried to find my mother, who no doubt was looking for us. As we walked down the stairs, my body still throbbing from what Cole had just done to me in the storage closet, he leaned over and kissed my temple. "Are you okay?"

"A hundred percent fine. I ended up exactly where I was supposed to be."

"You most certainly did."

ACKNOWLEDGMENTS

The words "thank you" don't seem like enough.

This book could never have happened without my mother, Serwah Quaynor. This book is a love letter to her and all the crazy antics that took place during my childhood and young adulthood. You are a force of nature, and I'm proud to be called your daughter.

Cuzi Love Collective, my family, my siblings, thank you for keeping me grounded and loving me.

For those of you who love stories of driven, hilarious, slightly messy women of color who still get to marry the billionaire, the race car driver, the movie star, the rock star—who love stories centered in joy for these women, thank you. With every single book, you have given me the love and confidence I needed to keep writing.

For my firstborn, Dadaba, Ghana girls who've never seen themselves between the pages, this book is for you. I hope you see what has always been possible. You belong in every room, and you are deserving of a love that is passionate, unbridled, out loud, and all-consuming.

I also want to thank Gallery Books and Simon & Schuster, especially Carrie Feron, for believing in this book and understanding my vision. Thank you to my agent, Jen Marshall, and Aevitas Creative Management, for being my avengers.

And to my friends in the trenches with me. I love you. Y'all are real ones. Kennedy Ryan, Sierra Simone, Lisa Lang Blakeney, Minx Malone, Theodora Taylor, and Kenya Wright—all of you have been so integral in getting me to this point.